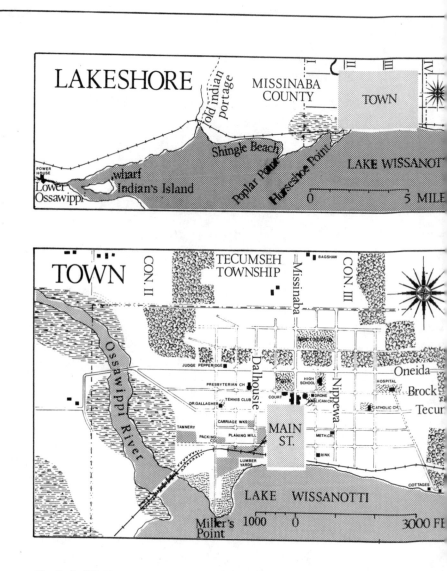

MARIPOSA, ONTARIO, C. 1910

STEPHEN LEACOCK'S

SMALL TOWN IMAGE

D.A. NORRIS,

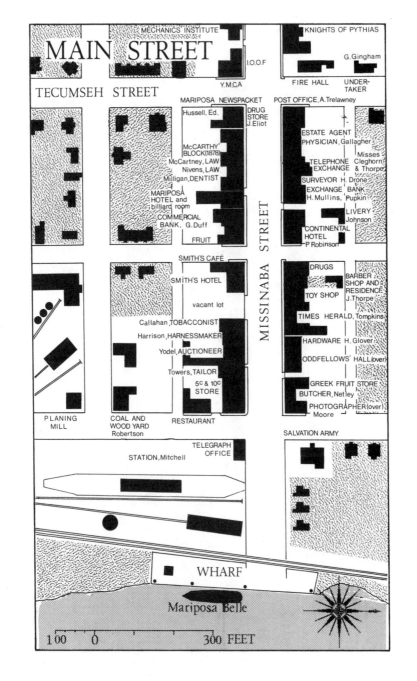

MAIN STREET

MECHANICS INSTITUTE

KNIGHTS OF PYTHIAS

I.O.O.F

G.Gingham

Y.M.C.A

FIRE HALL   UNDER-TAKER

TECUMSEH STREET

MARIPOSA NEWSPACKET

POST OFFICE, A.Trelawney

Hussell, Ed.

DRUG STORE J.Eliot

ESTATE AGENT

PHYSICIAN, Gallagher

McCARTHY BLOCK(1878)

McCartney, LAW

Nivens, LAW

Milligan, DENTIST

Misses Cleghorn & Thorpe

TELEPHONE EXCHANGE

SURVEYOR H. Drone

MARIPOSA HOTEL and billiard room

EXCHANGE BANK H. Mullins, Pupkin

COMMERCIAL BANK, G.Duff

LIVERY Johnson

FRUIT

CONTINENTAL HOTEL P Robinson

MISSINABA STREET

SMITH'S CAFÉ

DRUGS

BARBER SHOP AND RESIDENCE J.Thorpe

SMITH'S HOTEL

TOY SHOP

vacant lot

TIMES HERALD, Tompkins

Callahan, TOBACCONIST

Harrison, HARNESSMAKER

HARDWARE H. Glover

Yodel, AUCTIONEER

ODDFELLOWS' HALL (over)

Towers, TAILOR

GREEK FRUIT STORE

5c & 10c STORE

BUTCHER, Netley

PHOTOGRAPHER (over) Moore

PLANING MILL

COAL AND WOOD YARD Robertson

RESTAURANT

SALVATION ARMY

TELEGRAPH OFFICE

STATION, Mitchell

WHARF

Mariposa Belle

100   0   300 FEET

079

Sunshine Sketches
of a
Little Town

Canadian Critical Editions

General Editors

John Moss and Gerald Lynch

Canadian Critical Editions offer, for academic study and the interested reader, authoritative texts of significant Canadian works within a comprehensive critical setting. Where appropriate, each edition provides extensive biographical and bibliographical background, reprints of documents, commentary to illuminate the context of its creation and the history of its reception, new essays written from a variety of critical perspectives, and a bibliography. These critical editions provide an excellent opportunity for appreciation of the works themselves, for understanding their place in the developing tradition, and for participating in the critical discourse surrounding each work. Making the best accessible, this is the key concept behind Canadian Critical Editions.

Sunshine Sketches of a Little Town

by
Stephen Leacock

A Critical Edition

Edited by
Gerald Lynch

The Tecumseh Press Ltd.
Ottawa, Canada
1996

Copyright © by The Tecumseh Press Ltd., 1996
2nd printing, 1997
3rd printing, 2004

Canada

*The Publishers gratefully acknowledge the financial assistance of the
Government of Canada through the Book Publishing Industry
Development Program (BPIDP) for our publishing activities.*

Canadian Cataloguing in Publication Program

Leacock, Stephen, 1869-1944
    Sunshine sketches of a little town : a critical edition

(Critical series : 1)
Includes biographical references
ISBN 1-896133-32-0 (bound) -
ISBN 1-896133-34-7 (pbk.)

    1. Lynch, Gerald, 1953.   II. Title.   III. Series.

P38523.E15S83 1996   C813' 52   C96-900256-4
PR6023 E15S81 1996

*Copyright permission has been sought for all reprinted items.
See notes to titles in Documentary and Criticism sections. For any
omissions please contact the Publishers.

Cover art from the frontispiece by Cyrus Cuneo
to the first edition of 1912.

The map of Mariposa was composed by Darrel A. Norris and
appeared originally in *Journal of Canadian Studies*,
17 (Summer 1982). Used by permission,

Printed and bound in Canada.

for
David Bentley

… sitting reading in a quiet corner somewhere
such a book as the present one.

Contents

Editor's Preface   ix

The Text of *Sunshine Sketches of a Little Town*

Preface   xv

Chap.

I	The Hostelry of Mr. Smith	1
II	The Speculations of Jefferson Thorpe	21
III	The Marine Excursion of the Knights of Pythias	35
IV	The Ministrations of the Rev. Mr. Drone	53
V	The Whirlwind Campaign in Mariposa	67
VI	The Beacon on the Hill	74
VII	The Extraordinary Entanglement of Mr. Pupkin	83
VIII	The Fore-Ordained Attachment of Zena	
	Pepperleigh and Peter Pupkin	93
IX	The Mariposa Bank Mystery	104
X	The Great Election in Missinaba County	118
XI	The Candidacy of Mr. Smith	128
XII	*L'Envoi*. The Train to Mariposa	141

Biography

James Doyle, Deeps and Shallows: The Elusive
Life of Stephen Leacock 147

Documentary

B.K. Sandwell, How the "Sketches" Started 162
Arthur Lower, The Mariposa Belle 164
Douglas Bush, Small-Town Ontario 169

Criticism

Peter McArthur, Praise and Caution 176
Desmond Pacey, The Eighteenth-Century Tory 180
R.E. Watters, Leacock's Canadian Humour 184
Silver Donald Cameron, The Ironist 192
Robertson Davies, The Satirist 196
Alan Bowker, The Social Scientist 198
William H. Magee, The Local Colourist 204
Gerald Lynch, The Train to Mariposa 212

Bibliography 223

Editor's Preface

I know no way in which an editor may more fittingly preface a new edition of *Sunshine Sketches of a Little Town* than by adopting Malcolm Ross's attitude to prefacing the first (1960) New Canadian Library edition. This way, some self-consciousness can be shifted onto the capable shoulders of Professor Ross:

> Who, then, in these latter days dares to 'introduce' *Sunshine Sketches of a Little Town*? Not I. This is a preface, not an introduction, written in the belief that the editor's job (and the publisher's) is simply to keep the book going ad infinitum—for people who want to read it for the hundredth time, as well as for yesterday's crop of three-year-olds who may want to read it as though for the first time.

There are few (though sufficient, and growing) works of Canadian fiction that have been kept going ad infinitum, and relevant longevity is, surely, one reliable measure of a literary classic. What else might qualify a text as indispensable to its culture and therefore continuously deserving of new editions? It is still read widely for the sheer pleasure of it; it is studied; it serves as a national touchstone. *Sunshine Sketches* is all of these, and (as the advertisers say) much much more. For instance, it is funny, very funny, and written in a style that quietly proclaims in every sentence the touch of a master.

Canadians, ever wiser than they let on (and wise in their reticence), wisely take this book personally. I am always taken aback by the number of my students who know people who knew Leacock. Some are themselves distantly related (and doubtless Levesque and Laverty are variations of Leacock). The number of converts grows as we proceed through *Sunshine Sketches*, and such charmed students will sometimes bear witness to their conversion by asking what Leacock has published lately. Just about all claim immediate familiarity with Mariposa ("Yeah, my old man says he heard Dylan play there, a *long* time ago"). And having published a critical book on Leacock's writings, and suffered the reactions of a number of affronted Canadian reviewers —Who dares explain these jokes? Who appropriates Uncle Stevie?—I am fully qualified indeed to sympathize with Malcolm Ross's anxiety over editing and introducing a new edition of *Sunshine Sketches of a Little Town*. Regardless, it is worth wondering a little further: Why is it

Canadians think they know Leacock, that ironic seer who, as Ross first recognized and expressed so well, "loved what he hated," and Mariposa, that alleged site of centrism and waspish patriarchy that nonetheless still feels cognate with "home"?

A part of any answer to everyone's presumed familiarity is, I think, that the narrator himself so frequently presumes on our complicity—"you" are everywhere addressed—and is finally so accommodating in introducing us to this mythical place expressedly dear to Leacock's own heart. Or perhaps it's just that Leacock's narrator is not the kind with whom one would want to disagree. Mostly, though, I believe we know Mariposa because once upon a time so many of us did come from the Little Town in the Sunshine, whether it went by the name of Esterhazy, Saskatchewan or St. Urbain Street, Montreal. Leacock knew we were all rushing headlong for the Mausoleum Club, and as the unsurpassed "L'Envoi" shows, he gave us (hopefully, I think) *Sunshine Sketches of a Little Town* for a kind of reminder and pricking comfort.

The Criticism section of the background materials which conclude the present edition is intended to give a sense of the critical history of *Sunshine Sketches*, from Peter McArthur's first extensive study in 1923 to my own analysis of "L'Envoi" in 1988. Most are excerpts from longer works, and a line of spaced periods has been inserted to indicate omitted material. The section of criticism does not presume to be definitively representative; the selective process means that it represents this editor's opinion of what is most valuable to an initial acquaintance with *Sunshine Sketches*. From there, students and other readers are encouraged to proceed guided by their own critical-theoretical interests.

In his author's preface to *Sunshine Sketches*, Leacock jokes that for many years it was found impossible to print his first two books of humour, *Literary Lapses* (1910) and *Nonsense Novels* (1911), because "the compositors fell back from their task suffocated with laughter and gasping for air. Nothing but the invention of the linotype machine—or rather, of the kind of men who operate it—made it possible to print these books." Like so many of Leacock's nonsensical remarks, this seeming exaggeration is actually true to experience. I don't know how many times I've read this book, but in closely checking and re-checking the proofs against the first published edition of the book, I had to stop again and again, and for long stretches I simply smiled till it hurt, and had to rest.

Which is to say: the present edition is based on the first edition of *Sunshine Sketches of a Little Town* published in book form (London and New York: John Lane; Toronto: Bell & Cockburn, 1912). Although Leacock revisited Mariposa in his fiction (as part of a Second World War bonds drive), there is no evidence that he ever revised the first-edition text of *Sunshine Sketches*. The present edition is not a variorum editon, though there does remain much to be learned from, say, a comparison of the serialized version of *Sunshine Sketches* published originally in the *Montreal Star* (17 Feb. 1912-22 June 1912) and the first edition.

There have been so very few silent changes of inarguable errors ("devices" for "advices"; missing end punctuation, and similar typos) that it was thought unnecessary to dignify them in a list of editorial emendations. Where the original edition indents the initial paragraphs following section breaks, the present one begins them flush left. Otherwise the present edition faithfully reproduces the text Leacock approved, preserving all idiosyncrasies of capitalization and punctuation in the belief that such conventions help convey a sense of the fiction's historical context.

In closing I gratefully acknowledge the guidance and support of my Department of English colleagues here at the University of Ottawa: Glenn Clever, Frank Tierney, and my co-General Editor in this critical edition series, John Moss. Thanks also for the computer help generously provided by Daniel Lefebvre of the School of Graduate Studies and Research at the University of Ottawa; the staff at the Computing Help Centre, University of Ottawa; and the computing skills of Marie Tremblay-Chénier.

Stephen Leacock (1869-1944) was the English-speaking world's best-known humorist for the period roughly 1910-1925. Born in England, he moved with his family to a bush farm near Lake Simcoe when he was five. He was educated at Upper Canada College, the University of Toronto, and the University of Chicago (Ph.D. 1903). From 1903 until his retirement in 1936, he taught Political Economy at McGill University, spending his summers in Orillia, Ontario, the town that inspired the creation of Mariposa in *Sunshine Sketches of a Little Town*. In total, Leacock published some eighty books and pamphlets on a remarkably wide range of subjects: economics, history, the British Empire, politics, biography, teaching, humour, and writing. However, it is as a writer of humorous fiction that he will most likely continue to be remembered and read. Beginning with *Literary Lapses* in 1910, he averaged a book of humour a year until his death.

Portrait of Stephen Leacock by Richard Jack. Photograph by V. Tetley-Miller. Used by permission of the University Club of Montreal and the Jack estate.

Sunshine Sketches

of a Little Town

by

Stephen Leacock

Preface

I know no way in which a writer may more fittingly introduce his work to the public than by giving a brief account of who and what he is. By this means some of the blame for what he has done is very properly shifted to the extenuating circumstances of his life.

I was born at Swanmoor, Hants, England, on December 30, 1869. I am not aware that there was any particular conjunction of the planets at the time, but should think it extremely likely. My parents migrated to Canada in 1876, and I decided to go with them. My father took up a farm near Lake Simcoe, in Ontario. This was during the hard times of Canadian farming, and my father was just able by great diligence to pay the hired men and, in years of plenty, to raise enough grain to have seed for the next year's crop without buying any. By this process my brothers and I were inevitably driven off the land, and have become professors, business men, and engineers, instead of being able to grow up as farm labourers. Yet I saw enough of farming to speak exuberantly in political addresses of the joy of early rising and the deep sleep, both of body and intellect, that is induced by honest manual toil.

I was educated at Upper Canada College, Toronto, of which I was head boy in 1887. From there I went to the University of Toronto, where I graduated in 1891. At the University I spent my entire time in the acquisition of languages, living, dead, and half-dead, and knew nothing of the outside world. In this diligent pursuit of words I spent about sixteen hours of each day. Very soon after graduation I had forgotten the languages, and found myself intellectually bankrupt. In other words I was what is called a distinguished graduate, and, as such, I took to school teaching as the only trade I could find that needed neither experience nor intellect. I spent my time from 1891 to 1899 on the staff of Upper Canada College, an experience which has left me with a profound sympathy for the many gifted and brilliant men who are compelled to spend their lives in the most dreary, the most thankless, and the worst paid profession in the world. I have noted that of my pupils, those who seemed the laziest and the least enamoured of books are now rising to eminence at the bar, in business, and in public life; the really promising boys who took all the prizes are now able with difficulty to earn the wages of a clerk in a summer hotel or a deck hand on a canal boat.

In 1899 I gave up school teaching in disgust, borrowed enough money to live upon for a few months, and went to the University of Chicago to study economics and political science. I was soon appointed to a Fellowship in political economy, and by means of this and some temporary employment by McGill University, I survived until I took the degree of Doctor of Philosophy in 1903. The meaning of this degree is that the recipient of instruction is examined for the last time in his life, and is pronounced completely full. After this, no new ideas can be imparted to him.

From this time, and since my marriage, which had occurred at this period, I have belonged to the staff of McGill University, first as lecturer in Political Science, and later as head of the department of Economics and Political Science. As this position is one of the prizes of my profession, I am able to regard myself as singularly fortunate. The emolument is so high as to place me distinctly above the policemen, postmen, street-car conductors, and other salaried officials of the neighbourhood, while I am able to mix with the poorer of the business men of the city on terms of something like equality. In point of leisure, I enjoy more in the four corners of a single year than a business man knows in his whole life. I thus have what the business man can never enjoy, an ability to think, and, what is still better, to stop thinking altogether for months at a time.

I have written a number of things in connection with my college life—a book on Political Science, and many essays, magazine articles, and so on. I belong to the Political Science Association of America, to the Royal Colonial Institute, and to the Church of England. These things, surely, are a proof of respectability. I have had some small connection with politics and public life. A few years ago I went all round the British Empire delivering addresses on Imperial organization. When I state that these lectures were followed almost immediately by the Union of South Africa, the Banana Riots in Trinidad, and the Turco-Italian war, I think the reader can form some idea of their importance. In Canada I belong to the Conservative party, but as yet I have failed entirely in Canadian politics, never having received a contract to build a bridge, or make a wharf, nor to construct even the smallest section of the Transcontinental Railway. This, however, is a form of national ingratitude to which one becomes accustomed in this Dominion.

Apart from my college work, I have written two books, one called "Literary Lapses" and the other "Nonsense Novels." Each of these is published by John Lane (London and New York), and either of them can be obtained, absurd though it sounds, for the mere sum of three shillings and sixpence. Any reader of this preface, for example, ridiculous though it appears, could walk into a bookstore and buy both of these books for seven shillings. Yet these works are of so humorous a character that for many years it was found impossible to print them. The compositors fell back from their task suffocated with laughter and gasping for air. Nothing but the invention of the linotype machine—or rather, of the kind of men who operate it—made it possible to print these books. Even now people have to be very careful in circulating them, and the books should never be put into the hands of persons not in robust health.

Many of my friends are under the impression that I write these humorous nothings in idle moments when the wearied brain is unable to perform the serious labours of the economist. My own experience is exactly the other way. The writing of solid, instructive stuff fortified by facts and figures is easy enough. There is no trouble in writing a scientific treatise on the folk-lore of Central China, or a statistical enquiry into the declining population of Prince Edward Island. But to write something out of one's own mind, worth reading for its own sake, is an arduous contrivance only to be achieved in fortunate moments, few and far between. Personally, I would sooner have written "Alice in Wonderland" than the whole Encyclopædia Britannica.

In regard to the present work I must disclaim at once all intention of trying to do anything so ridiculously easy as writing about a real place and real people. Mariposa is not a real town. On the contrary, it is about seventy or eighty of them. You may find them all the way from Lake Superior to the sea, with the same square streets and the same maple trees and the same churches and hotels, and everywhere the sunshine of the land of hope.

Similarly, the Reverend Mr. Drone is not one person, but about eight or ten. To make him I clapped the gaiters of one ecclesiastic round the legs of another, added the sermons of a third and the character of a fourth, and so let him start on his way in the book to pick up such individual attributes as he might find for himself. Mullins and Bagshaw and Judge Pepperleigh and the rest are, it is true, personal friends of mine. But I have known them in such a variety of forms, with such alternations of tall and short, dark and fair, that, individually, I should have much ado to know them. Mr. Pupkin is found whenever a Canadian bank opens a branch in a county town and needs a teller. As for Mr. Smith, with his two hundred and eighty pounds, his hoarse voice, his loud check suit, his diamonds, the roughness of his address and the goodness of his heart,—all of this is known by everybody to be a necessary and universal adjunct of the hotel business.

The inspiration of the book,—a land of hope and sunshine where little towns spread their square streets and their trim maple trees beside placid lakes almost within echo of the primeval forest,—is large enough. If it fails in its portrayal of the scenes and the country that it depicts the fault lies rather with an art that is deficient than in an affection that is wanting.

STEPHEN LEACOCK.

McGill University,
June, 1912.

Chapter I

The Hostelry of Mr. Smith

I don't know whether you know Mariposa. If not, it is of no consequence, for if you know Canada at all, you are probably well acquainted with a dozen towns just like it.

There it lies in the sunlight, sloping up from the little lake that spreads out at the foot of the hillside on which the town is built. There is a wharf beside the lake, and lying alongside of it a steamer that is tied to the wharf with two ropes of about the same size as they use on the Lusitania. The steamer goes nowhere in particular, for the lake is landlocked and there is no navigation for the Mariposa Belle except to "run trips" on the first of July and the Queen's Birthday, and to take excursions of the Knights of Pythias and the Sons of Temperance to and from the Local Option Townships.

In point of geography the lake is called Lake Wissanotti and the river running out of it the Ossawippi, just as the main street of Mariposa is called Missinaba Street and the county Missinaba County. But these names do not really matter. Nobody uses them. People simply speak of the "lake" and the "river" and the "main street," much in the same way as they always call the Continental Hotel, "Pete Robinson's" and the Pharmaceutical Hall, "Eliot's Drug Store." But I suppose this is just the same in every one else's town as in mine, so I need lay no stress on it.

The town, I say, has one broad street that runs up from the lake, commonly called the Main Street. There is no doubt about its width. When Mariposa was laid out there was none of that shortsightedness which is seen in the cramped dimensions of Wall Street and Piccadilly. Missinaba street is so wide that if you were to roll Jeff Thorpe's barber shop over on its face it wouldn't reach half way across. Up and down the Main Street are telegraph poles of cedar of colossal thickness, standing at a variety of angles and carrying rather more wires than are commonly seen at a transatlantic cable station.

On the Main Street itself are a number of buildings of extraordinary importance,—Smith's Hotel and the Continental and the

Mariposa House, and the two banks (the Commercial and the Exchange), to say nothing of McCarthy's Block (erected in 1878), and Glover's Hardware Store with the Oddfellows' Hall above it. Then on the "cross" street that intersects Missinaba Street at the main corner there is the Post Office and the Fire Hall and the Young Men's Christian Association and the office of the Mariposa Newspacket,—in fact, to the eye of discernment a perfect jostle of public institutions comparable only to Thread-needle Street or Lower Broadway. On all the side streets there are maple trees and broad sidewalks, trim gardens with upright calla lilies, houses with verandahs, which are here and there being replaced by residences with piazzas.

To the careless eye the scene on the Main Street of a summer afternoon is one of deep and unbroken peace. The empty street sleeps in the sunshine. There is a horse and buggy tied to the hitching post in front of Glover's hardware store. There is, usually and commonly, the burly figure of Mr. Smith, proprietor of Smith's Hotel, standing in his chequered waistcoat on the steps of his hostelry, and perhaps, further up the street Lawyer Mac-artney going for his afternoon mail, or the Rev. Mr. Drone, the Rural Dean of the Church of England Church, going home to get his fishing rod after a mothers' auxiliary meeting.

But this quiet is mere appearance. In reality and to those who know it, the place is a perfect hive of activity. Why, at Netley's butcher shop (established in 1882) there are no less than four men working on the sausage machines in the basement; at the News-packet office there are as many more job printing; there is a long distance telephone with four distracting girls on high stools wear-ing steel caps and talking incessantly; in the offices in McCar-thy's block are dentists and lawyers, with their coats off, ready to work at any moment; and from the big planing factory down beside the lake where the railroad siding is, you may hear all through the hours of the summer afternoon the long-drawn music of the running saw.

Busy—well, I should think so! Ask any of its inhabitants if Mariposa isn't a busy, hustling, thriving town. Ask Mullins, the manager of the Exchange Bank, who comes hustling over to his office from the Mariposa House every day at 10.30 and has scarcely time all morning to go out and take a drink with the manager of the Commercial; or ask—well, for the matter of that, ask any of them if they ever knew a more rushing go-a-head town than Mariposa.

Of course if you come to the place fresh from New York, you are deceived. Your standard of vision is all astray. You do think the place is quiet. You do imagine that Mr. Smith is asleep merely because he closes his eyes as he stands. But live in Mariposa for six months or a year and then you will begin to understand it better; the buildings get higher and higher; the Mariposa House grows more and more luxurious; McCarthy's block towers to the sky; the 'buses roar and hum to the station; the trains shriek; the traffic multiplies; the people move faster and faster; a dense crowd swirls to and fro in the post-office and the five and ten cent store—and amusements! well, now! lacrosse, baseball, excursions, dances, the Firemen's Ball every winter and the Catholic picnic every summer; and music—the town band in the park every Wednesday evening, and the Oddfellows' brass band on the street every other Friday; the Mariposa Quartette, the Salvation Army—why, after a few months' residence you begin to realize that the place is a mere mad round of gaiety.

In point of population, if one must come down to figures, the Canadian census puts the numbers every time at something round five thousand. But it is very generally understood in Mariposa that the census is largely the outcome of malicious jealousy. It is usual that after the census the editor of the Mariposa Newspacket makes a careful re-estimate (based on the data of relative non-payment of subscriptions), and brings the population up to 6,000. After that the Mariposa Times-Herald makes an estimate that runs the figures up to 6,500. Then Mr. Gingham, the undertaker, who collects the vital statistics for the provincial government, makes an estimate from the number of what he calls the "demised" as compared with the less interesting persons who are still alive, and brings the population to 7,000. After that somebody else works it out that it's 7,500; then the man behind the bar of the Mariposa House offers to bet the whole room that there are 9,000 people in Mariposa. That settles it, and the population is well on the way to 10,000, when down swoops the federal census taker on his next round and the town has to begin all over again.

Still, it is a thriving town and there is no doubt of it. Even the transcontinental railways, as any townsman will tell you, run through Mariposa. It is true that the trains mostly go through at night and don't stop. But in the wakeful silence of the summer night you may hear the long whistle of the through train for the west as it tears through Mariposa, rattling over the switches and past the semaphores and ending in a long, sullen roar as it takes the trestle bridge over the Ossawippi. Or, better still, on a winter evening about eight o'clock you will see the long row of the Pullmans and diners of the night express going north to the mining country, the windows flashing with brilliant light, and within them a vista of cut glass and snow-white table linen, smiling negroes and millionaires with napkins at their chins whirling past in the driving snowstorm.

I can tell you the people of Mariposa are proud of the trains, even if they don't stop! The joy of being on the main line lifts the Mariposa people above the level of their neighbours in such places as Tecumseh and Nichols Corners into the cosmopolitan atmosphere of through traffic and the larger life. Of course, they have their own train, too—the Mariposa Local, made up right there in the station yard, and running south to the city a hundred miles away. That, of course, is a real train, with a box stove on end in the passenger car, fed with cordwood upside down, and with seventeen flat cars of pine lumber set between the passenger car and the locomotive so as to give the train its full impact when shunting.

Outside of Mariposa there are farms that begin well but get thinner and meaner as you go on, and end sooner or later in bush and swamp and the rock of the north country. And beyond that again, as the background of it all, though it's far away, you are somehow aware of the great pine woods of the lumber country reaching endlessly into the north.

Not that the little town is always gay or always bright in the sunshine. There never was such a place for changing its character with the season. Dark enough and dull it seems of a winter night, wooden sidewalks creaking with the frost, and the lights burning dim behind the shop windows. In olden times the lights were coal oil lamps; now, of course, they are, or are supposed to be, electricity,—brought from the power house on the lower Ossawippi nineteen miles away. But, somehow, though it starts off as electricity from the Ossawippi rapids, by the time it gets to Mariposa and filters into the little bulbs behind the frosty windows of the shops, it has turned into coal oil again, as yellow and bleared as ever.

After the winter, the snow melts and the ice goes out of the lake, the sun shines high and the shanty-men come down from the lumber woods and lie round drunk on the sidewalk outside of Smith's Hotel—and that's spring time. Mariposa is then a fierce, dangerous lumber town, calculated to terrorize the soul of a newcomer who does not understand that this also is only an appearance and that presently the rough-looking shanty-men will change their clothes and turn back again into farmers.

Then the sun shines warmer and the maple trees come out and Lawyer Macartney puts on his tennis trousers, and that's summer time. The little town changes to a sort of summer resort. There are visitors up from the city. Every one of the seven cottages along the lake is full. The Mariposa Belle churns the waters of the Wissanotti into foam as she sails out from the wharf, in a cloud of flags, the band playing and the daughters and sisters of the Knights of Pythias dancing gaily on the deck.

That changes too. The days shorten. The visitors disappear. The golden rod beside the meadow droops and withers on its stem. The maples blaze in glory and die. The evening closes dark and chill, and in the gloom of the main corner of Mariposa the Salvation Army around a naphtha lamp lift up the confession of their sins—and that is autumn. Thus the year runs its round, moving and changing in Mariposa, much as it does in other places.

If, then, you feel that you know the town well enough to be admitted into the inner life and movement of it, walk down this June afternoon half way down the Main Street—or, if you like, half way up from the wharf—to where Mr. Smith is standing at the door of his hostelry. You will feel as you draw near that it is no ordinary man that you approach. It is not alone the huge bulk of Mr. Smith (two hundred and eighty pounds as tested on Netley's scales). It is not merely his costume, though the chequered waistcoat of dark blue with a flowered pattern forms, with his shepherd's plaid trousers, his grey spats and patent leather boots, a colour scheme of no mean order. Nor is it merely Mr. Smith's finely mottled face. The face, no doubt, is a notable one,—solemn, inexpressible, unreadable, the face of the heaven-born hotel keeper. It is more than that. It is the strange dominating

personality of the man that somehow holds you captive. I know
nothing in history to compare with the position of Mr. Smith
among those who drink over his bar, except, though in a lesser
degree, the relation of the Emperor Napoleon to the Imperial
Guard.

When you meet Mr. Smith first you think he looks like an
over-dressed pirate. Then you begin to think him a character.
You wonder at his enormous bulk. Then the utter hopelessness of
knowing what Smith is thinking by merely looking at his features
gets on your mind and makes the Mona Lisa seem an open book
and the ordinary human countenance as superficial as a puddle in
the sunlight. After you have had a drink in Mr. Smith's bar, and
he has called you by your Christian name, you realize that you
are dealing with one of the greatest minds in the hotel business.

Take, for instance, the big sign that sticks out into the street
above Mr. Smith's head as he stands. What is on it? Simply:
"JOS. SMITH, PROP." Nothing more, and yet the thing was a flash
of genius. Other men who had had the hotel before Mr. Smith
had called it by such feeble names as the Royal Hotel and the
Queen's and the Alexandria. Every one of them failed. When
Mr. Smith took over the hotel he simply put up the sign with
"JOS. SMITH, PROP.," and then stood underneath in the sunshine
as a living proof that a man who weighs nearly three hundred
pounds is the natural king of the hotel business.

But on this particular afternoon, in spite of the sunshine and
deep peace, there was something as near to profound concern and
anxiety as the features of Mr. Smith were ever known to express.

The moment was indeed an anxious one. Mr. Smith was
awaiting a telegram from his legal adviser who had that day
journeyed to the county town to represent the proprietor's interest
before the assembled License Commissioners. If you know
anything of the hotel business at all, you will understand that as
beside the decisions of the License Commissioners of Missinaba
County, the opinions of the Lords of the Privy Council are mere
trifles.

The matter in question was very grave. The Mariposa Court
had just fined Mr. Smith for the second time for selling liquors
after hours. The Commissioners, therefore, were entitled to
cancel the license.

Mr. Smith knew his fault and acknowledged it. He had broken

the law. How he had come to do so, it passed his imagination to recall. Crime always seems impossible in retrospect. By what sheer madness of the moment could he have shut up the bar on the night in question, and shut Judge Pepperleigh, the district judge of Missinaba County outside of it? The more so inasmuch as the closing up of the bar under the rigid license law of the province was a matter that the proprietor never trusted to any hands but his own. Punctually every night at 11 o'clock Mr. Smith strolled from the desk of the "rotunda" to the door of the bar. If it seemed properly full of people and all was bright and cheerful, then he closed it. If not, he kept it open a few minutes longer till he had enough people inside to warrant closing. But never, never unless he was assured that Pepperleigh, the judge of the court, and Macartney, the prosecuting attorney, were both safely in the bar, or the bar parlour, did the proprietor venture to close up. Yet on this fatal night Pepperleigh and Macartney had been shut out—actually left on the street without a drink, and compelled to hammer and beat at the street door of the bar to gain admittance.

This was the kind of thing not to be tolerated. Either a hotel must be run decently or quit. An information was laid next day and Mr. Smith convicted in four minutes, his lawyers practically refusing to plead. The Mariposa court, when the presiding judge was cold sober, and it had the force of public opinion behind it, was a terrible engine of retributive justice.

So no wonder that Mr. Smith awaited with anxiety the message of his legal adviser.

He looked alternately up the street and down it again, hauled out his watch from the depths of his embroidered pocket, and examined the hour hand and the minute hand and the second hand with frowning scrutiny.

Then wearily, and as one mindful that a hotel man is ever the servant of the public, he turned back into the hotel.

"Billy," he said to the desk clerk, "if a wire comes bring it into the bar parlour."

The voice of Mr. Smith is of a deep guttural such as Plancon or Edouard de Reske might have obtained had they had the advantages of the hotel business. And with that, Mr. Smith, as was his custom in off moments, joined his guests in the back room.

His appearance, to the untrained eye, was merely that of an extremely stout hotel-keeper walking from the rotunda to the back bar. In reality, Mr. Smith was on the eve of one of the most brilliant and daring strokes ever effected in the history of licensed liquor. When I say that it was out of the agitation of this situation that Smith's Ladies' and Gent's Café originated, anybody who knows Mariposa will understand the magnitude of the moment.

Mr. Smith, then, moved slowly from the doorway of the hotel through the "rotunda," or more simply the front room with the desk and the cigar case in it, and so to the bar and thence to the little room or back bar behind it. In this room, as I have said, the brightest minds of Mariposa might commonly be found in the quieter part of a summer afternoon.

To-day there was a group of four who looked up as Mr. Smith entered, somewhat sympathetically, and evidently aware of the perplexities of the moment.

Henry Mullins and George Duff, the two bank managers, were both present. Mullins is a rather short, rather round, smooth-shaven man of less than forty, wearing one of those round banking suits of pepper and salt, with a round banking hat of hard straw, and with the kind of gold tie-pin and heavy watch-chain and seals necessary to inspire confidence in matters of foreign exchange. Duff is just as round and just as short, and equally smoothly shaven, while his seals and straw hat are calculated to prove that the Commercial is just as sound a bank as the Exchange. From the technical point of view of the banking business, neither of them had any objection to being in Smith's Hotel or to taking a drink as long as the other was present. This, of course, was one of the cardinal principles of Mariposa banking.

Then there was Mr. Diston, the high school teacher, commonly known as the "one who drank." None of the other teachers ever entered a hotel unless accompanied by a lady or protected by a child. But as Mr. Diston was known to drink beer on occasions and to go in and out of the Mariposa House and Smith's Hotel, he was looked upon as a man whose life was a mere wreck. Whenever the School Board raised the salaries of the other teachers, fifty or sixty dollars per annum at one lift, it was well understood that public morality wouldn't permit of an increase for Mr. Diston.

Still more noticeable, perhaps, was the quiet, sallow looking man dressed in black, with black gloves and with black silk hat heavily craped and placed hollow-side-up on a chair. This was Mr. Golgotha Gingham, the undertaker of Mariposa, and his dress was due to the fact that he had just come from what he called an "interment." Mr. Gingham had the true spirit of his profession, and such words as "funeral" or "coffin" or "hearse" never passed his lips. He spoke always of "interments," of "caskets," and "coaches," using terms that were calculated rather to bring out the majesty and sublimity of death than to parade its horrors.

To be present at the hotel was in accord with Mr. Gingham's general conception of his business. No man had ever grasped the true principles of undertaking more thoroughly than Mr. Gingham. I have often heard him explain that to associate with the living, uninteresting though they appear, is the only way to secure the custom of the dead.

"Get to know people really well while they are alive," said Mr. Gingham; "be friends with them, close friends, and then when they die you don't need to worry. You'll get the order every time."

So, naturally, as the moment was one of sympathy, it was Mr. Gingham who spoke first.

"What'll you do, Josh," he said, "if the Commissioners go against you?"

"Boys," said Mr. Smith, "I don't rightly know. If I have to quit, the next move is to the city. But I don't reckon that I will have to quit. I've got an idee that I think's good every time."

"Could you run a hotel in the city?" asked Mullins.

"I could," said Mr. Smith. "I'll tell you. There's big things doin' in the hotel business right now, big chances if you go into it right. Hotels in the city is branching out. Why, you take the dining-room side of it," continued Mr. Smith, looking round at the group, "there's thousands in it. The old plan's all gone. Folks won't eat now in an ordinary dining-room with a high ceiling and windows. You have to get 'em down underground in a room with no windows and lots of sawdust round and waiters that can't speak English. I seen them places last time I was in the city. They call 'em Rats' Coolers. And for light meals they want a

Caff, a real French Caff, and for folks that come in late another place that they call a Girl Room that don't shut up at all. If I go to the city that's the kind of place I mean to run. What's yours, Gol? It's on the house?"

And it was just at the moment when Mr. Smith said this that Billy, the desk clerk, entered the room with the telegram in his hand.

But stop—it is impossible for you to understand the anxiety with which Mr. Smith and his associates awaited the news from the Commissioners, without first realizing the astounding progress of Mr. Smith in the three past years and the pinnacle of public eminence to which he had attained.

Mr. Smith had come down from the lumber country of the Spanish River, where the divide is toward the Hudson Bay,— "back north" as they called it in Mariposa.

He had been, it was said, a cook in the lumber shanties. To this day Mr. Smith can fry an egg on both sides with a lightness of touch that is the despair of his own "help."

After that, he had run a river driver's boarding-house.

After that, he had taken a food contract for a gang of railroad navvies on the transcontinental.

After that, of course, the whole world was open to him.

He came down to Mariposa and bought out the "inside" of what had been the Royal Hotel.

Those who are educated understand that by the "inside" of a hotel is meant everything except the four outer walls of it—the fittings, the furniture, the bar, Billy the desk-clerk, the three dining-room girls, and above all the license granted by King Edward VII., and ratified further by King George, for the sale of intoxicating liquors.

Till then the Royal had been a mere nothing. As "Smith's Hotel" it broke into a blaze of effulgence.

From the first, Mr. Smith, as a proprietor, was a wild, rapturous success.

He had all the qualifications.

He weighed two hundred and eighty pounds.

He could haul two drunken men out of the bar each by the scruff of the neck without the faintest anger or excitement.

He carried money enough in his trousers pockets to start a bank, and spent it on anything, bet it on anything, and gave it away in handfuls.

He was never drunk, and, as a point of chivalry to his customers, never quite sober. Anybody was free of the hotel who cared to come in. Anybody who didn't like it could go out. Drinks of all kinds cost five cents, or six for a quarter. Meals and beds were practically free. Any persons foolish enough to go to the desk and pay for them, Mr. Smith charged according to the expression of their faces.

At first the loafers and the shanty men settled down on the place in a shower. But that was not the "trade" that Mr. Smith wanted. He knew how to get rid of them. An army of charwomen, turned into the hotel, scrubbed it from top to bottom. A vacuum cleaner, the first seen in Mariposa, hissed and screamed in the corridors. Forty brass beds were imported from the city, not, of course, for the guests to sleep in, but to keep them out. A bar-tender with a starched coat and wicker sleeves was put behind the bar.

The loafers were put out of business. The place had become too "high toned" for them.

To get the high class trade, Mr. Smith set himself to dress the part. He wore wide cut coats of filmy serge, light as gossamer; chequered waistcoats with a pattern for every day in the week; fedora hats light as autumn leaves; four-in-hand ties of saffron and myrtle green with a diamond pin the size of a hazel nut. On his fingers there were as many gems as would grace a native prince of India; across his waistcoat lay a gold watch-chain in huge square links and in his pocket a gold watch that weighed a pound and a half and marked minutes, seconds and quarter seconds. Just to look at Josh Smith's watch brought at least ten men to the bar every evening.

Every morning Mr. Smith was shaved by Jefferson Thorpe, across the way. All that art could do, all that Florida water could effect, was lavished on his person.

Mr. Smith became a local character. Mariposa was at his feet. All the reputable business men drank at Mr. Smith's bar, and in the little parlour behind it you might find at any time a group of the brightest intellects in the town.

Not but what there was opposition at first. The clergy, for example, who accepted the Mariposa House and the Continental as a necessary and useful evil, looked askance at the blazing lights and the surging crowd of Mr. Smith's saloon. They preached against him. When the Rev. Dean Drone led off with a sermon on the text "Lord be merciful even unto this publican Matthew Six," it was generally understood as an invitation to strike Mr. Smith dead. In the same way the sermon at the Presbyterian church the week after was on the text "Lo what now doeth Abiram in the land of Melchisideck Kings Eight and Nine?" and it was perfectly plain that what was meant was, "Lo, what is Josh Smith doing in Mariposa?"

But this opposition had been countered by a wide and sagacious philanthropy. I think Mr. Smith first got the idea of that on the night when the steam merry-go-round came to Mariposa. Just below the hostelry, on an empty lot, it whirled and whistled, steaming forth its tunes on the summer evening while the children crowded round it in hundreds. Down the street strolled Mr. Smith, wearing a soft fedora to indicate that it was evening.

"What d'you charge for a ride, boss?" said Mr. Smith.

"Two for a nickel," said the man

"Take that," said Mr. Smith, handing out a ten-dollar bill from a roll of money, "and ride the little folks free all evening."

That night the merry-go-round whirled madly till after midnight, freighted to capacity with Mariposa children, while up in Smith's Hotel, parents, friends and admirers, as the news spread, were standing four deep along the bar. They sold forty dollars' worth of lager alone that night, and Mr. Smith learned, if he had not already suspected it, the blessedness of giving.

The uses of philanthropy went further. Mr. Smith subscribed to everything, joined everything, gave to everything. He became an Oddfellow, a Forester, a Knight of Pythias and a Workman. He gave a hundred dollars to the Mariposa Hospital and a hundred dollars to the Young Men's Christian Association.

He subscribed to the Ball Club, the Lacrosse Club, the Curling Club, to anything, in fact, and especially to all those things which needed premises to meet in and grew thirsty in their discussions.

As a consequence the Oddfellows held their annual banquet at Smith's Hotel and the Oyster Supper of the Knights of Pythias was celebrated in Mr. Smith's dining-room.

Even more effective, perhaps, were Mr. Smith's secret

benefactions, the kind of giving done by stealth of which not a
soul in town knew anything, often, for a week after it was done.
It was in this way that Mr. Smith put the new font in Dean
Drone's church, and handed over a hundred dollars to Judge Pepperleigh for the unrestrained use of the Conservative party.

So it came about that, little by little, the antagonism had died
down. Smith's Hotel became an accepted institution in Mariposa.
Even the temperance people were proud of Mr. Smith as a sort
of character who added distinction to the town. There were moments, in the earlier quiet of the morning, when Dean Drone
would go so far as to step in to the "rotunda" and collect a sub-
scription. As for the Salvation Army, they ran in and out all the
time unreproved.

On only one point difficulty still remained. That was the
closing of the bar. Mr. Smith could never bring his mind to
it,—not as a matter of profit, but as a point of honour. It was too
much for him to feel that Judge Pepperleigh might be out on the
sidewalk thirsty at midnight, that the night hands of the Times-
Herald on Wednesday might be compelled to go home dry. On
this point Mr. Smith's moral code was simplicity itself,—do what
is right and take the consequences. So the bar stayed open.

Every town, I suppose, has its meaner spirits. In every genial
bosom some snake is warmed,—or, as Mr. Smith put it to Golgotha Gingham—"there are some fellers even in this town skunks
enough to inform."

At first the Mariposa court quashed all indictments. The
presiding judge, with his spectacles on and a pile of books in
front of him, threatened the informer with the penitentiary. The
whole bar of Mariposa was with Mr. Smith. But by sheer itera-
tion the informations had proved successful. Judge Pepperleigh
learned that Mr. Smith had subscribed a hundred dollars for the
Liberal party and at once fined him for keeping open after hours.
That made one conviction. On the top of this had come the unto-
ward incident just mentioned and that made two. Beyond that was
the deluge. This then was the exact situation when Billy, the desk
clerk, entered the back bar with the telegram in his hand.

"Here's your wire, sir," he said.

"What does it say?" said Mr. Smith.

He always dealt with written documents with a fine air of

detachment. I don't suppose there were ten people in Mariposa who knew that Mr. Smith couldn't read.

Billy opened the message and read, "Commissioners give you three months to close down."

"Let me read it," said Mr. Smith, "that's right, three months to close down."

There was dead silence when the message was read. Everybody waited for Mr. Smith to speak. Mr. Gingham instinctively assumed the professional air of hopeless melancholy.

As it was afterwards recorded, Mr. Smith stood and "studied" with the tray in his hand for at least four minutes. Then he spoke.

"Boys," he said, "I'll be darned if I close down till I'm ready to close down. I've got an idee. You wait and I'll show you."

And beyond that, not another word did Mr. Smith say on the subject.

But within forty-eight hours the whole town knew that something was doing. The hotel swarmed with carpenters, bricklayers and painters. There was an architect up from the city with a bundle of blue prints in his hand. There was an engineer taking the street level with a theodolite, and a gang of navvies with shovels digging like fury as if to dig out the back foundations of the hotel.

"That'll fool 'em," said Mr. Smith.

Half the town was gathered round the hotel crazy with excitement. But not a word would the proprietor say.

Great dray loads of square timber, and two-by-eight pine joists kept arriving from the planing mill. There was a pile of matched spruce sixteen feet high lying by the sidewalk.

Then the excavation deepened and the dirt flew, and the beams went up and the joists across, and all the day from dawn till dusk the hammers of the carpenters clattered away, working overtime at time and a half.

"It don't matter what it costs," said Mr. Smith; "get it done."

Rapidly the structure took form. It extended down the side street, joining the hotel at a right angle. Spacious and graceful it looked as it reared its uprights into the air.

Already you could see the place where the row of windows was to come, a veritable palace of glass, it must be, so wide and commodious were they. Below it, you could see the basement shaping itself, with a low ceiling like a vault and big beams running across, dressed, smoothed, and ready for staining. Already in the street there were seven crates of red and white awning.

And even then nobody knew what it was, and it was not till the seventeenth day that Mr. Smith, in the privacy of the back bar, broke the silence and explained.

"I tell you, boys," he says, "it's a caff—like what they have in the city—a ladies' and gents' caff, and that underneath (what's yours, Mr. Mullins?) is a Rats' Cooler. And when I get her started, I'll hire a French Chief to do the cooking, and for the winter I will put in a 'girl room,' like what they have in the city hotels. And I'd like to see who's going to close her up then."

Within two more weeks the plan was in operation. Not only was the caff built but the very hotel was transformed. Awnings had broken out in a red and white cloud upon its face, its every window carried a box of hanging plants, and above in glory floated the Union Jack. The very stationery was changed. The place was now Smith's Summer Pavilion. It was advertised in the city as Smith's Tourists' Emporium, and Smith's Northern Health Resort. Mr. Smith got the editor of the Times-Herald to write up a circular all about ozone and the Mariposa pine woods, with illustrations of the maskinonge (piscis mariposis) of Lake Wissanotti.

The Saturday after that circular hit the city in July, there were men with fishing rods and landing nets pouring in on every train, almost too fast to register. And if, in the face of that, a few little drops of whiskey were sold over the bar, who thought of it?

But the caff! that, of course, was the crowning glory of the thing, that and the Rats' Cooler below.

Light and cool, with swinging windows open to the air, tables with marble tops, palms, waiters in white coats—it was the standing marvel of Mariposa. Not a soul in the town except Mr. Smith, who knew it by instinct, ever guessed that waiters and palms and marble tables can be rented over the long distance telephone.

Mr. Smith was as good as his word. He got a French Chief with an aristocratic saturnine countenance, and a moustache and imperial that recalled the late Napoleon III. No one knew where Mr. Smith got him. Some people in the town said he was a French marquis. Others said he was a count and explained the difference.

No one in Mariposa had ever seen anything like the caff. All down the side of it were the grill fires, with great pewter dish covers that went up and down on a chain, and you could walk along the row and actually pick out your own cutlet and then see the French marquis throw it on to the broiling iron; you could watch a buckwheat pancake whirled into existence under your eyes and see fowls' legs devilled, peppered, grilled, and tormented till they lost all semblance of the original Mariposa chicken.

Mr. Smith, of course, was in his glory.

"What have you got to-day, Alf?" he would say, as he strolled over to the marquis. The name of the Chief was, I believe, Alphonse, but "Alf" was near enough for Mr. Smith.

The marquis would extend to the proprietor the menu, "Voilà, m'sieu, la carte du jour."

Mr. Smith, by the way, encouraged the use of the French language in the caff. He viewed it, of course, solely in its relation to the hotel business, and, I think, regarded it as a recent invention.

"It's comin' in all the time in the city," he said, "and y'aint expected to understand it."

Mr. Smith would take the carte between his finger and thumb and stare at it. It was all covered with such devices as Potage à la Mariposa—Filet Mignon à la proprietaire—Côtelette à la Smith, and so on.

But the greatest thing about the caff were the prices. Therein lay, as everybody saw at once, the hopeless simplicity of Mr. Smith.

The prices stood fast at 25 cents a meal. You could come in and eat all they had in the caff for a quarter.

"No, sir," Mr. Smith said stoutly, "I ain't going to try to raise no prices on the public. The hotel's always been a quarter and the caff's a quarter."

Full? Full of people?

Well, I should think so! From the time the caff opened at 11 till it closed at 8.30, you could hardly find a table. Tourists, visitors, travellers, and half the people of Mariposa crowded at the little tables; crockery rattling, glasses tinkling on trays, corks popping, the waiters in their white coats flying to and fro,

Alphonse whirling the cutlets and pancakes into the air, and in and through it all, Mr. Smith, in a white flannel suit and a broad crimson sash about his waist. Crowded and gay from morning to night, and even noisy in its hilarity.

Noisy, yes; but if you wanted deep quiet and cool, if you wanted to step from the glare of a Canadian August to the deep shadow of an enchanted glade,—walk down below into the Rats' Cooler. There you had it; dark old beams (who could believe they were put there a month ago?) great casks set on end with legends such as Amontillado Fino done in gilt on a black ground, tall steins filled with German beer soft as moss, and a German waiter noiseless as moving foam. He who entered the Rats' Cooler at three of a summer afternoon was buried there for the day. Mr. Golgotha Gingham spent anything from four to seven hours there of every day. In his mind the place had all the quiet charm of an interment, with none of its sorrows.

But at night, when Mr. Smith and Billy, the desk clerk, opened up the cash register and figured out the combined losses of the caff and the Rats' Cooler, Mr. Smith would say:

"Billy, just wait till I get the license renood, and I'll close up this damn cam so tight they'll never know what hit her. What did that lamb cost? Fifty cents a pound, was it? I figure it, Billy, that every one of them hogs eats about a dollar's worth a grub for every twenty-five cents they pay on it. As for Alf—by gosh, I'm through with him."

But that, of course, was only a confidential matter as between Mr. Smith and Billy.

I don't know at what precise period it was that the idea of a petition to the License Commissioners first got about the town. No one seemed to know just who suggested it. But certain it was that public opinion began to swing strongly towards the support of Mr. Smith. I think it was perhaps on the day after the big fish dinner that Alphonse cooked for the Mariposa Canoe Club (at twenty cents a head) that the feeling began to find open expression. People said it was a shame that a man like Josh Smith should be run out of Mariposa by three license commissioners. Who were the license commissioners, anyway? Why, look at the license system they had in Sweden; yes, and in Finland and in South America. Or, for the matter of that, look at the French and

Italians, who drink all day and all night. Aren't they all right?
Aren't they a musical people? Take Napoleon, and Victor Hugo;
drunk half the time, and yet look what they did.

I quote these arguments not for their own sake, but merely to
indicate the changing temper of public opinion in Mariposa. Men
would sit in the caff at lunch perhaps for an hour and a half and
talk about the license question in general, and then go down into
the Rats' Cooler and talk about it for two hours more.

It was amazing the way the light broke in in the case of particular individuals, often the most unlikely, and quelled their opposition.

Take, for example, the editor of the Newspacket. I suppose
there wasn't a greater temperance advocate in town. Yet Alphonse queered him with an Omelette à la License in one meal.

Or take Pepperleigh himself, the judge of the Mariposa court.
He was put to the bad with a game pie,—pâté normand aux fines
herbes—the real thing, as good as a trip to Paris in itself. After
eating it, Pepperleigh had the common sense to realize that it was
sheer madness to destroy a hotel that could cook a thing like that.

In the same way, the secretary of the School Board was
silenced with a stuffed duck à la Ossawippi.

Three members of the town council were converted with a
Dindon farci à la Josh Smith.

And then, finally, Mr. Diston persuaded Dean Drone to
come, and as soon as Mr. Smith and Alphonse saw him they
landed him with a fried flounder that even the apostles would
have appreciated.

After that, every one knew that the license question was
practically settled. The petition was all over the town. It was
printed in duplicate at the Newspacket and you could see it lying
on the counter of every shop in Mariposa. Some of the people
signed it twenty or thirty times.

It was the right kind of document too. It began—"Whereas in
the bounty of providence the earth putteth forth her luscious fruits
and her vineyards for the delight and enjoyment of mankind—"
It made you thirsty just to read it. Any man who read that petition over was wild to get to the Rats' Cooler.

When it was all signed up they had nearly three thousand
names on it.

Then Nivens, the lawyer, and Mr. Gingham (as a provincial

official) took it down to the county town, and by three o'clock that afternoon the news had gone out from the long distance telephone office that Smith's license was renewed for three years.

Rejoicings! Well, I should think so! Everybody was down wanting to shake hands with Mr. Smith. They told him that he had done more to boom Mariposa than any ten men in town. Some of them said he ought to run for the town council, and others wanted to make him the Conservative candidate for the next Dominion election. The caff was a mere babel of voices, and even the Rats' Cooler was almost floated away from its moorings.

And in the middle of it all, Mr. Smith found time to say to Billy, the desk clerk: "Take the cash registers out of the caff and the Rats' Cooler and start counting up the books."

And Billy said: "Will I write the letters for the palms and the tables and the stuff to go back?"

And Mr. Smith said: "Get 'em written right away."

So all evening the laughter and the chatter and the congratulations went on, and it wasn't till long after midnight that Mr. Smith was able to join Billy in the private room behind the "rotunda." Even when he did, there was a quiet and a dignity about his manner that had never been there before. I think it must have been the new halo of the Conservative candidacy that already radiated from his brow. It was, I imagine, at this very moment that Mr. Smith first realised that the hotel business formed the natural and proper threshold of the national legislature.

"Here's the account of the cash registers," said Billy.

"Let me see it," said Mr. Smith. And he studied the figures without a word.

"And here's the letters about the palms, and here's Alphonse up to yesterday—"

And then an amazing thing happened.

"Billy," said Mr. Smith, "tear 'em up. I ain't going to do it. It ain't right and I won't do it. They got me the license for to keep the caff and I'm going to keep the caff. I don't need to close her. The bar's good for anything from forty to a hundred a day now, with the Rats' Cooler going good, and that caff will stay right here."

And stay it did.

There it stands, mind you, to this day. You've only to step round the corner of Smith's Hotel on the side street and read the sign: LADIES' AND GENT'S CAFÉ, just as large and as imposing as ever.

Mr. Smith said that he'd keep the caff, and when he said a thing he meant it!

Of course there were changes, small changes.

I don't say, mind you, that the fillet de beef that you get there now is perhaps quite up to the level of the filet de bœufs aux champignons of the days of glory.

No doubt the lamb chops in Smith's Caff are often very much the same, nowadays, as the lamb chops of the Mariposa House or the Continental.

Of course, things like Omelette aux Trufles practically died out when Alphonse went. And, naturally, the leaving of Alphonse was inevitable. No one knew just when he went, or why. But one morning he was gone. Mr. Smith said that "Alf had to go back to his folks in the old country."

So, too, when Alf left, the use of the French language, as such, fell off tremendously in the caff. Even now they use it to some extent. You can still get fillet de beef, and saucisson au juice, but Billy the desk clerk has considerable trouble with the spelling.

The Rats' Cooler, of course, closed down, or rather Mr. Smith closed it for repairs, and there is every likelihood that it will hardly open for three years. But the caff is there. They don't use the grills, because there's no need to, with the hotel kitchen so handy.

The "girl room," I may say, was never opened. Mr. Smith promised it, it is true, for the winter, and still talks of it. But somehow there's been a sort of feeling against it. Every one in town admits that every big hotel in the city has a "girl room" and that it must be all right. Still, there's a certain—well, you know how sensitive opinion is in a place like Mariposa.

Chapter II

The Speculations of Jefferson Thorpe

It was not until the mining boom, at the time when everybody went simply crazy over the Cobalt and Porcupine mines of the new silver country near the Hudson Bay, that Jefferson Thorpe reached what you might call public importance in Mariposa.

Of course everybody knew Jeff and his little barber shop that stood just across the street from Smith's Hotel. Everybody knew him and everybody got shaved there. From early morning, when the commercial travellers off the 6.30 express got shaved into the resemblance of human beings, there were always people going in and out of the barber shop.

Mullins, the manager of the Exchange Bank, took his morning shave from Jeff as a form of resuscitation, with enough wet towels laid on his face to stew him and with Jeff moving about in the steam, razor in hand, as grave as an operating surgeon.

Then, as I think I said, Mr. Smith came in every morning and there was a tremendous outpouring of Florida water and rums, essences and revivers and renovators, regardless of expense. What with Jeff's white coat and Mr. Smith's flowered waistcoat and the red geranium in the window and the Florida water and the double extract of hyacinth, the little shop seemed multi-coloured and luxurious enough for the annex of a Sultan's harem.

But what I mean is that, till the mining boom, Jefferson Thorpe never occupied a position of real prominence in Mariposa. You couldn't, for example, have compared him with a man like Golgotha Gingham, who, as undertaker, stood in a direct relation to life and death, or to Trelawney, the postmaster, who drew money from the Federal Government of Canada, and was regarded as virtually a member of the Dominion Cabinet.

Everybody knew Jeff and liked him, but the odd thing was that till he made money nobody took any stock in his ideas at all. It was only after he made the "clean up" that they came to see what a splendid fellow he was. "Level-headed" I think was the term; indeed in the speech of Mariposa, the highest form of endowment was to have the head set on horizontally as with a theodolite.

As I say, it was when Jeff made money that they saw how gifted he was, and when he lost it,—but still, there's no need to go into that. I believe it's something the same in other places, too.

The barber shop, you will remember, stands across the street from Smith's Hotel, and stares at it face to face.

It is one of those wooden structures—I don't know whether you know them—with a false front that sticks up above its real height and gives it an air at once rectangular and imposing. It is a form of architecture much used in Mariposa and understood to be in keeping with the pretentious and artificial character of modern business. There is a red, white and blue post in front of the shop and the shop itself has a large square window out of proportion to its little flat face.

Painted on the panes of the window is the remains of a legend that once spelt BARBER SHOP, executed with the flourishes that prevailed in the golden age of sign painting in Mariposa. Through the window you can see the geraniums in the window shelf and behind them Jeff Thorpe with his little black skull cap on and his spectacles drooped upon his nose as he bends forward in the absorption of shaving.

As you open the door, it sets in violent agitation a coiled spring up above and a bell that almost rings. Inside, there are two shaving chairs of the heavier, or electrocution pattern, with mirrors in front of them and pigeon holes with individual shaving mugs. There must be ever so many of them, fifteen or sixteen. It is the current supposition of each of Jeff's customers that everyone else but himself uses a separate mug. One corner of the shop is partitioned off and bears the sign: HOT AND COLD BATHS, 50 cents. There has been no bath inside the partition for twenty years—only old newspapers and a mop. Still, it lends distinction somehow, just as do the faded cardboard signs that hang against the mirror with the legends: TURKISH SHAMPOO, 75 cents, and ROMAN MASSAGE, $1.00.

They said commonly in Mariposa that Jeff made money out of the barber shop. He may have, and it may have been that that turned his mind to investment. But it's hard to see how he could. A shave cost five cents, and a hair-cut fifteen (or the two, if you liked, for a quarter), and at that it is hard to see how he could make money, even when he had both chairs going and shaved first in one and then in the other.

You see, in Mariposa, shaving isn't the hurried, perfunctory thing that it is in the city. A shave is looked upon as a form of physical pleasure and lasts anywhere from twenty-five minutes to three-quarters of an hour.

In the morning hours, perhaps, there was a semblance of haste about it, but in the long quiet of the afternoon, as Jeff leaned forward towards the customer and talked to him in a soft confidential monotone, like a portrait painter, the razor would go slower and slower, and pause and stop, move and pause again, till the shave died away into the mere drowse of conversation.

At such hours, the Mariposa barber shop would become a very Palace of Slumber, and as you waited your turn in one of the wooden arm-chairs beside the wall, what with the quiet of the hour, and the low drone of Jeff's conversation, the buzzing of the flies against the window pane and the measured tick of the clock above the mirror, your head sank dreaming on your breast, and the Mariposa Newspacket rustled unheeded on the floor. It makes one drowsy just to think of it!

The conversation, of course, was the real charm of the place. You see, Jefferson's forte, or specialty, was information. He could tell you more things within the compass of a half-hour's shave than you get in days of laborious research in an encyclopædia. Where he got it all, I don't know, but I am inclined to think it came more or less out of the newspapers.

In the city, people never read the newspapers, not really, only little bits and scraps of them. But in Mariposa it's different. There they read the whole thing from cover to cover, and they build up on it, in the course of years, a range of acquirement that would put a college president to the blush. Anybody who has ever heard Henry Mullins and Peter Glover talk about the future of China will know just what I mean.

And, of course, the peculiarity of Jeff's conversation was that he could suit it to his man every time. He had a kind of divination about it. There was a certain kind of man that Jeff would size up sideways as he stropped the razor, and in whose ear he would whisper: "I see where Saint Louis has took four straight games off Chicago,"—and so hold him fascinated to the end.

In the same way he would say to Mr. Smith: "I see where it

says that this 'Flying Squirl' run a dead heat for the King's Plate."

To a humble intellect like mine he would explain in full the relations of the Keesar to the German Rich Dog.

But first and foremost, Jeff's specialty in the way of conversation was finance and the money market, the huge fortunes that a man with the right kind of head could make.

I've known Jefferson to pause in his shaving with the razor suspended in the air as long as five minutes while he described, with his eye half closed, exactly the kind of a head a man needed in order to make a "haul" or a "clean up." It was evidently simply a matter of the head, and as far as one could judge, Jeff's own was the very type required.

I don't know just at what time or how Jefferson first began his speculative enterprises. It was probably in him from the start. There is no doubt that the very idea of such things as Traction Stock and Amalgamated Asbestos went to his head: and whenever he spoke of Mr. Carnegie and Mr. Rockefeller, the yearning tone of his voice made it as soft as lathered soap.

I suppose the most rudimentary form of his speculation was the hens. That was years ago. He kept them out at the back of his house,—which itself stood up a grass plot behind and beyond the barber shop,—and in the old days Jeff would say, with a certain note of pride in his voice, that The Woman had sold as many as two dozen eggs in a day to the summer visitors.

But what with reading about Amalgamated Asbestos and Consolidated Copper and all that, the hens began to seem pretty small business, and, in any case, the idea of two dozen eggs at a cent apiece almost makes one blush. I suppose a good many of us have felt just as Jeff did about our poor little earnings. Anyway, I remember Jeff telling me one day that he could take the whole lot of the hens and sell them off and crack the money into Chicago wheat on margin and turn it over in twenty-four hours. He did it too. Only somehow when it was turned over it came upside down on top of the hens.

After that the hen house stood empty and The Woman had to throw away chicken feed every day, at a dead loss of perhaps a shave and a half. But it made no difference to Jeff, for his mind had floated away already on the possibilities of what he called "displacement" mining on the Yukon.

So you can understand that when the mining boom struck Mariposa, Jefferson Thorpe was in it right from the very start. Why, no wonder; it seemed like the finger of Providence. Here was this great silver country spread out to north of us, where people had thought there was only a wilderness. And right at our very doors! You could see, as I saw, the night express going north every evening; for all one knew Rockefeller or Carnegie or anyone might be on it! Here was the wealth of Calcutta, as the Mariposa Newspacket put it, poured out at our very feet.

So no wonder the town went wild! All day in the street you could hear men talking of veins, and smelters and dips and deposits and faults,—the town hummed with it like a geology class on examination day. And there were men about the hotels with mining outfits and theodolites and dunnage bags, and at Smith's bar they would hand chunks of rock up and down, some of which would run as high as ten drinks to the pound.

The fever just caught the town and ran through it! Within a fortnight they put a partition down Robertson's Coal and Wood Office and opened the Mariposa Mining Exchange, and just about every man on the Main Street started buying scrip. Then presently young Fizzlechip, who had been teller in Mullins's Bank and that everybody had thought a worthless jackass before, came back from the Cobalt country with a fortune, and loafed round in the Mariposa House in English khaki and a horizontal hat, drunk all the time, and everybody holding him up as an example of what it was possible to do if you tried.

They all went in. Jim Eliot mortgaged the inside of the drug store and jammed it into Twin Tamagami. Pete Glover at the hardware store bought Nippewa stock at thirteen cents and sold it to his brother at seventeen and bought it back in less than a week at nineteen. They didn't care! They took a chance. Judge Pepperleigh put the rest of his wife's money into Temiskaming Common, and Lawyer Macartney got the fever, too, and put every cent that his sister possessed into Tulip Preferred.

And even when young Fizzlechip shot himself in the back room of the Mariposa House, Mr. Gingham buried him in a casket with silver handles and it was felt that there was a Monte Carlo touch about the whole thing.

They all went in—or all except Mr. Smith. You see, Mr. Smith had come down from there, and he knew all about rocks and mining and canoes and the north country. He knew what it was to eat flour-baked dampers under the lee side of a canoe propped among the underbrush, and to drink the last drop of whiskey within fifty miles. Mr. Smith had mighty little use for the north. But what he did do, was to buy up enough early potatoes to send fifteen carload lots into Cobalt at a profit of five dollars a bag.

Mr. Smith, I say, hung back. But Jeff Thorpe was in the mining boom right from the start. He bought in on the Nippewa mine even before the interim prospectus was out. He took a "block" of 100 shares of Abbitibbi Development at fourteen cents, and he and Johnson, the livery stable-keeper next door, formed a syndicate and got a thousand shares of Metagami Lake at 3 1-4 cents and then "unloaded" them on one of the sausage men at Netley's butcher shop at a clear cent per cent. advance.

Jeff would open the little drawer below the mirror in the barber shop and show you all kinds and sorts of Cobalt country mining certificates,—blue ones, pink ones, green ones, with outlandish and fascinating names on them that ran clear from the Mattawa to the Hudson Bay.

And right from the start he was confident of winning.

"There ain't no difficulty to it," he said, there's lots of silver up there in that country and if you buy some here and some there you can't fail to come out somewhere. I don't say," he used to continue, with the scissors open and ready to cut, "that some of the greenhorns won't get bit. But if a feller knows the country and keeps his head level, he can't lose."

Jefferson had looked at so many prospectuses and so many pictures of mines and pine trees and smelters, that I think he'd forgotten that he'd never been in the country. Anyway, what's two hundred miles!

To an onlooker it certainly didn't seem so simple. I never knew the meanness, the trickery, of the mining business, the sheer obstinate determination of the bigger capitalists not to make money when they might, till I heard the accounts of Jeff's different mines. Take the case of the Corona Jewel. There was a good mine, simply going to ruin for lack of common sense.

"She ain't been developed," Jeff would say. "There's silver enough in her so you could dig it out with a shovel. She's full of it. But they won't get at her and work her."

Then he'd take a look at the pink and blue certificates of the Corona Jewel and slam the drawer on them in disgust.

Worse than that was the Silent Pine,—a clear case of stupid incompetence! Utter lack of engineering skill was all that was keeping the Silent Pine from making a fortune for its holders.

"The only trouble with that mine," said Jeff, "is they won't go deep enough. They followed the vein down to where it kind o' thinned out and then they quit. If they'd just go right into her good, they'd get it again. She's down there all right."

But perhaps the meanest case of all was the Northern Star. That always seemed to me every time I heard of it, a straight case for the criminal law. The thing was so evidently a conspiracy.

"I bought her," said Jeff, "at thirty-two, and she stayed right there tight, like she was stuck. Then a bunch of these fellers in the city started to drive her down and they got her pushed down to twenty-four, and I held on to her and they shoved her down to twenty-one. This morning they've got her down to sixteen, but I don't mean to let go. No, sir."

In another fortnight they shoved her, the same unscrupulous crowd, down to nine cents, and Jefferson still held on.

"They're working her down," he admitted, "but I'm holding her."

No conflict between vice and virtue was ever grimmer.

"She's at six," said Jeff, "but I've got her. They can't squeeze me."

A few days after that, the same criminal gang had her down further than ever.

"They've got her down to three cents," said Jeff, "but I'm with her. Yes, sir, they think they can shove her clean off the market, but they can't do it. I've boughten in Johnson's shares, and the whole of Netley's, and I'll stay with her till she breaks."

So they shoved and pushed and clawed her down—that unseen nefarious crowd in the city—and Jeff held on to her and they writhed and twisted at his grip, and then—

And then—well, that's just the queer thing about the mining business. Why, sudden as a flash of lightning, it seemed, the news came over the wire to the Mariposa Newspacket, that they had struck a vein of silver in the Northern Star as thick as a sidewalk, and that the stock had jumped to seventeen dollars a share, and even at that you couldn't get it! And Jeff stood there flushed and half-staggered against the mirror of the little shop, with a bunch of mining scrip in his hand that was worth forty thousand dollars!

Excitement! It was all over the town in a minute. They ran off a news extra at the Mariposa Newspacket, and in less than no time there wasn't standing room in the barber shop, and over in Smith's Hotel they had three extra bar-keepers working on the lager beer pumps.

They were selling mining shares on the Main Street in Mariposa that afternoon and people were just clutching for them. Then at night there was a big oyster supper in Smith's caff, with speeches and the Mariposa band outside.

And the queer thing was that the very next afternoon was the funeral of young Fizzlechip, and Dean Drone had to change the whole text of his Sunday sermon at two days' notice for fear of offending public sentiment.

But I think what Jeff liked best of it all was the sort of public recognition that it meant. He'd stand there in the shop, hardly bothering to shave, and explain to the men in the arm-chairs how he held her, and they shoved her, and he clung to her, and what he'd said to himself—a perfect Iliad—while he was clinging to her.

The whole thing was in the city papers a few days after with a photograph of Jeff, taken specially at Ed Moore's studio (upstairs over Netley's). It showed Jeff sitting among palm trees, as all mining men do, with one hand on his knee, and a dog, one of those regular mining dogs, at his feet, and a look of piercing intelligence in his face that would easily account for forty thousand dollars.

I say that the recognition meant a lot to Jeff for its own sake. But no doubt the fortune meant quite a bit to him too on account of Myra.

Did I mention Myra, Jeff's daughter? Perhaps not. That's the trouble with the people in Mariposa; they're all so separate and so different—not a bit like the people in the cities—that unless you hear about them separately and one by one you can't for a moment understand what they're like.

Myra had golden hair and a Greek face and would come

bursting through the barber shop in a hat at least six inches wider than what they wear in Paris. As you saw her swinging up the street to the Telephone Exchange in a suit that was straight out of the Delineator and brown American boots, there was style written all over her,—the kind of thing that Mariposa recognised and did homage to. And to see her in the Exchange,—she was one of the four girls that I spoke of,—on her high stool with a steel cap on, —jabbing the connecting plugs in and out as if electricity cost nothing—well, all I mean is that you could understand why it was that the commercial travellers would stand round in the Exchange calling up all sorts of impossible villages, and waiting about so pleasant and genial!—it made one realize how naturally good-tempered men are. And then when Myra would go off duty and Miss Cleghorn, who was sallow, would come on, the commercial men would be off again like autumn leaves.

It just shows the difference between people. There was Myra who treated lovers like dogs and would slap them across the face with a banana skin to show her utter independence. And there was Miss Cleghorn, who was sallow, and who bought a forty cent Ancient History to improve herself: and yet if she'd hit any man in Mariposa with a banana skin, he'd have had her arrested for assault.

Mind you, I don't mean that Myra was merely flippant and worthless. Not at all. She was a girl with any amount of talent. You should have heard her recite "The Raven," at the Methodist Social! Simply genius! And when she acted Portia in the Trial Scene of the Merchant of Venice at the High School concert, everybody in Mariposa admitted that you couldn't have told it from the original.

So, of course, as soon as Jeff made the fortune, Myra had her resignation in next morning and everybody knew that she was to go to a dramatic school for three months in the fall and become a leading actress.

But, as I said, the public recognition counted a lot for Jeff. The moment you begin to get that sort of thing it comes in quickly enough. Brains, you know, are recognized right away. That was why, of course, within a week from this Jeff received the first big packet of stuff from the Cuban Land Development Company, with coloured pictures of Cuba, and fields of bananas, and haciendas and insurrectos with machetes and Heaven knows what. They heard of him, somehow,—it wasn't for a modest man like Jefferson to say how. After all, the capitalists of the world are just one and the same crowd. If you're in it, you're in it, that's all! Jeff realized why it is that of course men like Carnegie or Rockefeller and Morgan all know one another. They have to.

For all I know, this Cuban stuff may have been sent from Morgan himself. Some of the people in Mariposa said yes, others said no. There was no certainty.

Anyway, they were fair and straight, this Cuban crowd that wrote to Jeff. They offered him to come right in and be one of themselves. If a man's got the brains, you may as well recognize it straight away. Just as well write him to be a director now as wait and hesitate till he forces his way into it.

Anyhow, they didn't hesitate, these Cuban people that wrote to Jeff from Cuba—or from a post-office box in New York—it's all the same thing, because Cuba being so near to New York the mail is all distributed from there. I suppose in some financial circles they might have been slower, wanted guarantees of some sort, and so on, but these Cubans, you know, have got a sort of Spanish warmth of heart that you don't see in business men in America, and that touches you. No, they asked no guarantee. Just send the money—whether by express order or by bank draft or cheque, they left that entirely to oneself, as a matter between Cuban gentlemen.

And they were quite frank about their enterprise—bananas and tobacco in the plantation district reclaimed from the insurrectos. You could see it all there in the pictures—the tobacco plants and the insurrectos—everything. They made no rash promises, just admitted straight out that the enterprise might realise 400 per cent. or might conceivably make less. There was no hint of more.

So within a month, everybody in Mariposa knew that Jeff Thorpe was "in Cuban lands" and would probably clean up half a million by New Year's. You couldn't have failed to know it. All round the little shop there were pictures of banana groves and the harbour of Habana, and Cubans in white suits and scarlet sashes, smoking cigarettes in the sun and too ignorant to know that you can make four hundred per cent. by planting a banana tree.

I liked it about Jeff that he didn't stop shaving. He went on just the same. Even when Johnson, the livery stable man, came in with five hundred dollars and asked him to see if the Cuban Board of Directors would let him put it in, Jeff laid it in the drawer and then shaved him for five cents, in the same old way. Of course, he must have felt proud when, a few days later, he got a letter from the Cuban people, from New York, accepting the money straight off without a single question, and without knowing anything more of Johnson except that he was a friend of Jeff's. They wrote most handsomely. Any friends of Jeff's were friends of Cuba. All money they might send would be treated just as Jeff's would be treated.

One reason, perhaps, why Jeff didn't give up shaving was because it allowed him to talk about Cuba. You see, everybody knew in Mariposa that Jeff Thorpe had sold out of Cobalts and had gone into Cuban Renovated Lands—and that spread round him a kind of halo of wealth and mystery and outlandishness— oh, something Spanish. Perhaps you've felt it about people that you know. Anyhow, they asked him about the climate, and yellow fever and what the negroes were like and all that sort of thing.

"This Cubey, it appears, is an island," Jeff would explain. Of course, everybody knows how easily islands lend themselves to making money,—"and for fruit, they say it comes up so fast you can't stop it." And then he would pass into details about the Hash-enders and the resurrectos and technical things like that till it was thought a wonder how he could know it. Still, it was realized that a man with money has got to know these things. Look at Morgan and Rockefeller and all the men that make a pile. They know just as much as Jeff did about the countries where they make it. It stands to reason.

Did I say that Jeff shaved in the same old way? Not quite. There was something even dreamier about it now, and a sort of new element in the way Jeff fell out of his monotone into lapses of thought that I, for one, misunderstood. I thought that perhaps getting so much money,—well, you know the way it acts on people in the larger cities. It seemed to spoil one's idea of Jeff that copper and asbestos and banana lands should form the goal of his thought when, if he knew it, the little shop and the sunlight of Mariposa was so much better.

In fact, I had perhaps borne him a grudge for what seemed to me his perpetual interest in the great capitalists. He always had some item out of the paper about them.

"I see where this here Carnegie has give fifty thousand dollars for one of them observatories," he would say.

And another day he would pause in the course of shaving, and almost whisper: "Did you ever *see* this Rockefeller?"

It was only by a sort of accident that I came to know that there was another side to Jefferson's speculation that no one in Mariposa ever knew, or will ever know now.

I knew it because I went in to see Jeff in his house one night. The house,—I think I said it,—stood out behind the barber shop. You went out of the back door of the shop, and through a grass plot with petunias beside it, and the house stood at the end. You could see the light of the lamp behind the blind, and through the screen door as you came along. And it was here that Jefferson used to sit in the evenings when the shop got empty.

There was a round table that The Woman used to lay for supper, and after supper there used to be a chequered cloth on it and a lamp with a shade. And beside it Jeff would sit, with his spectacles on and the paper spread out, reading about Carnegie and Rockefeller. Near him, but away from the table, was The Woman doing needlework, and Myra, when she wasn't working in the Telephone Exchange, was there too with her elbows on the table reading Marie Corelli—only now, of course, after the fortune, she was reading the prospectuses of Dramatic Schools.

So this night,—I don't know just what it was in the paper that caused it,—Jeff laid down what he was reading and started to talk about Carnegie.

"This Carnegie, I bet you, would be worth," said Jeff, closing up his eyes in calculation, "as much as perhaps two million dollars, if you was to sell him up. And this Rockefeller and this Morgan, either of them, to sell them up clean, would be worth another couple of million—"

I may say in parenthesis that it was a favourite method in Mariposa if you wanted to get at the real worth of a man, to imagine him clean sold up, put up for auction, as it were. It was the only way to test him.

"And now look at 'em," Jeff went on. "They make their money and what do they do with it? They give it away. And who do they give it to? Why, to those as don't want it, every time.

They give it to these professors and to this research and that, and do the poor get any of it? Not a cent and never will.

"I tell you, boys," continued Jeff (there were no boys present, but in Mariposa all really important speeches are addressed to an imaginary audience of boys)—"I tell you, if I was to make a million out of this Cubey, I'd give it straight to the poor, yes, sir— divide it up into a hundred lots of a thousand dollars each and give it to the people that hadn't nothing."

So always after that I knew just what those bananas were being grown for.

Indeed, after that, though Jefferson never spoke of his intentions directly, he said a number of things that seemed to bear on them. He asked me, for instance, one day, how many blind people it would take to fill one of these blind homes and how a feller could get ahold of them. And at another time he asked whether if a feller advertised for some of these incurables a feller could get enough of them to make a showing. I know for a fact that he got Nivens, the lawyer, to draw up a document that was to give an acre of banana land in Cuba to every idiot in Missinaba county.

But still,—what's the use of talking of what Jeff meant to do? Nobody knows or cares about it now.

The end of it was bound to come. Even in Mariposa some of the people must have thought so. Else how was it that Henry Mullins made such a fuss about selling a draft for forty thousand on New York? And why was it that Mr. Smith wouldn't pay Billy, the desk clerk, his back wages when he wanted to put it into Cuba?

Oh yes; some of them must have seen it. And yet when it came it seemed so quiet,—ever so quiet,—not a bit like the Northern Star mine and the oyster supper and the Mariposa band. It is strange how quiet these things look, the other way round.

You remember the Cuban Land frauds in New York—and Porforio Gomez shooting the detective, and him and Maximo Morez getting clear away with two hundred thousand? No, of course you don't; why, even in the city papers it only filled an inch or two of type, and anyway the names were hard to remember. That was Jeff's money—part of it. Mullins got the telegram, from a broker or someone, and he showed it to Jeff just as he was going up the street with an estate agent to look at a big empty

lot on the hill behind the town—the very place for these incurables.

And Jeff went back to the shop so quiet—have you ever seen
an animal that is stricken through, how quiet it seems to move?

Well, that's how he walked.

And since that, though it's quite a little while ago, the shop's
open till eleven every night now, and Jeff is shaving away to pay
back that five hundred that Johnson, the livery man, sent to the
Cubans, and—

Pathetic? tut! tut! You don't know Mariposa. Jeff has to work
pretty late, but that's nothing—nothing at all, if you've worked
hard all your lifetime. And Myra is back at the Telephone Exchange—they were glad enough to get her, and she says now that
if there's one thing she hates, it's the stage, and she can't see
how the actresses put up with it.

Anyway, things are not so bad. You see it was just at this
time that Mr. Smith's caff opened, and Mr. Smith came to Jeff's
Woman and said he wanted seven dozen eggs a day, and wanted
them handy, and so the hens are back, and more of them, and
they exult so every morning over the eggs they lay that if you
wanted to talk of Rockefeller in the barber shop you couldn't hear
his name for the cackling.

Chapter III

The Marine Excursion of the
Knights of Pythias

Half-past six on a July morning! The Mariposa Belle is at the wharf, decked in flags, with steam up ready to start.

Excursion day!

Half-past six on a July morning, and Lake Wissanotti lying in the sun as calm as glass. The opal colours of the morning light are shot from the surface of the water.

Out on the lake the last thin threads of the mist are clearing away like flecks of cotton wool.

The long call of the loon echoes over the lake. The air is cool and fresh. There is in it all the new life of the land of the silent pine and the moving waters. Lake Wissanotti in the morning sunlight! Don't talk to me of the Italian lakes, or the Tyrol or the Swiss Alps. Take them away. Move them somewhere else. I don't want them.

Excursion Day, at half-past six of a summer morning! With the boat all decked in flags and all the people in Mariposa on the wharf, and the band in peaked caps with big cornets tied to their bodies ready to play at any minute! I say! Don't tell me about the Carnival of Venice and the Delhi Durbar. Don't! I wouldn't look at them. I'd shut my eyes! For light and colour give me every time an excursion out of Mariposa down the lake to the Indian's Island out of sight in the morning mist. Talk of your Papal Zouaves and your Buckingham Palace Guard! I want to see the Mariposa band in uniform and the Mariposa Knights of Pythias with their aprons and their insignia and their picnic baskets and their five-cent cigars!

Half-past six in the morning, and all the crowd on the wharf and the boat due to leave in half an hour. Notice it!—in half an hour. Already she's whistled twice (at six, and at six fifteen), and at any minute now, Christie Johnson will step into the pilot house and pull the string for the warning whistle that the boat will leave in half an hour. So keep ready. Don't think of running back to

Smith's Hotel for the sandwiches. Don't be fool enough to try to go up to the Greek Store, next to Netley's, and buy fruit. You'll be left behind for sure if you do. Never mind the sandwiches and the fruit! Anyway, here comes Mr. Smith himself with a huge basket of provender that would feed a factory. There must be sandwiches in that. I think I can hear them clinking. And behind Mr. Smith is the German waiter from the caff with another basket—indubitably lager beer; and behind him, the bar-tender of the hotel, carrying nothing, as far as one can see. But of course if you know Mariposa you will understand that why he looks so nonchalant and empty-handed is because he has two bottles of rye whiskey under his linen duster. You know, I think, the peculiar walk of a man with two bottles of whiskey in the inside pockets of a linen coat. In Mariposa, you see, to bring beer to an excursion is quite in keeping with public opinion. But, whiskey,—well, one has to be a little careful.

Do I say that Mr. Smith is here? Why, everybody's here. There's Hussell the editor of the Newspacket, wearing a blue ribbon on his coat, for the Mariposa Knights of Pythias are, by their constitution, dedicated to temperance; and there's Henry Mullins, the manager of the Exchange Bank, also a Knight of Pythias, with a small flask of Pogram's Special in his hip pocket as a sort of amendment to the constitution. And there's Dean Drone, the Chaplain of the Order, with a fishing-rod (you never saw such green bass as lie among the rocks at Indian's Island), and with a trolling line in case of maskinonge, and a landing net in case of pickerel, and with his eldest daughter, Lilian Drone, in case of young men. There never was such a fisherman as the Rev. Rupert Drone.

Perhaps I ought to explain that when I speak of the excursion as being of the Knights of Pythias, the thing must not be understood in any narrow sense. In Mariposa practically everybody belongs to the Knights of Pythias just as they do to everything else. That's the great thing about the town and that's what makes it so different from the city. Everybody is in everything.

You should see them on the seventeenth of March, for example, when everybody wears a green ribbon and they're all laughing and glad,—you know what the Celtic nature is,—and talking about Home Rule.

On St. Andrew's Day every man in town wears a thistle and shakes hands with everybody else, and you see the fine old Scotch honesty beaming out of their eyes.

And on St. George's Day!—well, there's no heartiness like the good old English spirit, after all; why shouldn't a man feel glad that he's an Englishman?

Then on the Fourth of July there are stars and stripes flying over half the stores in town, and suddenly all the men are seen to smoke cigars, and to know all about Roosevelt and Bryan and the Philippine Islands. Then you learn for the first time that Jeff Thorpe's people came from Massachusetts and that his uncle fought at Bunker Hill (it must have been Bunker Hill,—anyway Jefferson will swear it was in Dakota all right enough); and you find that George Duff has a married sister in Rochester and that her husband is all right; in fact, George was down there as recently as eight years ago. Oh, it's the most American town imaginable is Mariposa,—on the fourth of July.

But wait, just wait, if you feel anxious about the solidity of the British connection, till the twelfth of the month, when everybody is wearing an orange streamer in his coat and the Orangemen (every man in town) walk in the big procession. Allegiance! Well, perhaps you remember the address they gave to the Prince of Wales on the platform of the Mariposa station as he went through on his tour to the west. I think that pretty well settled that question.

So you will easily understand that of course everybody belongs to the Knights of Pythias and the Masons and Oddfellows, just as they all belong to the Snow Shoe Club and the Girls' Friendly Society.

And meanwhile the whistle of the steamer has blown again for a quarter to seven:—loud and long this time, for any one not here now is late for certain, unless he should happen to come down in the last fifteen minutes.

What a crowd upon the wharf and how they pile on to the steamer! It's a wonder that the boat can hold them all. But that's just the marvellous thing about the Mariposa Belle.

I don't know,—I have never known,—where the steamers like the Mariposa Belle come from. Whether they are built by Harland and Wolff of Belfast, or whether, on the other hand, they are not built by Harland and Wolff of Belfast, is more than one would like to say offhand.

The Mariposa Belle always seems to me to have some of those strange properties that distinguish Mariposa itself. I mean, her size seems to vary so. If you see her there in the winter, frozen in the ice beside the wharf with a snowdrift against the windows of the pilot house, she looks a pathetic little thing the size of a butternut. But in the summer time, especially after you've been in Mariposa for a month or two, and have paddled alongside of her in a canoe, she gets larger and taller, and with a great sweep of black sides, till you see no difference between the Mariposa Belle and the Lusitania. Each one is a big steamer and that's all you can say.

Nor do her measurements help you much. She draws about eighteen inches forward, and more than that,—at least half an inch more, astern, and when she's loaded down with an excursion crowd she draws a good two inches more. And above the water, —why, look at all the decks on her! There's the deck you walk on to, from the wharf, all shut in, with windows along it, and the after cabin with the long table, and above that the deck with all the chairs piled upon it, and the deck in front where the band stand round in a circle, and the pilot house is higher than that, and above the pilot house is the board with the gold name and the flag pole and the steel ropes and the flags; and fixed in some-where on the different levels is the lunch counter where they sell the sandwiches, and the engine room, and down below the deck level, beneath the water line, is the place where the crew sleep. What with steps and stairs and passages and piles of cordwood for the engine,—oh no, I guess Harland and Wolff didn't build her. They couldn't have.

Yet even with a huge boat like the Mariposa Belle, it would be impossible for her to carry all of the crowd that you see in the boat and on the wharf. In reality, the crowd is made up of two classes,—all of the people in Mariposa who are going on the excursion and all those who are not. Some come for the one reason and some for the other.

The two tellers of the Exchange Bank are both there standing side by side. But one of them,—the one with the cameo pin and the long face like a horse,—is going, and the other,—with the other cameo pin and the face like another horse,—is not. In the same way, Hussell of the Newspacket is going, but his brother, beside him, isn't. Lilian Drone is going, but her sister can't; and so on all through the crowd.

And to think that things should look like that on the morning of a steamboat accident.

How strange life is!

To think of all these people so eager and anxious to catch the steamer, and some of them running to catch it, and so fearful that they might miss it,—the morning of a steamboat accident. And the captain blowing his whistle, and warning them so severely that he would leave them behind,—leave them out of the accident! And everybody crowding so eagerly to be in the accident.

Perhaps life is like that all through.

Strangest of all to think, in a case like this, of the people who were left behind, or in some way or other prevented from going, and always afterwards told of how they had escaped being on board the Mariposa Belle that day!

Some of the instances were certainly extraordinary.

Nivens, the lawyer, escaped from being there merely by the fact that he was away in the city.

Towers, the tailor, only escaped owing to the fact that, not intending to go on the excursion he had stayed in bed till eight o'clock and so had not gone. He narrated afterwards that waking up that morning at half-past five, he had thought of the excursion and for some unaccountable reason had felt glad that he was not going.

The case of Yodel, the auctioneer, was even more inscrutable. He had been to the Oddfellows' excursion on the train the week before and to the Conservative picnic the week before that, and had decided not to go on this trip. In fact, he had not the least intention of going. He narrated afterwards how the night before someone had stopped him on the corner of Nippewa and Tecumseh Streets (he indicated the very spot) and asked: "Are you going to take in the excursion to-morrow?" and he had said, just as simply as he was talking when narrating it: "No." And ten minutes after that, at the corner of Dalhousie and Brock Streets (he offered to lead a party of verification to the precise place) somebody else had stopped him and asked: "Well, are you going on the steamer trip to-morrow?" Again he had answered: "No," apparently almost in the same tone as before.

He said afterwards that when he heard the rumour of the accident it seemed like the finger of Providence, and he fell on his knees in thankfulness.

There was the similar case of Morison (I mean the one in Glover's hardware store that married one of the Thompsons). He said afterwards that he had read so much in the papers about accidents lately,—mining accidents, and aeroplanes and gasoline,—that he had grown nervous. The night before his wife had asked him at supper: "Are you going on the excursion?" He had answered: "No, I don't think I feel like it," and had added: "Perhaps your mother might like to go." And the next evening just at dusk, when the news ran through the town, he said the first thought that flashed through his head was: "Mrs. Thompson's on that boat."

He told this right as I say it—without the least doubt or confusion. He never for a moment imagined she was on the Lusitania or the Olympic or any other boat. He knew she was on this one. He said you could have knocked him down where he stood. But no one had. Not even when he got half-way down,—on his knees, and it would have been easier still to knock him down or kick him. People do miss a lot of chances.

Still, as I say, neither Yodel nor Morison nor anyone thought about there being an accident until just after sundown when they—

Well, have you ever heard the long booming whistle of a steamboat two miles out on the lake in the dusk, and while you listen and count and wonder, seen the crimson rockets going up against the sky and then heard the fire bell ringing right there beside you in the town, and seen the people running to the town wharf?

That's what the people of Mariposa saw and felt that summer evening as they watched the Mackinaw life-boat go plunging out into the lake with seven sweeps to a side and the foam clear to the gunwale with the lifting stroke of fourteen men!

But, dear me, I am afraid that this is no way to tell a story. I suppose the true art would have been to have said nothing about the accident till it happened. But when you write about Mariposa, or hear of it, if you know the place, it's all so vivid and real that a thing like the contrast between the excursion crowd in the morning and the scene at night leaps into your mind and you must think of it.

But never mind about the accident,—let us turn back again to the morning.

The boat was due to leave at seven. There was no doubt about the hour,—not only seven, but seven sharp. The notice in the Newspacket said: "The boat will leave sharp at seven;" and the advertising posters on the telegraph poles on Missinaba Street that began "Ho, for Indian's Island!" ended up with the words: "Boat leaves at seven sharp." There was a big notice on the wharf that said: "Boat leaves sharp on time."

So at seven, right on the hour, the whistle blew loud and long, and then at seven fifteen three short peremptory blasts, and at seven thirty one quick angry call,—just one,—and very soon after that they cast off the last of the ropes and the Mariposa Belle sailed off in her cloud of flags, and the band of the Knights of Pythias, timing it to a nicety, broke into the "Maple Leaf for Ever!"

I suppose that all excursions when they start are much the same. Anyway, on the Mariposa Belle everybody went running up and down all over the boat with deck chairs and camp stools and baskets, and found places, splendid places to sit, and then got scared that there might be better ones and chased off again. People hunted for places out of the sun and when they got them swore that they weren't going to freeze to please anybody; and the people in the sun said that they hadn't paid fifty cents to be roasted. Others said that they hadn't paid fifty cents to get covered with cinders, and there were still others who hadn't paid fifty cents to get shaken to death with the propeller.

Still, it was all right presently. The people seemed to get sorted out into the places on the boat where they belonged. The women, the older ones, all gravitated into the cabin on the lower deck and by getting round the table with needlework, and with all the windows shut, they soon had it, as they said themselves, just like being at home.

All the young boys and the toughs and the men in the band got down on the lower deck forward, where the boat was dirtiest and where the anchor was and the coils of rope.

And upstairs on the after deck there were Lilian Drone and

Miss Lawson, the high school teacher, with a book of German poetry,—Gothey I think it was,—and the bank teller and the younger men.

In the centre, standing beside the rail, were Dean Drone and Dr. Gallagher, looking through binocular glasses at the shore.

Up in front on the little deck forward of the pilot house was a group of the older men, Mullins and Duff and Mr. Smith in a deck chair, and beside him Mr. Golgotha Gingham, the undertaker of Mariposa, on a stool. It was part of Mr. Gingham's principles to take in an outing of this sort, a business matter, more or less,—for you never know what may happen at these water parties. At any rate, he was there in a neat suit of black, not, of course, his heavier or professional suit, but a soft clinging effect as of burnt paper that combined gaiety and decorum to a nicety.

"Yes," said Mr. Gingham, waving his black glove in a general way towards the shore, "I know the lake well, very well. I've been pretty much all over it in my time."

"Canoeing?" asked somebody.

"No," said Mr. Gingham, "not in a canoe." There seemed a peculiar and quiet meaning in his tone.

"Sailing, I suppose," said somebody else.

"No," said Mr. Gingham. "I don't understand it."

"I never knowed that you went on to the water at all, Gol," said Mr. Smith, breaking in.

"Ah, not now," explained Mr. Gingham; "it was years ago, the first summer I came to Mariposa. I was on the water practically all day. Nothing like it to give a man an appetite and keep him in shape."

"Was you camping?" asked Mr. Smith.

"We camped at night," assented the undertaker, "but we put in practically the whole day on the water. You see we were after a party that had come up here from the city on his vacation and gone out in a sailing canoe. We were dragging. We were up every morning at sunrise, lit a fire on the beach and cooked breakfast, and then we'd light our pipes and be off with the net for a whole day. It's a great life," concluded Mr. Gingham wistfully.

"Did you get him?" asked two or three together.

There was a pause before Mr. Gingham answered.

"We did," he said,—"down in the reeds past Horseshoe Point. But it was no use. He turned blue on me right away."

After which Mr. Gingham fell into such a deep reverie that the boat had steamed another half-mile down the lake before anybody broke the silence again.

Talk of this sort,—and after all what more suitable for a day on the water?—beguiled the way.

Down the lake, mile by mile over the calm water, steamed the Mariposa Belle. They passed Poplar Point where the high sandbanks are with all the swallows' nests in them, and Dean Drone and Dr. Gallagher looked at them alternately through the binocular glasses, and it was wonderful how plainly one could see the swallows and the banks and the shrubs,—just as plainly as with the naked eye.

And a little further down they passed the Shingle Beach, and Dr. Gallagher, who knew Canadian history, said to Dean Drone that it was strange to think that Champlain had landed there with his French explorers three hundred years ago; and Dean Drone, who didn't know Canadian history, said it was stranger still to think that the hand of the Almighty had piled up the hills and rocks long before that; and Dr. Gallagher said it was wonderful how the French had found their way through such a pathless wilderness; and Dean Drone said that it was wonderful also to think that the Almighty had placed even the smallest shrub in its appointed place. Dr. Gallagher said it filled him with admiration. Dean Drone said it filled him with awe. Dr. Gallagher said he'd been full of it ever since he was a boy; and Dean Drone said so had he.

Then a little further, as the Mariposa Belle steamed on down the lake, they passed the Old Indian Portage where the great grey rocks are; and Dr. Gallagher drew Dean Drone's attention to the place where the narrow canoe track wound up from the shore to the woods, and Dean Drone said he could see it perfectly well without the glasses.

Dr. Gallagher said that it was just here that a party of five hundred French had made their way with all their baggage and accoutrements across the rocks of the divide and down to the Great Bay. And Dean Drone said that it reminded him of Xenophon leading his ten thousand Greeks over the hill passes of

Armenia down to the sea. Dr. Gallagher said that he had often wished he could have seen and spoken to Champlain, and Dean Drone said how much he regretted to have never known Xenophon.

And then after that they fell to talking of relics and traces of the past, and Dr. Gallagher said that if Dean Drone would come round to his house some night he would show him some Indian arrow heads that he had dug up in his garden. And Dean Drone said that if Dr. Gallagher would come round to the rectory any afternoon he would show him a map of Xerxes' invasion of Greece. Only he must come some time between the Infant Class and the Mothers' Auxiliary.

So presently they both knew that they were blocked out of one another's houses for some time to come, and Dr. Gallagher walked forward and told Mr. Smith, who had never studied Greek, about Champlain crossing the rock divide.

Mr. Smith turned his head and looked at the divide for half a second and then said he had crossed a worse one up north back of the Wahnipitae and that the flies were Hades,—and then went on playing freezeout poker with the two juniors in Duff's bank.

So Dr. Gallagher realized that that's always the way when you try to tell people things, and that as far as gratitude and appreciation goes one might as well never read books or travel anywhere or do anything.

In fact, it was at this very moment that he made up his mind to give the arrows to the Mariposa Mechanics' Institute,—they afterwards became, as you know, the Gallagher Collection. But, for the time being, the doctor was sick of them and wandered off round the boat and watched Henry Mullins showing George Duff how to make a John Collins without lemons, and finally went and sat down among the Mariposa band and wished that he hadn't come.

So the boat steamed on and the sun rose higher and higher, and the freshness of the morning changed into the full glare of noon, and they went on to where the lake began to narrow in at its foot, just where the Indian's Island is,—all grass and trees and with a log wharf running into the water. Below it the Lower Ossawippi runs out of the lake, and quite near are the rapids, and you can see down among the trees the red brick of the power house and hear the roar of the leaping water.

The Indian's Island itself is all covered with trees and tangled vines, and the water about it is so still that it's all reflected double and looks the same either way up. Then when the steamer's whistle blows as it comes into the wharf, you hear it echo among the trees of the island, and reverberate back from the shores of the lake.

The scene is all so quiet and still and unbroken, that Miss Cleghorn,—the sallow girl in the telephone exchange, that I spoke of—said she'd like to be buried there. But all the people were so busy getting their baskets and gathering up their things that no one had time to attend to it.

I mustn't even try to describe the landing and the boat crunching against the wooden wharf and all the people running to the same side of the deck and Christie Johnson calling out to the crowd to keep to the starboard and nobody being able to find it. Everyone who has been on a Mariposa excursion knows all about that.

Nor can I describe the day itself and the picnic under the trees. There were speeches afterwards, and Judge Pepperleigh gave such offence by bringing in Conservative politics that a man called Patriotus Canadiensis wrote and asked for some of the invaluable space of the Mariposa Times-Herald and exposed it.

I should say that there were races too, on the grass on the open side of the island, graded mostly according to ages,—races for boys under thirteen and girls over nineteen and all that sort of thing. Sports are generally conducted on that plan in Mariposa. It is realized that a woman of sixty has an unfair advantage over a mere child.

Dean Drone managed the races and decided the ages and gave out the prizes; the Wesleyan minister helped, and he and the young student, who was relieving in the Presbyterian Church, held the string at the winning point.

They had to get mostly clergymen for the races because all the men had wandered off, somehow, to where they were drinking lager beer out of two kegs stuck on pine logs among the trees.

But if you've ever been on a Mariposa excursion you know all about these details anyway.

So the day wore on and presently the sun came through the trees on a slant and the steamer whistle blew with a great puff of white steam and all the people came straggling down to the wharf and pretty soon the Mariposa Belle had floated out on to the lake again and headed for the town, twenty miles away.

I suppose you have often noticed the contrast there is between an excursion on its way out in the morning and what it looks like on the way home.

In the morning everybody is so restless and animated and moves to and fro all over the boat and asks questions. But coming home, as the afternoon gets later and later and the sun sinks beyond the hills, all the people seem to get so still and quiet and drowsy.

So it was with the people on the Mariposa Belle. They sat there on the benches and the deck chairs in little clusters, and listened to the regular beat of the propeller and almost dozed off asleep as they sat. Then when the sun set and the dusk drew on, it grew almost dark on the deck and so still that you could hardly tell there was anyone on board.

And if you had looked at the steamer from the shore or from one of the islands, you'd have seen the row of lights from the cabin windows shining on the water and the red glare of the burning hemlock from the funnel, and you'd have heard the soft thud of the propeller miles away over the lake.

Now and then, too, you could have heard them singing on the steamer,—the voices of the girls and the men blended into unison by the distance, rising and falling in long-drawn melody: *"O— Can-a-da—O—Can-a-da."*

You may talk as you will about the intoning choirs of your European cathedrals, but the sound of "O Can-a-da," borne across the waters of a silent lake at evening is good enough for those of us who know Mariposa.

I think that it was just as they were singing like this: *"O—Can-a-da,"* that word went round that the boat was sinking.

If you have ever been in any sudden emergency on the water, you will understand the strange psychology of it,—the way in which what is happening seems to become known all in a moment without a word being said. The news is transmitted from one to the other by some mysterious process.

At any rate, on the Mariposa Belle first one and then the other heard that the steamer was sinking. As far as I could ever learn the first of it was that George Duff, the bank manager, came very quietly to Dr. Gallagher and asked him if he thought that the boat was sinking. The doctor said no, that he had thought so earlier in the day but that he didn't now think that she was.

After that Duff, according to his own account, had said to Macartney, the lawyer, that the boat was sinking, and Macartney said that he doubted it very much.

Then somebody came to Judge Pepperleigh and woke him up and said that there was six inches of water in the steamer and that she was sinking. And Pepperleigh said it was perfect scandal and passed the news on to his wife and she said that they had no business to allow it and that if the steamer sank that was the last excursion she'd go on.

So the news went all round the boat and everywhere the people gathered in groups and talked about it in the angry and excited way that people have when a steamer is sinking on one of the lakes like Lake Wissanotti.

Dean Drone, of course, and some others were quieter about it, and said that one must make allowances and that naturally there were two sides to everything. But most of them wouldn't listen to reason at all. I think, perhaps, that some of them were frightened. You see the last time but one that the steamer had sunk, there had been a man drowned and it made them nervous.

What? Hadn't I explained about the depth of Lake Wissanotti? I had taken it for granted that you knew; and in any case parts of it are deep enough, though I don't suppose in this stretch of it from the big reed beds up to within a mile of the town wharf, you could find six feet of water in it if you tried. Oh, pshaw! I was not talking about a steamer sinking in the ocean and carrying down its screaming crowds of people into the hideous depths of green water. Oh, dear me, no! That kind of thing never happens on Lake Wissanotti.

But what does happen is that the Mariposa Belle sinks every now and then, and sticks there on the bottom till they get things straightened up.

On the lakes round Mariposa, if a person arrives late anywhere and explains that the steamer sank, everybody understands the situation.

You see when Harland and Wolff built the Mariposa Belle, they left some cracks in between the timbers that you fill up with cotton waste every Sunday. If this is not attended to, the boat sinks. In fact, it is part of the law of the province that all the steamers like the Mariposa Belle must be properly corked,—I think that is the word,—every season. There are inspectors who visit all the hotels in the province to see that it is done.

So you can imagine now that I've explained it a little straighter, the indignation of the people when they knew that the boat had come uncorked and that they might be stuck out there on a shoal or a mud-bank half the night.

I don't say either that there wasn't any danger; anyway, it doesn't feel very safe when you realise that the boat is settling down with every hundred yards that she goes, and you look over the side and see only the black water in the gathering night.

Safe! I'm not sure now that I come to think of it that it isn't worse than sinking in the Atlantic. After all, in the Atlantic there is wireless telegraphy, and a lot of trained sailors and stewards. But out on Lake Wissanotti,—far out, so that you can only just see the lights of the town away off to the south,—when the propeller comes to a stop,—and you can hear the hiss of steam as they start to rake out the engine fires to prevent an explosion,—and when you turn from the red glare that comes from the furnace doors as they open them, to the black dark that is gathering over the lake,—and there's a night wind beginning to run among the rushes,—and you see the men going forward to the roof of the pilot house to send up the rockets to rouse the town,—safe? Safe yourself, if you like; as for me, let me once get back into Mariposa again, under the night shadow of the maple trees, and this shall be the last, last time I'll go on Lake Wissanotti.

Safe! Oh yes! Isn't it strange how safe other people's adventures seem after they happen. But you'd have been scared, too, if you'd been there just before the steamer sank, and seen them bringing up all the women on to the top deck.

I don't see how some of the people took it so calmly; how Mr. Smith, for instance, could have gone on smoking and telling how he'd had a steamer "sink on him" on Lake Nipissing and a still bigger one, a side-wheeler, sink on him in Lake Abbitibbi.

Then, quite suddenly, with a quiver, down she went. You could feel the boat sink, sink,—down, down,—would it never get to the bottom? The water came flush up to the lower deck, and then—thank heaven,—the sinking stopped and there was the Mariposa Belle safe and tight on a reed bank.

Really, it made one positively laugh! It seemed so queer and, anyway, if a man has a sort of natural courage, danger makes him laugh. Danger? pshaw! fiddlesticks! everybody scouted the idea. Why, it is just the little things like this that give zest to a day on the water.

Within half a minute they were all running round looking for sandwiches and cracking jokes and talking of making coffee over the remains of the engine fires.

I don't need to tell at length how it all happened after that.

I suppose the people on the Mariposa Belle would have had to settle down there all night or till help came from the town, but some of the men who had gone forward and were peering out into the dark said that it couldn't be more than a mile across the water to Miller's Point. You could almost see it over there to the left,—some of them, I think, said "off on the port bow," because you know when you get mixed up in these marine disasters, you soon catch the atmosphere of the thing.

So pretty soon they had the davits swung out over the side and were lowering the old lifeboat from the top deck into the water.

There were men leaning out over the rail of the Mariposa Belle with lanterns that threw the light as they let her down, and the glare fell on the water and the reeds. But when they got the boat lowered, it looked such a frail, clumsy thing as one saw it from the rail above, that the cry was raised: "Women and children first!" For what was the sense, if it should turn out that the boat wouldn't even hold women and children, of trying to jam a lot of heavy men into it?

So they put in mostly women and children and the boat pushed out into the darkness so freighted down it would hardly float.

In the bow of it was the Presbyterian student who was relieving the minister, and he called out that they were in the hands of Providence. But he was crouched and ready to spring out of them at the first moment.

So the boat went and was lost in the darkness except for the lantern in the bow that you could see bobbing on the water. Then presently it came back and they sent another load, till pretty soon the decks began to thin out and everybody got impatient to be gone.

It was about the time that the third boat-load put off that Mr.

Smith took a bet with Mullins for twenty-five dollars, that he'd be home in Mariposa before the people in the boats had walked round the shore.

No one knew just what he meant, but pretty soon they saw Mr. Smith disappear down below into the lowest part of the steamer with a mallet in one hand and a big bundle of marline in the other.

They might have wondered more about it, but it was just at this time that they heard the shouts from the rescue boat—the big Mackinaw lifeboat—that had put out from the town with fourteen men at the sweeps, when they saw the first rockets go up.

I suppose there is always something inspiring about a rescue at sea, or on the water.

After all, the bravery of the lifeboat man is the true bravery,—expended to save life, not to destroy it.

Certainly they told for months after of how the rescue boat came out to the Mariposa Belle.

I suppose that when they put her in the water the lifeboat touched it for the first time since the old Macdonald Government placed her on Lake Wissanotti.

Anyway, the water poured in at every seam. But not for a moment,—even with two miles of water between them and the steamer,—did the rowers pause for that.

By the time they were half-way there the water was almost up to the thwarts, but they drove her on. Panting and exhausted (for mind you, if you haven't been in a fool boat like that for years, rowing takes it out of you), the rowers stuck to their task. They threw the ballast over and chucked into the water the heavy cork jackets and lifebelts that encumbered their movements. There was no thought of turning back. They were nearer to the steamer than the shore.

"Hang to it, boys," called the crowd from the steamer's deck, and hang they did.

They were almost exhausted when they got them; men leaning from the steamer threw them ropes and one by one every man was hauled aboard just as the lifeboat sank under their feet.

Saved! by Heaven, saved, by one of the smartest pieces of rescue work ever seen on the lake.

There's no use describing it; you need to see rescue work of this kind by lifeboats to understand it.

Nor were the lifeboat crew the only ones that distinguished themselves.

Boat after boat and canoe after canoe had put out from Mariposa to the help of the steamer. They got them all.

Pupkin, the other bank teller, with a face like a horse, who hadn't gone on the excursion,—as soon as he knew that the boat was signalling for help and that Miss Lawson was sending up rockets,—rushed for a row boat, grabbed an oar (two would have hampered him), and paddled madly out into the lake. He struck right out into the dark with the crazy skiff almost sinking beneath his feet. But they got him. They rescued him. They watched him, almost dead with exhaustion, make his way to the steamer, where he was hauled up with ropes. Saved! Saved!!

They might have gone on that way half the night, picking up the rescuers, only, at the very moment when the tenth load of people left for the shore,—just as suddenly and saucily as you please, up came the Mariposa Belle from the mud bottom and floated.

Floated?

Why, of course she did. If you take a hundred and fifty people off a steamer that has sunk, and if you get a man as shrewd as Mr. Smith to plug the timber seams with mallet and marline, and if you turn ten bandsmen of the Mariposa band on to your hand pump on the bow of the lower decks—float? why, what else can she do?

Then, if you stuff in hemlock into the embers of the fire that you were raking out, till it hums and crackles under the boiler, it won't be long before you hear the propeller thud—thudding at the stern again, and before the long roar of the steam whistle echoes over to the town.

And so the Mariposa Belle, with all steam up again and with the long train of sparks careering from the funnel, is heading for the town.

But no Christie Johnson at the wheel in the pilot house this time.

"Smith! Get Smith!" is the cry.

Can he take her in? Well, now! Ask a man who has had steamers sink on him in half the lakes from Temiscaming to the Bay, if he can take her in? Ask a man who has run a York boat down the rapids of the Moose when the ice is moving, if he can grip the steering wheel of the Mariposa Belle? So there she steams safe and sound to the town wharf!

Look at the lights and the crowd! If only the federal census taker could count us now! Hear them calling and shouting back and forward from the deck to the shore! Listen! There is the rattle of the shore ropes as they get them ready, and there's the Mariposa band,—actually forming in a circle on the upper deck just as she docks, and the leader with his baton,—one—two—ready now,—

"0 CAN-A-DA!"

Chapter IV

The Ministrations of the Rev. Mr. Drone

The Church of England Church in Mariposa is on a side street, where the maple trees are thickest, a little up the hill from the heart of the town. The trees above the church and the grass plot that was once the cemetery, till they made the new one (the Necropolis, over the brow of the hill), fill out the whole corner. Down behind the church, with only the driving shed and a lane between, is the rectory. It is a little brick house with odd angles. There is a hedge and a little gate, and a weeping ash tree with red berries.

At the side of the rectory, churchward, is a little grass lawn with low hedges and at the side of that two wild plum trees, that are practically always in white blossom. Underneath them is a rustic table and chairs, and it is here that you may see Rural Dean Drone, the incumbent of the Church of England Church, sitting, in the chequered light of the plum trees that is neither sun nor shadow. Generally you will find him reading, and when I tell you that at the end of the grass plot where the hedge is highest there is a yellow bee hive with seven bees that belong to Dean Drone, you will realize that it is only fitting that the Dean is reading in the Greek. For what better could a man be reading beneath the blossom of the plum trees, within the very sound of the bees, than the Pastorals of Theocritus? The light trash of modern romance might put a man to sleep in such a spot, but with such food for reflection as Theocritus, a man may safely close his eyes and muse on what he reads without fear of dropping into slumber.

Some men, I suppose, terminate their education when they leave their college. Not so Dean Drone. I have often heard him say that if he couldn't take a book in the Greek out on the lawn in a spare half-hour, he would feel lost. It's a certain activity of the brain that must be stilled somehow. The Dean, too, seemed to have a native feeling for the Greek language. I have often heard people who might sit with him on the lawn, ask him to translate some of it. But he always refused. One couldn't translate it, he said. It lost so much in the translation that it was better not to try. It was far wiser not to attempt it. If you undertook to translate it, there was something gone, something missing immediately. I believe that many classical scholars feel this way, and like to read the Greek just as it is, without the hazard of trying to put it into so poor a medium as English. So that when Dean Drone said that he simply couldn't translate it, I believe he was perfectly sincere.

Sometimes, indeed, he would read it aloud. That was another matter. Whenever, for example, Dr. Gallagher—I mean, of course, old Dr. Gallagher, not the young doctor (who was always out in the country in the afternoon)—would come over and bring his latest Indian relics to show to the Dean, the latter always read to him a passage or two. As soon as the doctor laid his tomahawk on the table, the Dean would reach for his Theocritus. I remember that on the day when Dr. Gallagher brought over the Indian skull that they had dug out of the railway embankment, and placed it on the rustic table, the Dean read to him so long from Theocritus that the doctor, I truly believe, dozed off in his chair. The Dean had to wait and fold his hands with the book across his knee, and close his eyes till the doctor should wake up again. And the skull was on the table between them, and from above the plum blossoms fluttered down, till they made flakes on it as white as Dr. Gallagher's hair.

I don't want you to suppose that the Rev. Mr. Drone spent the whole of his time under the trees. Not at all. In point of fact, the rector's life was one round of activity which he himself might deplore but was powerless to prevent. He had hardly sat down beneath the trees of an afternoon after his mid-day meal when there was the Infant Class at three, and after that, with scarcely an hour between, the Mothers' Auxiliary at five, and the next morning the Book Club, and that evening the Bible Study Class, and the next morning the Early Workers' Guild at eleven-thirty. The whole week was like that, and if one found time to sit down for an hour or so to recuperate it was the most one could do. After all, if a busy man spends the little bit of leisure that he gets in advanced classical study, there is surely no harm in it. I suppose, take it all in all, there wasn't a busier man than the Rural Dean among the Anglican clergy of the diocese.

If the Dean ever did snatch a half-day from his incessant work, he spent it in fishing. But not always that, for as likely as not, instead of taking a real holiday he would put in the whole afternoon amusing the children and the boys that he knew, by making kites and toys and clockwork steamboats for them.

It was fortunate for the Dean that he had the strange interest and aptitude for mechanical devices which he possessed, or otherwise this kind of thing would have been too cruel an imposition. But the Rev. Mr. Drone had a curious liking for machinery. I think I never heard him preach a better sermon than the one on Aeroplanes (Lo, what now see you on high Jeremiah Two).

So it was that he spent two whole days making a kite with Chinese wings for Teddy Moore, the photographer's son, and closed down the infant class for forty-eight hours so that Teddy Moore should not miss the pleasure of flying it, or rather seeing it flown. It is foolish to trust a Chinese kite to the hands of a young child.

In the same way the Dean made a mechanical top for little Marjorie Trelawney, the cripple, to see spun: it would have been unwise to allow the afflicted girl to spin it. There was no end to the things that Mr. Drone could make, and always for the children. Even when he was making the sand-clock for poor little Willie Yodel (who died, you know) the Dean went right on with it and gave it to another child with just the same pleasure. Death, you know, to the clergy is a different thing from what it is to us. The Dean and Mr. Gingham used often to speak of it as they walked through the long grass of the new cemetery, the Necropolis. And when your Sunday walk is to your wife's grave, as the Dean's was, perhaps it seems different to anybody.

The Church of England Church, I said, stood close to the rectory, a tall, sweeping church, and inside a great reach of polished cedar beams that ran to the point of the roof. There used to stand on the same spot the little stone church that all the grown-up people in Mariposa still remember, a quaint little building in red and grey stone. About it was the old cemetery, but that was all smoothed out later into the grass plot round the new church, and the headstones laid out flat, and no new graves have been put there for ever so long. But the Mariposa children still walk round and read the headstones lying flat in the grass and look for the old ones,—because some of them are ever so old—forty or fifty years back.

Nor are you to think from all this that the Dean was not a man
with serious perplexities. You could easily convince yourself of
the contrary. For if you watched the Rev. Mr. Drone as he sat
reading in the Greek, you would notice that no very long period
ever passed without his taking up a sheet or two of paper that lay
between the leaves of the Theocritus and that were covered close
with figures.

And these the Dean would lay upon the rustic table, and he
would add them up forwards and backwards, going first up the
column and then down it to see that nothing had been left out,
and then down it again to see what it was that must have been left
out.

Mathematics, you will understand, were not the Dean's forte.
They never were the forte of the men who had been trained at the
little Anglican college with the clipped hedges and the cricket
ground, where Rupert Drone had taken the gold medal in Greek
fifty-two years ago. You will see the medal at any time lying
there in its open box on the rectory table, in case of immediate
need. Any of the Drone girls, Lilian, or Jocelyn, or Theodore,
would show it to you. But, as I say, mathematics were not the
rector's forte, and he blamed for it (in a Christian spirit, you will
understand) the memory of his mathematical professor, and often
he spoke with great bitterness. I have often heard him say that in
his opinion the colleges ought to dismiss, of course in a Christian
spirit, all the professors who are not, in the most reverential
sense of the term, fit for their jobs.

No doubt many of the clergy of the diocese had suffered more
or less just as the Dean had from lack of mathematical training.
But the Dean always felt that his own case was especially to be
lamented. For you see, if a man is trying to make a model aeroplane—for a poor family in the lower part of the town—and he is
brought to a stop by the need of reckoning the coefficient of
torsion of cast-iron rods, it shows plainly enough that the colleges
are not truly filling their divine mission.

But the figures that I speak of were not those of the model
aeroplane. These were far more serious. Night and day they had
been with the rector now for the best part of ten years, and they
grew, if anything, more intricate.

If, for example, you try to reckon the debt of a church—a large church with a great sweep of polished cedar beams inside, for the special glorification of the All Powerful, and with imported tiles on the roof for the greater glory of Heaven and with stained-glass windows for the exaltation of the All Seeing—if, I say, you try to reckon up the debt on such a church and figure out its interest and its present worth, less a fixed annual payment, it makes a pretty complicated sum. Then if you try to add to this the annual cost of insurance, and deduct from it three-quarters of a stipend, year by year, and then suddenly remember that three-quarters is too much, because you have forgotten the boarding-school fees of the littlest of the Drones (including French, as an extra—she must have it, all the older girls did), you have got a sum that pretty well defies ordinary arithmetic. The provoking part of it was that the Dean knew perfectly well that with the help of logarithms he could have done the thing in a moment. But at the Anglican college they had stopped short at that very place in the book. They had simply explained that Logos was a word and Arithmos a number, which, at the time, seemed amply sufficient.

So the Dean was perpetually taking out his sheets of figures, and adding them upwards and downwards, and they never came the same. Very often Mr. Gingham, who was a warden, would come and sit beside the rector and ponder over the figures, and Mr. Drone would explain that with a book of logarithms you could work it out in a moment. You would simply open the book and run your finger up the columns (he illustrated exactly the way in which the finger was moved), and there you were. Mr. Gingham said that it was a caution, and that logarithms (I quote his exact phrase) must be a terror.

Very often, too, Nivens, the lawyer, who was a sidesman, and Mullins, the manager of the Exchange Bank, who was the chairman of the vestry, would come and take a look at the figures. But they never could make much of them, because the stipend part was not a matter that one could discuss.

Mullins would notice the item for a hundred dollars due on fire insurance and would say, as a business man, that surely, that couldn't be fire insurance, and the Dean would say surely not, and change it: and Mullins would say surely there couldn't be fifty dollars for taxes, because there weren't any taxes, and the Dean would admit that of course it couldn't be for the taxes. In

fact, the truth is that the Dean's figures were badly mixed, and
the fault lay indubitably with the mathematical professor of two
generations back.

It was always Mullins's intention some day to look into the
finances of the church, the more so as his father had been with
Dean Drone at the little Anglican college with the cricket ground.
But he was a busy man. As he explained to the rector himself,
the banking business nowadays is getting to be such that a banker
can hardly call even his Sunday mornings his own. Certainly
Henry Mullins could not. They belonged largely to Smith's
Hotel, and during the fishing season they belonged away down
the lake, so far away that practically no one, unless it was
George Duff of the Commercial Bank, could see them.

But to think that all this trouble had come through the building
of the new church.

That was the bitterness of it.

For the twenty-five years that Rural Dean Drone had preached
in the little stone church, it had been his one aim, as he often put
it in his sermons, to rear a larger Ark in Gideon. His one hope
had been to set up a greater Evidence, or, very simply stated, to
kindle a Brighter Beacon. After twenty-five years of waiting, he
had been able at last to kindle it. Everybody in Mariposa remembers the building of the church. First of all they had demolished
the little stone church to make way for the newer Evidence. It
seemed almost a sacrilege, as the Dean himself said, to lay hands
on it. Indeed it was at first proposed to take the stone of it and
build it into a Sunday School, as a lesser testimony. Then, when
that proved impracticable, it was suggested that the stone be reverently fashioned into a wall that should stand as a token. And
when even that could not be managed, the stone of the little
church was laid reverently into a stone pile; afterwards it was
devoutly sold to a building contractor, and, like so much else in
life, was forgotten.

But the building of the church, no one, I think, will forget.
The Dean threw himself into the work. With his coat off and his
white shirtsleeves conspicuous among the gang that were working
at the foundations, he set his hand to the shovel, himself guided
the road-scraper, urging on the horses, cheering and encouraging
the men, till they begged him to desist. He mingled with the
stone-masons, advising, helping, and giving counsel, till they

pleaded with him to rest. He was among the carpenters, sawing, hammering, enquiring, suggesting, till they besought him to lay off. And he was night and day with the architect's assistants, drawing, planning, revising, till the architect told him to cut it out.

So great was his activity, that I doubt whether the new church would ever have been finished, had not the wardens and the vestry men insisted that Mr. Drone must take a holiday, and sent him on the Mackinaw trip up the lakes,—the only foreign travel of the Dean's life.

So in due time the New Church was built and it towered above the maple trees of Mariposa like a beacon on a hill. It stood so high that from the open steeple of it, where the bells were, you could see all the town lying at its feet, and the farmsteads to the south of it, and the railway like a double pencil line, and Lake Wissanotti spread out like a map. You could see and appreciate things from the height of the new church,—such as the size and the growing wealth of Mariposa,—that you never could have seen from the little stone church at all.

Presently the church was opened and the Dean preached his first sermon in it, and he called it a Greater Testimony, and he said that it was an earnest, or firstfruit of endeavour, and that it was a token or pledge, and he named it also a covenant. He said, too, that it was an anchorage and a harbour and a lighthouse as well as being a city set upon a hill; and he ended by declaring it an Ark of Refuge and notified them that the Bible Class would meet in the basement of it on that and every other third Wednesday.

In the opening months of preaching about it the Dean had called the church so often an earnest and a pledge and a guerdon and a tabernacle, that I think he used to forget that it wasn't paid for. It was only when the agent of the building society and a representative of the Hosanna Pipe and Steam Organ Co. (Limited), used to call for quarterly payments that he was suddenly reminded of the fact. Always after these men came round the Dean used to preach a special sermon on sin, in the course of which he would mention that the ancient Hebrews used to put unjust traders to death,—a thing of which he spoke with Christian serenity.

I don't think that at first anybody troubled much about the debt on the church. Dean Drone's figures showed that it was only a matter of time before it would be extinguished; only a little effort was needed, a little girding up of the loins of the congregation and they could shoulder the whole debt and trample it under their feet. Let them but set their hands to the plough and they could soon guide it into the deep water. Then they might furl their sails and sit every man under his own olive tree.

Meantime, while the congregation was waiting to gird up its loins, the interest on the debt was paid somehow, or, when it wasn't paid, was added to the principal.

I don't know whether you have had any experience with Greater Testimonies and with Beacons set on Hills. If you have, you will realize how, at first gradually, and then rapidly, their position from year to year grows more distressing. What with the building loan and the organ instalment, and the fire insurance,—a cruel charge,—and the heat and light, the rector began to realize as he added up the figures that nothing but logarithms could solve them. Then the time came when not only the rector, but all the wardens knew and the sidesmen knew that the debt was more than the church could carry; then the choir knew and the congregation knew and at last everybody knew; and there were special collections at Easter and special days of giving, and special weeks of tribulation, and special arrangements with the Hosanna Pipe and Steam Organ Co. And it was noticed that when the Rural Dean announced a service of Lenten Sorrow,—aimed more especially at the business men,—the congregation had diminished by forty per cent.

I suppose things are just the same elsewhere,—I mean the peculiar kind of discontent that crept into the Church of England congregation in Mariposa after the setting up of the Beacon. There were those who claimed that they had seen the error from the first, though they had kept quiet, as such people always do, from breadth of mind. There were those who had felt years before how it would end, but their lips were sealed from humility of spirit. What was worse was that there were others who grew dissatisfied with the whole conduct of the church.

Yodel, the auctioneer, for example, narrated how he had been to the city and had gone into a service of the Roman Catholic

church: I believe, to state it more fairly, he had "dropped in,"—
the only recognized means of access to such a service. He
claimed that the music that he had heard there was music, and
that (outside of his profession) the chanting and intoning could
not be touched.

Ed Moore, the photographer, also related that he had listened
to a sermon in the city, and that if anyone would guarantee him
a sermon like that he would defy you to keep him away from
church. Meanwhile, failing the guarantee, he stayed away.

The very doctrines were impeached. Some of the congregation
began to cast doubts on eternal punishment,—doubts so grave as
to keep them absent from the Lenten Services of Sorrow. Indeed,
Lawyer Macartney took up the whole question of the Athanasian
Creed one afternoon with Joe Milligan, the dentist, and hardly
left a clause of it intact.

All this time, you will understand, Dean Drone kept on with
his special services, and leaflets, calls, and appeals went out from
the Ark of Gideon like rockets from a sinking ship. More and
more with every month the debt of the church lay heavy on his
mind. At times he forgot it. At other times he woke up in the
night and thought about it. Sometimes as he went down the street
from the lighted precincts of the Greater Testimony and passed
the Salvation Army, praying around a naphtha lamp under the
open sky, it smote him to the heart with a stab.

But the congregation were wrong, I think, in imputing fault to
the sermons of Dean Drone. There I do think they were wrong.
I can speak from personal knowledge when I say that the rector's
sermons were not only stimulating in matters of faith, but con-
tained valuable material in regard to the Greek language, to
modern machinery and to a variety of things that should have
proved of the highest advantage to the congregation.

There was, I say, the Greek language. The Dean always
showed the greatest delicacy of feeling in regard to any translation in or out of it that he made from the pulpit. He was never
willing to accept even the faintest shade of rendering different
from that commonly given without being assured of the full con-
currence of the congregation. Either the translation must be una-
nimous and without contradiction, or he could not pass it. He
would pause in his sermon and would say: "The original Greek
is 'Hoson,' but perhaps you will allow me to translate it as equi-

valent to 'Hoyon.'" And they did. So that if there was any fault
to be found it was purely on the side of the congregation for not
entering a protest at the time.

It was the same way in regard to machinery. After all, what
better illustrates the supreme purpose of the All Wise than such
a thing as the dynamo or the reciprocating marine engine or the
pictures in the Scientific American?

Then, too, if a man has had the opportunity to travel and has
seen the great lakes spread out by the hand of Providence from
where one leaves the new dock at the Sound to where one arrives
safe and thankful with one's dear fellow-passengers in the spirit
at the concrete landing stage at Mackinaw—is not this fit and
proper material for the construction of an analogy or illustration?
Indeed, even apart from an analogy, is it not mighty interesting
to narrate, anyway? In any case, why should the churchwardens
have sent the rector on the Mackinaw trip, if they had not
expected him to make some little return for it?

I lay some stress on this point because the criticisms directed
against the Mackinaw sermons always seemed so unfair. If the
rector had described his experiences in the crude language of the
ordinary newspaper, there might, I admit, have been something
unfitting about it. But he was always careful to express himself
in a way that showed,—or, listen, let me explain with an
example.

"It happened to be my lot some years ago," he would say, "to
find myself a voyager, just as one is a voyager on the sea of life,
on the broad expanse of water which has been spread out to the
north-west of us by the hand of Providence, at a height of five
hundred and eighty-one feet above the level of the sea,—I refer,
I may say, to Lake Huron."

Now, how different that is from saying: "I'll never forget the
time I went on the Mackinaw trip." The whole thing has a
different sound entirely. In the same way the Dean would go on:

"I was voyaging on one of those magnificent leviathans of the
water,—I refer to the boats of the Northern Navigation Company,—and was standing beside the forward rail talking with a
dear brother in the faith who was journeying westward also—I
may say he was a commercial traveller,—and beside us was a
dear sister in the spirit seated in a deck chair, while near us were
two other dear souls in grace engaged in Christian pastime on the
deck,—I allude more particularly to the game of deck billiards."

I leave it to any reasonable man whether with that complete and fair-minded explanation of the environment, it was not perfectly proper to close down the analogy, as the rector did, with the simple words: "In fact, it was an extremely fine morning."

Yet there were some people, even in Mariposa, that took exception and spent their Sunday dinner time in making out that they couldn't understand what Dean Drone was talking about, and asking one another if they knew. Once, as he passed out from the doors of the Greater Testimony, the rector heard some one say: "The Church would be all right if that old mugwump was out of the pulpit." It went to his heart like a barbed thorn, and stayed there.

You know, perhaps, how a remark of that sort can stay and rankle, and make you wish you could hear it again to make sure of it, because perhaps you didn't hear it aright, and it was a mistake after all. Perhaps no one said it, anyway. You ought to have written it down at the time. I have seen the Dean take down the encyclopædia in the rectory, and move his finger slowly down the pages of the letter M, looking for mugwump. But it wasn't there. I have known him, in his little study upstairs, turn over the pages of the "Animals of Palestine," looking for a mugwump. But there was none there. It must have been unknown in the greater days of Judea.

So things went on from month to month, and from year to year, and the debt and the charges loomed like a dark and gathering cloud on the horizon. I don't mean to say that efforts were not made to face the difficulty and to fight it. They were. Time after time the workers of the congregation got together and thought out plans for the extinction of the debt. But somehow, after every trial, the debt grew larger with each year, and every system that could be devised turned out more hopeless than the last.

They began, I think, with the "endless chain" of letters of appeal. You may remember the device, for it was all-popular in clerical circles some ten or fifteen years ago. You got a number of people to write each of them three letters asking for ten cents from three each of their friends and asking each of them to send on three similar letters. Three each from three each, and three each more from each! Do you observe the wonderful ingenuity of it? Nobody, I think, has forgotten how the Willing Workers of the Church of England Church of Mariposa sat down in the vestry room in the basement with a pile of stationery three feet high, sending out the letters. Some, I know, will never forget it. Certainly not Mr. Pupkin, the teller in the Exchange Bank, for it was here that he met Zena Pepperleigh, the judge's daughter, for the first time; and they worked so busily that they wrote out ever so many letters—eight or nine—in a single afternoon, and they discovered that their handwritings were awfully alike, which was one of the most extraordinary and amazing coincidences, you will admit, in the history of chirography.

But the scheme failed—failed utterly. I don't know why. The letters went out and were copied, broadcast and recopied, till you could see the Mariposa endless chain winding its way towards the Rocky Mountains. But they never got the ten cents. The Willing Workers wrote for it in thousands, but by some odd chance they never struck the person who had it.

Then after that there came a regular winter of effort. First of all they had a bazaar that was got up by the Girls' Auxiliary and held in the basement of the church. All the girls wore special costumes that were brought up from the city, and they had booths, where there was every imaginable thing for sale—pincushion covers, and chair covers, and sofa covers, everything that you can think of. If the people had once started buying them, the debt would have been lifted in no time. Even as it was the bazaar only lost twenty dollars.

After that, I think, was the magic lantern lecture that Dean Drone gave on "Italy and her Invaders." They got the lantern and the slides up from the city; and it was simply splendid. Some of the slides were perhaps a little confusing, but it was all there,— the pictures of the dense Italian jungle and the crocodiles and the naked invaders with their invading clubs. It was a pity that it was such a bad night, snowing hard, and a curling match on, or they would have made a lot of money out of the lecture. As it was the loss, apart from the breaking of the lantern, which was unavoidable, was quite trifling.

I can hardly remember all the things that there were after that. I recollect that it was always Mullins who arranged about renting the hall and printing the tickets and all that sort of thing. His father, you remember, had been at the Anglican college with Dean Drone, and though the rector was thirty-seven years older than Mullins, he leaned upon him, in matters of business, as upon a staff; and though Mullins was thirty-seven years younger than the Dean, he leaned against him, in matters of doctrine, as against a rock.

At one time they got the idea that what the public wanted was not anything instructive but something light and amusing. Mullins said that people loved to laugh. He said that if you get a lot of people all together and get them laughing you can do anything you like with them. Once they start to laugh they are lost. So they got Mr. Dreery, the English Literature teacher at the high school, to give an evening of readings from the Great Humorists from Chaucer to Adam Smith. They came mighty near to making a barrel of money out of that. If the people had once started laughing it would have been all over with them. As it was I heard a lot of them say that they simply wanted to scream with laughter: they said they just felt like bursting into peals of laughter all the time. Even when, in the more subtle parts, they didn't feel like bursting out laughing, they said they had all they could do to keep from smiling. They said they never had such a hard struggle in their lives not to smile.

In fact the chairman said when he put the vote of thanks that he was sure if people had known what the lecture was to be like there would have been a much better "turn-out." But you see all that the people had to go on was just the announcement of the name of the lecturer, Mr. Dreery, and that he would lecture on English Humour All Seats Twenty-five Cents. As the chairman expressed it himself, if the people had had any idea, any idea at all, of what the lecture would be like they would have been there in hundreds. But how could they get an idea that it would be so amusing with practically nothing to go upon?

After that attempt things seemed to go from bad to worse. Nearly everybody was disheartened about it. What would have happened to the debt, or whether they would have ever paid it off, is more than I can say, if it hadn't occurred that light broke in on Mullins in the strangest and most surprising way you can imagine. It happened that he went away for his bank holidays, and while he was away he happened to be present in one of the big cities and saw how they went at it there to raise money. He came home in such a state of excitement that he went straight up from the Mariposa station to the rectory, valise and all, and he burst in one

April evening to where the Rural Dean was sitting with the three girls beside the lamp in the front room, and he cried out:

"Mr. Drone, I've got it,—I've got a way that will clear the debt before you're a fortnight older. We'll have a Whirlwind Campaign in Mariposa!"

But stay! The change from the depth of depression to the pinnacle of hope is too abrupt. I must pause and tell you in another chapter of the Whirlwind Campaign in Mariposa.

Chapter V

The Whirlwind Campaign in Mariposa

It was Mullins, the banker, who told Mariposa all about the plan of a Whirlwind Campaign and explained how it was to be done. He'd happened to be in one of the big cities when they were raising money by a Whirlwind Campaign for one of the universities, and he saw it all.

He said he would never forget the scene on the last day of it, when the announcement was made that the total of the money raised was even more than what was needed. It was a splendid sight,—the business men of the town all cheering and laughing and shaking hands, and the professors with the tears streaming down their faces, and the Deans of the Faculties, who had given money themselves, sobbing aloud.

He said it was the most moving thing he ever saw.

So, as I said, Henry Mullins, who had seen it, explained to the others how it was done. He said that first of all a few of the business men got together quietly,—very quietly, indeed the more quietly the better,—and talked things over. Perhaps one of them would dine,—just quietly,—with another one and discuss the situation. Then these two would invite a third man,—possibly even a fourth,—to have lunch with them and talk in a general way,— even talk of other things part of the time. And so on in this way things would be discussed and looked at in different lights and viewed from different angles and then when everything was ready they would go at things with a rush. A central committee would be formed and sub-committees, with captains of each group and recorders and secretaries, and on a stated day the Whirlwind Campaign would begin.

Each day the crowd would all agree to meet at some stated place and eat lunch together,—say at a restaurant or at a club or at some eating place. This would go on every day with the interest getting keener and keener, and everybody getting more and more excited, till presently the chairman would announce that the campaign had succeeded and there would be the kind of scene that Mullins had described.

So that was the plan that they set in motion in Mariposa.

I don't wish to say too much about the Whirlwind Campaign itself. I don't mean to say that it was a failure. On the contrary, in many ways it couldn't have been a greater success, and yet somehow it didn't seem to work out just as Henry Mullins had said it would. It may be that there are differences between Mariposa and the larger cities that one doesn't appreciate at first sight. Perhaps it would have been better to try some other plan.

Yet they followed along the usual line of things closely enough. They began with the regular system of some of the business men getting together in a quiet way.

First of all, for example, Henry Mullins came over quietly to Duff's rooms, over the Commercial Bank, with a bottle of rye whiskey, and they talked things over. And the night after that George Duff came over quietly to Mullins's rooms, over the Exchange Bank, with a bottle of Scotch whiskey. A few evenings after that Mullins and Duff went together, in a very unostentatious way, with perhaps a couple of bottles of rye, to Pete Glover's room over the hardware store. And then all three of them went up one night with Ed Moore, the photographer, to Judge Pepperleigh's house under pretence of having a game of poker. The very day after that, Mullins and Duff and Ed Moore, and Pete Glover and the judge got Will Harrison, the harness maker, to go out without any formality on the lake on the pretext of fishing. And the next night after that Duff and Mullins and Ed Moore and Pete Glover and Pepperleigh and Will Harrison got Alf Trelawney, the postmaster, to come over, just in a casual way, to the Mariposa House, after the night mail, and the next day Mullins and Duff and—

But, pshaw! you see at once how the thing is worked. There's no need to follow that part of the Whirlwind Campaign further. But it just shows the power of organization.

And all this time, mind you, they were talking things over, and looking at things first in one light and then in another light, —in fact, just doing as the big city men do when there's an important thing like this under way.

So after things had been got pretty well into shape in this way, Duff asked Mullins one night, straight out, if he would be chairman of the Central Committee. He sprung it on him and Mullins had no time to refuse, but he put it to Duff straight whether he would be treasurer. And Duff had no time to refuse.

That gave things a start, and within a week they had the whole organization on foot. There was the Grand Central Committee and six groups or sub-committees of twenty men each, and a captain for every group. They had it all arranged on the lines most likely to be effective.

In one group there were all the bankers, Mullins and Duff and Pupkin (with the cameo pin), and about four others. They had their photographs taken at Ed Moore's studio, taken in a line with a background of icebergs—a winter scene—and a pretty penetrating crowd they looked, I can tell you. After all, you know, if you get a crowd of representative bank men together in any financial deal, you've got a pretty considerable leverage right away.

In the second group were the lawyers, Nivens and Macartney and the rest—about as level-headed a lot as you'd see anywhere. Get the lawyers of a town with you on a thing like this and you'll find you've got a sort of brain power with you that you'd never get without them.

Then there were the business men—there was a solid crowd for you,—Harrison, the harness maker, and Glover, the hardware man, and all that gang, not talkers, perhaps, but solid men who can tell you to a nicety how many cents there are in a dollar. It's all right to talk about education and that sort of thing, but if want driving power and efficiency, get business men. They're seeing it every day in the city, and it's just the same in Mariposa. Why, in the big concerns in the city, if they found out a man was educated, they wouldn't have him,—wouldn't keep him there a minute. That's why the business men have to conceal it so much.

Then in the other teams there were the doctors and the newspaper men and the professional men like judge Pepperleigh and Yodel the auctioneer.

It was all organized so that every team had its headquarters, two of them in each of the three hotels—one upstairs and one down. And it was arranged that there would be a big lunch every day, to be held in Smith's caff, round the corner of Smith's Northern Health Resort and Home of the Wissanotti Angler,—you know the place. The lunch was divided up into tables, with a captain for each table to see about things to drink, and of course all the tables were in competition with one another. In fact the competition was the very life of the whole thing.

It's just wonderful how these things run when they're organized. Take the first luncheon, for example. There they all were, every man in his place, every captain at his post at the top of the table. It was hard, perhaps, for some of them to get there. They had very likely to be in their stores and banks and offices till the last minute and then make a dash for it. It was the cleanest piece of team work you ever saw.

You have noticed already, I am sure, that a good many of the captains and committee men didn't belong to the Church of England Church. Glover, for instance, was a Presbyterian, till they ran the picket fence of the manse two feet on to his property, and after that he became a free thinker. But in Mariposa, as I have said, everybody likes to be in everything and naturally a Whirlwind Campaign was a novelty. Anyway it would have been a poor business to keep a man out of the lunches merely on account of his religion. I trust that the day for that kind of religious bigotry is past.

Of course the excitement was when Henry Mullins at the head of the table began reading out the telegrams and letters and messages. First of all there was a telegram of good wishes from the Anglican Lord Bishop of the Diocese to Henry Mullins and calling him Dear Brother in Grace—the Mariposa telegraph office is a little unreliable and it read: "Dear Brother in grease," but that was good enough. The Bishop said that his most earnest wishes were with them.

Then Mullins read a letter from the Mayor of Mariposa—Pete Glover was mayor that year—stating that his keenest desires were with them: and then one from the Carriage Company saying that its heartiest good will was all theirs; and then one from the Meat Works saying that its nearest thoughts were next to them. Then he read one from himself, as head of the Exchange Bank, you understand, informing him that he had heard of his project and assuring him of his liveliest interest in what he proposed.

At each of these telegrams and messages there was round after round of applause, so that you could hardly hear yourself speak or give an order. But that was nothing to when Mullins got up again, and beat on the table for silence and made one of those

cracking, concise speeches—just the way business men speak—
the kind of speech that a college man simply can't make. I wish
I could repeat it all. I remember that it began: "Now boys, you
know what we're here for, gentlemen," and it went on just as
good as that all through.

When Mullins had done he took out a fountain pen and wrote
out a cheque for a hundred dollars, conditional on the fund reaching fifty thousand. And there was a burst of cheers all over the
room.

Just the moment he had done it, up sprang George Duff,—
you know the keen competition there is, as a straight matter of
business, between the banks in Mariposa,—up sprang George
Duff, I say, and wrote out a cheque for another hundred conditional on the fund reaching seventy thousand. You never heard
such cheering in your life.

And then when Netley walked up to the head of the table and
laid down a cheque for a hundred dollars conditional on the fund
reaching one hundred thousand the room was in an uproar. A
hundred thousand dollars! Just think of it! The figures fairly
stagger one. To think of a hundred thousand dollars raised in five
minutes in a little place like Mariposa!

And even that was nothing! In less than no time there was
such a crowd round Mullins trying to borrow his pen all at once
that his waistcoat was all stained with ink. Finally when they got
order at last, and Mullins stood up and announced that the
conditional fund had reached a quarter of a million, the whole
place was a perfect babel of cheering. Oh, these Whirlwind Campaigns are wonderful things!

I can tell you the Committee felt pretty proud that first day.
There was Henry Mullins looking a little bit flushed and excited,
with his white waistcoat and an American Beauty rose, and with
ink marks all over him from the cheque signing; and he kept
telling them that he'd known all along that all that was needed
was to get the thing started and telling again about what he'd seen
at the University Campaign and about the professors crying, and
wondering if the high school teachers would come down for the
last day of the meetings.

Looking back on the Mariposa Whirlwind, I can never feel
that it was a failure. After all, there is a sympathy and a brother-

hood in these things when men work shoulder to shoulder. If you had seen the canvassers of the Committee going round the town that evening shoulder to shoulder from the Mariposa House to the Continental and up to Mullins's rooms and over to Duff's, shoulder to shoulder, you'd have understood it.

I don't say that every lunch was quite such a success as the first. It's not always easy to get out of the store if you're a busy man, and a good many of the Whirlwind Committee found that they had just time to hurry down and snatch their lunch and get back again. Still, they came, and snatched it. As long as the lunches lasted, they came. Even if they had simply to rush in and grab something to eat and drink without time to talk to anybody, they came.

No, no, it was not lack of enthusiasm that killed the Whirlwind Campaign in Mariposa. It must have been something else. I don't just know what it was but I think it had something to do with the financial, the book-keeping side of the thing.

It may have been, too, that the organization was not quite correctly planned. You see, if practically everybody is on the committees, it is awfully hard to try to find men to canvass, and it is not allowable for the captains and the Committee men to canvass one another, because their gifts are spontaneous. So the only thing that the different groups could do was to wait round in some likely place—say the bar parlour of Smith's Hotel—in the hope that somebody might come in who could be canvassed.

You might ask why they didn't canvass Mr. Smith himself, but of course they had done that at the very start, as I should have said. Mr. Smith had given them two hundred dollars in cash conditional on the lunches being held in the caff of his hotel; and it's awfully hard to get a proper lunch—I mean the kind to which a Bishop can express regret at not being there—under a dollar twenty-five. So Mr. Smith got back his own money, and the crowd began eating into the benefactions, and it got more and more complicated whether to hold another lunch in the hope of breaking even, or to stop the campaign.

It was disappointing, yes. In spite of all the success and the sympathy, it was disappointing. I don't say it didn't do good. No doubt a lot of the men got to know one another better than ever they had before. I have myself heard Judge Pepperleigh say that after the campaign he knew all of Pete Glover that he wanted to.

There was a lot of that kind of complete satiety. The real trouble about the Whirlwind Campaign was that they never clearly understood which of them were the whirlwind and who were to be the campaign.

Some of them, I believe, took it pretty much to heart. I know that Henry Mullins did. You could see it. The first day he came down to the lunch, all dressed up with the American Beauty and the white waistcoat. The second day he only wore a pink carnation and a grey waistcoat. The third day he had on a dead daffodil and a cardigan undervest, and on the last day, when the high school teachers should have been there, he only wore his office suit and he hadn't even shaved. He looked beaten.

It was that night that he went up to the rectory to tell the news to Dean Drone. It had been arranged, you know, that the rector should not attend the lunches, so as to let the whole thing come as a surprise; so that all he knew about it was just scraps of information about the crowds at the lunch and how they cheered and all that. Once, I believe, he caught sight of the Newspacket with the two-inch headline: A QUARTER OF A MILLION, but he wouldn't let himself read further because it would have spoilt the surprise.

I saw Mullins, as I say, go up the street on his way to Dean Drone's. It was middle April and there was ragged snow on the streets, and the nights were dark still, and cold. I saw Mullins grit his teeth as he walked, and I know that he held in his coat pocket his own cheque for the hundred, with the condition taken off it, and he said that there were so many skunks in Mariposa that a man might as well be in the Head Office in the city.

The Dean came out to the little gate in the dark,—you could see the lamplight behind him from the open door of the rectory, —and he shook hands with Mullins and they went in together.

Chapter VI

The Beacon on the Hill

Mullins said afterward that it was ever so much easier than he thought it would have been. The Dean, he said, was so quiet. Of course if Mr. Drone had started to swear at Mullins, or tried to strike him, it would have been much harder. But as it was he was so quiet that part of the time he hardly seemed to follow what Mullins was saying. So Mullins was glad of that, because it proved that the Dean wasn't feeling disappointed as, in a way, he might have.

Indeed, the only time when the rector seemed animated and excited in the whole interview was when Mullins said that the campaign had been ruined by a lot of confounded mugwumps. Straight away the Dean asked if those mugwumps had really prejudiced the outcome of the campaign. Mullins said there was no doubt of it, and the Dean enquired if the presence of mugwumps was fatal in matters of endeavour, and Mullins said that it was. Then the rector asked if even one mugwump was, in the Christian sense, deleterious. Mullins said that one mugwump would kill anything. After that the Dean hardly spoke at all.

In fact, the rector presently said that he mustn't detain Mullins too long and that he had detained him too long already and that Mullins must be weary from his train journey and that in cases of extreme weariness nothing but a sound sleep was of any avail; he himself, unfortunately, would not be able to avail himself of the priceless boon of slumber until he had first retired to his study to write some letters; so that Mullins, who had a certain kind of social quickness of intuition, saw that it was time to leave, and went away.

It was midnight as he went down the street, and a dark, still night. That can be stated positively because it came out in court afterwards. Mullins swore that it was a dark night; he admitted, under examination, that there may have been the stars, or at least some of the less important of them, though he had made no attempt, as brought out on cross-examination, to count them: there may have been, too, the electric lights, and Mullins was not willing to deny that it was quite possible that there was more or less moonlight. But that there was no light that night in the form of sunlight, Mullins was absolutely certain. All that, I say, came out in court.

But meanwhile the rector had gone upstairs to his study and had seated himself in front of his table to write his letters. It was here always that he wrote his sermons. From the window of the room you looked through the bare white maple trees to the sweeping outline of the church shadowed against the night sky, and beyond that, though far off, was the new cemetery where the rector walked of a Sunday (I think I told you why): beyond that again, for the window faced the east, there lay, at no very great distance, the New Jerusalem. There were no better things that a man might look towards from his study window, nor anything that could serve as a better aid to writing.

But this night the Dean's letters must have been difficult indeed to write. For he sat beside the table holding his pen and with his head bent upon his other hand, and though he sometimes put a line or two on the paper, for the most part he sat motionless. The fact is that Dean Drone was not trying to write letters, but only one letter. He was writing a letter of resignation. If you have not done that for forty years it is extremely difficult to get the words.

So at least the Dean found it. First he wrote one set of words and then he sat and thought and wrote something else. But nothing seemed to suit.

The real truth was that Dean Drone, perhaps more than he knew himself, had a fine taste for words and effects, and when you feel that a situation is entirely out of the common, you naturally try, if you have that instinct, to give it the right sort of expression.

I believe that at the time when Rupert Drone had taken the medal in Greek over fifty years ago, it was only a twist of fate that had prevented him from becoming a great writer. There was a buried author in him just as there was a buried financier in Jefferson Thorpe. In fact, there were many people in Mariposa like that, and for all I know you may yourself have seen such elsewhere. For instance, I am certain that Billy Rawson, the telegraph operator at Mariposa, could easily have invented radium. In the same way one has only to read the advertisements of Mr. Gingham, the undertaker, to know that there is still in him a poet, who could have written on death far more attractive verses than the Thanatopsis of Cullen Bryant, and under a title less likely to offend the public and drive away custom. He has told me this himself.

So the Dean tried first this and then that and nothing would seem to suit. First of all he wrote:

"It is now forty years since I came among you, a youth full of life and hope and ardent in the work before me—" Then he paused, doubtful of the accuracy and clearness of the expression, read it over again and again in deep thought and then began again:

"It is now forty years since I came among you, a broken and melancholy boy, without life or hope, desiring only to devote to the service of this parish such few years as might remain of an existence blighted before it had truly begun—" And then again the Dean stopped. He read what he had written; he frowned; he crossed it through with his pen. This was no way to write, this thin egotistical strain of complaint. Once more he started:

"It is now forty years since I came among you, a man already tempered and trained, except possibly in mathematics—" And then again the rector paused and his mind drifted away to the memory of the Anglican professor that I spoke of, who had had so little sense of his higher mission as to omit the teaching of logarithms. And the rector mused so long that when he began again it seemed to him that it was simpler and better to discard the personal note altogether, and he wrote:

"There are times, gentlemen, in the life of a parish, when it comes to an epoch which brings it to a moment when it reaches a point—"

The Dean stuck fast again, but refusing this time to be beaten went resolutely on:

"—reaches a point where the circumstances of the moment make the epoch such as to focus the life of the parish in that time."

Then the Dean saw that he was beaten, and he knew that he not only couldn't manage the parish but couldn't say so in proper English, and of the two the last was the bitterer discovery.

He raised his head, and looked for a moment through the window at the shadow of the church against the night, so outlined that you could almost fancy that the light of the New Jerusalem was beyond it. Then he wrote, and this time not to the world at large but only to Mullins:

"My dear Harry, I want to resign my charge. Will you come over and help me?"

When the Dean at last rose from writing that, I think it was far on in the night. As he rose he looked again through the window, looked once and then once more, and so stood with widening eyes, and his face set towards what he saw.

What was that? That light in the sky there, eastward?—near or far he could not say. Was it already the dawn of the New Jerusalem brightening in the east, or was it—look—in the church itself,—what is that?—that dull red glow that shines behind the stained-glass windows, turning them to crimson? that fork of flame that breaks now from the casement and flashes upward, along the wood—and see—that sudden sheet of fire that springs from the windows of the church with the roar of splintered glass and surges upward into the sky, till the dark night and the bare trees and sleeping street of Mariposa are all illumined with its glow!

Fire! Fire! and the sudden sound of the bell now, breaking upon the night.

So stood the Dean erect, with one hand pressed against the table for support, while the Mariposa fire bell struck out its warning to the sleeping town,—stood there while the street grew loud with the tumult of voices,—with the roaring gallop of the fire brigade,—with the harsh note of the gong—and over all other sounds, the great seething of the flames that tore their way into the beams and rafters of the pointed church and flared above it like a torch into the midnight sky.

So stood the Dean, and as the church broke thus into a very beacon kindled upon a hill,—sank forward without a sign, his face against the table, stricken.

You need to see a fire in a place such as Mariposa, a town still half of wood, to know what fire means. In the city it is all different. To the onlooker, at any rate, a fire is only a spectacle, nothing more. Everything is arranged, organized, certain. It is only once perhaps in a century that fire comes to a large city as it comes to the little wooden town like Mariposa as a great Terror of the Night.

That, at any rate, is what it meant in Mariposa that night in April, the night the Church of England Church burnt down. Had the fire gained but a hundred feet, or less, it could have reached from the driving shed behind the church to the backs of the wooden shops of the Main Street, and once there not all the waters of Lake Wissanotti could stay the course of its destruction. It was for that hundred feet that they fought, the men of Mariposa, from the midnight call of the bell till the slow coming of the day.

They fought the fire, not to save the church, for that was doomed from the first outbreak of the flames, but to stop the spread of it and save the town. They fought it at the windows, and at the blazing doors, and through the yawning furnace of the open belfry; fought it, with the Mariposa engine thumping and panting in the street, itself aglow with fire like a servant demon fighting its own kind, with tall ladders reaching to the very roof, and with hose that poured their streams of tossing water foaming into the flames.

Most of all they fought to save the wooden driving shed behind the church from which the fire could leap into the heart of Mariposa. That was where the real fight was, for the life of the town. I wish you could have seen how they turned the hose against the shingles, ripping and tearing them from their places with the force of the driven water: how they mounted on the roof, axe in hand, and cut madly at the rafters to bring the building down, while the black clouds of smoke rolled in volumes about the men as they worked. You could see the fire horses harnessed with logging chains to the uprights of the shed to tear the building from its place.

Most of all I wish you could have seen Mr. Smith, proprietor, as I think you know, of Smith's Hotel, there on the roof with a fireman's helmet on, cutting through the main beam of solid cedar, twelve by twelve, that held tight still when the rafters and the roof tree were down already, the shed on fire in a dozen places, and the other men driven from the work by the flaming sparks, and by the strangle of the smoke. Not so Mr. Smith! See him there as he plants himself firm at the angle of the beams, and with the full impact of his two hundred and eighty pounds drives his axe into the wood! I tell you it takes a man from the pine country of the north to handle an axe! Right, left, left, right, down it comes, with never a pause or stay, never missing by a fraction of an inch the line of the stroke! At it, Smith! Down with it! Till with a shout from the crowd the beam gapes asunder, and Mr. Smith is on the ground again, roaring his directions to the men and horses as they haul down the shed, in a voice that dominates the fire itself.

Who made Mr. Smith the head and chief of the Mariposa fire brigade that night, I cannot say. I do not know even where he got the huge red helmet that he wore, nor had I ever heard till the night the church burnt down that Mr. Smith was a member of the fire brigade at all. But it's always that way. Your little narrow-chested men may plan and organize, but when there is something to be done, something real, then it's the man of size and weight that steps to the front every time. Look at Bismarck and Mr. Gladstone and President Taft and Mr. Smith,—the same thing in each case.

I suppose it was perfectly natural that just as soon as Mr. Smith came on the scene he put on somebody's helmet and shouted his directions to the men and bossed the Mariposa fire brigade like Bismarck with the German parliament.

The fire had broken out late, late at night, and they fought it till the day. The flame of it lit up the town and the bare grey maple trees, and you could see in the light of it the broad sheet of the frozen lake, snow covered still. It kindled such a beacon as it burned that from the other side of the lake the people on the night express from the north could see it twenty miles away. It lit up such a testimony of flame that Mariposa has never seen the like of it before or since. Then when the roof crashed in and the tall steeple tottered and fell, so swift a darkness seemed to come that the grey trees and the frozen lake vanished in a moment as if blotted out of existence.

When the morning came the great church of Mariposa was nothing but a ragged group of walls with a sodden heap of bricks and blackened wood, still hissing here and there beneath the hose with the sullen anger of a conquered fire.

Round the ruins of the fire walked the people of Mariposa next morning, and they pointed out where the wreck of the steeple had fallen, and where the bells of the church lay in a molten heap among the bricks, and they talked of the loss that it was and how many dollars it would take to rebuild the church, and whether it was insured and for how much. And there were at least fourteen people who had seen the fire first, and more than that who had given the first alarm, and ever so many who knew how fires of this sort could be prevented.

Most noticeable of all you could see the sidesmen and the wardens and Mullins, the chairman of the vestry, talking in little groups about the fire. Later in the day there came from the city the insurance men and the fire appraisers, and they too walked about the ruins, and talked with the wardens and the vestry men. There was such a luxury of excitement in the town that day that it was just as good as a public holiday.

But the strangest part of it was the unexpected sequel. I don't know through what error of the Dean's figures it happened, through what lack of mathematical training the thing turned out as it did. No doubt the memory of the mathematical professor was heavily to blame for it, but the solid fact is that the Church of England Church of Mariposa turned out to be insured for a hundred thousand, and there were the receipts and the vouchers, all signed and regular, just as they found them in a drawer of the rector's study. There was no doubt about it. The insurance people might protest as they liked. The straight, plain fact was that the church was insured for about twice the whole amount of the cost and the debt and the rector's salary and the boarding-school fees of the littlest of the Drones all put together.

There was a whirlwind Campaign for you! Talk of raising money, —that was something like! I wonder if the universities and the city institutions that go round trying to raise money by the slow and painful method called a Whirlwind Campaign, that takes perhaps all day to raise fifty thousand dollars, ever thought of anything so beautifully simple as this.

The Greater Testimony that had lain so heavily on the congregation went flaming to its end, and burned up its debts and its obligations and enriched its worshippers by its destruction. Talk of a beacon on a hill! You can hardly beat that one.

I wish you could have seen how the wardens and the sidesmen and Mullins, the chairman of the vestry, smiled and chuckled at the thought of it. Hadn't they said all along that all that was needed was a little faith and effort? And here it was just as they said, and they'd been right after all.

Protest from the insurance people? Legal proceedings to prevent payment? My dear sir! I see you know nothing about the Mariposa court, in spite of the fact that I have already said that it was one of the most precise instruments of British fair play ever established. Why, Judge Pepperleigh disposed of the case and dismissed the protest of the company in less than fifteen minutes! Just what the jurisdiction of Judge Pepperleigh's court is I don't know, but I do know that in upholding the rights of a Christian congregation—I am quoting here the text of the decision—against the intrigues of a set of infernal skunks that make too much money, anyway, the Mariposa court is without an equal. Pepperleigh even threatened the plaintiffs with the penitentiary, or worse.

How the fire started no one ever knew. There was a queer story that went about to the effect that Mr. Smith and Mr. Gingham's assistant had been seen very late that night carrying an automobile can of kerosene up the street. But that was amply disproved by the proceedings of the court, and by the evidence of Mr. Smith himself. He took his dying oath,—not his ordinary one as used in the License cases, but his dying one,—that he had not carried a can of kerosene up the street, and that anyway it was the rottenest kind of kerosene he had ever seen and no more use than so much molasses. So that point was settled.

Dean Drone? Did he get well again? Why, what makes you ask that? You mean, was his head at all affected after the stroke? No, it was not. Absolutely not. It was not affected in the least, though how anybody who knows him now in Mariposa could have the faintest idea that his mind was in any way impaired by the stroke is more than I can tell. The engaging of Mr. Uttermost, the curate, whom perhaps you have heard preach in the new church, had nothing whatever to do with Dean Drone's head. It was merely a case of the pressure of overwork. It was felt very generally by the wardens that, in these days of specialization, the rector was covering too wide a field, and that if he should abandon some of the lesser duties of his office, he might devote his energies more intently to the Infant Class. That was all. You may hear him there any afternoon, talking to them, if you will stand under the maple trees and listen through the open windows of the new Infant School.

And, as for audiences, for intelligence, for attention—well, if I want to find listeners who can hear and understand about the great spaces of Lake Huron, let me tell of it, every time face to face with the blue eyes of the Infant Class, fresh from the infinity of spaces greater still. Talk of grown-up people all you like, but for listeners let me have the Infant Class with their pinafores and their Teddy Bears and their feet not even touching the floor, and Mr. Uttermost may preach to his heart's content of the newer forms of doubt revealed by the higher criticism.

So you will understand that the Dean's mind is, if anything, even keener, and his head even clearer than before. And if you want proof of it, notice him there beneath the plum blossoms reading in the Greek: he has told me that he finds that he can read, with the greatest ease, works in the Greek that seemed difficult before. Because his head is so clear now.

And sometimes,—when his head is very clear,—as he sits there reading beneath the plum blossoms he can hear them singing beyond, and his wife's voice.

Chapter VII

The Extraordinary Entanglement of Mr. Pupkin

Judge Pepperleigh lived in a big house with hardwood floors and a wide piazza that looked over the lake from the top of Oneida Street.

Every day about half-past five he used to come home from his office in the Mariposa Court House. On some days as he got near the house he would call out to his wife:

"Almighty Moses, Martha! who left the sprinkler on the grass?"

On other days he would call to her from quite a little distance off: "Hullo, mother! Got any supper for a hungry man?"

And Mrs. Pepperleigh never knew which it would be.

On the days when he swore at the sprinkler you could see his spectacles flash like dynamite. But on the days when he called: "Hullo, mother," they were simply irradiated with kindliness.

Some days, I say, he would cry out with a perfect whine of indignation: "Suffering Caesar! has that infernal dog torn up those geraniums again?" And other days you would hear him singing out: "Hullo, Rover! Well, doggie, well, old fellow!"

In the same way at breakfast, the judge, as he looked over the morning paper, would sometimes leap to his feet with a perfect howl of suffering, and cry: "Everlasting Moses! the Liberals have carried East Elgin." Or else he would lean back from the breakfast table with the most good-humoured laugh you ever heard and say: "Ha! ha! the Conservatives have carried South Norfolk."

And yet he was perfectly logical, when you come to think of it. After all, what is more annoying to a sensitive, highly- strung man than an infernal sprinkler playing all over the place, and what more agreeable to a good-natured, even-tempered fellow than a well-prepared supper? Or, what is more likeable than one's good, old, affectionate dog bounding down the path from sheer delight at seeing you,—or more execrable than an infernal whelp that has torn up the geraniums and is too old to keep, anyway?

As for politics, well, it all seemed reasonable enough. When the Conservatives got in anywhere, Pepperleigh laughed and enjoyed it, simply because it does one good to see a straight, fine, honest fight where the best man wins. When a Liberal got in, it made him mad, and he said so,—not, mind you, from any political bias, for his office forbid it,—but simply because one can't bear to see the country go absolutely to the devil.

I suppose, too, it was partly the effect of sitting in court all day listening to cases. One gets what you might call the judicial temper of mind. Pepperleigh had it so strongly developed that I've seen him kick a hydrangea pot to pieces with his foot because the accursed thing wouldn't flower. He once threw the canary cage clear into the lilac bushes because the "blasted bird wouldn't stop singing." It was a straight case of judicial temper. Lots of judges have it, developed in just the same broad, all-round way as with Judge Pepperleigh.

I think it must be passing sentences that does it. Anyway, Pepperleigh had the aptitude for passing sentences so highly perfected that he spent his whole time at it inside of court and out. I've heard him hand out sentences for the Sultan of Turkey and Mrs. Pankhurst and the Emperor of Germany that made one's blood run cold. He would sit there on the piazza of a summer evening reading the paper, with dynamite sparks flying from his spectacles as he sentenced the Czar of Russia to ten years in the salt mines—and made it fifteen a few minutes afterwards. Pepperleigh always read the foreign news—the news of things that he couldn't alter—as a form of wild and stimulating torment.

So you can imagine that in some ways the judge's house was a pretty difficult house to go to. I mean you can see how awfully hard it must have been for Mr. Pupkin. I tell you it took some nerve to step up on that piazza and say, in a perfectly natural, off-hand way: "Oh, how do you do, judge? Is Miss Zena in? No, I won't stay, thanks; I think I ought to be going. I simply called." A man who can do that has got to have a pretty fair amount of savoir what do you call it, and he's got to be mighty well shaved and have his cameo pin put in his tie at a pretty undeniable angle before he can tackle it. Yes, and even then he may need to hang round behind the lilac bushes for half an hour first, and cool off. And he's apt to make pretty good time down Oneida Street on the way back.

Still, that's what you call love, and if you've got it, and are well shaved, and your boots well blacked, you can do things that seem almost impossible. Yes, you can do anything, even if you do trip over the dog in getting off the piazza.

Don't suppose for a moment that Judge Pepperleigh was an unapproachable or a harsh man always and to everybody. Even Mr. Pupkin had to admit that that couldn't be so. To know that, you had only to see Zena Pepperleigh put her arm round his neck and call him Daddy. She would do that even when there were two or three young men sitting on the edge of the piazza. You know, I think, the way they sit on the edge in Mariposa. It is meant to indicate what part of the family they have come to see. Thus when George Duff, the bank manager, came up to the Pepperleigh house, he always sat in a chair on the verandah and talked to the judge. But when Pupkin or Mallory Tompkins or any fellow like that came, he sat down in a sidelong fashion on the edge of the boards and then they knew exactly what he was there for. If he knew the house well, he leaned his back against the verandah post and smoked a cigarette. But that took nerve.

But I am afraid that this is a digression, and, of course, you know all about it just as well as I do. All that I was trying to say was that I don't suppose that the judge had ever spoken a cross word to Zena in his life.—Oh, he threw her novel over the grape-vine, I don't deny that, but then why on earth should a girl read trash like the *Errant Quest of the Palladin Pilgrim,* and the *Life of Sir Galahad,* when the house was full of good reading like *The Life ol Sir John A. Macdonald,* and *Pioneer Days in Tecumseh Township?*

Still, what I mean is that the judge never spoke harshly to Zena, except perhaps under extreme provocation; and I am quite sure that he never, never had to Neil. But then what father ever would want to speak angrily to such a boy as Neil Pepperleigh? The judge took no credit to himself for that; the finest grown boy in the whole county and so broad and big that they took him into the Missinaba Horse when he was only seventeen. And clever,—so clever that he didn't need to study; so clever that he used to come out at the foot of the class in mathematics at the Mariposa high school through sheer surplus of brain power. I've heard the judge explain it a dozen times. Why, Neil was so clever that he used to be able to play billiards at the Mariposa House all evening when the other boys had to stay at home and study.

Such a powerful looking fellow, too! Everybody in Mariposa remembers how Neil Pepperleigh smashed in the face of Peter McGinnis, the Liberal organizer, at the big election—you recall it—when the old Macdonald Government went out. Judge Pepperleigh had to try him for it the next morning—his own son. They say there never was such a scene even in the Mariposa court. There was, I believe, something like it on a smaller scale in Roman history, but it wasn't half as dramatic. I remember Judge Pepperleigh leaning forward to pass the sentence,—for a judge is bound, you know, by his oath,—and how grave he looked and yet so proud and happy, like a man doing his duty and sustained by it, and he said:

"My boy, you are innocent. You smashed in Peter McGinnis's face, but you did it without criminal intent. You put a face on him, by Jehoshaphat! that he won't lose for six months, but you did it without evil purpose or malign design. My boy, look up! Give me your hand! You leave this court without a stain upon your name."

They said it was one of the most moving scenes ever enacted in the Mariposa Court.

But the strangest thing is that if the judge had known what every one else in Mariposa knew, it would have broken his heart. If he could have seen Neil with the drunken flush on his face in the billiard room of the Mariposa House,—if he had known, as every one else did, that Neil was crazed with drink the night he struck the Liberal organizer when the old Macdonald Government went out,—if he could have known that even on that last day Neil was drunk when he rode with the Missinaba Horse to the station to join the Third Contingent for the war, and all the street of the little town was one, great roar of people,—

But the judge never knew, and now he never will. For if you could find it in the meanness of your soul to tell him, it would serve no purpose now except to break his heart, and there would rise up to rebuke you the pictured vision of an untended grave somewhere in the great silences of South Africa.

Did I say above, or seem to imply, that the judge sometimes

spoke harshly to his wife? Or did you gather for a minute that her lot was one to lament over or feel sorry for? If so, it just shows that you know nothing about such things, and that marriage, at least as it exists in Mariposa, is a sealed book to you. You are as ignorant as Miss Spiffkins, the biology teacher at the high school, who always says how sorry she is for Mrs. Pepperleigh. You get that impression simply because the judge howled like an Algonquin Indian when he saw the sprinkler running on the lawn. But are you sure you know the other side of it? Are you quite sure when you talk like Miss Spiffkins does about the rights of it, that you are taking all things into account? You might have thought differently perhaps of the Pepperleighs, anyway, if you had been there that evening when the judge came home to his wife with one hand pressed to his temple and in the other the cablegram that said that Neil had been killed in action in South Africa. That night they sat together with her hand in his, just as they had sat together thirty years ago when he was a law student in the city.

Go and tell Miss Spiffkins that! Hydrangeas, canaries,—temper,—blazes! What does Miss Spiffkins know about it all?

But in any case, if you tried to tell Judge Pepperleigh about Neil now he wouldn't believe it. He'd laugh it to scorn. That is Neil's Picture, in uniform, hanging in the dining-room beside the Fathers of Confederation. That military-looking man in the picture beside him is General Kitchener, whom you may perhaps have heard of, for he was very highly spoken of in Neil's letters. All round the room, in fact, and still more in the judge's library upstairs, you will see pictures of South Africa and the departure of the Canadians (there are none of the return), and of Mounted Infantry and of Unmounted Cavalry and a lot of things that only soldiers and the fathers of soldiers know about.

So you can realize that for a fellow who isn't military, and who wears nothing nearer to a uniform than a daffodil tennis blazer, the judge's house is a devil of a house to come to.

I think you remember young Mr. Pupkin, do you not? I have referred to him several times already as the junior teller in the Exchange Bank. But if you know Mariposa at all you have often seen him. You have noticed him, I am sure, going for the bank mail in the morning in an office suit effect of clinging grey with a gold neck-tie pin shaped like a riding whip. You have seen him often enough going down to the lake front after supper, in tennis things, smoking a cigarette and with a paddle and a crimson canoe cushion under his arm. You have seen him entering Dean Drone's church in a top hat and a long frock coat nearly to his feet. You have seen him, perhaps, playing poker in Peter Glover's room over the hardware store and trying to look as if he didn't hold three aces,—in fact, giving absolutely no sign of it beyond the wild flush in his face and the fact that his hair stands on end.

That kind of reticence is a thing you simply have to learn in banking. I mean, if you've got to be in a position where you know for a fact that the Mariposa Packing Company's account is overdrawn by sixty-four dollars, and yet daren't say anything about it, not even to the girls that you play tennis with,—I don't say, not a casual hint as a reference, but not really tell them, not, for instance, bring down the bank ledger to the tennis court and show them,—you learn a sort of reticence and self-control that people outside of banking circles never can attain.

Why, I've known Pupkin at the Firemen's Ball lean against the wall in his dress suit and talk away to Jim Eliot, the druggist, without giving the faintest hint or indication that Eliot's note for twenty-seven dollars had been protested that very morning. Not a hint of it. I don't say he didn't mention it, in a sort of way, in the supper room, just to one or two, but I mean there was nothing in the way he leant up against the wall to suggest it.

But, however, I don't mention that as either for or against Mr. Pupkin. That sort of thing is merely the A B C of banking, as he himself told me when explaining why it was that he hesitated to divulge the exact standing of the Mariposa Carriage Company. Of course, once you get past the A B C you can learn a lot that is mighty interesting.

So I think that if you know Mariposa and understand even the rudiments of banking, you are perfectly acquainted with Mr. Pupkin. What? You remember him as being in love with Miss Lawson, the high school teacher? In love with HER? What a ridiculous idea. You mean merely because on the night when the Mariposa Belle sank with every soul on board, Pupkin put off from the town in a skiff to rescue Miss Lawson. Oh, but you're quite wrong. That wasn't LOVE. I've heard Pupkin explain it himself a dozen times. That sort of thing,—paddling out to a sinking steamer at night in a crazy skiff,—may indicate a sort of

attraction, but not real love, not what Pupkin came to feel afterwards. Indeed, when he began to think of it, it wasn't even attraction, it was merely respect,—that's all it was. And anyway, that was long before, six or seven months back, and Pupkin admitted that at the time he was a mere boy.

Mr. Pupkin, I must explain, lived with Mallory Tompkins in rooms over the Exchange Bank, on the very top floor, the third, with Mullins's own rooms below them. Extremely comfortable quarters they were, with two bedrooms and a sitting-room that was all fixed up with snowshoes and tennis rackets on the walls and dance programmes and canoe club badges and all that sort of thing.

Mallory Tompkins was a young man with long legs and check trousers who worked on the Mariposa Times-Herald. That was what gave him his literary taste. He used to read Ibsen and that other Dutch author—Bumstone Bumstone, isn't it?—and you can judge that he was a mighty intellectual fellow. He was so intellectual that he was, as he himself admitted, a complete eggnostic. He and Pupkin used to have the most tremendous arguments about creation and evolution, and how if you study at a school of applied science you learn that there's no hell beyond the present life.

Mallory Tompkins used to prove absolutely that the miracles were only electricity, and Pupkin used to admit that it was an awfully good argument, but claimed that he had heard it awfully well answered in a sermon, though unfortunately he had forgotten how.

Tompkins used to show that the flood was contrary to geology, and Pupkin would acknowledge that the point was an excellent one, but that he had read a book,—the title of which he ought to have written down,—which explained geology away altogether.

Mallory Tompkins generally got the best of the merely logical side of the arguments, but Pupkin—who was a tremendous Christian—was much stronger in the things he had forgotten. So the discussions often lasted till far into the night, and Mr. Pupkin would fall asleep and dream of a splendid argument, which would have settled the whole controversy, only unfortunately he couldn't recall it in the morning.

Of course, Pupkin, would never have thought of considering himself on an intellectual par with Mallory Tompkins. That would have been ridiculous. Mallory Tompkins had read all sorts of things and had half a mind to write a novel himself—either that or a play. All he needed, he said, was to have a chance to get away somewhere by himself and think. Every time he went away to the city Pupkin expected that he might return with the novel all finished; but though he often came back with his eyes red from thinking, the novel as yet remained incomplete.

Meantime, Mallory Tompkins, as I say, was a mighty intellectual fellow. You could see that from the books on the bamboo bookshelves in the sitting-room. There was, for instance, the "Encyclopædia Metropolitana" in forty volumes, that he bought on the instalment plan for two dollars a month. Then when they took that away, there was the "History of Civilization," in fifty volumes at fifty cents a week for fifty years. Tompkins had read in it half-way through the Stone Age before they took it from him. After that there was the "Lives of the Painters," one volume at a time—a splendid thing in which you could read all about Aahrens, and Aachenthal, and Aax and men of that class. After all, there's nothing like educating oneself. Mallory Tompkins knew about the opening period of all sorts of things, and in regard to people whose names began with "A" you couldn't stick him.

I don't mean that he and Mr. Pupkin lived a mere routine of studious evenings. That would be untrue. Quite often their time was spent in much less commendable ways than that, and there were poker parties in their sitting-room that didn't break up till nearly midnight. Card-playing, after all, is a slow business, unless you put money on it, and, besides, if you are in a bank and are handling money all day, gambling has a fascination.

I've seen Pupkin and Mallory Tompkins and Joe Milligan, the dentist, and Mitchell the ticket agent, and the other "boys" sitting round the table with matches enough piled up in front of them to stock a factory. Ten matches counted for one chip and ten chips made a cent—so you see they weren't merely playing for the fun of the thing. Of course it's a hollow pleasure. You realize that when you wake up at night parched with thirst, ten thousand matches to the bad. But banking is a wild life and everybody knows it.

Sometimes Pupkin would swear off and keep away from the cursed thing for weeks, and then perhaps he'd see by sheer accident a pile of matches on the table, or a match lying on the floor and it would start the craze in him. I am using his own words—a "craze"—that's what he called it when he told Miss Lawson all about it, and she promised to cure him of it. She would have, too. Only, as I say, Pupkin found that what he had mistaken for attraction was only respect. And there's no use worrying a woman that you respect about your crazes.

It was from Mallory Tompkins that Pupkin learned all about the Mariposa people, because Pupkin came from away off—somewhere down in the Maritime Provinces—and didn't know a soul. Mallory Tompkins used to tell him about Judge Pepperleigh, and what a wonderfully clever man he was and how he would have been in the Supreme Court for certain if the Conservative Government had stayed in another fifteen or twenty years instead of coming to a premature end. He used to talk so much about the Pepperleighs, that Pupkin was sick of the very name. But just as soon as he had seen Zena Pepperleigh he couldn't hear enough of them. He would have talked with Tompkins for hours about the judge's dog Rover. And as for Zena, if he could have brought her name over his lips, he would have talked of her forever.

He first saw her—by one of the strangest coincidences in the world—on the Main Street of Mariposa. If he hadn't happened to be going up the street and she to be coming down it, the thing wouldn't have happened. Afterwards they both admitted that it was one of the most peculiar coincidences they ever heard of. Pupkin owned that he had had the strangest feeling that morning as if something were going to happen—a feeling not at all to be classed with the one of which he had once spoken to Miss Lawson, and which was, at the most, a mere anticipation of respect.

But, as I say, Pupkin met Zena Pepperleigh on the 26th of June, at twenty-five minutes to eleven. And at once the whole world changed. The past was all blotted out. Even in the new forty volume edition of the "Instalment Record of Humanity" that Mallory Tompkins had just received—Pupkin wouldn't have bothered with it.

She—that word henceforth meant Zena—had just come back from her boarding-school, and of all times of year for coming back from a boarding-school and for wearing a white shirt waist and a crimson tie and for carrying a tennis racket on the stricken street of a town—commend me to the month of June in Mariposa.

And, for Pupkin, straight away the whole town was irradiated with sunshine, and there was such a singing of the birds, and such a dancing of the rippled waters of the lake, and such a kindliness in the faces of all the people, that only those who have lived in Mariposa, and been young there, can know at all what he felt.

The simple fact is that just the moment he saw Zena Pepperleigh, Mr. Pupkin was clean, plumb, straight, flat, absolutely in love with her.

Which fact is so important that it would be folly not to close the chapter and think about it.

Chapter VIII

The Fore-ordained Attachment
of Zena Pepperleigh and
Peter Pupkin

Zena Pepperleigh used to sit reading novels on the piazza of the judge's house, half hidden by the Virginia creepers. At times the book would fall upon her lap and there was such a look of unstilled yearning in her violet eyes that it did not entirely disappear even when she picked up the apple that lay beside her and took another bite out of it.

With hands clasped she would sit there dreaming, all the beautiful day-dreams of girlhood. When you saw that far-away look in her eyes, it meant that she was dreaming that a plumed and armoured knight was rescuing her from the embattled keep of a castle beside the Danube. At other times she was being borne away by an Algerian corsair over the blue waters of the Mediterranean and was reaching out her arms towards France to say farewell to it.

Sometimes when you noticed a sweet look of resignation that seemed to rest upon her features, it meant that Lord Ronald de Chevereux was kneeling at her feet, and that she was telling him to rise, that her humbler birth must ever be a bar to their happiness, and Lord Ronald was getting into an awful state about it, as English peers do at the least suggestion of anything of the sort.

Or, if it wasn't that, then her lover had just returned to her side, tall and soldierly and sunburned, after fighting for ten years in the Soudan for her sake, and had come back to ask her for her answer and to tell her that for ten years her face had been with him even in the watches of the night. He was asking her for a sign, any kind of sign,—ten years in the Soudan entitles them to a sign,—and Zena was plucking a white rose, just one, from her hair, when she would hear her father's step on the piazza and make a grab for the *Pioneers of Tecumseh Township,* and start reading it like mad.

She was always, as I say, being rescued and being borne away, and being parted, and reaching out her arms to France and to Spain, and saying good-bye forever to Valladolid or the old grey towers of Hohenbranntwein.

And I don't mean that she was in the least exceptional or romantic, because all the girls in Mariposa were just like that. An Algerian corsair could have come into the town and had a dozen of them for the asking, and as for a wounded English officer,— well, perhaps it's better not to talk about it outside or the little town would become a regular military hospital.

Because, mind you, the Mariposa girls are all right. You've only to look at them to realize that. You see, you can get in Mariposa a print dress of pale blue or pale pink for a dollar twenty that looks infinitely better than anything you ever see in the city,—especially if you can wear with it a broad straw hat and a background of maple trees and the green grass of a tennis court. And if you remember, too, that these are cultivated girls who have all been to the Mariposa high school and can do decimal fractions, you will understand that an Algerian corsair would sharpen his scimitar at the very sight of them.

Don't think either that they are all dying to get married; because they are not. I don't say they wouldn't take an errant knight, or a buccaneer or a Hungarian refugee, but for the ordinary marriages of ordinary people they feel nothing but a pitying disdain. So it is that each one of them in due time marries an enchanted prince and goes to live in one of the little enchanted houses in the lower part of the town.

I don't know whether you know it, but you can rent an enchanted house in Mariposa for eight dollars a month, and some of the most completely enchanted are the cheapest. As for the enchanted princes, they find them in the strangest places, where you never expected to see them, working—under a spell, you understand,—in drug-stores and printing offices, and even selling things in shops. But to be able to find them you have first to read ever so many novels about Sir Galahad and the Errant Quest and that sort of thing.

Naturally then Zena Pepperleigh, as she sat on the piazza, dreamed of bandits and of wounded officers and of Lord Ronalds riding on foam-flecked chargers. But that she ever dreamed of a junior bank teller in a daffodil blazer riding past on a bicycle, is pretty hard to imagine. So, when Mr. Pupkin came tearing past up the slope of Oneida Street at a speed that proved that he wasn't riding there merely to pass the house, I don't suppose that Zena Pepperleigh was aware of his existence.

That may be a slight exaggeration. She knew, perhaps, that he was the new junior teller in the Exchange Bank and that he came from the Maritime Provinces, and that nobody knew who his people were, and that he had never been in a canoe in his life till he came to Mariposa, and that he sat four pews back in Dean Drone's church, and that his salary was eight hundred dollars. Beyond that, she didn't know a thing about him. She presumed, however, that the reason why he went past so fast was because he didn't dare to go slow.

This, of course, was perfectly correct. Ever since the day when Mr. Pupkin met Zena in the Main Street he used to come past the house on his bicycle just after bank hours. He would have gone past twenty times a day but he was afraid to. As he came up Oneida Street, he used to pedal faster and faster,—he never meant to, but he couldn't help it,—till he went past the piazza where Zena was sitting at an awful speed with his little yellow blazer flying in the wind. In a second he had disappeared in a buzz and a cloud of dust, and the momentum of it carried him clear out into the country for miles and miles before he ever dared to pause or look back.

Then Mr. Pupkin would ride in a huge circuit about the country, trying to think he was looking at the crops, and sooner or later his bicycle would be turned towards the town again and headed for Oneida Street, and would get going quicker and quicker and quicker, till the pedals whirled round with a buzz and he came past the judge's house again, like a bullet out of a gun. He rode fifteen miles to pass the house twice, and even then it took all the nerve that he had.

The people on Oneida Street thought that Mr. Pupkin was crazy, but Zena Pepperleigh knew that he was not. Already, you see, there was a sort of dim parallel between the passing of the bicycle and the last ride of Tancred the Inconsolable along the banks of the Danube.

I have already mentioned, I think, how Mr. Pupkin and Zena Pepperleigh first came to know one another. Like everything else about them, it was a sheer matter of coincidence, quite inexplicable unless you understand that these things are foreordained.

That, of course, is the way with foreordained affairs and
that's where they differ from ordinary love.

I won't even try to describe how Mr. Pupkin felt when he first
spoke with Zena and sat beside her as they copied out the "endless chain" letter asking for ten cents. They wrote out, as I said,
no less than eight of the letters between them, and they found out
that their handwritings were so alike that you could hardly tell
them apart, except that Pupkin's letters were round and Zena's
letters were pointed and Pupkin wrote straight up and down and
Zena wrote on a slant. Beyond that the writing was so alike that
it was the strangest coincidence in the world. Of course when
they made figures it was different and Pupkin explained to Zena
that in the bank you have to be able to make a seven so that it
doesn't look like a nine.

So, as I say, they wrote the letters all afternoon and when it
was over they walked up Oneida Street together, ever so slowly.
When they got near the house, Zena asked Pupkin to come in to
tea, with such an easy off-hand way that you couldn't have told
that she was half an hour late and was taking awful chances on
the judge. Pupkin hadn't had time to say yes before the judge
appeared at the door, just as they were stepping up on to the
piazza, and he had a table napkin in his hand and the dynamite
sparks were flying from his spectacles as he called out:

"Great heaven! Zena, why in everlasting blazes can't you get
in to tea at a Christian hour?"

Zena gave one look of appeal to Pupkin, and Pupkin looked
one glance of comprehension, and turned and fled down Oneida
Street. And if the scene wasn't quite as dramatic as the renuncia-
tion of Tancred the Troubadour, it at least had something of the
same elements in it.

Pupkin walked home to his supper at the Mariposa House on
air, and that evening there was a gentle distance in his manner
towards Sadie, the dining-room girl, that I suppose no bank clerk
in Mariposa ever showed before. It was like Sir Galahad talking
with the tire-women of Queen Guinevere and receiving huckleberry pie at their hands.

After that Mr. Pupkin and Zena Pepperleigh constantly met
together. They played tennis as partners on the grass court behind
Dr. Gallagher's house,—the Mariposa Tennis Club rent it, you

remember, for fifty cents a month,—and Pupkin used to perform perfect prodigies of valour, leaping in the air to serve with his little body hooked like a letter S. Sometimes, too, they went out on Lake Wissanotti in the evening in Pupkin's canoe, with Zena sitting in the bow and Pupkin paddling in the stern and they went out ever so far and it was after dark and the stars were shining before they came home. Zena would look at the stars and say how infinitely far away they seemed, and Pupkin would realize that a girl with a mind like that couldn't have any use for a fool such as he. Zena used to ask him to point out the Pleiades and Jupiter and Ursa minor, and Pupkin showed her exactly where they were. That impressed them both tremendously because Pupkin didn't know that Zena remembered the names out of the astronomy book at her boarding-school, and Zena didn't know that Pupkin simply took a chance on where the stars were.

And ever so many times they talked so intimately that Pupkin came mighty near telling her about his home in the Maritime Provinces and about his father and mother, and then kicked himself that he hadn't the manliness to speak straight out about it and take the consequences.

Please don't imagine from any of this that the course of Mr. Pupkin's love ran smooth. On the contrary, Pupkin himself felt that it was absolutely hopeless from the start.

There were, it might be admitted, certain things that seemed to indicate progress.

In the course of the months of June and July and August, he had taken Zena out in his canoe thirty-one times. Allowing an average of two miles for each evening, Pupkin had paddled Zena sixty-two miles, or more than a hundred thousand yards. That surely was something.

He had played tennis with her on sixteen afternoons. Three times he had left his tennis racket up at the judge's house in Zena's charge, and once he had, with her full consent, left his bicycle there all night. This must count for something. No girl could trifle with a man to the extent of having his bicycle leaning against the verandah post all night and mean nothing by it.

More than that—he had been to tea at the judge's house fourteen times, and seven times he had been asked by Lilian Drone to the rectory when Zena was coming, and five times by Nora Gallagher to tea at the doctor's house because Zena was there.

Altogether he had eaten so many meals where Zena was that his meal ticket at the Mariposa lasted nearly double its proper time, and the face of Sadie, the dining-room girl, had grown to wear a look of melancholy resignation, sadder than romance.

Still more than that, Pupkin had bought for Zena, reckoning it altogether, about two buckets of ice cream and perhaps half a bushel of chocolate. Not that Pupkin grudged the expense of it. On the contrary, over and above the ice cream and the chocolate he had bought her a white waistcoat and a walking stick with a gold top, a lot of new neckties and a pair of patent leather boots—that is, they were all bought on account of her, which is the same thing.

Add to all this that Pupkin and Zena had been to the Church of England Church nearly every Sunday evening for two months, and one evening they had even gone to the Presbyterian Church "for fun," which, if you know Mariposa, you will realize to be a wild sort of escapade that ought to speak volumes.

Yet in spite of this, Pupkin felt that the thing was hopeless: which only illustrates the dreadful ups and downs, the wild alternations of hope and despair that characterise an exceptional affair of this sort.

Yes, it was hopeless.

Every time that Pupkin watched Zena praying in church, he knew that she was too good for him. Every time that he came to call for her and found her reading Browning and Omar Khayyam he knew that she was too clever for him. And every time that he saw her at all he realized that she was too beautiful for him.

You see, Pupkin knew that he wasn't a hero. When Zena would clasp her hands and talk rapturously about crusaders and soldiers and firemen and heroes generally, Pupkin knew just where he came in. Not in it, that was all. If a war could have broken out in Mariposa, or the judge's house been invaded by the Germans, he might have had a chance, but as it was—hopeless.

Then there was Zena's father. Heaven knows Pupkin tried hard to please the judge. He agreed with every theory that Judge Pepperleigh advanced, and that took a pretty pliable intellect in itself. They denounced female suffrage one day and they favoured it the next. One day the judge would claim that the labour movement was eating out the heart of the country, and the next day he would hold that the hope of the world lay in the organization of the toiling masses. Pupkin shifted his opinions like the glass in a kaleidoscope. Indeed, the only things on which he was allowed to maintain a steadfast conviction were the purity of the Conservative party of Canada and the awful wickedness of the recall of judges.

But with all that the judge was hardly civil to Pupkin. He hadn't asked him to the house till Zena brought him there, though, as a rule, all the bank clerks in Mariposa treated Judge Pepperleigh's premises as their own. He used to sit and sneer at Pupkin after he had gone till Zena would throw down the *Pioneers of Tecumseh Township* in a temper and flounce off the piazza to her room. After which the judge's manner would change instantly and he would relight his corn cob pipe and sit and positively beam with contentment. In all of which there was something so mysterious as to prove that Mr. Pupkin's chances were hopeless.

Nor was that all of it. Pupkin's salary was eight hundred dollars a year and the Exchange Bank limit for marriage was a thousand.

I suppose you are aware of the grinding capitalistic tyranny of the banks in Mariposa whereby marriage is put beyond the reach of ever so many mature and experienced men of nineteen and twenty and twenty-one, who are compelled to go on eating on a meal ticket at the Mariposa House and living over the bank to suit the whim of a group of capitalists.

Whenever Pupkin thought of this two hundred dollars he understood all that is meant by social unrest. In fact, he interpreted all forms of social discontent in terms of it. Russian Anarchism, German Socialism, the Labour Movement, Henry George, Lloyd George,—he understood the whole lot of them by thinking of his two hundred dollars.

When I tell you that at this period Mr. Pupkin read *Memoirs of the Great Revolutionists* and even thought of blowing up Henry Mullins with dynamite, you can appreciate his state of mind.

But not even by all these hindrances and obstacles to his love for Zena Pepperleigh would Peter Pupkin have been driven to commit suicide (oh, yes; he committed it three times, as I'm going to tell you), had it not been for another thing that he knew stood once and for all and in cold reality between him and Zena.

He felt it in a sort of way, as soon as he knew her. Each time that he tried to talk to her about his home and his father and mother and found that something held him back, he realized more and more the kind of thing that stood between them. Most of all did he realize it, with a sudden sickness of heart, when he got word that his father and mother wanted to come to Mariposa to see him and he had all he could do to head them off from it.

Why? Why stop them? The reason was, simple enough, that Pupkin was ashamed of them, bitterly ashamed. The picture of his mother and father turning up in Mariposa and being seen by his friends there and going up to the Pepperleighs' house made him feel faint with shame.

No, I don't say it wasn't wrong. It only shows what difference of fortune, the difference of being rich and being poor, means in this world. You perhaps have been so lucky that you cannot appreciate what it means to feel shame at the station of your own father and mother. You think it doesn't matter, that honesty and kindliness of heart are all that counts. That only shows that you have never known some of the bitterest feelings of people less fortunate than yourself.

So it was with Mr. Pupkin. When he thought of his father and mother turning up in Mariposa, his face reddened with unworthy shame.

He could just picture the scene! He could see them getting out of their Limousine touring car, with the chauffeur holding open the door for them, and his father asking for a suite of rooms,— just think of it, a suite of rooms!—at the Mariposa House.

The very thought of it turned him ill.

What! You have mistaken my meaning? Ashamed of them because they were poor? Good heavens, no, but because they were rich! And not rich in the sense in which they use the term in Mariposa, where a rich person merely means a man who has money enough to build a house with a piazza and to have every-thing he wants; but rich in the other sense,—motor cars, Ritz hotels, steam yachts, summer islands and all that sort of thing.

Why, Pupkin's father,—what's the use of trying to conceal it any longer?—was the senior partner in the law firm of Pupkin, Pupkin and Pupkin. If you know the Maritime Provinces at all, you've heard of the Pupkins. The name is a household word from Chedabucto to Chidabecto. And, for the matter of that, the law

firm and the fact that Pupkin senior had been an Attorney
General was the least part of it. Attorney General! Why, there's
no money in that! It's no better than the Senate. No, no, Pupkin
senior, like so many lawyers, was practically a promoter, and he
blew companies like bubbles, and when he wasn't in the Maritime Provinces he was in Boston and New York raising money
and floating loans, and when they had no money left in New
York he floated it in London: and when he had it, he floated on
top of it big rafts of lumber on the Miramichi and codfish on the
Grand Banks and lesser fish in the Fundy Bay. You've heard
perhaps of the Tidal Transportation Company, and Fundy Fisheries Corporation, and the Paspebiac Pulp and Paper Unlimited?
Well, all of those were Pupkin senior under other names. So just
imagine him in Mariposa! Wouldn't he be utterly foolish there?
Just imagine him meeting Jim Eliot and treating him like a druggist merely because he ran a drug store! Or speaking to Jefferson
Thorpe as if he were a barber simply because he shaved for
money! Why, a man like that could ruin young Pupkin in Mariposa in half a day, and Pupkin knew it.

That wouldn't matter so much, but think of the Pepperleighs
and Zena! Everything would be over with them at once. Pupkin
knew just what the judge thought of riches and luxuries. How
often had he heard the judge pass sentences of life imprisonment
on Pierpont Morgan and Mr. Rockefeller. How often had Pupkin
heard him say that any man who received more than three thousand dollars a year (that was the judicial salary in the Missinaba
district) was a mere robber, unfit to shake the hand of an honest
man. Bitter! I should think he was! He was not so bitter, perhaps,
as Mr. Muddleson, the principal of the Mariposa high school,
who said that any man who received more than fifteen hundred
dollars was a public enemy. He was certainly not so bitter as
Trelawney, the post-master, who said that any man who got from
society more than thirteen hundred dollars (apart from a legiti-
mate increase in recognition of a successful election) was a
danger to society. Still, he was bitter. They all were in Mariposa.
Pupkin could just imagine how they would despise his father!

And Zena! That was the worst of all. How often had Pupkin
heard her say that she simply hated diamonds, wouldn't wear
them, despised them, wouldn't give a thank you for a whole tiara
of them! As for motor cars and steam yachts,—well, it was pretty

plain that that sort of thing had no chance with Zena Pepperleigh. Why, she had told Pupkin one night in the canoe that she would only marry a man who was poor and had his way to make and would hew down difficulties for her sake. And when Pupkin couldn't answer the argument she was quite cross and silent all the way home.

What was Peter Pupkin doing, then, at eight hundred dollars in a bank in Mariposa? If you ask that, it means that you know nothing of the life of the Maritime Provinces and the sturdy temper of the people. I suppose there are no people in the world who hate luxury and extravagance and that sort of thing quite as much as the Maritime Province people, and, of them, no one hated luxury more than Pupkin senior.

Don't mistake the man. He wore a long sealskin coat in winter, yes; but mark you, not as a matter of luxury, but merely as a question of his lungs. He smoked, I admit it, a thirty-five cent cigar, not because he preferred it, but merely through a delicacy of the thorax that made it imperative. He drank champagne at lunch, I concede the point, not in the least from the enjoyment of it, but simply on account of a peculiar affection of the tongue and lips that positively dictated it. His own longing—and his wife shared it—was for the simple, simple life—an island somewhere, with birds and trees. They had bought three or four islands—one in the St. Lawrence, and two in the Gulf, and one off the coast of Maine—looking for this sort of thing. Pupkin senior often said that he wanted to have some place that would remind him of the little old farm up the Aroostook where he was brought up. He often bought little old farms, just to try them, but they always turned out to be so near a city that he cut them into real estate lots, without even having had time to look at them.

But—and this is where the emphasis lay—in the matter of luxury for his only son, Peter, Pupkin senior was a Maritime Province man right to the core, with all the hardihood of the United Empire Loyalists ingrained in him. No luxury for that boy! No, sir! From his childhood, Pupkin senior had undertaken, at the least sign of luxury, to "tan it out of him," after the fashion still in vogue in the provinces. Then he sent him to an old-fashioned school to get it "thumped out of him," and after that he had put him for a year on a Nova Scotia schooner to get it "knocked out of him." If, after all that, young Pupkin, even when he came to Mariposa, wore cameo pins and daffodil blazers, and broke out into ribbed silk saffron ties on pay day, it only shows that the old Adam still needs further tanning even in the Maritime Provinces.

Young Pupkin, of course, was to have gone into law. That was his father's cherished dream and would have made the firm Pupkin, Pupkin, Pupkin, and Pupkin, as it ought to have been. But young Peter was kept out of the law by the fool system of examinations devised since his father's time. Hence there was nothing for it but to sling him into a bank; "sling him" was, I think, the expression. So his father decided that if Pupkin was to be slung, he should be slung good and far—clean into Canada (you know the way they use that word in the Maritime Provinces). And to sling Pupkin he called in the services of an old friend, a man after his own heart, just as violent as himself, who used to be at the law school in the city with Pupkin senior thirty years ago. So this friend, who happened to live in Mariposa, and who was a violent man, said at once: "Edward, by Jehosephat! send the boy up here."

So that is how Pupkin came to Mariposa. And if, when he got there, his father's friend gave no sign, and treated the boy with roughness and incivility, that may have been, for all I know, a continuation of the "tanning" process of the Maritime people.

Did I mention that the Pepperleigh family, generations ago, had taken up land near the Aroostook, and that it was from there the judge's father came to Tecumseh township? Perhaps not, but it doesn't matter.

But surely after such reminiscences as these, the awful things that are impending over Mr. Pupkin must be kept for another chapter.

Chapter IX

The Mariposa Bank Mystery

Suicide is a thing that ought not to be committed without very careful thought. It often involves serious consequences, and in some cases brings pain to others than oneself.

I don't say that there is no justification for it. There often is. Anybody who has listened to certain kinds of music, or read certain kinds of poetry, or heard certain kinds of performances upon the concertina, will admit that there are some lives which ought not to be continued, and that even suicide has its brighter aspects.

But to commit suicide on grounds of love is at the best a very dubious experiment. I know that in this I am expressing an opinion contrary to that of most true lovers who embrace suicide on the slightest provocation as the only honourable termination of an existence that never ought to have begun.

I quite admit that there is a glamour and a sensation about the thing which has its charm, and that there is nothing like it for causing a girl to realize the value of the heart that she has broken and which breathed forgiveness upon her at the very moment when it held in its hand the half-pint of prussic acid that was to terminate its beating for ever.

But apart from the general merits of the question, I suppose there are few people, outside of lovers, who know what it is to commit suicide four times in five weeks.

Yet this was what happened to Mr. Pupkin, of the Exchange Bank of Mariposa.

Ever since he had known Zena Pepperleigh he had realized that his love for her was hopeless. She was too beautiful for him and too good for him; her father hated him and her mother despised him; his salary was too small and his own people were too rich.

If you add to all that that he came up to the judge's house one night and found a poet reciting verses to Zena, you will understand the suicide at once. It was one of those regular poets with a solemn jackass face, and lank parted hair and eyes like puddles

of molasses. I don't know how he came there—up from the city, probably—but there he was on the Pepperleighs' verandah that August evening. He was reciting poetry—either Tennyson's or Shelley's, or his own, you couldn't tell—and about him sat Zena with her hands clasped and Nora Gallagher looking at the sky and Jocelyn Drone gazing into infinity, and a little tubby woman looking at the poet with her head falling over sideways—in fact, there was a whole group of them.

I don't know what it is about poets that draws women to them in this way. But everybody knows that a poet has only to sit and saw the air with his hands and recite verses in a deep stupid voice, and all the women are crazy over him. Men despise him and would kick him off the verandah if they dared, but the women simply rave over him.

So Pupkin sat there in the gloom and listened to this poet reciting Browning and he realized that everybody understood it but him. He could see Zena with her eyes fixed on the poet as if she were hanging on to every syllable (she was; she needed to), and he stood it just about fifteen minutes and then slid off the side of the verandah and disappeared without even saying good-night.

He walked straight down Oneida Street and along the Main Street just as hard as he could go. There was only one purpose in his mind,—suicide. He was heading straight for Jim Eliot's drug store on the main corner and his idea was to buy a drink of chloroform and drink it and die right there on the spot.

As Pupkin walked down the street, the whole thing was so vivid in his mind that he could picture it to the remotest detail. He could even see it all in type, in big headings in the newspapers of the following day:

APPALLING SUICIDE.
PETER PUPKIN POISONED.

He perhaps hoped that the thing might lead to some kind of public enquiry and that the question of Browning's poetry and whether it is altogether fair to allow of its general circulation would be fully ventilated in the newspapers.

Thinking all that, Pupkin came to the main corner.

On a warm August evening the drug store of Mariposa, as you

know, is all a blaze of lights. You can hear the hissing of the soda-water fountain half a block away, and inside the store there are ever so many people—boys and girls and old people too—all drinking sarsaparilla and chocolate sundaes and lemon sours and foaming drinks that you take out of long straws. There is such a laughing and a talking as you never heard, and the girls are all in white and pink and cambridge blue, and the soda fountain is of white marble with silver taps, and it hisses and sputters, and Jim Eliot and his assistant wear white coats with red geraniums in them, and it's all just as gay as gay.

The foyer of the opera in Paris may be a fine sight, but I doubt if it can compare with the inside of Eliot's drug store in Mariposa—for real gaiety and joy of living.

This night the store was especially crowded because it was a Saturday and that meant early closing for all the hotels, except, of course, Smith's. So as the hotels were shut, the people were all in the drug store, drinking like fishes. It just shows the folly of Local Option and the Temperance Movement and all that. Why, if you shut the hotels you simply drive the people to the soda fountains and there's more drinking than ever, and not only of the men, too, but the girls and young boys and children. I've seen little things of eight and nine that had to be lifted up on the high stools at Eliot's drug store, drinking great goblets of lemon soda, enough to burst them—brought there by their own fathers, and why? Simply because the hotel bars were shut.

What's the use of thinking you can stop people drinking merely by cutting off whiskey and brandy? The only effect is to drive them to taking lemon sour and sarsaparilla and cherry pectoral and caroka cordial and things they wouldn't have touched before. So in the long run they drink more than ever. The point is that you can't prevent people having a good time, no matter how hard you try. If they can't have it with lager beer and brandy, they'll have it with plain soda and lemon pop, and so the whole gloomy scheme of the temperance people breaks down, anyway.

But I was only saying that Eliot's drug store in Mariposa on a Saturday night is the gayest and brightest spot in the world.

And just imagine what a fool of a place to commit suicide in!

Just imagine going up to the soda-water fountain and asking for five cents' worth of chloroform and soda! Well, you simply can't, that's all.

That's the way Pupkin found it. You see, as soon as he came in, somebody called out: "Hello, Pete!" and one or two others called: "Hullo, Pup!" and some said: "How goes it?" and others: "How are you toughing it?" and so on, because you see they had all been drinking more or less and naturally they felt jolly and glad-hearted.

So the upshot of it was that instead of taking chloroform, Pupkin stepped up to the counter of the fountain and he had a bromo-seltzer with cherry soda, and after that he had one of those aerated seltzers, and then a couple of lemon seltzers and a bromophizzer.

I don't know if you know the mental effect of a bromo-seltzer.

But it's a hard thing to commit suicide on.

You can't.

You feel so buoyant.

Anyway, what with the phizzing of the seltzer and the lights and the girls, Pupkin began to feel so fine that he didn't care a cuss for all the Browning in the world, and as for the poet—oh, to blazes with him! What's poetry, anyway?—only rhymes.

So, would you believe it, in about ten minutes Peter Pupkin was off again and heading straight for the Pepperleighs' house, poet or no poet, and, what was more to the point, he carried with him three great bricks of Eliot's ice cream—in green, pink and brown layers. He struck the verandah just at the moment when Browning was getting too stale and dreary for words. His brain was all sizzling and jolly with the bromo-seltzer, and when he fetched out the ice cream bricks and Zena ran to get plates and spoons to eat it with, and Pupkin went with her to help fetch them and they picked out the spoons together, they were so laughing and happy that it was just a marvel. Girls, you know, need no bromo-seltzer. They're full of it all the time.

And as for the poet—well, can you imagine how Pupkin felt when Zena told him that the poet was married, and that the tubby little woman with her head on sideways was his wife?

So they had the ice cream, and the poet ate it in bucketsful. Poets always do. They need it. And after it the poet recited some stanzas of his own and Pupkin saw that he had misjudged the man, because it was dandy poetry, the very best. That night

Pupkin walked home on air and there was no thought of chloroform, and it turned out that he hadn't committed suicide, but like all lovers he had commuted it.

I don't need to describe in full the later suicides of Mr. Pupkin, because they were all conducted on the same plan and rested on something the same reasons as above.

Sometimes he would go down at night to the offices of the bank below his bedroom and bring up his bank revolver in order to make an end of himself with it. This, too, he could see headed up in the newspapers as:

BRILLIANT BOY BANKER BLOWS OUT BRAINS.

But blowing your brains out is a noisy, rackety performance, and Pupkin soon found that only special kinds of brains are suited for it. So he always sneaked back again later in the night and put the revolver in its place, deciding to drown himself instead. Yet every time that he walked down to the Trestle Bridge over the Ossawippi he found it was quite unsuitable for drowning—too high, and the water too swift and black, and the rushes too gruesome—in fact, not at all the kind of place for a drowning.

Far better, he realized, to wait there on the railroad track and throw himself under the wheels of the express and be done with it. Yet, though Pupkin often waited in this way for the train, he was never able to pick out a pair of wheels that suited him. Anyhow, it's awfully hard to tell an express from a fast freight.

I wouldn't mention these attempts at suicide if one of them hadn't finally culminated in making Peter Pupkin a hero and solving for him the whole perplexed entanglement of his love affair with Zena Pepperleigh. Incidentally it threw him into the very centre of one of the most impenetrable bank mysteries that ever baffled the ingenuity of some of the finest legal talent that ever adorned one of the most enterprising communities in the country.

It happened one night, as I say, that Pupkin decided to go down into the office of the bank and get his revolver and see if it would blow his brains out. It was the night of the Firemen's Ball and Zena had danced four times with a visitor from the city, a man who was in the fourth year at the University and who knew everything. It was more than Peter Pupkin could bear. Mallory Tompkins was away that night, and when Pupkin came home he was all alone in the building, except for Gillis, the caretaker, who lived in the extension at the back.

He sat in his room for hours brooding. Two or three times he picked up a book—he remembered afterwards distinctly that it was *Kant's Critique of Pure Reason*—and tried to read it, but it seemed meaningless and trivial. Then with a sudden access of resolution he started from his chair and made his way down the stairs and into the office room of the bank, meaning to get a revolver and kill himself on the spot and let them find his body lying on the floor.

It was then far on in the night and the empty building of the bank was as still as death. Pupkin could hear the stairs creak under his feet, and as he went he thought he heard another sound like the opening or closing of a door. But it sounded not like the sharp ordinary noise of a closing door but with a dull muffled noise as if some one had shut the iron door of a safe in a room under the ground. For a moment Pupkin stood and listened with his heart thumping against his ribs. Then he kicked his slippers from his feet and without a sound stole into the office on the ground floor and took the revolver from his teller's desk. As he gripped it, he listened to the sounds on the back-stairway and in the vaults below.

I should explain that in the Exchange Bank of Mariposa the offices are on the ground floor level with the street. Below this is another floor with low dark rooms paved with flagstones, with unused office desks and with piles of papers stored in boxes. On this floor are the vaults of the bank, and lying in them in the autumn—the grain season—there is anything from fifty to a hundred thousand dollars in currency tied in bundles. There is no other light down there than the dim reflection from the lights out on the street, that lies in patches on the stone floor.

I think as Peter Pupkin stood, revolver in hand, in the office of the bank, he had forgotten all about the maudlin purpose of his first coming. He had forgotten for the moment all about heroes and love affairs, and his whole mind was focussed, sharp and alert, with the intensity of the nighttime, on the sounds that he heard in the vault and on the back-stairway of the bank.

Straight away, Pupkin knew what it meant as plainly as if it were written in print. He had forgotten, I say, about being a hero and he only knew that there was sixty thousand dollars in the vault of the bank below, and that he was paid eight hundred dollars a year to look after it.

As Peter Pupkin stood there listening to the sounds in his stockinged feet, his face showed grey as ashes in the light that fell through the window from the street. His heart beat like a hammer against his ribs. But behind its beatings was the blood of four generations of Loyalists, and the robber who would take that sixty thousand dollars from the Mariposa bank must take it over the dead body of Peter Pupkin, teller.

Pupkin walked down the stairs to the lower room, the one below the ground with the bank vault in it, with as fine a step as any of his ancestors showed on parade. And if he had known it, as he came down the stairway in the front of the vault room, there was a man crouched in the shadow of the passage way by the stairs at the back. This man, too, held a revolver in his hand, and, criminal or not, his face was as resolute as Pupkin's own. As he heard the teller's step on the stair, he turned and waited in the shadow of the doorway without a sound.

There is no need really to mention all these details. They are only of interest as showing how sometimes a bank teller in a corded smoking jacket and stockinged feet may be turned into such a hero as even the Mariposa girls might dream about.

All of this must have happened at about three o'clock in the night. This much was established afterwards from the evidence of Gillis, the caretaker. When he first heard the sounds he had looked at his watch and noticed that it was half-past two; the watch he knew was three-quarters of an hour slow three days before and had been gaining since. The exact time at which Gillis heard footsteps in the bank and started downstairs, pistol in hand, became a nice point afterwards in the cross-examination.

But one must not anticipate. Pupkin reached the iron door of the bank safe, and knelt in front of it, feeling in the dark to find the fracture of the lock. As he knelt, he heard a sound behind him, and swung round on his knees and saw the bank robber in the half light of the passage way and the glitter of a pistol in his hand. The rest was over in an instant. Pupkin heard a voice that was his own, but that sounded strange and hollow, call out: "Drop that, or I'll fire!" and then just as he raised his revolver, there came a blinding flash of light before his eyes, and Peter

Pupkin, junior teller of the bank, fell forward on the floor and knew no more.

At that point, of course, I ought to close down a chapter, or volume, or, at least, strike the reader over the head with a sandbag to force him to stop and think. In common fairness one ought to stop here and count a hundred or get up and walk round a block, or, at any rate, picture to oneself Peter Pupkin lying on the floor of the bank, motionless, his arms distended, the revolver still grasped in his hand. But I must go on.

By half-past seven on the following morning it was known all over Mariposa that Peter Pupkin the junior teller of the Exchange had been shot dead by a bank robber in the vault of the building. It was known also that Gillis, the caretaker, had been shot and killed at the foot of the stairs, and that the robber had made off with fifty thousand dollars in currency; that he had left a trail of blood on the sidewalk and that the men were out tracking him with bloodhounds in the great swamps to the north of the town.

This, I say, and it is important to note it, was what they knew at half-past seven. Of course as each hour went past they learned more and more. At eight o'clock it was known that Pupkin was not dead, but dangerously wounded in the lungs. At eight-thirty it was known that he was not shot in the lungs, but that the ball had traversed the pit of his stomach.

At nine o'clock it was learned that the pit of Pupkin's stomach was all right, but that the bullet had struck his right ear and carried it away. Finally it was learned that his ear had not exactly been carried away, that is, not precisely removed by the bullet, but that it had grazed Pupkin's head in such a way that it had stunned him, and if it had been an inch or two more to the left it might have reached his brain. This, of course, was just as good as being killed from the point of view of public interest.

Indeed, by nine o'clock Pupkin could be himself seen on the Main Street with a great bandage sideways on his head, pointing out the traces of the robber. Gillis, the caretaker, too, it was known by eight, had not been killed. He had been shot through the brain, but whether the injury was serious or not was only a matter of conjecture. In fact, by ten o'clock it was understood that the bullet from the robber's second shot had grazed the side of the caretaker's head, but as far as could be known his brain was just as before. I should add that the first report about the bloodstains and the swamp and the bloodhounds turned out to be inaccurate. The stains may have been blood, but as they led to the cellar way of Netley's store they may have also been molasses, though it was argued, to be sure, that the robber might well have poured molasses over the bloodstains from sheer cunning.

It was remembered, too, that there were no bloodhounds in Mariposa, although, mind you, there are any amount of dogs there.

So you see that by ten o'clock in the morning the whole affair was settling into the impenetrable mystery which it ever since remained.

Not that there wasn't evidence enough. There was Pupkin's own story and Gillis's story, and the stories of all the people who had heard the shots and seen the robber (some said, the bunch of robbers) go running past (others said, walking past), in the night. Apparently the robber ran up and down half the streets of Mariposa before he vanished.

But the stories of Pupkin and Gillis were plain enough. Pupkin related that he heard sounds in the bank and came downstairs just in time to see the robber crouching in the passage-way, and that the robber was a large hulking, villainous looking man, wearing a heavy coat. Gillis told exactly the same story, having heard the noises at the same time, except that he first described the robber as a small thin fellow (peculiarly villainous looking, however, even in the dark), wearing a short jacket; but on thinking it over, Gillis realized that he had been wrong about the size of the criminal, and that he was even bigger, if anything, than what Mr. Pupkin thought. Gillis had fired at the robber; just at the same moment had Mr. Pupkin.

Beyond that, all was mystery, absolute and impenetrable.

By eleven o'clock the detectives had come up from the city under orders from the head of the bank.

I wish you could have seen the two detectives as they moved to and fro in Mariposa—fine looking, stern, impenetrable men that they were. They seemed to take in the whole town by instinct and so quietly. They found their way to Mr. Smith's Hotel just as quietly as if it wasn't design at all and stood there at the bar, picking up scraps of conversation—you know the way detectives do it. Occasionally they allowed one or two bystanders—confederates, perhaps—to buy a drink for them, and you could see from the way they drank it that they were still listening for a clue. If there had been the faintest clue in Smith's Hotel or in the Mariposa House or in the Continental, those fellows would have been at it like a flash.

To see them moving round the town that day—silent, massive, imperturbable—gave one a great idea of their strange, dangerous calling. They went about the town all day and yet in such a quiet peculiar way that you couldn't have realized that they were working at all. They ate their dinner together at Smith's café and took an hour and a half over it to throw people off the scent. Then when they got them off it, they sat and talked with Josh Smith in the back bar to keep them off. Mr. Smith seemed to take to them right away. They were men of his own size, or near it, and anyway hotel men and detectives have a general affinity and share in the same impenetrable silence and in their confidential knowledge of the weaknesses of the public.

Mr. Smith, too, was of great use to the detectives. "Boys," he said, "I wouldn't ask too close as to what folks was out late at night: in this town it don't do."

When those two great brains finally left for the city on the five-thirty, it was hard to realize that behind each grand, impassible face a perfect vortex of clues was seething.

But if the detectives were heroes, what was Pupkin? Imagine him with his bandage on his head standing in front of the bank and talking of the midnight robbery with that peculiar false modesty that only heroes are entitled to use.

I don't know whether you have ever been a hero, but for sheer exhilaration there is nothing like it. And for Mr. Pupkin, who had gone through life thinking himself no good, to be suddenly exalted into the class of Napoleon Bonaparte and John Maynard and the Charge of the Light Brigade—oh, it was wonderful. Because Pupkin was a brave man now and he knew it and acquired with it all the brave man's modesty. In fact, I believe he was heard to say that he had only done his duty, and that what he did was what any other man would have done: though when somebody else said: "That's so, when you come to think of it," Pupkin turned on him that quiet look of the wounded hero, bitterer than words.

And if Pupkin had known that all of the afternoon papers in the city reported him dead, he would have felt more luxurious still.

That afternoon the Mariposa court sat in enquiry,—technically it was summoned in inquest on the dead robber—though they hadn't found the body—and it was wonderful to see them lining up the witnesses and holding cross-examinations. There is something in the cross-examination of great criminal lawyers like Nivens, of Mariposa, and in the counter examinations of presiding judges like Pepperleigh that thrills you to the core with the astuteness of it.

They had Henry Mullins, the manager, on the stand for an hour and a half, and the excitement was so breathless that you could have heard a pin drop. Nivens took him on first.

"What is your name?" he said.

"Henry Augustus Mullins."

"What position do you hold?"

"I am manager of the Exchange Bank."

"When were you born?"

"December 30, 1869."

After that, Nivens stood looking quietly at Mullins. You could feel that he was thinking pretty deeply before he shot the next question at him.

"Where did you go to school?"

Mullins answered straight off: "The high school down home," and Nivens thought again for a while and then asked:

"How many boys were at the school?"

"About sixty."

"How many masters?"

"About three."

After that Nivens paused a long while and seemed to be digesting the evidence, but at last an idea seemed to strike him and he said:

"I understand you were not on the bank premises last night. Where were you?"

"Down the lake duck shooting."

You should have seen the excitement in the court when Mullins said this. The judge leaned forward in his chair and broke in at once.

"Did you get any, Harry?" he asked.

"Yes," Mullins said, "about six."

"Where did you get them? What? In the wild rice marsh past the river? You don't say so! Did you get them on the sit or how?"

All of these questions were fired off at the witness from the court in a single breath. In fact, it was the knowledge that the first ducks of the season had been seen in the Ossawippi marsh that led to the termination of the proceedings before the afternoon was a quarter over. Mullins and George Duff and half the witnesses were off with shotguns as soon as the court was cleared.

I may as well state at once that the full story of the robbery of the bank at Mariposa never came to the light. A number of arrests —mostly of vagrants and suspicious characters—were made, but the guilt of the robbery was never brought home to them. One man was arrested twenty miles away, at the other end of Missinaba county, who not only corresponded exactly with the description of the robber, but, in addition to this, had a wooden leg. Vagrants with one leg are always regarded with suspicion in places like Mariposa, and whenever a robbery or a murder happens they are arrested in batches.

It was never even known just how much money was stolen from the bank. Some people said ten thousand dollars, others more. The bank, no doubt for business motives, claimed that the contents of the safe were intact and that the robber had been foiled in his design.

But none of this matters to the exaltation of Mr. Pupkin. Good fortune, like bad, never comes in small instalments. On that wonderful day, every good thing happened to Peter Pupkin at once. The morning saw him a hero. At the sitting of the court, the judge publicly told him that his conduct was fit to rank among the annals of the pioneers of Tecumseh Township, and asked him to his house for supper. At five o'clock he received the telegram of promotion from the head office that raised his salary to a thousand dollars, and made him not only a hero but a marriageable man. At six o'clock he started up to the judge's house with his resolution nerved to the most momentous step of his life.

His mind was made up.

He would do a thing seldom if ever done in Mariposa. He would propose to Zena Pepperleigh. In Mariposa this kind of step, I say, is seldom taken. The course of love runs on and on through all its stages of tennis playing and dancing and sleigh riding, till by sheer notoriety of circumstance an understanding is reached. To propose straight out would be thought priggish and affected and is supposed to belong only to people in books.

But Pupkin felt that what ordinary people dare not do, heroes are allowed to attempt. He would propose to Zena, and more than that, he would tell her in a straight, manly way that he was rich and take the consequences.

And he did it.

That night on the piazza, where the hammock hangs in the shadow of the Virginia creeper, he did it. By sheer good luck the judge had gone indoors to the library, and by a piece of rare good fortune Mrs. Pepperleigh had gone indoors to the sewing room, and by a happy trick of coincidence the servant was out and the dog was tied up—in fact, no such chain of circumstances was ever offered in favour of mortal man before.

What Zena said—beyond saying yes—I do not know. I am sure that when Pupkin told her of the money, she bore up as bravely as so fine a girl as Zena would, and when he spoke of diamonds she said she would wear them for his sake.

They were saying these things and other things—ever so many other things—when there was such a roar and a clatter up Oneida Street as you never heard, and there came bounding up to the house one of the most marvellous Limousine touring cars that ever drew up at the home of a judge on a modest salary of three thousand dollars. When it stopped there sprang from it an excited man in a long sealskin coat—worn not for the luxury of it at all but from the sheer chilliness of the autumn evening. And it was, as of course you know, Pupkin's father. He had seen the news of his son's death in the evening paper in the city. They drove the car through, so the chauffeur said, in two hours and a quarter, and behind them there was to follow a special trainload of detectives and emergency men, but Pupkin senior had cancelled all that by telegram half way up when he heard that Peter was still living.

For a moment as his eye rested on young Pupkin you would almost have imagined, had you not known that he came from the Maritime Provinces, that there were tears in them and that he was about to hug his son to his heart. But if he didn't hug Peter to his heart, he certainly did within a few moments clasp Zena to it, in that fine fatherly way in which they clasp pretty girls in the Maritime Provinces. The strangest thing is that Pupkin senior seemed to understand the whole situation without any explanations at all.

Judge Pepperleigh, I think, would have shaken both of Pupkin senior's arms off when he saw him; and when you heard them call one another "Ned" and "Phillip" it made you feel that they were boys again attending classes together at the old law school in the city.

If Pupkin thought that his father wouldn't make a hit in Mariposa, it only showed his ignorance. Pupkin senior sat there on the judge's verandah smoking a corn cob pipe as if he had never heard of Havana cigars in his life. In the three days that he spent in Mariposa that autumn, he went in and out of Jeff Thorpe's barber shop and Eliot's drug store, shot black ducks in the marsh and played poker every evening at a hundred matches for a cent as if he had never lived any other life in all his days. They had to send him telegrams enough to fill a satchel to make him come away.

So Pupkin and Zena in due course of time were married, and went to live in one of the enchanted houses on the hillside in the newer part of the town, where you may find them to this day.

You may see Pupkin there at any time cutting enchanted grass on a little lawn in as gaudy a blazer as ever.

But if you step up to speak to him or walk with him into the enchanted house, pray modulate your voice a little—musical though it is—for there is said to be an enchanted baby on the premises whose sleep must not lightly be disturbed.

Chapter X

The Great Election in Missinaba County

Don't ask me what election it was, whether Dominion or Provincial or Imperial or Universal, for I scarcely know.

It must, of course, have been going on in other parts of the country as well, but I saw it all from Missinaba County which, with the town of Mariposa, was, of course, the storm centre and focus point of the whole turmoil.

I only know that it was a huge election and that on it turned issues of the most tremendous importance, such as whether or not Mariposa should become part of the United States, and whether the flag that had waved over the school house at Tecumseh Township for ten centuries should be trampled under the hoof of an alien invader, and whether Britons should be slaves, and whether Canadians should be Britons, and whether the farming class would prove themselves Canadians, and tremendous questions of that kind.

And there was such a roar and a tumult to it, and such a waving of flags and beating of drums and flaring of torchlights that such parts of the election as may have been going on elsewhere than in Missinaba county must have been quite unimportant and didn't really matter.

Now that it is all over, we can look back at it without heat or passion. We can see,—it's plain enough now,—that in the great election Canada saved the British Empire, and that Missinaba saved Canada and that the vote of the Third Concession of Tecumseh Township saved Missinaba County, and that those of us who carried the third concession,—well, there's no need to push it further. We prefer to be modest about it. If we still speak of it, it is only quietly and simply and not more than three or four times a day.

But you can't understand the election at all, and the conventions and the campaigns and the nominations and the balloting, unless you first appreciate the peculiar complexion of politics in Mariposa.

Let me begin at the beginning. Everybody in Mariposa is

either a Liberal or a Conservative or else is both. Some of the people are or have been Liberals or Conservatives all their lives and are called dyed-in-the-wool Grits or old-time Tories and things of that sort. These people get from long training such a swift penetrating insight into national issues that they can decide the most complicated question in four seconds: in fact, just as soon as they grab the city papers out of the morning mail, they know the whole solution of any problem you can put to them. There are other people whose aim it is to be broad-minded and judicious and who vote Liberal or Conservative according to their judgment of the questions of the day. If their judgment of these questions tells them that there is something in it for them in voting Liberal, then they do so. But if not, they refuse to be the slaves of a party or the henchmen of any political leader. So that anybody looking for henches has got to keep away from them.

But the one thing that nobody is allowed to do in Mariposa is to have no politics. Of course there are always some people whose circumstances compel them to say that they have no politics. But that is easily understood. Take the case of Trelawney, the postmaster. Long ago he was a letter carrier under the old Mackenzie Government, and later he was a letter sorter under the old Macdonald Government, and after that a letter stamper under the old Tupper Government, and so on. Trelawney always says that he has no politics, but the truth is that he has too many.

So, too, with the clergy in Mariposa. They have no politics— absolutely none. Yet Dean Drone round election time always announces as his text such a verse as: "Lo! is there not one righteous man in Israel?" or: "What ho! is it not time for a change?" And that is a signal for all the Liberal business men to get up and leave their pews.

Similarly over at the Presbyterian Church, the minister says that his sacred calling will not allow him to take part in politics and that his sacred calling prevents him from breathing even a word of harshness against his fellow man, but that when it comes to the elevation of the ungodly into high places in the commonwealth (this means, of course, the nomination of the Conservative candidate) then he's not going to allow his sacred calling to prevent him from saying just what he thinks of it. And by that time, having pretty well cleared the church of Conservatives, he proceeds to show from the scriptures that the ancient Hebrews

were Liberals to a man, except those who were drowned in the
flood or who perished, more or less deservedly, in the desert.

There are, I say, some people who are allowed to claim to
have no politics,—the office holders, and the clergy and the
school teachers and the hotel keepers. But beyond them, anybody
in Mariposa who says that he has no politics is looked upon as
crooked, and people wonder what it is that he is "out after."

In fact, the whole town and county is a hive of politics, and
people who have only witnessed gatherings such as the House of
Commons at Westminster and the Senate at Washington and
never seen a Conservative Convention at Tecumseh Corners or
a Liberal Rally at the Concession school house, don't know what
politics means.

So you may imagine the excitement in Mariposa when it
became known that King George had dissolved the parliament of
Canada and had sent out a writ or command for Missinaba
County to elect for him some other person than John Henry Bagshaw because he no longer had confidence in him.

The king, of course, is very well known, very favourably
known, in Mariposa. Everybody remembers how he visited the
town on his great tour in Canada, and stopped off at the Mariposa
station. Although he was only a prince at the time, there was
quite a big crowd down at the depot and everybody felt what a
shame it was that the prince had no time to see more of Mariposa, because he would get such a false idea of it, seeing only the
station and the lumber yards. Still, they all came to the station
and all the Liberals and Conservatives mixed together perfectly
freely and stood side by side without any distinction, so that the
prince should not observe any party differences among them. And
he didn't,—you could see that he didn't. They read him an address all about the tranquillity and loyalty of the Empire, and they
purposely left out any reference to the trouble over the town
wharf or the big row there had been about the location of the new
post-office. There was a general decent feeling that it wouldn't
be fair to disturb the prince with these things: later on, as king,
he would, of course, *have* to know all about them, but meanwhile
it was better to leave him with the idea that his empire was
tranquil.

So they deliberately couched the address in terms that were
just as reassuring as possible and the prince was simply delighted

with it. I am certain that he slept pretty soundly after hearing that address. Why, you could see it taking effect even on his aides-de-camp and the people round him, so imagine how the prince must have felt!

I think in Mariposa they understand kings perfectly. Every time that a king or a prince comes, they try to make him see the bright side of everything and let him think that they're all united. Judge Pepperleigh walked up and down arm in arm with Dr. Gallagher, the worst Grit in the town, just to make the prince feel fine.

So when they got the news that the king had lost confidence in John Henry Bagshaw, the sitting member, they never questioned it a bit. Lost confidence? All right, they'd elect him another right away. They'd elect him half a dozen if he needed them. They don't mind; they'd elect the whole town man after man rather than have the king worried about it.

In any case, all the Conservatives had been wondering for years how the king and the governor-general and men like that had tolerated such a man as Bagshaw so long.

Missinaba County, I say, is a regular hive of politics, and not the miserable, crooked, money-ridden politics of the cities, but the straight, real old-fashioned thing that is an honour to the country side. Any man who would offer to take a bribe or sell his convictions for money, would be an object of scorn. I don't say they wouldn't take money,—they would, of course, why not?— but if they did they would take it in a straight fearless way and say nothing about it. They might,—it's only human,—accept a job or a contract from the government, but if they did, rest assured it would be in a broad national spirit and not for the sake of the work itself. No, sir. Not for a minute.

Any man who wants to get the votes of the Missinaba farmers and the Mariposa business men has got to persuade them that he's the right man. If he can do that,—if he can persuade any one of them that he is the right man and that all the rest know it, then they'll vote for him.

The division, I repeat, between the Liberals and the Conservatives, is intense. Yet you might live for a long while in the town, between elections, and never know it. It is only when you get to understand the people that you begin to see that there is a cross division running through them that nothing can ever remove. You gradually become aware of fine subtle distinctions that miss your observation at first. Outwardly, they are all friendly enough. For instance, Joe Milligan the dentist is a Conservative, and has been for six years, and yet he shares the same boat-house with young Dr. Gallagher, who is a Liberal, and they even bought a motor boat between them. Pete Glover and Alf McNichol were in partnership in the hardware and paint store, though they belonged on different sides.

But just as soon as elections drew near, the differences in politics became perfectly apparent. Liberals and Conservatives drew away from one another. Joe Milligan used the motor boat one Saturday and Dr. Gallagher the next, and Pete Glover sold hardware on one side of the store and Alf McNichol sold paint on the other. You soon realized too that one of the newspapers was Conservative and the other was Liberal, that there was a Liberal drug store and a Conservative drug store, and so on. Similarly round election time, the Mariposa House was the Liberal Hotel, and the Continental Conservative, though Mr. Smith's place, where they always put on a couple of extra bar tenders, was what you might call Independent-Liberal-Conservative, with a dash of Imperialism thrown in. Mr. Gingham, the undertaker, was, as a natural effect of his calling, an advanced Liberal, but at election time he always engaged a special assistant for embalming Conservative customers.

So now, I think, you understand something of the general political surroundings of the great election in Missinaba County.

John Henry Bagshaw was the sitting member, the Liberal member, for Missinaba County.

The Liberals called him the old war horse, and the old battle-axe, and the old charger and the old champion and all sorts of things of that kind. The Conservatives called him the old jackass and the old army mule and the old booze fighter and the old grafter and the old scoundrel.

John Henry Bagshaw was, I suppose, one of the greatest political forces in the world. He had flowing white hair crowned with a fedora hat, and a smooth statesmanlike face which it cost the country twenty-five cents a day to shave.

Altogether the Dominion of Canada had spent over two thousand dollars in shaving that face during the twenty years that Bagshaw had represented Missinaba County. But the result had been well worth it.

Bagshaw wore a long political overcoat that it cost the country twenty cents a day to brush, and boots that cost the Dominion fifteen cents every morning to shine.

But it was money well spent.

Bagshaw of Mariposa was one of the most representative men of the age, and it's no wonder that he had been returned for the county for five elections running, leaving the Conservatives nowhere. Just think how representative he was. He owned two hundred acres out on the Third Concession and kept two men working on it all the time to prove that he was a practical farmer. They sent in fat hogs to the Missinaba County Agricultural Exposition and World's Fair every autumn, and Bagshaw himself stood beside the pig pens with the judges, and wore a pair of corduroy breeches and chewed a straw all afternoon. After that if any farmer thought that he was not properly represented in Parliament, it showed that he was an ass.

Bagshaw owned a half share in the harness business and a quarter share in the tannery and that made him a business man. He paid for a pew in the Presbyterian Church and that represented religion in Parliament. He attended college for two sessions thirty years ago, and that represented education and kept him abreast with modem science, if not ahead of it. He kept a little account in one bank and a big account in the other, so that he was a rich man or a poor man at the same time.

Add to that that John Henry Bagshaw was perhaps the finest orator in Mariposa. That, of course, is saying a great deal. There are speakers there, lots of them that can talk two or three hours at a stretch, but the old war horse could beat them all. They say that when John Henry Bagshaw got well started, say after a couple of hours of talk, he could speak as Pericles or Demosthenes or Cicero never could have spoken.

You could tell Bagshaw a hundred yards off as a member of the House of Commons. He wore a pepper-and-salt suit to show that he came from a rural constituency, and he wore a broad gold watch-chain with dangling seals to show that he also represents a town. You could see from his quiet low collar and white tie that his electorate were a God-fearing, religious people, while the horseshoe pin that he wore showed that his electorate were not without sporting instincts and knew a horse from a jackass.

Most of the time, John Henry Bagshaw had to be at Ottawa (though he preferred the quiet of his farm and always left it, as he said, with a sigh). If he was not in Ottawa, he was in Washington, and of course at any time they might need him in London, so that it was no wonder that he could only be in Mariposa about two months in the year.

That is why everybody knew, when Bagshaw got off the afternoon train one day early in the spring, that there must be something very important coming and that the rumours about a new election must be perfectly true.

Everything that he did showed this. He gave the baggage man twenty-five cents to take the check off his trunk, the 'bus driver fifty cents to drive him up to the Main Street, and he went into Callahan's tobacco store and bought two ten-cent cigars and took them across the street and gave them to Mallory Tompkins of the Times-Herald as a present from the Prime Minister.

All that afternoon, Bagshaw went up and down the Main Street of Mariposa, and you could see, if you knew the signs of it, that there was politics in the air. He bought nails and putty and glass in the hardware store, and harness in the harness shop, and drugs in the drug store and toys in the toy shop, and all the things like that that are needed for a big campaign.

Then when he had done all this he went over with McGinnis the Liberal organizer and Mallory Tompkins, the Times-Herald man, and Gingham (the great Independent-Liberal undertaker) to the back parlour in the Mariposa House.

You could tell from the way John Henry Bagshaw closed the door before he sat down that he was in a pretty serious frame of mind.

"Gentlemen," he said, "the election is a certainty. We're going to have a big fight on our hands and we've got to get ready for it."

"Is it going to be on the tariff?" asked Tompkins.

"Yes, gentlemen, I'm afraid it is. The whole thing is going to turn on the tariff question. I wish it were otherwise. I think it madness, but they're bent on it, and we got to fight it on that line. Why they can't fight it merely on the question of graft," continued the old war horse, rising from his seat and walking up and down, "Heaven only knows. I warned them. I appealed to them. I said, fight the thing on graft and we can win easy. Take this constituency, why not have fought the thing out on whether I spent too much money on the town wharf or the post-office? What better issues could a man want? Let them claim that I am crooked, and let me claim that I'm not. Surely that was good enough without dragging in the tariff. But now, gentlemen, tell me about things in the constituency. Is there any talk yet of who is to run?"

Mallory Tompkins lighted up the second of the Prime Minister's cigars and then answered for the group:

"Everybody says that Edward Drone is going to run."

"Ah!" said the old war horse, and there was joy upon his face, "is he? At last! That's good, that's good—now what platform will he run on?"

"Independent."

"Excellent," said Mr. Bagshaw. "Independent, that's fine. On a programme of what?"

"Just simple honesty and public morality."

"Come now," said the member, "that's splendid: that will help enormously. Honesty and public morality! The very thing! If Drone runs and makes a good showing, we win for a certainty. Tompkins, you must lose no time over this. Can't you manage to get some articles in the other papers hinting that at the last election we bribed all the voters in the county, and that we gave out enough contracts to simply pervert the whole constituency. Imply that we poured the public money into this county in bucketsful and that we are bound to do it again. Let Drone have plenty of material of this sort and he'll draw off every honest unbiassed vote in the Conservative party.

"My only fear is," continued the old war horse, losing some of his animation, "that Drone won't run after all. He's said it so often before and never has. He hasn't got the money. But we must see to that. Gingham, you know his brother well; you must work it so that we pay Drone's deposit and his campaign expenses. But how like Drone it is to come out at this time!"

It was indeed very like Edward Drone to attempt so misguided a thing as to come out an Independent candidate in Missinaba County on a platform of public honesty. It was just the sort of thing that anyone in Mariposa would expect from him.

Edward Drone was the Rural Dean's younger brother,—young Mr. Drone, they used to call him, years ago, to distinguish him from the rector. He was a somewhat weaker copy of his elder brother, with a simple, inefficient face and kind blue eyes. Edward Drone was, and always had been, a failure. In training he had been, once upon a time, an engineer and built dams that broke and bridges that fell down and wharves that floated away in the spring floods. He had been a manufacturer and failed, had been a contractor and failed, and now lived a meagre life as a sort of surveyor or land expert on goodness knows what.

In his political ideas Edward Drone was and, as everybody in Mariposa knew, always had been crazy. He used to come up to the autumn exercises at the high school and make speeches about the ancient Romans and Titus Manlius and Quintus Curtius at the same time when John Henry Bagshaw used to make a speech about the Maple Leaf and ask for an extra half holiday. Drone used to tell the boys about the lessons to be learned from the lives of the truly great, and Bagshaw used to talk to them about the lessons learned from the lives of the extremely rich. Drone used to say that his heart filled whenever he thought of the splendid patriotism of the ancient Romans, and Bagshaw said that whenever he looked out over this wide Dominion his heart overflowed.

Even the youngest boy in the school could tell that Drone was foolish. Not even the school teachers would have voted for him.

"What about the Conservatives?" asked Bagshaw presently; "is there any talk yet as to who they'll bring out?"

Gingham and Mallory Tompkins looked at one another. They were almost afraid to speak.

"Hadn't you heard?" said Gingham; "they've got their man already."

"Who is it?" said Bagshaw quickly.

"They're going to put up Josh Smith."

"Great Heaven!" said Bagshaw, jumping to his feet; "Smith! the hotel keeper."

"Yes, sir," said Mr. Gingham, "that's the man."

Do you remember, in history, how Napoleon turned pale when he heard that the Duke of Wellington was to lead the allies in Belgium? Do you remember how, when Themistocles heard that Aristogiton was to lead the Spartans, he jumped into the sea? Possibly you don't, but it may help you to form some idea of what John Henry Bagshaw felt when he heard that the Conservatives had selected Josh Smith, proprietor of Smith's Hotel.

You remember Smith. You've seen him there on the steps of his hotel,—two hundred and eighty pounds in his stockinged feet. You've seen him selling liquor after hours through sheer public spirit, and you recall how he saved the lives of hundreds of people on the day when the steamer sank, and how he saved the town from being destroyed the night when the Church of England Church burnt down. You know that hotel of his, too, half way down the street, Smith's Northern Health Resort, though already they were beginning to call it Smith's British Arms.

So you can imagine that Bagshaw came as near to turning pale as a man in federal politics can.

"I never knew Smith was a Conservative," he said faintly; "he always subscribed to our fund."

"He is now," said Mr. Gingham ominously; "he says the idea of this reciprocity business cuts him to the heart."

"The infernal liar!" said Mr. Bagshaw.

There was a silence for a few moments. Then Bagshaw spoke again.

"Will Smith have anything else in his platform besides the trade question?"

"Yes," said Mr. Gingham gloomily, "he will."

"What is it?"

"Temperance and total prohibition!"

John Henry Bagshaw sank back in his chair as if struck with a club. There let me leave him for a chapter.

Chapter XI

The Candidacy of Mr. Smith

"Boys," said Mr. Smith to the two hostlers, stepping out on to the sidewalk in front of the hotel,—"hoist that there British Jack over the place and hoist her up good."

Then he stood and watched the flag fluttering in the wind.

"Billy," he said to the desk clerk, "get a couple more and put them up on the roof of the caff behind the hotel. Wire down to the city and get a quotation on a hundred of them. Take them signs *'American Drinks'* out of the bar. Put up noo ones with *'British Beer at all Hours;'* clear out the rye whiskey and order in Scotch and Irish, and then go up to the printing office and get me them placards."

Then another thought struck Mr. Smith.

"Say, Billy," he said, "wire to the city for fifty pictures of King George. Get 'em good, and get 'em coloured. It don't matter what they cost."

"All right, sir," said Billy.

"And Billy," called Mr. Smith, as still another thought struck him (indeed, the moment Mr. Smith went into politics you could see these thoughts strike him like waves), "get fifty pictures of his father, old King Albert."

"All right, sir."

"And say, I tell you, while you're at it, get some of the old queen, Victorina, if you can. Get 'em in mourning, with a harp and one of them lions and a three-pointed prong."

It was on the morning after the Conservative Convention. Josh Smith had been chosen the candidate. And now the whole town was covered with flags and placards and there were bands in the streets every evening, and noise and music and excitement that went on from morning till night.

Election times are exciting enough even in the city. But there the excitement dies down in business hours. In Mariposa there aren't any business hours and the excitement goes on all the time.

Mr. Smith had carried the Convention before him. There had been a feeble attempt to put up Nivens. But everybody knew that he was a lawyer and a college man and wouldn't have a chance by a man with a broader outlook like Josh Smith.

So the result was that Smith was the candidate and there were placards out all over the town with SMITH AND BRITISH ALLEGIANCE in big letters, and people were wearing badges with Mr. Smith's face on one side and King George's on the other, and the fruit store next to the hotel had been cleaned out and turned into committee rooms with a gang of workers smoking cigars in it all day and half the night.

There were other placards, too, with BAGSHAW AND LIBERTY, BAGSHAW AND PROSPERITY, VOTE FOR THE OLD MISSINABA STANDARD BEARER, and up town beside the Mariposa House there were the Bagshaw committee rooms with a huge white streamer across the street, and with a gang of Bagshaw workers smoking their heads off.

But Mr. Smith had an estimate made which showed that nearly two cigars to one were smoked in his committee rooms as compared with the Liberals. It was the first time in five elections that the Conservatives had been able to make such a showing as that.

One might mention, too, that there were Drone placards out,—five or six of them,—little things about the size of a pocket handkerchief, with a statement that "Mr. Edward Drone solicits the votes of the electors of Missinaba County." But you would never notice them. And when Drone tried to put up a streamer across the Main Street with DRONE AND HONESTY the wind carried it away into the lake.

The fight was really between Smith and Bagshaw, and everybody knew it from the start.

I wish that I were able to narrate all the phases and the turns of the great contest from the opening of the campaign till the final polling day. But it would take volumes.

First of all, of course, the trade question was hotly discussed in the two newspapers of Mariposa, and the Newspacket and the Times-Herald literally bristled with statistics. Then came interviews with the candidates and the expression of their convictions in regard to tariff questions.

"Mr. Smith," said the reporter of the Mariposa Newspacket, "we'd like to get your views of the effect of the proposed reduction of the differential duties."

"By gosh, Pete," said Mr. Smith, "you can search me. Have

a cigar."

"What do you think, Mr. Smith, would be the result of lowering the *ad valorem* British preference and admitting American goods at a reciprocal rate?"

"It's a corker, ain't it?" answered Mr. Smith. "What'll you take, lager or domestic?"

And in that short dialogue Mr. Smith showed that he had instantaneously grasped the whole method of dealing with the press. The interview in the paper next day said that Mr. Smith, while unwilling to state positively that the principle of tariff discrimination was at variance with sound fiscal science, was firmly of opinion that any reciprocal interchange of tariff preferences with the United States must inevitably lead to a serious per capita reduction of the national industry.

"Mr. Smith," said the chairman of a delegation of the manufacturers of Mariposa, "what do you propose to do in regard to the tariff if you're elected?"

"Boys," answered Mr. Smith, "I'll put her up so darned high they won't never get her down again."

"Mr. Smith," said the chairman of another delegation, "I'm an old free trader—"

"Put it there," said Mr. Smith, "so'm I. There ain't nothing like it."

"What do you think about imperial defence?" asked another questioner.

"Which?" said Mr. Smith.

"Imperial defence."

"Of what?"

"Of everything."

"Who says it?" said Mr. Smith.

"Everybody is talking of it."

"What do the Conservative boys at Ottaway think about it?" answered Mr. Smith.

"They're all for it."

"Well, I'm fer it too," said Mr. Smith.

These little conversations represented only the first stage, the argumentative stage of the great contest. It was during this period, for example, that the Mariposa Newspacket absolutely proved that the price of hogs in Mariposa was decimal six higher than the price of oranges in Southern California and that the average decennial import of eggs into Missinaba County had increased four decimal six eight two in the last fifteen years more than the import of lemons in New Orleans.

Figures of this kind made the people think. Most certainly.

After all this came the organizing stage and after that the big public meetings and the rallies. Perhaps you have never seen a county being "organized." It is a wonderful sight. First of all the Bagshaw men drove through crosswise in top buggies and then drove through it again lengthwise. Whenever they met a farmer they went in and ate a meal with him, and after the meal they took him out to the buggy and gave him a drink. After that the man's vote was absolutely solid until it was tampered with by feeding a Conservative.

In fact, the only way to show a farmer that you are in earnest is to go in and eat a meal with him. If you can't eat it, he won't vote for you. That is the recognized political test.

But, of course, just as soon as the Bagshaw men had begun to get the farming vote solidified, the Smith buggies came driving through in the other direction, eating meals and distributing cigars and turning all the farmers back into Conservatives.

Here and there you might see Edward Drone, the Independent candidate, wandering round from farm to farm in the dust of the political buggies. To each of the farmers he explained that he pledged himself to give no bribes, to spend no money and to offer no jobs, and each one of them gripped him warmly by the hand and showed him the way to the next farm.

After the organization of the county there came the period of the public meetings and the rallies and the joint debates between the candidates and their supporters.

I suppose there was no place in the whole Dominion where the trade question,—the Reciprocity question—was threshed out quite so thoroughly and in quite such a national patriotic spirit as in Mariposa. For a month, at least, people talked of nothing else. A man would stop another in the street and tell him that he had read last night that the average price of an egg in New York was decimal ought one more than the price of an egg in Mariposa, and the other man would stop the first one later in the day and tell him that the average price of a hog in Idaho was point six of a cent per pound less (or more,—he couldn't remember which for the moment) than the average price of beef in Mariposa.

People lived on figures of this sort, and the man who could remember most of them stood out as a born leader.

But of course it was at the public meetings that these things were most fully discussed. It would take volumes to do full justice to all the meetings that they held in Missinaba County. But here and there single speeches stood out as masterpieces of convincing oratory. Take, for example, the speech of John Henry Bagshaw at the Tecumseh Corners School House. The Mariposa Times-Herald said next day that that speech would go down in history, and so it will,—ever so far down.

Anyone who has heard Bagshaw knows what an impressive speaker he is, and on this night when he spoke with the quiet dignity of a man old in years and anxious only to serve his country, he almost surpassed himself. Near the end of his speech somebody dropped a pin, and the noise it made in falling fairly rattled the windows.

"I am an old man now, gentlemen," Bagshaw said, "and the time must soon come when I must not only leave politics, but must take my way towards that goal from which no traveller returns."

There was a deep hush when Bagshaw said this. It was understood to imply that he thought of going to the United States.

"Yes, gentlemen, I am an old man, and I wish, when my time comes to go, to depart leaving as little animosity behind me as possible. But before I *do* go, I want it pretty clearly understood that there are more darn scoundrels in the Conservative party than ought to be tolerated in any decent community. I bear," he continued, "malice towards none and I wish to speak with gentleness to all, but what I will say is that how any set of rational responsible men could nominate such a skunk as the Conservative candidate passes the bounds of my comprehension. Gentlemen, in the present campaign there is no room for vindictive abuse. Let us rise to a higher level than that. They tell me that my opponent, Smith, is a common saloon keeper. Let it pass. They tell me that he has stood convicted of horse stealing, that he is a notable perjurer, that he is known as the blackest-hearted liar in

Missinaba County. Let us not speak of it. Let no whisper of it pass our lips.

"No, gentlemen," continued Bagshaw, pausing to take a drink of water, "let us rather consider this question on the high plane of national welfare. Let us not think of our own particular interests but let us consider the good of the country at large. And to do this, let me present to you some facts in regard to the price of barley in Tecumseh Township."

Then, amid a deep stillness, Bagshaw read off the list of prices of sixteen kinds of grain in sixteen different places during sixteen years.

"But let me turn," Bagshaw went on to another phase of the national subject, "and view for a moment the price of marsh hay in Missinaba County—"

When Bagshaw sat down that night it was felt that a Liberal vote in Tecumseh Township was a foregone conclusion.

But here they hadn't reckoned on the political genius of Mr. Smith. When he heard next day of the meeting, he summoned some of his leading speakers to him and he said:

"Boys, they're beating us on them statissicks. Ourn ain't good enough."

Then he turned to Nivens and he said:

"What was them figures you had here the other night?"

Nivens took out a paper and began reading.

"Stop," said Mr. Smith, "what was that figure for bacon?"

"Fourteen million dollars," said Nivens.

"Not enough," said Mr. Smith, "make it twenty. They'll stand for it, them farmers."

Nivens changed it.

"And what was that for hay?"

"Two dollars a ton."

"Shove it up to four," said Mr. Smith. "And I tell you," he added, "if any of them farmers says the figures ain't correct, tell them to go to Washington and see for themselves; say that if any man wants the proof of your figures let him go over to England and ask,—tell him to go straight to London and see it all for himself in the books."

After this, there was no more trouble over statistics. I must say though that it is a wonderfully convincing thing to hear trade figures of this kind properly handled. Perhaps the best man on this sort of thing in the campaign was Mullins, the banker. A man of his profession simply has to have figures of trade and population and money at his fingers' ends and the effect of it in public speaking is wonderful.

No doubt you have listened to speakers of this kind, but I question whether you have ever heard anything more typical of the sort of effect that I allude to than Mullins's speech at the big rally at the Fourth Concession.

Mullins himself, of course, knows the figures so well that he never bothers to write them into notes and the effect is very striking.

"Now, gentlemen," he said very earnestly, "how many of you know just to what extent the exports of this country have increased in the last ten years? How many could tell what per cent. of increase there has been in one decade of our national importation?"—then Mullins paused and looked round. Not a man knew it.

"I don't recall," he said, "exactly the precise amount myself, —not at this moment,—but it must be simply tremendous. Or take the question of population," Mullins went on, warming up again as a born statistician always does at the proximity of figures, "how many of you know, how many of you can state, what has been the decennial percentage increase in our leading cities—?"

There he paused, and would you believe it, not a man could state it.

"I don't recall the exact figures," said Mullins, "but I have them at home and they are positively colossal."

But just in one phase of the public speaking, the candidacy of Mr. Smith received a serious set-back.

It had been arranged that Mr. Smith should run on a platform of total prohibition. But they soon found that it was a mistake. They had imported a special speaker from the city, a grave man with a white tie, who put his whole heart into the work and would take nothing for it except his expenses and a sum of money for each speech. But beyond the money, I say, he would take nothing.

He spoke one night at the Tecumseh Corners social hall at the same time when the Liberal meeting was going on at the Tecumseh Corners school house.

"Gentlemen," he said, as he paused half way in his speech,— "while we are gathered here in earnest discussion, do you know what is happening over at the meeting place of our opponents? Do you know that seventeen bottles of rye whiskey were sent out from the town this afternoon to that innocent and unsuspecting school house? Seventeen bottles of whiskey hidden in between the blackboard and the wall, and every single man that attends that meeting,—mark my words, every single man,—will drink his fill of the abominable stuff at the expense of the Liberal candidate!"

Just as soon as the speaker said this, you could see the Smith men at the meeting look at one another in injured surprise, and before the speech was half over the hall was practically emptied.

After that the total prohibition plank was changed and the committee substituted a declaration in favour of such a form of restrictive license as should promote temperance while encouraging the manufacture of spirituous liquors, and by a severe regulation of the liquor traffic should place intoxicants only in the hands of those fitted to use them.

Finally there came the great day itself, the Election Day that brought, as everybody knows, the crowning triumph of Mr. Smith's career. There is no need to speak of it at any length, because it has become a matter of history.

In any case, everybody who has ever seen Mariposa knows just what election day is like. The shops, of course, are, as a mater of custom, all closed, as the bar rooms are all closed by law so that you have to go in by the back way. All the people are in their best clothes and at first they walk up and down the street in a solemn way just as they do on the twelfth of July and on St. Patrick's Day, before the fun begins. Everybody keeps looking in at the different polling places to see if anybody else has voted yet, because, of course, nobody cares to vote first for fear of being fooled after all and voting on the wrong side.

Most of all did the supporters of Mr. Smith, acting under his instructions, hang back from the poll in the early hours. To Mr. Smith's mind voting was to be conducted on the same plan as bear-shooting.

"Hold back your votes, boys," he said, "and don't be too eager. Wait till when she begins to warm up and then let 'em have it good and hard."

In each of the polling places in Mariposa there is a returning officer and with him are two scrutineers, and the electors, I say, peep in and out like mice looking into a trap. But if once the scrutineers get a man well into the polling booth, they push him in behind a little curtain and make him vote. The voting, of course, is by secret ballot, so that no one except the scrutineers and the returning officer and the two or three people who may be round the poll can possibly tell how a man has voted.

That's how it comes about that the first results are often so contradictory and conflicting. Sometimes the poll is badly arranged and the scrutineers are unable to see properly just how the ballots are being marked and they count up the Liberals and Conservatives in different ways. Often, too, a voter makes his mark so hurriedly and carelessly that they have to pick it out of the ballot box and look at it to see what it is.

I suppose that may have been why it was that in Mariposa the results came out at first in such a conflicting way.

Perhaps that was how it was that the first reports showed that Edward Drone the Independent candidate was certain to win. You should have seen how the excitement grew upon the streets when the news was circulated. In the big rallies and meetings of the Liberals and Conservatives, everybody had pretty well forgotten all about Drone, and when the news got round at about four o'clock that the Drone vote was carrying the poll, the people were simply astounded. Not that they were not pleased. On the contrary. They were delighted. Everybody came up to Drone and shook hands and congratulated him and told him that they had known all along that what the country wanted was a straight, honest, non-partisan representation. The Conservatives said openly that they were sick of party, utterly done with it, and the Liberals said that they hated it. Already three or four of them had taken Drone aside and explained that what was needed in the town was a straight, clean, non-partisan post-office, built on a piece of ground of a strictly non-partisan character, and con- structed under contracts that were not tainted and smirched with party affiliation. Two or three men were willing to show to Drone just where a piece of ground of this character could be bought. They told him too that in the matter of the postmastership itself they had nothing against Trelawney, the present postmaster, in any personal sense, and would say nothing against him except merely that he was utterly and hopelessly unfit for his job and that if Drone believed, as he had said he did, in a purified civil service, he ought to begin by purifying Trelawney.

Already Edward Drone was beginning to feel something of what it meant to hold office and there was creeping into his manner the quiet self-importance which is the first sign of conscious power.

In fact, in that brief half-hour of office, Drone had a chance to see something of what it meant. Henry McGinnis came to him and asked straight out for a job as federal census-taker on the ground that he was hard up and had been crippled with rheumatism all winter. Nelson Williamson asked for the post of wharf master on the plea that he had been laid up with sciatica all winter and was absolutely fit for nothing. Erasmus Archer asked him if he could get his boy Pete into one of the departments at Ottawa, and made a strong case of it by explaining that he had tried his cussedest to get Pete a job anywhere else and it was simply impossible. Not that Pete wasn't a willing boy, but he was slow,—even his father admitted it,—slow as the devil, blast him, and with no head for figures and unfortunately he'd never had the schooling to bring him on. But if Drone could get him in at Ottawa, his father truly believed it would be the very place for him. Surely in the Indian Department or in the Astronomical Branch or in the New Canadian Navy there must be any amount of opening for a boy like this? And to all of these requests Drone found himself explaining that he would take the matter under his very earnest consideration and that they must remember that he had to consult his colleagues and not merely follow the dictates of his own wishes. In fact, if he had ever in his life had any envy of Cabinet Ministers, he lost it in this hour.

But Drone's hour was short. Even before the poll had closed in Mariposa, the news came sweeping in, true or false, that Bagshaw was carrying the county. The second concession had gone for Bagshaw in a regular landslide,—six votes to only two for Smith,—and all down the township line road (where the hay farms are) Bagshaw was said to be carrying all before him.

Just as soon as that news went round the town, they launched the Mariposa band of the Knights of Pythias (every man in it is a Liberal) down the Main Street with big red banners in front of it with the motto BAGSHAW FOREVER in letters a foot high.

Such rejoicing and enthusiasm began to set in as you never saw. Everybody crowded round Bagshaw on the steps of the Mariposa House and shook his hand and said they were proud to see the day and that the Liberal party was the glory of the Dominion and that as for this idea of non-partisan politics the very thought of it made them sick. Right away in the committee rooms they began to organize the demonstration for the evening with lantern slides and speeches and they arranged for a huge bouquet to be presented to Bagshaw on the platform by four little girls (all Liberals) all dressed in white.

And it was just at this juncture, with one hour of voting left, that Mr. Smith emerged from his committee rooms and turned his voters on the town, much as the Duke of Wellington sent the whole line to the charge at Waterloo. From every committee room and sub-committee room they poured out in flocks with blue badges fluttering on their coats.

"Get at it, boys," said Mr. Smith, "vote and keep on voting till they make you quit."

Then he turned to his campaign assistant. "Billy," he said, "wire down to the city that I'm elected by an overwhelming majority and tell them to wire it right back. Send word by telephone to all the polling places in the county that the hull town has gone solid Conservative and tell them to send the same news back here. Get carpenters and tell them to run up a platform in front of the hotel; tell them to take the bar door clean off its hinges and be all ready the minute the poll quits."

It was that last hour that did it. Just as soon as the big posters went up in the windows of the Mariposa Newspacket with the telegraphic despatch that Josh Smith was reported in the city to be elected, and was followed by the messages from all over the county, the voters hesitated no longer. They had waited, most of them, all through the day, not wanting to make any error in their vote, but when they saw the Smith men crowding into the polls and heard the news from the outside, they went solid in one great stampede, and by the time the poll was declared closed at five o'clock there was no shadow of doubt that the county was saved and that Josh Smith was elected for Missinaba.

I wish you could have witnessed the scene in Mariposa that evening. It would have done your heart good,—such joy, such public rejoicing as you never saw. It turned out that there wasn't really a Liberal in the whole town and that there never had been. They were all Conservatives and had been for years and years. Men who had voted, with pain and sorrow in their hearts, for the Liberal party for twenty years, came out that evening and owned up straight that they were Conservatives. They said they could stand the strain no longer and simply had to confess. Whatever the sacrifice might mean, they were prepared to make it.

Even Mr. Golgotha Gingham, the undertaker, came out and admitted that in working for John Henry Bagshaw he'd been going straight against his conscience. He said that right from the first he had had his misgivings. He said it had haunted him. Often at night when he would be working away quietly, one of these sudden misgivings would overcome him so that he could hardly go on with his embalming. Why, it appeared that on the very first day when reciprocity was proposed, he had come home and said to Mrs. Gingham that he thought it simply meant selling out the country. And the strange thing was that ever so many others had just the same misgivings. Trelawney admitted that he had said to Mrs. Trelawney that it was madness, and Jeff Thorpe, the barber, had, he admitted, gone home to his dinner, the first day reciprocity was talked of, and said to Mrs. Thorpe that it would simply kill business in the country and introduce a cheap, shoddy, American form of hair-cut that would render true loyalty impossible. To think that Mrs. Gingham and Mrs. Trelawney and Mrs. Thorpe had known all this for six months and kept quiet about it! Yet I think there were a good many Mrs. Ginghams in the country. It is merely another proof that no woman is fit for politics.

The demonstration that night in Mariposa will never be forgotten. The excitement in the streets, the torchlights, the music of the band of the Knights of Pythias (an organization which is conservative in all but name), and above all the speeches and the patriotism.

They had put up a big platform in front of the hotel, and on it were Mr. Smith and his chief workers, and behind them was a perfect forest of flags. They presented a huge bouquet of flowers to Mr. Smith, handed to him by four little girls in white, —the same four that I spoke of above, for it turned out that they were all Conservatives.

Then there were the speeches. Judge Pepperleigh spoke and said that there was no need to dwell on the victory that they had achieved, because it was history; there was no occasion to speak of what part he himself had played, within the limits of his official position, because what he had done was henceforth a matter of history; and Nivens, the lawyer, said that he would only say just a few words, because anything that he might have done was now history; later generations, he said, might read it but it was not for him to speak of it, because it belonged now to the history of the country. And, after them, others spoke in the same strain and all refused absolutely to dwell on the subject (for more than half an hour) on the ground that anything that they might have done was better left for future generations to investigate. And no doubt this was very true, as to some things, anyway.

Mr. Smith, of course, said nothing. He didn't have to,—not for four years,—and he knew it.

Chapter XII

L'Envoi. The Train to Mariposa

It leaves the city every day about five o'clock in the evening, the train for Mariposa. Strange that you did not know of it, though you come from the little town—or did, long years ago.

Odd that you never knew, in all these years, that the train was there every afternoon, puffing up steam in the city station, and that you might have boarded it any day and gone home. No, not "home,"—of course you couldn't call it "home" now; "home" means that big red sandstone house of yours in the costlier part of the city. "Home" means, in a way, this Mausoleum Club where you sometimes talk with me of the times that you had as a boy in Mariposa.

But of course "home" would hardly be the word you would apply to the little town, unless perhaps, late at night, when you'd been sitting reading in a quiet corner somewhere such a book as the present one.

Naturally you don't know of the Mariposa train now. Years ago, when you first came to the city as a boy with your way to make, you knew of it well enough, only too well. The price of a ticket counted in those days, and though you knew of the train you couldn't take it, but sometimes from sheer homesickness you used to wander down to the station on a Friday afternoon after your work, and watch the Mariposa people getting on the train and wish that you could go.

Why, you knew that little train at one time better, I suppose, than any other single thing in the city, and loved it too for the little town in the sunshine that it ran to.

Do you remember how when you first began to make money you used to plan that just as soon as you were rich, really rich, you'd go back home again to the little town and build a great big house with a fine verandah,—no stint about it, the best that money could buy, planed lumber, every square foot of it, and a fine picket fence in front of it.

It was to be one of the grandest and finest houses that thought could conceive; much finer, in true reality, than that vast palace of sandstone with the porte cochère and the sweeping conservatories that you afterwards built in the costlier part of the city.

But if you have half forgotten Mariposa, and long since lost the way to it, you are only like the greater part of the men here in this Mausoleum Club in the city. Would you believe it that practically every one of them came from Mariposa once upon a time, and that there isn't one of them that doesn't sometimes dream in the dull quiet of the long evening here in the club, that some day he will go back and see the place.

They all do. Only they're half ashamed to own it.

Ask your neighbour there at the next table whether the partridge that they sometimes serve to you here can be compared for a moment to the birds that he and you, or he and some one else, used to shoot as boys in the spruce thickets along the lake. Ask him if he ever tasted duck that could for a moment be compared to the black ducks in the rice marsh along the Ossawippi. And as for fish, and fishing,—no, don't ask him about that, for if he ever starts telling you of the chub they used to catch below the mill dam and the green bass that used to lie in the water-shadow of the rocks beside the Indian's Island, not even the long dull evening in this club would be long enough for the telling of it.

But no wonder they don't know about the five o'clock train for Mariposa. Very few people know about it. Hundreds of them know that there is a train that goes out at five o'clock, but they mistake it. Ever so many of them think it's just a suburban train. Lots of people that take it every day think it's only the train to the golf grounds, but the joke is that after it passes out of the city and the suburbs and the golf grounds, it turns itself little by little into the Mariposa train, thundering and pounding towards the north with hemlock sparks pouring out into the darkness from the funnel of it.

Of course you can't tell it just at first. All those people that are crowding into it with golf clubs, and wearing knickerbockers and flat caps, would deceive anybody. That crowd of suburban people going home on commutation tickets and sometimes standing thick in the aisles, those are, of course, not Mariposa people. But look round a little bit and you'll find them easily enough. Here and there in the crowd those people with the clothes that are perfectly all right and yet look odd in some way, the women with the peculiar hats and the—what do you say?—last year's fashions? Ah yes, of course, that must be it.

Anyway, those are the Mariposa people all right enough. That man with the two-dollar panama and the glaring spectacles is one of the greatest judges that ever adorned the bench of Missinaba County. That clerical gentleman with the wide black hat, who is explaining to the man with him the marvellous mechanism of the new air brake (one of the most conspicuous illustrations of the divine structure of the physical universe), surely you have seen him before. Mariposa people! Oh yes, there are any number of them on the train every day.

But of course you hardly recognize them while the train is still passing through the suburbs and the golf district and the outlying parts of the city area. But wait a little, and you will see that when the city is well behind you, bit by bit the train changes its character. The electric locomotive that took you through the city tunnels is off now and the old wood engine is hitched on in its place. I suppose, very probably, you haven't seen one of these wood engines since you were a boy forty years ago,—the old engine with a wide top like a hat on its funnel, and with sparks enough to light up a suit for damages once in every mile.

Do you see, too, that the trim little cars that came out of the city on the electric suburban express are being discarded now at the way stations, one by one, and in their place is the old familiar car with the stuff cushions in red plush (how gorgeous it once seemed!) and with a box stove set up in one end of it? The stove is burning furiously at its sticks this autumn evening, for the air sets in chill as you get clear away from the city and are rising up to the higher ground of the country of the pines and the lakes.

Look from the window as you go. The city is far behind now and right and left of you there are trim farms with elms and maples near them and with tall windmills beside the barns that you can still see in the gathering dusk. There is a dull red light from the windows of the farmstead. It must be comfortable there after the roar and clatter of the city, and only think of the still quiet of it.

As you sit back half dreaming in the car, you keep wondering why it is that you never came up before in all these years. Ever so many times you planned that just as soon as the rush and strain of business eased up a little, you would take the train and go back to the little town to see what it was like now, and if things had changed much since your day. But each time when your holidays came, somehow you changed your mind and went down to Naragansett or Nagahuckett or Nagasomething, and left over the visit to Mariposa for another time.

It is almost night now. You can still see the trees and the fences and the farmsteads, but they are fading fast in the twilight. They have lengthened out the train by this time with a string of flat cars and freight cars between where we are sitting and the engine. But at every crossway we can hear the long muffled roar of the whistle, dying to a melancholy wail that echoes into the woods; the woods, I say, for the farms are thinning out and the track plunges here and there into great stretches of bush,—tall tamarack and red scrub willow and with a tangled undergrowth of brush that has defied for two generations all attempts to clear it into the form of fields.

Why, look, that great space that seems to open out in the half-dark of the falling evening,—why, surely yes,—Lake Ossawippi, the big lake, as they used to call it, from which the river runs down to the smaller lake,—Lake Wissanotti,—where the town of Mariposa has lain waiting for you there for thirty years.

This is Lake Ossawippi surely enough. You would know it anywhere by the broad, still, black water with hardly a ripple, and with the grip of the coming frost already on it. Such a great sheet of blackness it looks as the train thunders along the side, swinging the curve of the embankment at a breakneck speed as it rounds the corner of the lake.

How fast the train goes this autumn night! You have travelled, I know you have, in the Empire State Express, and the New Limited and the Maritime Express that holds the record of six hundred whirling miles from Paris to Marseilles But what are they to this, this mad career, this breakneck speed, this thundering roar of the Mariposa local driving hard to its home! Don't tell me that the speed is only twenty-five miles an hour. I don't care what it is. I tell you, and you can prove it for yourself if you will, that that train of mingled flat cars and coaches that goes tearing into the night, its engine whistle shrieking out its warning into the silent woods and echoing over the dull still lake, is the fastest train in the whole world.

Yes, and the best too,—the most comfortable, the most reliable, the most luxurious and the speediest train that ever turned a wheel.

And the most genial, the most sociable too. See how the passengers all turn and talk to one another now, as they get nearer and nearer to the little town. That dull reserve that seemed to hold the passengers in the electric suburban has clean vanished and gone. They are talking,—listen,—of the harvest, and the late election, and of how the local member is mentioned for the cabinet and all the old familiar topics of the sort. Already the conductor has changed his glazed hat for an ordinary round Christie and you can hear the passengers calling him and the brakesman "Bill" and "Sam" as if the were all one family.

What is it now—nine thirty? Ah, then we must be nearing the town,—this big bush that we are passing through, you remember it surely as the great swamp just this side of the bridge over the Ossawippi? There is the bridge itself, and the long roar of the train as it rushes sounding over the trestle work that rises above the marsh. Hear the clatter as we pass the semaphores and the switch lights! We must be close in now!

What? it feels nervous and strange to be coming here again after all these years? It must indeed. No, don't bother to look at the reflection of your face in the window-pane shadowed by the night outside. Nobody could tell you now after all these years. Your face has changed in these long years of money-getting in the city. Perhaps if you had come back now and again, just at odd times, it wouldn't have been so.

There,—you hear it?—the long whistle of the locomotive, one, two, three! You feel the sharp slackening of the train as it swings round the curve of the last embankment that brings it to the Mariposa station. See, too, as we round the curve, the row of the flashing lights, the bright windows of the depôt.

How vivid and plain it all is. Just as it used to be thirty years ago. There is the string of the hotel 'buses, drawn up all ready for the train, and as the train rounds in and stops hissing and panting at the platform, you can hear above all other sounds the cry of the brakesmen and the porters:

"MARIPOSA! MARIPOSA!"

And as we listen, the cry grows fainter and fainter in our ears and we are sitting here again in the leather chairs of the Mausoleum Club, talking of the little Town in the Sunshine that once we knew.

Biography

James Doyle
Deeps and Shallows: The Elusive Life of Stephen Leacock

"My life is, I think, uninteresting to other people," Stephen Leacock replied to The London Press and Publicity Service in 1935, in response to a suggestion that he write his autobiography (draft of letter, Leacock Museum). Yet the suggestion worked on Leacock's mind over the remaining nine years of his life, and he left a 40,000-word manuscript of reminiscence among his incomplete literary projects at his death, edited and published posthumously as *The Boy I Left Behind Me*. If he believed that his own life was uninteresting, he did not apply the generalization to all authors' lives, for he wrote biographies of two of his favourites, Charles Dickens and Mark Twain.

Yet in spite of his interest in biography and autobiography and his recognition of their importance in literature, Leacock remained reticent about his own life. Like many writers, he developed the habit of saving some of his papers, but what he preserved is often frustratingly unrevealing. In the Leacock Museum at Orillia, the MacLennan Library of McGill University, and the National Archives of Canada, there is a vast amount of biographical documentation that includes school reports, tax returns, receipts, lecture tour itineraries, business correspondence, desk memoranda and literary manuscripts—but very little in the way of personal revelation. All his life, Leacock protected from the public gaze his most private feelings and intimate relationships. As far as the written record is concerned, he is totally silent about the woman he married and almost equally reserved about his son. There are no confidential diaries, no love letters, few personal letters of any kind. Even his unfinished memoir is more a collection of random opinions and historical notes based on his reading than the beginning of a genuine autobiography.

Such reticence only stimulates the curiosity of biographers, and Leacock has probably had more biographers than any other figure in Canadian literary history. Leacock's personal reserve has also encouraged gossip and legend, sometimes traceable to relatives and friends of the writer, sometimes originating in no discoverable source, but perpetuated because of a seeming appropriateness to Leacock's character. But much of what is known about Leacock for certain is what he himself has chosen to reveal, and his preferred medium of revelation is the facetious voice of the narrator of his comic writings, supplemented only by the hodge-podge of financial and professional documents he selected for preservation.

Ironically, in the voice of his literary works Leacock seems garrulously fond of talking about himself. He made his first venture into telling his readers about his own life as early as 1912, in his preface to *Sunshine Sketches*. Although the preface is a more-or-less factual recitation of the events of his early life, it is also an obvious burlesque of the clichés of autobiography. "I was born at Swanmoor [usual modern spelling: Swanmore], Hants, England, on December 30, 1869," he begins. "My parents migrated to Canada in 1876, and I decided to go with them" (xv). The parents, Agnes and Peter Leacock, were born into prosperous families, but Peter evidently had more charm than intelligence or sense of responsibility. After failed attempts at farming in South Africa and the United States, he and Agnes settled in 1876 on a rugged plot of land in Georgina Township, Ontario, inland from the south shore of Lake Simcoe, a few miles from the village of Sutton. It remained for the older Agnes to sustain the marriage as well as the family through twenty years of struggles to make a go at farming, until Peter abandoned farm, wife and eleven children for good in 1887.

Stephen was the third-born son, but he soon became the person his mother most often turned to for support in place of her unreliable husband. Stephen, his niece claimed years later, "having taken over the responsibility for his mother and his younger brothers and sisters when he was only sixteen, was always considered the actual head of the house despite having two older brothers." "Quite aside from filial regard and love," Leacock "was very close to his mother intellectually," a closeness that endured until Agnes Leacock's death in 1934 at the age of ninety (Kimball 23, 90). This impression of Stephen's ascendancy in the family is illustrated by a legend reported by his first biographer that in 1887 sixteen-year-old Stephen drove his departing father to the railway station, and with a final flourish of the buggy whip threatened him with death if he ever came back (Curry 41).

With the father gone and money scarce, Stephen and the older boys were subjected to the arduous regimen of physical labor typical of subsistence farming in nineteenth-century Canada. "I saw enough of farming," Leacock says in one of the most frequently quoted comments in the Preface to *Sunshine Sketches*, "to speak exuberantly ... of the joy of early rising and the deep sleep, both of body and intellect, that is induced by honest manual toil" (xv). But thanks largely to his strong-willed mother, Stephen was not allowed to grow up with either body or intellect asleep. After discovering the limitations of country schoolhouses and home tutoring, Agnes managed to scrape together the means to send Stephen and two of his brothers to the prestigious private boys' school in Toronto, Upper Canada College. Here Stephen distinguished himself both academically and socially, graduating as "head boy" in 1887.

In the fall of the same year he entered the University of Toronto, intending to follow a comprehensive course of study in classical and modern languages and literature. But this project proved too much for the family's strained resources, and like many another young person in similar circumstances, Stephen had to fall back on school-teaching. The next ten years left him with a life-long distaste for teaching at any level lower than university. Most young men, he later wrote, take up the work because they are incapable of doing anything better, or because like himself they need the money to pursue higher education ("The Lot of the Schoolmaster" 140-43). Yet Leacock's teaching years were not a complete loss. He was good at his job, as he was good at just about everything he turned his hand to. As he had already demonstrated as a student, he had a talent for public speaking and debate, abilities that served him well at the front of a classroom. These skills, plus his academic record, secured him an appointment to the faculty of Upper Canada College in 1889.

At Upper Canada, he had congenial intellectual companionship, leisure to read, and access to the university and city libraries. Having enrolled part-time at the university, with characteristic energy he completed the necessary courses in record time, receiving his honours B.A. in 1891. Now fully qualified, Leacock might have had a distinguished career at Upper Canada, but his ambitions were still aimed beyond school teaching. In the next few years, he began looking in two directions, toward a literary career as a writer of comic prose, and toward a career as a university teacher and scholar—not, however, as a professor of language and literature, but in the relatively new social scientific field of political economy.

Leacock's attraction to humorous writing was an extension of his personality. His friend, Upper Canada schoolmate and fellow teacher Pelham Edgar, recalled that Leacock was an ebullient person with a ready laugh and an active sense of humour, traits shared, according to a family friend, with his mother and siblings (Edgar 94-95; Robert B. Pattison, "Stephen Leacock at Play," ms., n.d., Leacock Museum). Like many another ambitious young author, Leacock probably took to writing from the conviction that he could produce better work than much of the stuff he saw in the popular magazines. He had written for school and university publications, but now he tried for the more challenging professional market—and succeeded very quickly, placing material in the Toronto humorous magazine *Grip*, then the New York periodicals *Life* and *Truth*. Several of the sketches collected in his first book *Literary Lapses* (1910) appeared in periodicals between 1895-97, including the well-known "My Financial Career," "The Awful Fate of Melpomenus Jones," and "Boarding-House Geometry."

But his comic writing remained for the time being an avocation. His serious ambitions were directed toward his growing fascination with economics and political science. It is not surprising that such an active mind as Leacock's should switch from a traditional humanistic subject of study to a modern social scientific one at a time of growing interest in new academic disciplines. Nor is it surprising that someone with his outstanding academic record should aspire to advanced post-graduate status on the basis of private study in a discipline in which he lacked official academic standing. Like many young would-be intellectuals at the turn of the century, he was attracted to the multi-disciplinary writings of American social philosopher Thorstein Veblen, then a faculty member at the University of Chicago. Veblen's ideas were later to influence much of Leacock's serious writing on politics and economics, as well as some of his comic work, such as his satire on the modern urban world in *Arcadian Adventures with the Idle Rich* (1914).

Armed with strong recommendations and with distinguished performance on admission examinations, in 1899 Leacock entered the Ph.D. program at the University of Chicago. For the next ten years, the course of his life followed that of an academically brilliant young man consolidating his professional and personal successes. In the summer of 1900, he returned to Canada to marry. His bride was Beatrix Hamilton, daughter of a wealthy Toronto businessman, whose family maintained a summer home on the south shore of Lake Simcoe, near the summer cottage of the Leacock family. That summer Leacock also took up a sessional appointment as a lecturer in Economics and Political Science at McGill University. He had hoped to return as a teacher to his alma mater, but the head of the department of Political Economy at the University of Toronto had inexplicably taken a dislike to him, and blocked his attempts at winning the desired appointment (Edgar 94). McGill was a reluctant second choice, although over the years he would come to develop considerable affection for the university and the city of Montreal.

Alternating semesters between Chicago and Montreal for the next two years, Leacock finished his thesis on "The Doctrine of Laissez-faire" in 1903, and was awarded the Ph.D. All his life Leacock remained proud of his post-graduate academic record, but no biographical comment can improve on his own statements in the Preface to *Sunshine Sketches*: "The meaning of this degree is that the recipient of instruction is examined for the last time in his life, and is pronounced completely full. After this, no new ideas can be imparted to him" (xvi).

In spite of such jokes, this was the beginning, not the end, of Leacock's intellectual life. Appointed to a full-time position as assistant professor at McGill, he soon began to excel as a teacher, scholar, and public speaker. One of his lifelong political preoccupations was the unity of the British Empire, a theme he developed in scholarly articles, and took to the public lecture platform in schools and service clubs in Quebec and Ontario. In 1906, he published *Elements of Political Science*, which became a standard text in universities throughout North America and, as Leacock often liked to point out, his most profitable book. In 1907, his growing reputation as a scholar and speaker secured him an appointment from the Rhodes Trust to undertake a speaking tour on imperial unity which took him to England, Australia, New Zealand, and South Africa. "When I state that these lectures were followed almost immediately by the Union of South Africa, the Banana Riots in Trinidad, and the Turco-Italian war," said Leacock in the *Sunshine Sketches* Preface, "I think the reader can form some idea of their importance" (xvi-xvii). But if the Empire tour did not substantially improve the state of the world, it certainly improved Leacock's professional status. On his return to McGill he was appointed William Dow Professor of Political Economy and chairman of the Department of Economics and Political Science, a position he held until his retirement almost thirty years later.

His reputation as a scholar firmly established by a second book, the historical study *Baldwin, Lafontaine, Hincks: Responsible Government* (1907), Leacock had earned the right to settle into a more leisurely life. Still much attached to the region where he grew up, he purchased a thirty-three acre plot of land on "Old Brewery Bay" on Lake Couchiching, near the town of Orillia, where he had a spacious cottage built. Here he was to spend almost every summer for the rest of his life. But Leacock was not the sort of person who could sit back and relax. The summer home was soon equipped with a writing studio—at first the attic of a boathouse, later a sunroom in the main house. Looking for a change from the scholarly work that had occupied him for the past ten years, he took up the comic sketches he had produced in the 1890s, and after writing some new ones, put them all into a slim book manuscript entitled "Literary Lapses." Unable to interest the publisher of his academic books in this unexpected tangent of his writing energies, Leacock subsidized the publication and distribution himself. Subsequent events, although evidently true, sound almost as fantastic as the ironic accidents of his fictional "Simple Stories of Success" (in *Frenzied Fiction*, 1919). The obscure little book was spotted on a railway newstand by the British publisher John Lane, who offered the author a contract for British publication rights. The work was a best-seller in England and North America.

By 1910, at age forty, Leacock had achieved more than most people do in a much longer lifetime. A respected scholar in economics and political science, he was also an extremely successful teacher and public speaker, as well as a best-selling writer. It is difficult to discern a clear personality from this explosion of activity that threw out essays on economics, political science, history and literature, public lectures on imperial unity and conservative economic policies, comic sketches and narratives, and at least one book almost every year for the next thirty years, all the while maintaining a full academic schedule as a university teacher and head of his department. Nor is it easy to understand why Leacock seemed to be compelled to fill almost every waking moment with work, a trait he displayed from boyhood. A friend from summer vacations when Leacock was in his twenties recalls how the young Leacock was devoted to physical sports, especially tennis, cricket and sailing, as well as to socializing and academic study, all of which activities he pursued not only with equal vigour, but almost simultaneously. "He mixed tennis and geometry with ease," sometimes even pausing in a game to jot down a mathematical problem or some other academic memorandum prompted by his musings during play (Pattison).

This zeal for work enabled him to easily repeat the success of *Literary Lapses* with *Nonsense Novels* (1911), a series of short parodies of various literary genres that Leacock had grown up with and that were still familiar to a substantial readership: tales of mystery and the supernatural, romantic stories of adventure and love, American parables of success, Utopian fantasy narratives. Although in the Preface to *Sunshine Sketches* he insists that writing "something out of one's own mind" is much more difficult than the writing of "solid, instructive stuff fortified with facts and figures" (xvii), most of the casual ridicule of easy targets in his first two humorous books probably cost Leacock little effort. He would continue producing collections like this, with little thought except to sales and to the mild amusement of a not-very-demanding readership, for the next thirty years.

The early signs of Leacock's mechanical attitude to literary production make all the more surprising the appearance, only a year after *Nonsense Novels,* of his literary masterpiece, *Sunshine Sketches*. Written with his usual energy, most of the chapters appeared as a serial in the *Montreal Star* from January to June, 1912, before being issued as a book by John Lane's Bodley Head publishing. *Sunshine Sketches* is one of Leacock's most personal books, yet at the same time rather elusively impersonal as a biographical document. In part, it expresses nostalgia for a village world that seemed to be passing away in the twentieth century, a world based on his own boyhood and on his summer experiences in Orillia. Its portraits of small-town people are consistently amusing, sometimes affectionate, and sometimes witheringly satirical. Insofar as *Sunshine Sketches* suggests anything about its author, it suggests a man who lived both within and without the world of Mariposa, longing for the simplicity of village life yet making fun of the simplicity when he found it; setting up this life as an ideal yet discovering many signs of corruption within it.

Whatever ambivalences of attitude the author may have had about his material, there was little doubt of his readers' responses. *Sunshine Sketches* was a popular and critical success in Canada, England, and the United States. American and British readers and reviewers were sometimes mystified by the Canadian references, but most of the images of small-town life were universal enough to appeal to readers all over the world.

A great deal of speculation has been devoted to the question of Leacock's relationship with the people of Orillia, especially after the publication of *Sunshine Sketches*. One frequently propagated opinion holds that the townspeople never forgave him for his accusations of their dishonesty and hypocrisy. Some commentators have suggested, on the other hand, that Orillians were among the most amused readers of the *Sketches*. Another possibility is that few of the local citizens even read the book, or were more than vaguely aware of who Leacock was. "I personally never realized that the man was a writer," one local old-timer was quoted as saying (Anderson 153-56).

The success of *Sunshine Sketches* encouraged Leacock to produce *Arcadian Adventures with the Idle Rich*, which directs its satire at life in an unnamed North American city, unmistakably based on Leacock's other main stamping ground, Montreal. The charlatans and fools of big business, religion, and upper-crust society bear a good deal of resemblance to their rustic counterparts in Mariposa, but the satire now takes on a sharpness that leaves no room for the affection that the *Sunshine Sketches* narrator finds for the little town. The two books taken together suggest

Leacock's preference for the "home town" he freely chose to spend his idyllic summers in, over the city to which he was committed out of professional necessity.

In addition to *Arcadian Adventures*, in 1914 Leacock produced three small books on early Canadian history for the popular Chronicles of Canada series, as well as his usual annual complement of scholarly and journalistic articles. This prolific publication schedule was only slightly disrupted by the outbreak of the First World War, when Leacock entered a new stage of his career by taking to the public lecture platform to give a series of comic talks and readings in Canada and the United States for the benefit of the Belgian Relief Fund. The war affected Leacock profoundly, and his obsession with it is reflected for several years in both his comic writing such as the sketches collected in *The Hohenzollerns in America* (1919), and his more serious work such as *Essays and Literary Studies* (1916).

Pessimism about the war also undoubtedly strengthened his fervently conservative political, social and economic opinions, which were entrenched in the British imperial heritage and its sometimes archaic and aristocratic values. Throughout his life Leacock remained outspokenly opposed to such modern harbingers of historical change as women's suffrage, republicanism, and immigration of non-European peoples. His published opinions on such subjects are the frequent source of the critical distaste expressed for his work. Yet as a thinker and commentator on the modern world, Leacock was actually ambivalent, even paradoxical. Although a professed British imperialist, he was an enthusiastic admirer of the United States, and spent a great deal of time on his lecture tours as an uncritical observer of the ethnic cosmopolitanism and casual manners of the republican way of life. If his commitment to his British heritage helped preserve his belief in the value of the past, his experience of the supposedly forward-looking and exuberant modern American way of life seems to have helped him to overcome some of the gloom he felt about the devastating effects of the European war.

But if his thoughts on the public prospects of the world could be ambivalent or pessimistic, he was greatly cheered in his personal life by the birth of his only child on 19 August, 1915. Although a mysterious condition affecting the child's growth was to cause Leacock much anxiety in later years, he could write his mother happily on the day of birth that Stephen Jr., "Stevie," was "a fine big boy ... in fact a regular corker" (letter to Agnes Leacock, 19 Aug. 1915, Leacock Museum). The birth interrupted his public speaking schedule, but by February 1916 he was off again on his travels, through southern Ontario and the United States. Although the volunteer war work was unpaid, Leacock had by this time moved into a very comfortable financial bracket. In 1917, his gross annual income, according to tax work sheets he preserved, was fourteen thousand dollars—a handsome figure if seen in the context of the fact that his professor's salary at McGill amounted to only about four thousand a year. With this kind of income, he could enjoy fully his dual life as McGill scholar and Orillia gentleman farmer.

Although he was a founding member of the Canadian Authors' Association in 1921, Leacock had little contact with other members of the Canadian literary milieu. He occasionally encouraged younger authors who wrote fan letters to him or who emerged from among his McGill students, but on the whole he much preferred the company of his academic colleagues or his non-literary friends and acquaintances in Orillia. This isolation is perhaps partly the result of his lifelong indifference to twenti-eth-century literary trends, and his preference for going his own way, writing in an idiom that derived from his Victorian reading tastes (evident in the large remnant of his personal library that survives at the Leacock Museum) and his academic interests. But it was also a matter of personal inclination, the genuine prefer-ence of a congenial person for a simple, non-competitive social circle where he could seek relief from the pressures of his liter-ary and academic activities.

Leacock's devotion to the male pursuits of billiards at the Montreal University Club in the winter and fishing in the summer add support to the allegations that he neglected his wife and child. If such allegations are true, his self-indulgent life was tragically disrupted in 1925, when Beatrix Leacock developed cancer. When doctors in Canada held out no hope, Leacock took her on a vain search for a miracle cure in England, where she died in hospital in December. Leacock left no surviving written com-ments on this personal calamity; only a bundle of carefully preserved letters and telegrams of sympathy, plus his subsequent vigorous commitment of time and money to cancer charities, suggest the intensity of his grief. Perhaps wisely, he returned to his regular working routine soon after the bereavement. To manage his household and to look after ten-year-old Stevie, he hired a secretary-housekeeper, a position filled from 1927 to 1937 by his niece and eventual literary executor, Barbara Nimmo (née Ulrichson). Perhaps partly as an attempt to rid himself of painful memories, in 1928 he had the house at Old Brewery Bay demolished and replaced by a new, larger one—the house that still stands as the Leacock Museum and Memorial Home.

But above all, he returned with vigour to his writing desk. There was no collected volume of humorous pieces in 1925, but he published several magazine articles that year. His articles on history, politics and economics were seldom written now for scholarly journals, but for popular magazines such as the American *Collier*'s and *Harper's*, or the Canadian *Maclean's*. With the zeal of a missionary, Leacock was anxious to take his ideas to the widest possible audience. He was also eager to influence public policy, an eagerness that reached a literary climax in 1930 with the publication of his *Economic Prosperity in the British Empire*, in which he attempted to apply his conservative political ideals to the current economic crisis.

In spite of his conviction that he had cures for the economic ills of the world, or at least of the British Empire, Leacock was concerned about his own financial situation. Although reasonably secure in his academic employment and his income from royalties, he had invested heavily, and worried about over-extending himself. Early in the Depression he wrote to his Canadian publisher, Hugh Eayrs of the Macmillan Company, to complain about his much reduced income. Although he claimed that he had "lost in ... investments as little as anybody of sense would lose," he was unhappy with his diminishing royalties and with the reluctance of publishers to produce and promote his books with the vigour to which he felt they were entitled (draft of letter, n.d., Leacock Museum). Perhaps his worry about personal money troubles and the worsening state of the world led Leacock to write in the 1930s some of his most serious books. Even comic writing itself became a serious subject in his *Humour: Its Theory and Technique* (1935). A general mood of reminiscence focusing on some of his past literary enthusiasms led to two biographies, *Mark Twain* (1932) and *Charles Dickens: His Life and Work* (1933). The latter book is negligible compared to the much more scholarly lives of Dickens in print by the 1930s, but it is significant in relation to Leacock's own life, for Dickens was not only Leacock's favourite author, but also a person with whom he personally identified. Like Leacock, Dickens was a prolific writer, successful public lecturer and reader, congenial socializer but inattentive husband and father, with all the vagaries of emotion and behaviour that inevitably go with such a busy personality. Leacock might have been referring to himself when he wrote that Dickens was difficult "to live with and to live up to. It was not alone the sheer exuberance of his energy, the intensity of his mental life, his thought, his conversation. It was, as he grew older, his impatient temperament, his inability to brook criticism or contradiction, his inordinate desire to be always right" (*Charles Dickens* 214).

Leacock's impatient and vain temperament emerged more and more frequently in the 1930s. In 1935, he indulged in an unworthy squabble with his mother-in-law, Mrs. Kate Hamilton, over some trust fund money left by Beatrix for the benefit of Stevie (Leacock to Mrs. Hamilton, 29 June 1935, Leacock Museum). In the same year, he engaged in a much more public argument with the McGill administration when the university imposed compulsory retirement on him. Although the university was enforcing regulations that Leacock himself had supported, the abrupt and undiplomatic tone of the official notice of retirement enraged him. Before finally withdrawing gracefully from the university with accolades from colleagues and students, he carried on a drawn-out and ultimately futile war of words in the community and campus media ("Senility Gang Execution" 8).

Within months after retirement, however, he seemed reconciled to his new life, and was busier than ever with new books of humour, articles on economics and politics, and a speaking tour of western Canada, a trip recorded in *My Discovery of the West* (1937), for which he won the newly created Governor-General's Award. This volume was a rather incongruous combination of travel humour and serious discussion of the economic ills of the western Canadian provinces, far from one of Leacock's best books, but good enough to be an occasion for this much-overdue official recognition of his literary achievements.

Although retirement was a blow to his ego, it also gave him a release of time which he could amply fill at his writing desk. The "business of growing old," as he described it light-heartedly in a 1940 article ("Three Score and Ten"), disturbed him as he experienced the inconveniences of physical decline and the sometimes callous treatment of the elderly in modern society. But the mere passing of years could not slow his literary output. In the eight years following his retirement he produced no less than seventeen new books, and about ten times that many shorter periodical pieces.

His retirement years were also a time of accolades. "I have had so many honorary degrees & the other day a gold medal that the peerage is all I need," he wrote to a friend in 1936 (letter to Frank [?], copy, n.d., Leacock Museum). After the western tour, he gave up his career as a public speaker, but his books and articles sustained his international reputation, even though his continuing belief in Victorian values such as imperialism, political conservatism, and anti-feminism increasingly alienated him from certain segments of the reading public. The Second World War dismayed him—"I did not realize that it was coming," he lamented (letter to James Keddie, n.d., McGill)—but it revived pro-British sentiment in the Commonwealth countries, and created a demand for such books as Leacock now turned his hand to, *Our British Empire* (1940), *Our Heritage of Liberty* (1942), and *Canada and the Sea* (1944).

In his seventies, Leacock still prided himself on the energy and precision of his literary abilities. "I can hit 3,500 words, to a syllable, knowing [the required length] beforehand," he boasted to an editor who gave him a commission for an article (letter to Mr. Irwin, 5 Feb. 1943, Leacock Museum). But his physical capacities could not be expected to keep pace with his intellect and imagination forever. The inevitable infirmities of old age meant more and more frequent indispositions, spells of hospitalization, and enforced rest. Early in 1944, a persistent sore throat was diagnosed as cancer. The predictably futile surgery followed, and Leacock died in a Montreal hospital on 28 March. In fulfilment of his wishes, he was buried in the Leacock family plot at Jackson's Point, near his mother's grave, and within a few miles of the old family farm.

Critics of Leacock's prodigious literary output have been kept busy for many years with the question of whether he was a great artist or only an entertainer. Much inconclusive commentary has also accumulated from the questions raised by his life story. Was he, as the most vitriolic gossip about him suggests, an egotist who drank too much, neglected his family, preferred the company of his mother or his male cronies to that of his wife and child, and used his literary talents as a means of retreating from more mundane responsibilities? Leacock himself gazes from his remoteness on such questions with the familiar mischievous smile of the many photographic portraits taken of him at the height of his fame. In the end, it is by his literary output that he wanted to be judged. And this output is filled with many deeps and shallows, with as much ephemera as substance, with outmoded and offensive opinions, but often distinguished by moral sensitivity and imaginative brilliance. If such a summary can validly epitomize his achievement as a writer, perhaps it can serve also as an evaluation of his life.

Works Cited

Anderson, Allan. *Remembering Leacock: An Oral History*. Ottawa: Deneau, 1983.

Curry, Ralph L. *Stephen Leacock: Humorist and Humanist*. Garden City, NY: Doubleday, 1959.

Doyle, James. *Stephen Leacock: The Sage of Orillia*. Toronto: ECW, 1992.

Edgar, Pelham. *Across My Path*. Toronto: Ryerson, 1952.

Kimball, Elizabeth. *My Uncle, Stephen Leacock* [original title: *The Man in the Panama Hat*]. 1970. Halifax: Goodread-Formac, 1983.

Leacock, Stephen. *The Boy I Left Behind Me*. Garden City, NY: Doubleday, 1946.

_____. *Charles Dickens: His Life and Work*. Garden City, NY: Doubleday, 1933.

_____. "The Lot of the Schoolmaster." *Essays and Literary Studies*. London and New York: Lane, 1916.

_____. Preface to the Original Edition. *Sunshine Sketches of a Little Town*.

_____. "Three Score and Ten." *My Remarkable Uncle and Other Sketches*. 1942. Toronto: McClelland & Stewart, 1989.

_____. Unpublished letters and other papers. Leacock Museum (Orillia), MacLennan Library (McGill University), National Archives of Canada, Orillia Public Library.

Legate, David M. *Stephen Leacock: A Biography*. Toronto: Doubleday, 1970.

Moritz, Albert and Theresa Moritz. *Leacock: A Biography*. Toronto: Stoddart, 1985.

"'Senility Gang Execution' Described by Leacock." *Montreal Daily Star* 25 March 1936: 35.

Documentary

B.K. Sandwell
How the "Sketches" Started[1]

A writer in the Toronto *Telegram* recently expressed the view that there might be some doubt whether the Little Town of Leacock's *Sunshine Sketches* was actually Orillia, Ont. I do not think there can ever have been any doubt about that in the mind of anybody who was a friend of Leacock's at the time when the *Sketches* were written; but it is satisfactory to learn that there exists a letter in the humorist-economist's own highly characteristic handwriting, which makes the truth indisputably clear. This of course does not preclude the possibility of incidents having been transferred to "Mariposa" which actually occurred somewhere else in the Lake Simcoe district—as is very probably the case with the stranding of the excursion steamer *Mariposa Belle*, as has been suggested by Professor Lower.

The letter, of which a photostat copy exists in the Leacock Section of the Orillia Public Library, was published for the first time by the Orillia *Packet and Times* last month in an article replying to the *Telegram*'s suggestions. It was written in 1943, to George Rapley Banting, a relative of George Rapley, one-time manager of the Traders' Bank in Orillia, and reads in part:

> When I wrote my Sunshine Sketches as a serial story in the Montreal Star (1912), I put George under the name of George Papley. This and many of the other names were too transparent, such as Judge John McGan for John McCosh, etc.
>
> A lawyer friend of mine, Mel Tudhope, of Orillia, now Judge Tudhope, wrote me a mock letter threatening to sue me for libel against these people. It was only fun, but it led the publisher to think it wiser to alter the names so in the book edition they are changed and George Rapley appears under the harmless name of Mullins.

---

[1] From *Saturday Night* (August 1951), p. 7. Used by permission.

But in my book 'Too Much College' (1939) George appears
as George Rapley in the story 'Bass Fishing on Lake Simcoe'.

This will be no news to those of us who heard Leacock tell
practically every one of the Sunshine Sketches as dinner-table
anecdotes, always with the most explicit reference to Orillia and
to Orillian personages. But it is always as well to have things
down in black and white, so that they do not depend on fallible
human memory.

I think I can claim to have been a sort of godfather of the
Sunshine Sketches. My two most intimate friends in Montreal at
that time were Leacock and Edward Beck, who for a short time
around 1912 became Managing Editor of the Montreal *Star*. All
three of us were natives of England who had come out to Canada
in boyhood. Leacock had taught me at Upper Canada College in
1891-3, and we both arrived in Montreal about the same time
around 1901, he as a junior professor in Economics and I as a
reporter on the Montreal *Herald*. Beck arrived several years later
as Managing Editor of the *Herald* after a brilliant journalistic
career in Detroit. As he looked like making the *Herald* a serious
competitor of the *Star*, Lord Atholstan, pursuing his usual policy,
proceeded to buy him away with an irresistible salary offer; but
the salary was the only satisfactory thing about the job, and Beck
remained with the *Star* only for a couple of years, leaving it to
start the Montreal *Financial Times* in association with T. Kelly
Dickinson and myself and with the money of D. Lorne Mc-
Gibbon, then a very active industrial promoter. Beck eventually
became manager of the Pulp and Paper Association.

While Beck was top man at the *Star* (so far as Lord Atholstan
would permit him to be), Leacock achieved his two startling successes with *Literary Lapses* (1910) and *Nonsense Novels* (1911).
This gave Beck the idea of getting Leacock to write a series of
skits for the Saturday issue of the *Star*, and he asked me to bring
the two of them together, which I did. My recollection is that up
to that time they had not met, for Beck had not been very long in
Montreal, and the separation between the academic world of the
McGill campus and the journalistic world of St. James Street was
notoriously complete.

The result of the negotiations was the only really large-scale
commission that Leacock ever received for a fictional job to be
done for a purely Canadian audience. I do not know what the

figure was, but it was probably not large enough to have interested him a few years later, when he was swamped with commis-
sions from American magazines and syndicates; but in 1912 it
was adequate and he had a wealth of material which was not too
suitable for his American buyers and which he was delighted to
have a chance of using. As the letter indicates, he took no trouble
to disguise either the locality or the personages about whom he
was writing. All the stories were shaped out at the dinner-table
in the Leacock home on Côte des Neiges Road, where my wife
and I were frequent guests, and it was a fascinating business to
watch them developing in the telling.

   One of the most effective qualities of the Leacock style is its
close resemblance to that of the spoken story. I can never read a
Leacock piece even now without forming a mental picture of
Stephen talking.

Arthur Lower
The Mariposa Belle[2]

Readers of Stephen Leacock will recall that one of his *Sunshine
Sketches* tells of the sinking of the *Mariposa Belle*, a small
steamer on an inland lake. He gives a playful account of an
excursion, hitting off with skill the various local characters who
are on board and managing to convey through them the impression that, for pure adventure, the excursion ranks with an ex-
pedition to the South Seas. At a critical point an emergency arises
and the ship begins to sink. Amid scenes of terror she settles
slowly down. Yet hope flickers when a boat is sighted, pulling
frantically from the shore. The rescuer draws nearer and nearer.
Unfortunately, by the time he reaches her, the *Mariposa Belle*
has settled to the bottom. It is only a Leacockian tragedy,
however, for the water proves but a few feet in depth and the
little boat sits comfortably on the mud. As for the rescuer, he
puts so much zeal into his effort that when he comes alongside,
he is done for, and it is not the shipwrecked passengers who must

---

[2] From *Queen's Quarterly*, 58 (Summer 1951), pp. 220-26. Used
by permission.

be rescued, but the rescuer.

Leacock's good-humoured satire signalizes the passing of an epoch—that period between the early pioneer days and our modern urban civilisation, when the primitive methods of getting about had been superseded and the ubiquitous gas engine had not come in. It was preëminently the age of steam, and by the steam engine, installed in anything that would float, the back-country of Ontario was opened up. All the way along 'the front', as the shores of the St. Lawrence and the lower lakes were termed, settlement worked back into the bush, supported by steamers wherever lake or river allowed them.

These little inland steamers might be anything—ambitious boats or hardly more than scows with engines. For two generations or more, or until the seventies, when the interior railway system of the province had become fairly complete, they carried the goods, the crops, the animals and the persons of the people in the back townships. After the railways displaced them as common carriers, they were used for pleasure traffic and tried to keep going by means of 'excursions'. The period of the 'excursion steamer' on the secondary waters of Ontario lasted from about 1880 until 1910 or 1915. By the latter year, the internal combustion engine was putting automobiles on the roads and gasoline launches on the water. Everybody could then make his own 'excursion' and the steamer rapidly lost its customers.

Many of these little boats, when they ceased to pay, were tied up to wharves, and they and the wharf rotted away together. Others burned. But it remained for one to achieve the distinction, if not of being shipwrecked, at least of sinking.

That one was the original of the *Mariposa Belle*. Her name was the *Enterprise*.

Leacock was an Orillian, and being such, was, as every citizen of the neighbouring and fairer town of Barrie knows, capable of appropriating any of the unconsidered trifles of the region and building them into the greater glory of his home town. The true centre of light in Simcoe County, however, was the county town, Barrie. There, Lake Simcoe was to be seen at its best; the long reach of Kempenfelt Bay, blue in the sunshine, with the clear line of the horizon opening out at its end, contrasted sharply with the shallow limestone basin, Lake Couchiching, beside which Orillia was built. In those days neither town had a literary man to celebrate it, but when Leacock, on his way to fame, came out with his *Sunshine Sketches*, he made up for lost time. Since then, Orillia has never ceased to pat itself on the back for being the sleepy little town of his sketches.

Orillians apparently will pat themselves on the back at the slightest provocation, for if anyone should suggest to them that their town really is sleepy, he would be run out. This egregious place, not far from the wilderness of the Canadian Shield, grew up as a 'jumping-off point' for the bush: it has never entirely lost the marks of its origin. To this day, I am told, it is full of effervescent, incandescent people who form the strongest possible contrast to their dignified and stable neighbours in Barrie. Anxious to stand in the spotlight, however slender its claims to that position, Orillia, I learn, has sought to add to its fame as a sleepy little town the purely accidental renown of a visit from the great Champlain. It is possible that the explorer passed through "The Narrows" (where Lake Simcoe empties into Lake Couchiching) on his way from the Georgian Bay to the Bay of Quinté, but that seems hardly sufficient reason for erecting a pretentious monument to him on a spot in which he could have had no interest whatsoever. Citizens of Barrie would not erect a monument to the Angel Gabriel, even if a visit from him should actually have taken place. They are their own best monuments, and feel no need of support from men like Champlain. Had Leacock lived in Barrie, he would, as a native son, have been ostentatiously ignored.

In view of the foregoing and in common justice to Barrie, the history of the *Mariposa Belle* incident should be set down correctly.

During the steamboat age, the jealousy between the two towns naturally extended to the boats which plied from them. Orillia's pride was the *Islay*, and toward her Barrieites showed scant respect. Their favourite was the *Enterprise*, a noble bluff-bowed old lady that pushed half the lake along in front of her and covered everyone with cinders when she came in to the wharf. Between supporters of the rival vessels, two major points were under frequent discussion. One related to the question of speed. It was rumoured that the *Islay* could do ten knots (though few knew exactly what a 'knot' was), and alleged that the *Enterprise* could do only nine. As against this, there were eye-witness accounts of how the *Enterprise* had won races, as it were, by a nose. Considerable reliance was also placed on logic: the *Enter-*

prise had two engines, was actually twin-screwed, like a liner. That should have settled it.

The other contentious matter concerned seaworthiness. The inhabitants of the shores of Lake Simcoe were, in the mass, a good deal more familiar with the plough than with the deck of a ship, and in consequence, if they found themselves farther from the shore than the distance you could throw a stone, they became apprehensive. The average excursionist sought above all else placid water and safety. Any minor mishap, such as a little engine trouble, was sufficient to ruin a boat's reputation, for, if such things could happen, she could not be 'safe'. Every excursionist, with certain bold exceptions—persons looked on as not entirely normal, such as the rector whom Leacock depicts (I remember that he was not entirely normal)—went on the waters of Lake Simcoe with a delightful sense of dangerous adventure. On one occasion, a small steamer, caught in a wind between Snake and Fox Islands, began to roll, and the passengers, terrified, called on the Reverend Mr. Blank, who happened to be among them, to lead in prayer. He did so, and they all sang *For Those in Peril on the Sea*. Lake Simcoe was no ordinary lake, and the ships that ploughed it, no ordinary ships. The flat, round *Enterprise*, it was felt, compared with the long, sneaky *Islay*, was definitely 'safe'.

Where these two boats went for the winter, the small boys of Barrie could never discover, but for those boys, it used to be the great event of the year when word went round in the spring that a steamer was coming up the bay. If she should prove to be the *Islay*, that was taken as no great matter, for she was only an old boat from Orillia, but if it were the *Enterprise*, then, indeed, worth had triumphed.

The incident which Leacock purloined for Orillia in connection with his *Mariposa Belle*, occurred in the summer of 1902. The actual facts I here set down.

In the early August of that summer, I was a member of a group of young savages camping down at Big Bay Point, where Kempenfelt Bay joins the open lake. We had, for the first time in our lives, shaken free of our parents, and were shifting, quite satisfactorily, for ourselves. Yet I was glad to learn one day that my mother was coming down from Barrie on the *Enterprise* and that I was to go with her over to Jackson's Point, and return. It was by no means my first trip across the lake, for my earliest memories were of such expeditions. When I was a babe in arms, my grandmother had come out from England to live with us, and one of her favourite diversions was to take a big covered basket of sandwiches and 'go on the boat'. She always took me along with her. So Big Bay Point, Jackson's Point, Belle Ewart, Roche's Point, were familiar excursion calls to me from earliest days.

On this particular trip, I duly met my mother, and we went across the lake to Jackson's Point. It was a beautiful blue and silver day, with not a ripple on the surface. The ten miles across took about an hour. We had our picnic supper, got on board again and the boat pulled out. Returning was as uneventful as going. From Big Bay Point up to Barrie, the boat cut over to the north shore of the bay, and kept fairly close in. This was unusual, for crossing the bay instead of taking a direct course added a couple of miles to the length of the trip.

As we came up the bay, we crept closer and closer to the shore. Then, when we reached the town, an extraordinary thing happened. In those days Barrie had two wharves, one, the more easterly, at the foot of Mulcaster Street; the other, invariably used, at the foot of Bayfield Street. The *Enterprise* put in at Mulcaster Street: in a small boy's eyes, this was as though a C.P.R. liner should dock at St. John's, Newfoundland, instead of coming up to Montreal.

The puzzled passengers went ashore. Nothing unusual was observed aboard the boat. But in the morning, there she was, lying at the wharf, and sitting on the bottom!

Her bows were up, and the great square doors in them, through which her hawsers came out, made her look like a big dead fish. Her stern was well under. There was no doubt about it. She had sunk!

Within a few days she was patched up and pumped out. So far as I could gather, what had happened was that a shaft-bearing had given way and opened up the stuffing-box, which is the point at which the shaft passes through the hull. This had allowed too much water to enter for the pumps to cope with. Many another vessel has suffered such accidents and survived to sail another day. Not so the *Enterprise*. She quietly took flight and never returned. She was not 'safe'. Her Orillian rival had won, and remained to ply the lake in lonely grandeur for another dozen years. That sinking marks the closing of an era. It symbolizes the passing of the little steamboats, the end of navigation on the inland lakes of Ontario.

And may I add my best compliments to the shade of that rare master, Leacock, for the successful and shameless way in which he stole for his town the very weakness of the Barrie steamer, her death in fact? It is true that he talks of outlandish places like Mariposa, Lake Wissanotti, the Lower Ossawippi and other synthetic Indian remainders, but those in the secret know well enough where that stretch of the lake is 'from the big reed beds to within a mile of the town wharf': it is suspiciously close to Orillia—the waters of the rival town are clear and cold and deep. To take a really noble ship—Leacock himself says that after you've been in Mariposa for a month or two and paddled alongside the *Mariposa Belle* in a canoe, you see no difference between her and the *Lusitania*—and reduce her to a mere scow on a shallow little lake, after she had been breasting for decades the waves of one of Canada's minor inland seas, to advertise her last sad trip in that unmistakably Orillian journal, the *Newspacket*, all this, I contend, as a Barrieite, was a typically Orillian piece of work.

Douglas Bush
Small-Town Ontario[3]

... Not being a disciple of Henry James, Leacock did not worry about "point of view." His omniscient narrator can indeed combine contradictory roles. As the agent of the author's enveloping irony, he must be far enough above Mariposans in sophistication to make gentle fun of naive simplicity that poses as sophistication and to explain things a stranger might not understand. A visitor from New York, for instance, might think Mariposa the sleepiest of country towns, whereas it is actually "a mere mad round of gaiety." But the superior role shifts easily into and out of that of a typical Mariposan who shares the limited outlook of most of his fellow citizens. Now and then he touches a cultural nadir, as

[3] From *The Canadian Imagination: Dimensions of a Literary Culture*, ed. David Staines (Cambridge: Harvard University Press, 1977), pp. 123-51. Editor's title.

when he reports that on the excursion boat Lilian Drone and Miss
Lawson, the teacher, have "a book of German poetry,—Gothey
I think it was." But when Dean Drone has heard one of his flock
say that "the Church would be all right if that old mugwump was
out of the pulpit" and has been cut to the heart by the mysterious
word, the narrator—who can report that he has "seen" the Dean
searching the encyclopedia and has "known" him to turn over
Animals of Palestine in vain quest of the deadly creature—the
narrator rises above even his own superior level to remark that
"It must have been unknown in the greater days of Judea." Quite
often the tone of an item is such that it may be taken as either
superior irony or irony veiled as Mariposan simple-mindedness:
Peter Glover, the hardware dealer, "was a Presbyterian, till they
ran the picket fence of the manse two feet on to his property, and
after that he became a freethinker." The author could hardly have
achieved the rich, mellow flavor and atmosphere that pervade the
book if the narrator had not thus been allowed to shift his two or
three masks with entire freedom—somewhat like the men of
Mariposa, who all belong to all fraternal organizations, including
the Orange order, and celebrate with equal gusto the days allotted
to national saints, St. Patrick, St. Andrew, and St. George, and
the Fourth of July as well. The last sentence of the book, as we
shall see, gives a clue to the narrator's real status—and to his use
of the spontaneous speaking voice which so largely sets the tone
of the whole.

A very few Mariposans have some intellectual pretensions,
still fewer have any intellect. One marginal exception is that
"complete eggnostic," Mallory Tompkins, the young man who
works on the *Mariposa Times-Herald* and is a great reader. He
is always buying huge encyclopedias on the installment plan and
is an expert on anything beginning with the letter *A*, because the
volumes are always reclaimed by the salesman before reading has
got any further. Another intellectual is Dr. Gallagher, who, looking out from the *Mariposa Belle*, thinks of the journeys of Champlain, while Dean Drone, beside him, thinks of the wonders of
creation and of Xenophon's long march; the one wishes that he
could have known Champlain, the other that he could have
known Xenophon.

Other people have less disinterested dreams, some fulfilled
(for Peter Pupkin and Josh Smith), some not (for Mallory
Tompkins and Jeff Thorpe). Dean Drone is a special case.

Through years of preaching in the little old church he had hoped "to rear a larger Ark in Gideon, ... to set up a greater Evidence, or, very simply stated, to kindle a Brighter Beacon." The dream was in time fulfilled, though it brought that ever-worsening nightmare of debt which haunted the Dean's mind. He is surely Leacock's richest creation; he yields continual amusement, yet all his weaknesses are viewed by the author, and hence by us, with a benevolent, indeed an affectionate, eye. One would like to quote every word said by and about him.

The Dean's dream may not be wholly unrelated to the less exalted dreaming of the people whose civic pride and ambition aspire to the size and standing of a city, a status achieved in inflationary talk, in spite of the census. Jeff Thorpe's speculative enterprises (undone by rascals in New York), the idea—which the bank manager brought back from the city—of the Whirlwind Campaign to pay off the church's debt, the shady doings in everyday life of such a mastermind as Josh Smith, and his opponent's tactics in the election—these endeavors attest the more energetic citizens' craving to emulate urban ways and become bigger than they are. Even small, backward Mariposa was stirred by the Canadian "boom" of the period. In the remote Maritime Provinces Peter Pupkin's father, the builder of a far-flung financial empire, could cherish conflicting dreams. He had such a longing for the simple life that "He often bought little old farms, just to try them, but they always turned out to be so near a city that he cut them into real estate lots, without ever having had time to look at them." Yet, on his flying visit to Mariposa at the time of the bank robbery, this giant of finance quickly became "one of the boys."

The attractions of littleness and bigness come together, and move apart, in the last chapter. "*L'Envoi*. The Train to Mariposa" is both a fond farewell to the little town and a sort of anticipation of *Arcadian Adventures*. For the fact is that the tycoons of Toronto and Montreal had been boys in Mariposa and are always thinking of going back to see the old place. As the train approaches the town and the passengers begin to recognize the once familiar scenes, they forget the rat race of money-getting in the city and grow chummy with the conductor and brakemen. But all this is nostalgic dreaming. The passengers, the dreamers, are really "sitting here again in the leather chairs of the Mausoleum Club, talking of the little Town in the Sunshine that once we knew"—"we," for the narrator, who has such intimate, loving knowledge of Mariposa, is an urban émigré too. If the reader, who fully shares such nostalgic bewitchment, would not care to live out his life in what the harsh light of common day reveals as a cultural desert, it is none the less a far more attractive one than the Plutoria Avenue of *Arcadian Adventures*.

But before we come to that book, which is set in the United States, we may ask a question, less easy to answer than it seems, about the unmistakably Canadian quality of *Sunshine Sketches*. Anyone who grew up in such an Ontario community in the early 1900s can attest that, for all the bits of farcical extravagance Leacock could never resist, in spirit and most of the time in data the book is thoroughly authentic, so far as it goes. This last proviso is put in because, as the word *Sunshine* indicates, Leacock's portrait allows no really disfiguring warts. Comic realism there is in abundance, but not the sober realism of, say, the smaller Ontario village recreated in Robertson Davies' *Fifth Business*. Mariposa is nearer, if not very near, to Thornton Wilder's "Our Town" than to Sherwood Anderson's Winesburg—and a world away from Masters's Spoon River. Some of Leacock's characters and incidents could perhaps have appeared, with little change, in a picture of a small town in the United States, but although he normally wrote with an eye on the American scene and the American market, *Sunshine Sketches* was in countless ways so essentially Canadian that, outside Canada, it seems to have had far less appeal than *Nonsense Novels* and other books mainly compounded of crackling foolery.

One may be hard put to it to define the meaning of "Canadian" in general or in regard to *Sunshine Sketches*. In an area where many and more informed people than I have not, so far as I know, had much success, I could not hope to do much better than Dean Drone in his vain efforts to write a letter of resignation. To raise the problem to a higher level and a greater theologian, I find myself in the same situation as St. Augustine when he sought to define time: "What is time then? If nobody asks me, I know: but if I were desirous to explain it to one that should ask me, plainly I know not." One may indeed doubt whether, in the early 1900s (or now, for that matter), Canada was or is a sufficiently old, stable, homogeneous, and cohesive nation to have a definable national character. It would be—or rather, in the early 1900s it would have been—easier to define the varying characters of the nine provinces. Ontario had, we may be sure, many little towns like Leacock's Orillia, but we may also be pretty sure that there were few or none in any other province. Except perhaps in its eastern and northern extremities, Ontario was predominantly Anglo-Saxon and Protestant. This most populous and prosperous province had many descendants of Untied Empire Loyalists, that is, people who had left the American colonies rather than support the Revolution; it had had also a steady stream of emigrants from Britain (including the Leacocks) who perpetuated British ways, from class consciousness down to cockney accents and "fish and chips." Toronto, now so large and multinational, was, in its conception, almost the heart of the Empire, and most towns and villages were more or less proudly if dimly conscious of Canada's filial relationship: "Daughter am I in my mother's house, / But mistress in my own"—an attitude much altered in later years. "Everybody remembers," says the narrator in *Sunshine Sketches* (and I remember), the Canadian tour of the Duke of York (later George V). Mariposans regretted that he would get such a false idea of the town from seeing only the railway station and the lumber yards; in their loyal address they considerately refrained from alluding to the trouble over the town wharf and the row about the location of the new post office. Aged Canadians have too a different kind of memory: of the general response—outside Quebec—to the South African war and, above all, the crusading spirit of multitudes of young men who volunteered for a better cause, the First World War. And Canada joined at once in the Second—we may recall Colonel Lindbergh's protest.

As for peacetime activities, painting and music and little theaters flourished in Toronto and lesser cities and some towns. Imaginative writing was, with a few notable exceptions, inadequately nursed by patriotic and parochial sentiment, and such products could make small headway against the flood of American publications. Since those days, sophisticated writers have multiplied and Canadian literature has gained a place—a modest place, to be sure—in the contemporary world.

In small towns politics and religion were of much general concern. In politics there were the two traditional British parties: to adapt Sir William Gilbert's words, every boy and every gal born in Canada alive was either a little Liberal or else a little Conservative. (In Mariposa party spirit ran high around election time. Even the pacific Dean Drone preached from such texts as

"Lo! is there not one righteous man in Israel?"—which was "a signal for all the liberal business men to get up and leave their pews." On the other hand the Presbyterian minister, denouncing "the elevation of the ungodly into high places in the commonwealth," proceeded "to show from the scriptures that the ancient Hebrews were Liberals to a man, except those who were drowned in the flood or who perished, more or less deservedly, in the desert.") The emotions I recall did not reach that feverish intensity; and I might say that my own town engendered one of Ontario's premiers, Sir James Whitney, a man of complete honesty far above Leacock's Josh Smith or John Henry Bagshaw.

The religious spectrum was much wider than the political. My very small town, hardly half the size of Mariposa, had thriving Anglican, Methodist, Presbyterian, Lutheran, and Roman Catholic churches. After a particularly destructive fire the colorful Catholic priest, anathematizing from his pulpit the primitive fire brigade, declared that "a couple of little dogs could have done as much." The Anglican church was a massive, handsome stone edifice, without a shadow of debt, thanks to a large congregation and a zealously active rector. Every summer he chartered a steamer for a money-making excursion on the St. Lawrence, an event attended by the prolonged whistle-blowing and other phenomena (except sinking) that Leacock records of the excursion on the *Mariposa Belle*. Ecumenical spirit was in advance of its time: parades of the Knights of Columbus had the use of the Orangemen's drum (or perhaps it was the other way about). I recall a kindred display of civic magnanimity: on the death of a rich and prominent alcoholic, our town council toured New York State in quest of a model for a drinking fountain to be put up in his honor.

In little Ontario towns many people had an old-fashioned, wholesome steadiness, integrity, and dignity, a good share of what bourgeois intellectuals now stigmatize as "bourgeois virtues." And, whatever the cultural deficiencies, gentility was not altogether lacking: matrons of standing had their "day" for receiving callers (armed with cards), and some elderly husbands wore silk hats and Prince Alberts to church—as Leacock's Peter Pupkin does, though I never beheld a young bank teller in such attire. In general there was, so to speak, a mixture of the sedate proprieties of, say, Mrs. Gaskell's Cranford and the raw, contagious energies of Canada's mighty neighbor; both strains contribute their incongruities to the overflowing humor and comedy of life in Mariposa. Possibly, to echo Leacock's phrase again, the self-indulgent garrulousness of my reminiscences may help a bit to confirm if not to define the Canadianism of *Sunshine Sketches*. The book should have been and should be, outside as well as inside Canada, the uniquely beloved work in the Leacock canon because its account of people and their ways is a very funny, very warm-hearted Canadian or Ontario version of humanity as it was in almost any small town in the Western world.

Criticism

Peter McArthur
Praise and Caution[4]

... Mr. Leacock's most ambitious book is the series of "Sunshine Sketches" that reveal the town of Mariposa and its typical inhabitants. In commenting on it himself he points out all the faults that could be pointed out by the most censorious critic. "I wrote this book with considerable difficulty. I can invent characters quite easily, but I have no notion as to how to make things happen to them. Indeed I see no reason why anything should. I could write awfully good short stories if it were only permissible merely to introduce some extremely original character, and at the end of two pages announce that at this point a brick fell on his head and killed him. If there were room for a school of literature of this kind I should offer to lead it. I do not mean that the hero would always and necessarily be killed by a brick. One might sometimes use two. Such feeble plots as there are in this book were invented by brute force, after the characters had been introduced. Hence the atrocious clumsiness of the construction all through."

As a story, "Sunshine Sketches" has no plot. Very well. After reading it, we prefer our novels that way. The reader is satisfied, even though nothing happens. It has no suspended interest. True, but it has a sustained chuckle that keeps us going from page to page without any thought of skipping or stopping. And often the fun of the book bubbles over in hilarious nonsense, as when Mr. Bagshaw, on his return from Ottawa, "Went into Callahan's tobacco store and bought two ten cent cigars and took them across the street and gave them to Mallory Tompkins of the *Times-Herald* as a present from the Prime Minister."

The characters are such as you would find in any small town,

---

[4] From *Stephen Leacock* (Toronto: Ryerson Press, 1923), pp. 136-39, 158-63. Editor's title.

and the things they say and do and think in the book are the things they are saying and doing and thinking in a thousand small towns to-day. But in real life we have no chuckling master of ceremonies to bring them out and show their weaknesses and absurdities—and human decency. The people of Mariposa are revealed in another sunshine than of the every-day sun—the sunshine of a spirit that is wise and tolerant and amused. He reveals the law-breaking and cunning of Josh Smith—now legally extinct—as ruthlessly as if he were an investigator of the muck-raking period, yet makes the fat rascal so human and deep-read in human frailty that we know he must be descended from a younger scion of the Falstaff family who adventured to the New World in the days of Elizabeth or James. The prohibition wave may have swept the saloon from existence, but it breaks in vain against the colossal figure of "JOS. SMITH, PROP." And it is doubtful if the waves of time will submerge him any more than the prohibition wave.

There is not a character in this book that is not in place in a New World small town, and nothing happens that would not happen in any other small town. Only a touch of literary gloom would be needed to make this picture of contemporary life as sordid and mean and futile as any to be found in the most depressing "best seller." But the sunshine in which it is revealed has transfigured it. And the sunshine never fails. Judge Pepperleigh and Dean Drone and Henry Mullins, and all the rest of them, move through the years, aureoled in kindly light and laughter. The art of "Sunshine Sketches" successfully blends the keen observation of the realist with the glamour of the idealist. Whether the book ranks as a classic time alone can tell, but for the present it is very satisfying.

. . . .

But there is one point that gives me some disquietude. Mr. Leacock has poked fun at everything and everybody—except the modern enterprising publisher. And yet the publisher has deserved his satire more than any one else. If any one has done Mr. Leacock harm it is the publishers, syndicate managers and directors of lecture bureaus. It is true that he gives them a love tap in his essay on O. Henry. This shows that he is aware of the danger of listening to their blandishments, and that is a hopeful sign. But they have already tried to direct the current of his literary output, as is shown in the following announcement which ushered "Winsome Winnie and other Nonsense Novels" to the public:

"It is in response to repeated requests that these new novels have been written."

Quite so. Because "Nonsense Novels" were a wonderful success the publisher wanted more of them. I can imagine him beside Leacock's desk, "squat like a toad," and urging the certain profits to be made from a new book of burlesques. Or perhaps he took him to the top of a high mountain and showed him the world full of people laughing at "Nonsense Novels"—and the rich royalties pouring into the bank account of the author. If so, it is a pity that Leacock did not push him over a cliff and watch him land in a squashy mess among the fossils and geological specimens in the talus at its base.

The curse of modern literature is the enterprising publisher. If one book succeeds, every publisher tries to lure or bulldoze the author, and every other author over whom he has influence, to write another book like it that will be a sure winner. And if the harried author cannot do it the enterprising publisher takes whatever book he writes and puts a jacket on it that will fool the public into thinking that it is like the prosperous best seller of the hour.

Some day an enterprising publisher will undertake to publish the Bible along up-to-date lines. When a society novel makes a hit and sets the fashion, he will issue the Bible with a jacket my Montgomery Flagg, showing Vashti or the Shulamite. When "he man" stories are the rage, he will issue it with a Lyendecker jacket, showing Samson leaning on the jaw-bone after doing his day's work. A rage for "Back-to-Nature" novels will inspire a new edition with a jacket by Livingstone Bull, showing Nebuchadnezzar out to pasture.

Up to the present the publisher has not done Mr. Leacock as much harm as he has to most modern authors who have had a measure of success, but I shall not feel satisfied until he turns and rends him. Only then can we be sure that he has realized the danger and that his genius is free to develop along its own lines.

Not that the later burlesques are without merit. The trouble is that they are following an indicated line of success—and that way badness lies. Although Mr. Leacock's later books have been hailed with delight and an unvarying chorus of laughter, there are many sketches that have as much pathos as humor. Take the "Hohenzollerns in America," for instance. The study of the deposed Kaiser is essentially pathetic, and, although it may seem to many a broadly comic touch to marry off the faithful princess to the iceman, one cannot help hoping and believing that she lived happily ever after.

If the publishers and the public could get over their hysterical demand for comedy and read Stephen Leacock's writings with discernment, they would soon realize that his power of pathos is never less artistically sure than his command of laughter. His great danger is that he may be misled by an insistent and profitable demand into the modern evil of specialization—an evil with which he has dealt in his literary essays—and will give too free a rein to his genius for fun. As matters stand he is one of the truest interpreters of American and Canadian life that we have had; but by giving free play to all his powers he may finally win recognition as a broad and sympathetic interpreter of life as a whole.

In the classical masterpieces of the past great scenes and speeches and characterizations were shown against a background prepared by the poet or literary artist. In the lapse of time the great passages tend to become separated from their matrix and are enjoyed by themselves without the cumbersome machinery by which they were introduced. The conditions of modern literary expression—through magazines and serial publications—are such that a writer elaborates his fine scenes without other background than the evanescent interests of his own time, that may or may not have served as their inspiration. To the casual student this gives to much contemporary writing a fragmentary aspect. It may even give a sense of discouragement to the artist himself. Mr. Leacock somewhere expresses a sense of the trivial character of his sketches, as compared with the broad canvases of the great masters of the past. This dissatisfaction is unwarranted, for against the background of his own time the mass of his productions has a scope and richness that will enable it to bear comparison with the work of master artists working in other times and in other circumstances. As time passes, his finest work will tend to enter into comparison with the great passages that embody the literature of the past. How it will bear this comparison no critic can determine, but Mr. Leacock need not fear for the future of his work on the ground that it lacks breadth and volume. He has produced under the conditions and limitations of his own time, just as the acknowledged masters produced under the conditions and limitations of their times, and in the final verdict of mankind his work will be judged with the same impartiality as that of the established master writers, whose power he admires and applauds.

Desmond Pacey
The Eighteenth-Century Tory[5]

... Leacock's next book was his greatest: *Sunshine Sketches of a Little Town*. Here Leacock the gentle ironist and satirist found the ideal subject, and the ideal approach to it. All his best qualities—his benevolence, his common sense, his humanity, his whimsical yet ironic observation—come to a focus in this book. His eighteenth century values and preferences are also quite clearly displayed here. He creates an idyll of a small community based on the farming life of the surrounding area, and for the closest approach to the picture which emerges we must go to the "sweet Auburn" whose passing Oliver Goldsmith so movingly lamented. In Mariposa, life moves at a snail's pace, and there is time for the courtesy and contemplation which have been crowded out in the industrial metropolis. Dean Drone, sitting in his garden over a book of Theocritus, is more like the parson of Auburn than the modern go-getting cleric whom Leacock was later to pillory in *Arcadian Adventures with the Idle Rich*. Josh Smith, with his "chequered waistcoat of dark blue with a flowered pattern," "his shepherd's plaid trousers," "his grey spats and patent leather boots," is an innkeeper whom Fielding would have recognized or Dickens seized upon as a survivor from an earlier and more ample day.

---

[5] From *Creative Writing in Canada: A Short History of English-Canadian Literature* (Toronto: Ryerson, 1952; rev. 1962), pp. 113-15, 117-18. Title from article by Pacey.

But of course Mariposa is not merely an eighteenth century English or Irish village transferred to twentieth century Canada: it is also recognizably a Canadian small town. There were, and happily there still are, such communities in which the noises of the contemporary industrial era are heard only as a faint and distant murmur, and out of them, as we have seen, dozens of Canadian regional novelists were making their novels. Leacock could write as nostalgically, as sentimentally and more sincerely than any of them about the beauties of the region. He wasn't joking when he wrote, in "The Marine Excursion of the Knights of Pythias," that "You may talk as you will about the intoning choirs of your European cathedrals, but the sound of 'O Canada' borne across the waters of a silent lake at evening is good enough for those of us who know Mariposa."

He wasn't joking—or was he? It is the ambiguity, the subtle irony of *Sunshine Sketches* which makes it such a fascinating book. Leacock was aware of the sunshine of Mariposa, but he was also aware of its littleness—for there is irony in the title as everywhere. In contrast with big cities like Montreal and New York, Mariposa is a utopia, a blessed spot which the tide of industrialism has almost completely passed by. When "The Whirlwind Campaign in Mariposa" fails to produce the results that a similar financial drive had achieved in the city, Leacock drily comments: "It may be that there are differences between Mariposa and the larger cities that one doesn't appreciate at first sight." And the flaws in Mariposa life are chiefly things which, like the whirlwind campaign, arise from a misguided desire to ape the cities. Mariposa isn't content to be a sleepy small town: it wants itself to become a metropolis. Hence we get genial satire such as this:

> In point of population, if one must come down to figures, the Canadian census puts the numbers every time at something round five thousand. But it is very generally understood in Mariposa that the census is largely the outcome of malicious jealousy. It is usual that after the census the editor of the Mariposa Newspacket makes a careful re-estimate ... and brings the population up to 6,000. After that the Mariposa Times-Herald makes an estimate that runs the figure up to 6,500. Then Mr. Gingham, the undertaker, who collects the vital statistics for the provincial government, makes an estimate from the number of

what he calls the "demised" as compared with the less interesting persons who are still alive, and brings the population to
7,000. After that somebody else works it out that it's 7,500;
then the man behind the bar of the Mariposa House offers to bet
the whole room that there are 9,000 people in Mariposa. That
settles it, and the population is well on the way to 10,000, when
down swoops the federal census taker on his next round and the
town has to begin all over again.

The best sustained chapter in *Sunshine Sketches*—"The Spec-
ulations of Jefferson Thorpe"—is perhaps the clearest example of
this satire upon the corrupting influence of modern industrialism
and the worship of material success. This chapter describes the
effect upon Mariposa of one of the great financial booms which
were characteristic of this generation of Canadian life—the boom
occasioned by the discovery of silver deposits in the Cobalt area.
The town goes wild, the young bank teller commits suicide and
the laconic barber, Jefferson Thorpe himself, loses all his
savings. Of course the dominant tone of the piece is farcical, but
it is the kind of farce which T.S. Eliot detected in *The Jew of
Malta*—farce with a bite to it.

The theme is absent from the tedious chapters of nonsense
dealing with the love affairs of young Pupkin, but it reappears in
the sketches describing the 1911 election in Mariposa. In election
time, Mariposa is inevitably caught up in the stream of the
national life. The town exhibits, on a small scale, all the cheap
rhetoric which distinguished that most malicious election campaign in Canada's history. How neatly, by the slightest of
exaggerations, Leacock suggests the falseness of it all:

> I only knew that it was a huge election and that on it turned
> issues of the most tremendous importance, such as whether or
> not Mariposa should become part of the United States, and
> whether the flag, that had waved over the school house at
> Tecumseh Township for ten centuries, should be trampled under
> the hoof of an alien invader, and whether Britons should be
> slaves....

It is Josh Smith who wins the election—Josh Smith, the hotel
keeper, running as a Tory on a temperance ticket—and he wins
by a trick, as the result of a premature election report coming,

characteristically, from the city!

. . . .

Leacock was, in outlook and in actual political affiliation, a Tory; but he was a Tory of the eighteenth century rather than of the twentieth. His Toryism had nothing of the cynical callousness of Big Business; it was the Toryism of Goldsmith and of Burke, which saw in the traditional decencies and duties of an agricultural society the proper basis for community. His literary role was similar to that of Chaucer, seeking to preserve amid the growing commercialism and corruption of his century the values of feudal solidarity, chivalric courtesy and the ancestral faith; similar also to that of Addison, attempting to persuade the new middle class to take on something of the culture and humanity of the landed gentry; similar to that of Dickens, calling amid a squalid industrialism for the colour and kindness of a slower age; similar, finally to that of Twain, yearning amid the tinsel of the Gilded Age for the simple virtues of pioneer America.

It was from such men that Leacock learned, and it is with them that he has his closest affiliations. Like him, they were all genial satirists, laughing philosophers, but in them all, as in him, there was a serious underlying purpose. Was Leacock their equal? That is, perhaps, an idle question: time alone can answer it. The late Dr. G. G. Sedgwick came as close to an answer as anyone is likely to come for decades when he declared: "He is not one of the Great Ones, but he may sit at the same table."

If he was not "one of the Great Ones"—and it is true that the vast bulk of his work is ephemeral and that even his best books leave one with the feeling that the man who wrote these could have written better—it was at least in part because of the nature of Canadian society in his period. The prevailing materialism was too strong even for him, for any one man, to resist. In most of his books he went along with the crowd and wrote the kind of nonsense for which they were willing to pay. Canadian culture—as a glance at his literary contemporaries reveals—was still too shallow to support a great artist. But Leacock came much closer to greatness than any other Canadian writer of his generation, and in *Sunshine Sketches of a Little Town* the period found its chief literary justification.

R.E. Watters
Leacock's Canadian Humour[6]

... My conviction is that Leacock wrote Canadian humour, that our national characteristics shaped it, and that they are, in turn, revealed by it. Just as American humour can be distinguished from English, so can Leacock's be distinguished from both. Since Leacock himself was interested in the national characteristics of humour he cannot be numbered among those who consider the "national" quality of a work of literature as either regrettable or irrelevant. Of course, he readily admitted that humour everywhere has a common basis and warned that national distinctions could be overdrawn. Nevertheless, he firmly believed that "the various circumstances of environment, of national character, and of language, at least emphasize and make salient certain aspects of national humour."[7] Repeatedly he addressed himself to the challenge of distinguishing between English and American humour. In 1914 he saw in the jokes of the two countries a "divergence of national taste" which he considered "really fundamental": "The Englishman loves what is literal .... The American ... tries to convey the same idea by exaggeration."[8] His remarks here were followed over the years by many more, too many for me to summarize. For instance, he is reported to have once told Cyril Clemens that "English humour is always based on fact, whereas American humour often deals with what really could never have happened except in the imagination."[9] He has an entire chapter on "National Characteristics" in his *Humour, Its Theory and Technique* (1935), and he had further comments to make a couple of years later in *Humour and Humanity* (1937). In this book he goes into social history to explain the greater popularity of the pun in English humour than in American, and

---

[6] From *Canadian Literature* 5 (Summer 1960): 22-27, 31-32.

[7] His article on "Humour" in *Encyclopedia Britannica* (1945), 11:885.

[8] "American Humour," *Nineteenth Century*, 76: 455-456 (Aug. 1914).

[9] Cyril Clemens, "An Evening with Stephen Leacock," *Catholic World*, 159:240 (June 1940).

to explain why the humour of bad spelling, once so prevalent in the United States, never caught on in England.[10] He analyzes typical English and American jokes to demonstrate the national differences. "There is," he says, "a broad distinction to be made between jokes that proceed by telling the truth and thus landing us in a sort of impossibility, and jokes that proceed to state an impossibility and land us in a truth. These contrasted types correspond very much to the *formal* aspect (not the inner) of typical British and American jokes."[11]

Unfortunately, Leacock seldom talked directly about the characteristics of his own humour, and said even less about Canadian humour generally. It is certain, however, that he never grouped himself with English humorists. Instead, he spoke of himself as an "American" humorist, though he used the word in its continental rather than national sense. The fact that he often contrasted the humour of Britain with that of the United States, but never (so far as I know) made Canada a partner in any contrast, suggests to me nothing more than his awareness of what would most interest his international public. As for his national public, Canadian interest must have seemed negligible, if he took as a sign the amount of attention given to discussion of Canadian humour in our periodicals.

Critics and reviewers in England seem more perceptive than those in the United States of certain differences in Leacock's humour from both British and American. As with Canadian speech, the "American" characteristics in things Canadian are plainly evident to Englishmen. But British characteristics were also readily found in the humour, perhaps because English readers wished to have some claim on the man (after all, his first six years were lived in England!). The Americans felt no such need to discriminate, to look for differences; unlike the English they had nothing to gain, and had no need to placate their neighbour to the north. Canada had never asserted her rights in any aggressive manner; some Canadians, indeed, still think of Leacock as

---

[10] *Humour and Humanity* (London, Butterworth, 1937), pp. 42-49.

[11] *Ibid.*, p. 219.

an Englishman in exile.

But the perceptiveness of English critics, with one notable exception, had more width than depth. Leacock was regarded as something like a literary mason, skillfully applying English craftsmanship to American materials. No thought was given to the possibility that he might have quarried some of his own stone, invented some of his own methods, originated some of the final design. Sir Owen Seaman (of *Punch*) once spoke of Leacock's humour as being "British by heredity" with "something of the spirit of American humour by force of association."[12] Another English critic described Canada as "a sort of half-way house in letters between U.K. and U.S.A.," and therefore found no surprise in Leacock's having discovered "the hilarious mean between American and English humour":

> His fantastical ideas are often in the nature of American hyperbole—but they are developed in English fashion as a rule, in a quiet and close-knit narrative which has none of the exuberance of the typical American humorist.[13]

The notable exception is J.B. Priestley, who finds specific and positive Canadian qualities in Leacock's "outlook, manner, and style," which, he says, not only "belong to the man but ... to the nation":

> Very adroitly he aimed at both British and American audiences, but he never identified himself with either; always, at least when he is at his best, he remains a Canadian ....
>
> The best of Leacock exists somewhere between—though at a slight angle from—the amiable nonsense of characteristic British humour (e.g. Wodehouse) and the hard cutting wit and almost vindictive satire of much American humour ....
>
> It is in fact the satirical humour of a very shrewd but essentially good-natured and eupeptic man, anything but an angry reformer. And two sorts of readers may find it unsatisfactory;

---

[12] Quoted by Ralph L. Curry, *Stephen Leacock: Humorist and Humanist* (Garden City, N.Y.: Doubleday, 1959), p. 152.

[13] *The Living Age*, 311:353 (Nov. 1921). [An anonymous article reprinted in *The Living Age* from *The Morning Post* of Sept. 29, 1921.]

namely, those who prefer humour to be the nonsense of dream-land, in the Wodehouse manner, and those who regard humour as a weapon with which to attack the world.[14]

Beside these words we might place an extract from Lister Sinclair's essay entitled "The Canadian Idiom":

> We are beginning to realize our position in the world, and it is precarious. We lie between the greatest and grimmest of the Grim Great Powers ... and in the middle of the night we some-times dream of hot breath quietly playing on the backs of our necks .... We are very small in population ... [yet] we wish to be influential; we have a small voice, but we wish to make it heard.[15]

Mr. Sinclair also refers to what he calls the "calculated diffi-dence" of Canadians as being a kind of "protective colouration," and goes on to assert that the characteristic Canadian method of making our small voice heard is the use of irony, "the jiu-jitsu of literature ... the weapon of Socrates ... the principle of letting the giants destroy one another by their strength."[16]

Not only in the mid-twentieth century but throughout our history Canada's position has been "precarious." With inner tensions between our bi-racial cultures and provincial section-alisms; with geographic, economic, and military forces pulling vertically within the continent, and with historical, nostalgic, and institutional ones pulling horizontally across the Atlantic; with our vast territory and strenuous climate dwarfing and threatening our numbers and our energies; with all the complexities, in short, which we fully recognize but cannot wholly command, the out-look of Canadians on the world and on human relations is far from identical with that of Englishmen and Americans. We have

---

[14] *The Bodley Head Leacock*, Edited and Introduced by J.B. Priestley (London, The Bodley Head, 1957), pp. 10-12.

[15] Malcolm Ross (ed.), *Our Sense of Identity* (Toronto, Ryerson, 1954), pp. 236-237.

[16] *Ibid.*, p. 240.

never known the easy national security and laurelled self-confidence out of which may issue the "amiable nonsense" of a Wodehouse, nor have we ever had the wealth and strength which can both provoke and withstand the iconoclastic satire of a Sinclair Lewis. While one's home is being shaken by violent winds, one neither blows bubbles nor batters another member of the household.

As a people bent on self-preservation, Canadians have had to forego two luxuries: that of forgetting themselves in gay abandon and that of losing their tempers in righteous wrath. Yet there is a kind of humour that combines full understanding of the contending forces with a wry recognition of one's ineffectiveness in controlling them—a humour in which one sees himself as others see him but without any admission that this outer man is a truer portrait than the inner—a humour based on the incongruity between the real and the ideal, in which the ideal is repeatedly thwarted by the real but never quite annihilated. Such humour is Canadian.

What Lister Sinclair calls our "calculated diffidence" would never draw attention to itself in humour by exuberant slapstick or by linguistic pranks in the form of explosive wisecracks—and there is little of either in Leacock. The Socratic irony of letting the giants destroy themselves by their own utterances is a standard device of Leacock—witness, for example, the self-destruction so wrought amongst university administrators and professors, high financiers, clean-government reformers, and church boardmen in his *Arcadian Adventures With the Idle Rich*. Here Leacock may be, in Priestley's phrase, "anything but an angry reformer," yet a reformer he unmistakably is. So also with the *Sunshine Sketches*. Both these books display neither the "amiable nonsense" of a Wodehouse nor the "hard cutting wit and almost vindictive satire of much American humour." Good-tempered restraint is less easy to detect than slashing attack, and is perhaps less colourful to watch, but it has its own unique value. Given Canada's "precarious" situation of inner and outer relationships, self-restraint means self-preservation. We cannot enforce change or reform with a scourge or bludgeon, because the tightrope we walk is no place for flailing arms. The Canadian satirical weapon is, of necessity, the scalpel of the cool surgeon or the quick flip of the judo expert.

In his recent biography of Leacock, Ralph L. Curry frequently refers to Leacock's "favorite character, the little man in the society too complex for him," who preserves "his dignity by continuing, in his ignorance, to act like a man."[17] Wearing his American spectacles, Mr. Curry has misread Leacock, for the "little man" he describes is portrayed by various American humorists but not by Leacock. In the light of his own description, it is rather surprising that Mr. Curry cites "My Financial Career" as a good portrait of Leacock's "little man." The protagonist of this most famous of all Leacock's sketches is certainly not an innocent overwhelmed by an environment too complex for his understanding.

The truth is very simple: Leacock's "favorite character" was indeed a "little man" but he was a Canadian type, not an American; and "My Financial Career" *is* a good portrait of him but only when its Canadian subject is properly identified and described. In this sketch Leacock introduces us to a somewhat diffident young man who, he tells us, knows "beforehand" what is likely to happen but who nevertheless enters the bank undeterred by this knowledge. The young man has formed an ideal of saving his money and he considers the bank the best place to accomplish his purpose. He understands the essentials of banking, if not the details; he understands how he appears to others (confused, incompetent, helpless, etc.) and also *why* he appears so; he understands what he does wrong while he does it; and above all he understands himself thoroughly, past and present, both his inner self and his outer appearance. Far from preserving any "dignity" by "continuing in his ignorance, to act like a man," he is acutely handicapped by the very completeness of his knowledge. It is true that he cannot control his nervous reactions any more than he can change the atmosphere of the bank—the humour lies in just this ineffectiveness.

. . . .

All these "little men" know their environment, know themselves, know what is expected of them; sometimes they cannot conform, sometimes they will not, but invariably they draw their

---

[17] *Op. cit.*, p. 242 *et al.*

strength from within themselves. The world they choose to live in is a huge one, just as the clothes Stephen Leacock chose to wear were always several sizes too big for him. Yet the essential size and identity of the man inside is unaffected by the bigness outside, even though to outsiders the appearance may seem ridiculously dwarfing.

Leacock's Canadian archetype is therefore radically different in outlook from such a character as Benchley's befuddled little man in an incomprehensible world, or Thurber's Walter Mitty, who can live only by escaping into a fantasy of his own making. To Leacock's "little man" the world is not incomprehensible, nor does he want to escape into fantasy. He wants to continue living in this complex world, preferably by making changes in it to suit himself, but if this is impossible—as it usually is—then to live in this world somehow without sacrificing his self-respect, his principles, or his continuing identity. In an ideal world one should be able to reconcile, through knowledge of both, the outer pressures and the inner desires. But in the real world the actual power to shape and achieve may be lacking. Incongruity between the real and the ideal is everywhere a basis of humour—but which aspect of the real and which aspect of the ideal are not everywhere given the same emphasis. As Leacock said: "The various circumstances of environment, of national character, and of language, at least emphasize and make salient certain aspects of national humour."[18] If my analysis of some pieces of Leacock's work is valid, then certain salient characteristics of his humour are unmistakably national. In our precarious and complicated circumstances, and given our national character, Canadians must either cry with frustration or laugh with Leacock.

All through our history, the favourite intellectual game of Canadians has been to measure ourselves against the British on the one hand and the Americans on the other. We have tended to define what we are almost exclusively by detecting our differences from both. Consequently, if any people anywhere should be especially skilled in the comparative study of human beings considered as groups or types rather than as individuals, it should be us. And we should also be equipped to tell the world whatever

---

[18] See footnote 10, *supra*.

insights into general human nature such processes provide. Now consider what Leacock says:

> Comparison is the very soul of humour .... It is the discovery of resemblance and the lack of it that builds up the contrasts, discrepancies and incongruities on which ... humour depends.

As Leacock well knew, poetic imagery also springs from the perception of similarities and differences; but humour, not poetry, builds upon the resultant discrepancies and incongruities, particularly as applied to types of human nature and typical human behaviour. For generations, then, Canadians have cultivated the soil from which humour springs, and we therefore should not be surprised that out of Canada have come two great humorists to whom the world has given its approval. Men everywhere can detect and savour a special "tang" without caring about its special ingredients or even its origins.

It is noteworthy that Haliburton's humour is almost entirely the result of scrutinizing the differences between Americans, Nova Scotians, and Englishmen. The neglect into which Haliburton's humour has fallen is usually attributed to the lost appeal of dialect humour. A better reason may be that he concocted his Canadian humour for too restricted a contemporary market—for the provincial societies of England, the Eastern United States, and Nova Scotia; his "tang" is too crude for general modern taste. Leacock's blending is much subtler—he left out almost entirely such a strong ingredient as dialectal differences—and thereby he provided a refined seasoning for the humorous feasts of the entire western world, not merely for the Atlantic fringe. Canada has other humorists besides Haliburton and Leacock; they are lesser men, perhaps, but some day the world may discover them too.

Silver Donald Cameron
The Ironist[19]

... Although Leacock's vision in *Sunshine Sketches* appears at
first to be satiric, and although a large element of the book is
undoubtedly satiric, its overall vision is ironic, and in its best
passages the reader must be aware, however indistinctly, that he
is in the presence of basic questions about the nature of truth and
the nature of man. Leacock usually begins with an external view
of his characters and comes gradually to suggest their inner lives
as well; he begins in satire but he ends in irony. Pathos and
humour Leacock considered an ideal blend:

> United, each tempers and supports the other: pathos keeps
> humour from breaking into guffaws and humour keeps pathos
> from subsiding into sobs. It is like the union of two metals,
> one too hard, the other too soft for use alone. (*HH* 233)

Leacock satirizes the romantic illusions of Zena Pepperleigh:

> With hands clasped she would sit there dreaming all the beau-
> tiful day-dreams of girlhood. When you saw that far-away
> look in her eyes, it meant that she was dreaming that a
> plumed and armoured knight was rescuing her from the
> embattled keep of a castle beside the Danube. At other times
> she was being borne away by an Algerian corsair over the
> blue waters of the Mediterranean and was reaching out her
> arms towards France to say farewell to it. (*SS* 93)

During several more paragraphs of roughly the same kind,
Leacock broadens his satire to include the girls of Mariposa in

---

[19] From *Faces of Leacock* (Toronto: Ryerson Press, 1967), pp.
124-28. Used by permission of the author. *HH* refers to Leacock's
Humour and Humanity (London: Thornton Butterworth, 1937); *Leaves*
to *Last Leaves* (New York: Dodd Mead, 1945); *CD* to *Charles Dickens*
(London: Peter Davies, 1933); *AA* to *Arcadian Adventures with the
Idle Rich* (Toronto: McClelland and Stewart–NCL, 1959); and *SS* to
the present text of *Sunshine Sketches*.

general: "... all the girls in Mariposa were just like that." The edge of the satire is sharpened by his contrasting the girls' dreams with their actual situation—gently at first (they are seen against "a background of maple trees and the green grass of a tennis court") and then more incisively:

> And if you remember, too, that these are cultivated girls who have all been to the Mariposa high school and can do decimal fractions, you will understand that an Algerian corsair would sharpen his scimitar at the very sight of them. (*SS* 94)

We are seeing these girls from the outside, and we continue to do so until the last sentence of the next paragraph.

> don't think either that they are all dying to get married; because they are not. I don't say they wouldn't take an errant knight, or a buccaneer or a Hungarian refugee, but for the ordinary marriages of ordinary people they feel nothing but a pitying disdain. So it is that each one of them in due time marries an enchanted prince and goes to live in one of the little enchanted houses in the lower part of the town.

Something has changed; the illusion has become the reality. Leacock has gone over to the girls' point of view and is looking at the world through their eyes; the world as they find it really is the romantic place they thought it was, they are not disappointed in their hopes. When we were laughing at illusion, moreover, we were actually laughing at truth; the laughter now must be at our own expense, since we ourselves seem to have mistaken truth for illusion. To make it even more clear, Leacock continues:

> I don't know whether you know it, but you can rent an enchanted house in Mariposa for eight dollars a month, and some of the most completely enchanted are the cheapest. As for the enchanted princes, they find them in the strangest places, where you never expected to see them, working—under a spell, you understand—in drug-stores and printing offices, and even selling things in shops. But to be able to find them you have first to read ever so many novels about Sir Galahad and the Errant Quest and that sort of thing. (*SS* 94)

Clearly, Leacock is giving us an inside view of the girls' world;

from their viewpoint, what we have considered to be appearance
has become reality. But there is a further twist of the irony here.
So far Leacock has been saying, essentially, that there is no way
to say that one view of the girls' dreams is truer than the other;
it is a purely subjective question. But the passage began by dis-
cussing Zena Pepperleigh in particular, and as the story unfolds
we discover that her dream of marrying an enchanted prince is
literally true, if on a limited scale; Pupkin, the man she does
eventually marry, is working as a bank clerk, more or less
incognito. His father, one of the wealthiest men in the Maritimes
and a former Attorney-General, is a financier who "blew companies like bubbles" and who owns Tidal Transportation Company,
Fundy Fisheries Corporation and the Paspebiac Pulp and Paper
Unlimited. Pupkin, the only son and heir apparent, who has been
sent into the world to make his own name and fortune, is in
actual fact a merchant prince.[20]

The motif of the enchanted houses reappears as we leave that
part of the book which centres around Pupkin and Zena:

> So Pupkin and Zena in due course of time were married;
> and went to live in one of the enchanted houses on the hillside
> in the new part of the town, where you may find them to this
> day.
> You may see Pupkin there at any time cutting enchanted
> grass on a little lawn in as gaudy a blazer as ever.
> But if you step up to speak to him or walk with him into the
> enchanted house, pray modulate your voice a little—musical
> though it is—for there is said to be an enchanted baby on the
> premises whose sleep must not lightly be disturbed. (*SS* 117)

It is still funny: Pupkin is still a comic character, and once again
the reader himself is partially the object of the fun. But the passage is irradiated with Leacock's feeling for both the outside of the

---

[20] A further irony, which I think strained: Pupkin has been sent to
Mariposa at the suggestion of a friend of his father, a friend who
ignores Pupkin in Mariposa. This turns out to be Judge Pepperleigh,
Pupkin's future father-in-law, who has terrified the young man. So the
"foreordained" attachment really is foreordained, though not, perhaps,
in heaven.

house, which is comic, and the inside, the wonder and joy of marriage and family. The humour is based on a paradox: the lover as seen by other men is absurdly foolish and richly comic, but at the same time he inhabits a world which for him is utterly transformed into something fresh, golden and magnificent. That Leacock did see his lovers this way is confirmed by a passage in his own voice:

> For you see, it is the illusion that is the real reality. I think that there are only two people who see clearly (at least as to one another), and these are two young lovers, newly fallen in love. They see one another just as they really are, namely, a Knight Errant and a Fairy. But who realizes that that old feller shuffling along in spats is a Knight Errant, too, and that other is a Fairy, that bent old woman knitting in the corner.
>   This illusion, greater than reality, we grasp easily in the form of what we call art—our books, our plays. (*Leaves* 89)

The book as a whole reveals that Leacock's characters are often developed in the same manner as Pupkin and Zena, a process which reflects in part Leacock's sense of the nature of man in society.

> Human beings are made of aspects, not of realities. Each of us is such and such things from certain angles and in certain lights. We are many things to many people and show to the occasion and the hour a different aspect of our being. It is the art of genius to seize the deceiving aspects of real people and turn them into the realities of imaginary ones. (*CD* 126-27)

Pepperleigh, for instance, seems at first to be a simple caricature of the country judge; he is rabidly Conservative, ill-tempered and pompous, and his judgments are clearly dictated by his private interests—he acquits his son of an assault charge, and he forces the insurance company to pay for the burnt church. Yet when his son is killed in South Africa, Pepperleigh's pain and the support he derives from his wife reveal "a human personality" which for Leacock meant "a soul looking out from the infinite depth of the human eye." (*AA* 87)

Similarly, Josh Smith makes dramatic changes in his hotel in order to draw people so that his liquor licence will be renewed by popular request; he is cynically manipulating his fellow citizens, he intends to close the Caff and the Rats' Cooler as soon as the licence is renewed. Yet the kindly, sympathetic side of the man becomes visible when, at the crucial moment, he does not close up, because to do so would be petty and ungrateful. Jeff Thorpe seems to be a selfish, acquisitive little man, but Leacock reveals that he intends to use his wealth for the poor and the disabled —though Jeff's generous spirit is undercut by making his arithmetic suspiciously faulty. (*SS* 33) The recognition of each other's humanity is an impulse which Mariposa consciously values. Thus Pupkin is terrified that his wealthy father will come to Mariposa and fail to see the human beings living inside the roles and stereotypes. "Just imagine him meeting Jim Eliot and treating him like a druggist merely because he ran a drug store! or speaking to Jefferson Thorpe as if he were a barber simply because he shaved for money! Why, a man like that could ruin young Pupkin in half a day, and Pupkin knew it." (*SS* 101) This pattern is no formula, but it is pervasive; it represents one of Leacock's chief beliefs about his characters.

Robertson Davies
The Satirist[21]

... Certainly *Sunshine Sketches* looks like a move toward writing novels, as Leacock's heroes and exemplars, Dickens and Mark Twain, had done. The godlike view, the assumption by the writer of a power to judge his characters, certainly leads toward the composition of novels of a particular kind. If he had persisted, Leacock might have written another kind of novel—the kind in which characters are described from the inside, instead of being examined from the outside; *David Copperfield* and *Huckleberry Finn* are such novels, known to him and admired by him. But something happened that seems to have warned Leacock away from this sort of work. The Little Town sharply resented the way

---

[21] From *Stephen Leacock* (Toronto: McClelland and Stewart, 1970), pp. 25-26. Used by permission of the author. Editor's title.

in which it had been examined; the author's idea of sunshine seemed to it much more like an inquisitor's spotlight. Only a man of Leacock's remarkable self-confidence and lack of sensitivity toward other people could have thought that it would be otherwise. Strip the book of its humour, and what have we? A community in which the acknowledged leaders are windbags and self-serving clowns, and where the real leader is an illiterate saloon-keeper; a community that sees financial acuity in a lucky little barber who makes a one-in-a-thousand killing in the stock-market; a community that will not support a church, but will swindle an insurance company with a fraudulent fire; a community in which an election is shamelessly rigged; to say nothing of a community where a school- teacher who takes an occasional glass of beer is "the one who drinks" (and thus an unfit person to receive a raise in pay), where the captain of the lake-boat cannot keep it off a shoal, and where a chance encounter between a night watchman and a bank clerk becomes a tale of heroism. We may all know of towns where some of these things or others of the same kind are true, but which of us would boast of being the original of Dean Drone, Judge Pepper-leigh, or John Henry Bagshaw? The Little Town was very angry, and some of its citizens were still angry after Leacock died. It was later that he became a tourist attraction and the occasion of an annual award and banquet to which his own pen could do proper satiric justice.

During the greater part of his career Leacock reiterated, at intervals, his conviction that true humour springs from kindliness and gives no pain. He must have known, in his heart of hearts, that humour is a razor, and even in the most skilled hand it sometimes cuts. The humorist, if we take the word seriously, is akin to the writer of tragedy in his ability to see beneath the surface of life and to see what other men do not see. Of both the comic and the tragic writer people of commonplace outlook say the same thing—that he has exaggerated. Many artists, both in comedy and tragedy, are so naïve as to expect that humanity will be grateful to them for showing how absurd or how desperate human life can be. Leacock showed such naïveté toward Orillia and seems to have been both astonished and warned by the fury and hurt feelings he provoked. He never struck so truly again. He wanted to be liked, and that is a serious weakness in an artist of any kind. He gained his desire, for he was greatly liked—even loved, as time wore on. But his artistry was nipped by an early frost that succeeded the sunshine of the Little Town.

Alan Bowker
The Social Scientist[22]

... Thus all the ideas or institutions which might have put a brake on the human selfishness set loose by the rise of individualism, or might have modified or ameliorated its worst aspects, were in fact destroyed by progress. At the same time, Leacock was chronicling the corruption of politics and government, which were likewise succumbing to the blandishments of a material age. The ideas of materialism, individualism, and mastery of nature were supreme in North America. The result was a dynamic, but increasingly one- dimensional society, a society without critics, without opposition, in which man, pursuing his selfish individual ends in the name of an ideology which perpetuated injustice, headed for moral breakdown and social catastrophe. "The new government of the money power," he wrote in 1917,

> was without a soul. It knew nothing of the ancient pride of place and race that dictated a certain duty towards those below. The creed that was embodied in the words *noblesse oblige* has vanished with the nobility. The plutocrat, unfettered by responsibility, seem[s] as rapacious and remorseless as the machinery that has made him.[23]

This depressing picture was given force and depth in Leacock's most ambitious works of fiction, *Arcadian Adventures with the Idle Rich* and *Sunshine Sketches of a Little Town*. In *Arcadian*

---

[22] From *The Social Criticism of Stephen Leacock*, ed. Alan Bowker (Toronto: University of Toronto Press, 1973), pp.xxix-xxx, xxxii-xxxiii, xxxvii-xl. Used by permission. Editor's title.

[23] "Democracy and Social Progress," in *The New Era in Canada*, ed. J. O. Miller (Toronto: Dent, 1917), pp. 15-16.

Adventures the gloom of the essays is translated into a corrosive satire of an imaginary City in which the values of the age of progress have achieved untrammelled sway. The rich have amassed great wealth, and have arranged the City, and nature itself, according to their will. They live on the 'best' street at the top of the hill, where only 'the most expensive kinds of birds'[24] sing in the trees. Their lives are spent at the Mausoleum Club, an artificial environment of rubber plants, electric lighting, white linen, and soft carpets. They are described as wholly predatory creatures, glaring at each other like greedy and suspicious animals. The slums are kept carefully hidden from them, though the rich are uncomfortably aware of their presence. In general the poor accept their lot, and share the values of the rich.

The plutocrats were not always the inhuman denizens of the Mausoleum Club. They lost their moral sense, taste, and capacity for love during the climb from the slums, or from Mariposa, where many of them originated. This process of transition is depicted in 'L'Envoi' of *Sunshine Sketches,* which connects the two books. We are told that when the plutocrat first came to the City from Mariposa to make his fortune, he dreamed of returning as a rich man to build a frame house on the main street. But when he made money, he built instead a sandstone house in the costlier part of the City, and forgot the small town. Many years later, he and the narrator are going home on the train to Mariposa. 'No,' the narrator tells him, 'don't bother to look at the reflection of your face in the windowpane shadowed by the night outside. Nobody could tell you now after all these years. Your face has changed in these long years of money-getting in the city' (142). In other words, the rich master not only nature but themselves; they suppress all values non-essential to money-making, and identify themselves with what they make and do. In the process they cut themselves off from their own pasts, and from history in general. Life becomes an eternal 'now,' dynamic, fluid, in which everyone and everything is judged by present worth and utility, and discarded when these are gone.

---

[24] *Arcadian Adventures with the Idle Rich* (Toronto: McClelland and Stewart-New Canadian Library, 1959), 1.

The institutions which might have preserved a sense of the past are powerless in this society, and are captured and moulded by its values. The family is merely a group of people under the same roof, with the father making money, the mother pursuing pseudo- avocations, and sons and daughters seeking pleasure. The university, the churches, and the government are treated in more detail. In each case Leacock is careful not only to describe the institution, but to show how it got that way.

. . . .

The City of *Arcadian Adventures* is thus a kind of hell in which the rich, along with the poor and the professional classes, are compelled to exist in a state in which every decent emotion of man hides its opposite, in which, cut off from history, with everything judged by its money value and its utility, men go through the motions of being doctors, professors, ministers, lawyers, and businessmen, with little or no conception of what they are doing or why they are doing it, only that they must continue in order to survive. It is a jungle, but one without beauty or purpose. Leacock allows no affirmations in this book. Like Diogenes, he shines his lantern into every dark corner seeking honesty and finding only corruption and hypocrisy.

Is Mariposa any different? Of course, it is a happier and more innocent place, which has not yet become Plutoria Avenue. But fundamentally, both places believe in the same things: materialism, individualism, and mastery of nature. 'Ask any of its inhabitants if Mariposa isn't a busy, hustling, thriving town. ... ask any of them if they ever knew a more rushing go-ahead town than Mariposa' (2), says the narrator. Mariposa is the boyhood home of the plutocrat; it is the historical antecedent of the City; and at present it is the satellite of the City, aping its values, styles, and ideas, and certainly no more high-minded in religion or in politics. 'It is not for nothing that Mr. Leacock is a student of economics and sociology,' said the august *Review of Historical Publications Relating to Canada* (breaking this once its rule of never reviewing fiction):

> he has been able to grasp many of the typical features of the
> Ontario town. ... Students of Canadian political conditions
> would do well to ponder Mr. Leacock's account of the
> political career of Mr. Josh Smith ... they will find it to

> contain more instructive matter than many a treatise of a
> more pretentious character.

Mariposans, Leacock seems to say, should enjoy the sunshine
while they can.

. . . .

Stephen Leacock was part of that curious and perhaps indige-
nously Canadian species which has been given the name of 'Red
Tory.'[25] Troubled by the intellectual and physical results of the
age of progress, he refused to live in the past, yet feared the
social upheaval rapid change might cause. While we may feel that
at times Leacock doubted too much and hoped too little, we cannot question his sincerity in ardently promoting those measures
of reform which he felt were within the limits of the possible. His
imperialism, his essays, and his best humour all show various
aspects of this social concern, and each serves to deepen our
understanding of the others. Leacock the humorist no less than
Leacock the man is not fully comprehensible unless his intellectual preoccupations and his relationship to the age in which he
lived are clearly understood.

Literary critics for a generation have vexed themselves with
the question: Why didn't Leacock write the Great Canadian
Novel?[26] From a historical viewpoint, several other questions are
equally relevant. Why didn't he go into politics? ('I think that if
he had chosen to go into politics, he could easily have become
prime minister,' said his student and colleague Eugene Forsey;[27]
Leacock on several occasions was offered safe seats but declined,
though he did jokingly say that he would accept a seat in the
Canadian Senate at a moment's notice.) Why didn't he continue

---

[25] *Vide* G. Horowitz, *Canadian Labour in Politics* (Toronto 1968),
3-57.

[26] The best summary of the various positions in this debate, as well
as the most persuasive (but in my mind unconvincing) argument that
Leacock could have been a novelist, is found in D. Cameron, *Faces of
Leacock* (Toronto: Ryerson, 1967), pp. 138-54.

[27] *CBC Times*, 8-14 June 1958, 3.

as an essayist writing witty and biting pieces on all phases of Canadian life, like the ones in this book? Why didn't he fulfil the promise of *Elements* and become a great political scientist if not a great economist? The answers to all these questions have been suggested in this introduction; the point is that Leacock never achieved that supreme excellence which was potentially his in almost everything he did. By focussing attention exclusively on the question of novel-writing, these critics are adopting a highly arbitrary standard for judging human greatness, even literary greatness, and they are forcing upon the events of Leacock's life an order of importance which was not his.

Leacock the man cannot be brushed aside in favour of Leacock the humorist. Leacock the man was concerned with social and political problems, deeply involved in the affairs of his age. He used all his many and varied talents to define these problems to himself and his contemporaries, and to advocate solutions to them as persuasively as he knew how. Only after 1922 did he see himself primarily as a humorist; before this time, in large measure, his humour was but one of the weapons he brought to bear on social problems. He could not see his humour, or any of his other talents, in a vacuum, existing apart from the audiences he wanted to reach or the problems he wanted to solve. Whatever may be the relative literary merits of these writings, however much critics with their hindsight may lament that his genius moved in what seems to them a false direction, we must understand that, given the man Leacock was and the times in which he lived, the path which led from *Elements* through 'Greater Canada,' the essays, *Sunshine Sketches* and *Arcadian Adventures*, and the wartime humour and propaganda, to *The Unsolved Riddle*, was the only one he could have followed.

Even had novel-writing been high on Leacock's list of priorities, his genius probably did not lie in that direction. H.A. Innis, Canada's greatest economist, rightly remarks that the social sciences gave Leacock 'an interest in institutions rather than persons.'[28] The truth of this can best be illustrated by examining the two books which are alleged to be the sign that Leacock was

---

[28] Innis, 'Stephen Butler Leacock,' *Canadian Journal of Economics and Political Science*, X:223.

moving toward the writing of novels: *Sunshine Sketches* and *Arcadian Adventures*. In both books the human characters, however subtly and sympathetically drawn, serve primarily to illustrate the workings of social institutions. The real main characters which emerge are not any of the people, but Mariposa and the City themselves. And this was exactly what Leacock intended. What indication is there that he wanted to say more, or had more to say, about people or about humanity? Novel writing with its demands for psychological insight and rounded characterization would have been foreign both to Leacock's genius and to his major concerns.[29] If we really want to understand him we must cease to fantasize about the novelist who might have been and concentrate our attention on the social scientist who was; for it was a social scientist, not an embryo novelist, who wrote Leacock's best humour.

If we are thus forced to accept Leacock as a relatively stunted plant instead of the mighty oak which might (or might not) have been, there are compensations. To the historian, studying Leacock's many-faceted life against the backdrop of a dramatic and formative period in our history, Leacock's failure to write the Great Canadian Novel or to do any of the other things he might have done is no tragedy; it could be so only to those preoccupied with works and not with lives. If he had specialized more in any field Leacock might have left a more lasting monument, but he would have been a lesser man.

As a social scientist, with forays into politics, imperialism, and humour, Leacock stands out in the intellectual history of Canada. He anticipated several trends in later Canadian thought:

---

[29]Leacock himself recognized that he was not primarily interested in writing about people except as they represented types or the working of human institutions. 'I can invent characters quite easily,' he once wrote, 'but I have no notion as to how to make things happen to them. Indeed I see no reason why anything should. I could write awfully good short stories if it were only permissible, merely to introduce some extremely original character and at the end of two pages announce that at this point a brick fell on his head and killed him. If there was room for a school of literature of this kind I should offer to head it.' Quoted in Innis, 'Stephen Butler Leacock,' 224.

not only the 'Red Toryism' of Grant, but the preoccupation with technology and its relation to the Canadian identity which marked the later career of Innis and has produced Marshall McLuhan. Leacock was one of the first Canadian academics to fuse the insights of the American progressives with the British and Canadian conservative tradition in order to develop an analysis of the United States and North American society which was uniquely Canadian. He needs no apology for either his humour or his social science. 'There are simple minds,' said Harold Innis, 'which adopt Leacock's own statement that political economists regarded him as a humorist and that humorists regarded him as a political economist. According to the lights of this economist [Innis] he did much to save the soul of both in a period in which they were in grave danger.[30] Leacock the social scientist richly deserves Robertson Davies' description of Leacock the humorist: 'A great countryman of ours: a man to thank God for.'[31]

William H. Magee
The Local Colourist[32]

... Local colour, as developed by Maria Edgeworth and other Irish and Scottish novelists early in the nineteenth century, had attracted novelists of manners who wanted to exploit the untried literary topic of special ways of life as opposed to the typical manners of London society. Later novelists like Anthony Trollope in the Barsetshire series revelled in a local way of life as superior to that of London. In the works of the masters the artistic dangers of a concentration on local manners and a theme

---

[30] *Ibid.*, 226.

[31] Robertson Davies, 'Stephen Leacock,' in *Our Living Tradition*, First Series, ed. C.T. Bissell (Toronto: University of Toronto Press 1957), p. 149.

[32] From *Canadian Literature* 39 (Winter 1969): 35-41. Used by permission of the author. Editor's title.

of local perfection were overcome and hence not evident. Both new interests in fact resulted in a totally new kind of story-telling, one which stressed peculiar rather than representative traits. As a result characters by design look provincial rather than universal. In principle at least, the incidents which provide them with conflicts should involve distinctively local concerns. Descriptions need to point up the unique, which usually means taking pride in the manmade environment rather than the natural. Themes typically show the way to a "perfect" society, in which, as it is pictured, pastimes only too often cause more concern than work, and moral dogmatism underlies the portrayal of manners.

As developed in the United States and Canada late in the last century, local colour told of the life of the many small towns in countrysides where the frontier had been closed for at least a generation. In the United States hosts of local colourists described all the older regions of the country in the last generation of the nineteenth century. Writers like Sarah Orne Jewett brought out the distinctive features of New England life, and George Washington Cable recreated the special life of the Creoles in the Old South. In Canada too the local colourists were numerous and prolific. L.M. Montgomery idolized the quiet life of Prince Edward Island in more than a dozen novels. Duncan Campbell Scott wrote *In the Village of Viger* in praise of the self-contained life of a French-Canadian village soon and lamentably to be swallowed up by Montreal. In Ontario E.W. Thomson and Ralph Connor praised the manliness and moral integrity of Glengarry folk, and many another local colourist ransacked the rest of Southern Ontario for ideal small towns. So pervasive was this preoccupation in life and in literature that Hugh MacLennan a generation later chose the small town outlook and its moral Puritanism as his distinctive Canadian trait in *The Precipice*.

In the local colour fiction the small towns appear as islands of perfection in a generally undirected or even misdirected civilization. Behind this pride and optimism centered on small town life, there lurks in the more perceptive writings a dread of the changes appearing in the new big cities. No doubt, industrial routine and mass housing seemed to the small town onlookers to banish happiness, and, worse still, to lead to a flexible morality. Storytellers took two approaches to their topic. Militant local colourists like Ralph Connor used their fiction as a pulpit to

preach the way of perfection to a less fortunate people in the
cities, or sometimes on the frontier. They wrote vigorous stories
tightly unified by their underlying sermons, so that often their
works understandably became best-sellers in those Puritanical
times, even outside the small towns. The other local colourists,
like L.M. Montgomery, D.C. Scott, and E.W. Thomson were
complacent and gently humorous. They crammed their stories
with the placid atmosphere of the society they loved. They were
the local colourists who had no moralizing motives to interfere
with a purely artistic aim.

As artists these complacent local colourists faced two dilem-
mas. First, their absorption with features peculiar to a way of life
invited them to stress the local rather than the universal, and
usually they chose the superficial rather than the essential and
permanent. In characterization they often stressed the quaint, in
customs the bizarre. They were content with the charming in
scenery and the dogmatic in morality. Ministers and housewives
also were drawn as charming rather than devoted, except when
the perfection of their lives was stressed. Special customs like
gathering maple syrup provided incidents and scenery at once,
and so did special moral problems like the tavern, or social
phenomena like the Sunday School.

As a second dilemma, the complacent local colourists lacked
any obvious pattern or device to unify their stories. The staple unit
of local colour fiction is the self-contained anecdote or vignette, in
which an odd character does something peculiar. The most obvious
structure is a volume of independent sketches or loosely connected
stories, which when bound together can radiate the desired atmosphere of a charming and unchanging way of life. But the novel with
its larger plot requires a dynamic development rather than a series
of static situations. A plot depends on conflict and its conflict must
lead to change. Neither is inherent in complacent local colour, and
few if any of the writers who practised it at the turn of the century
had the ingenuity to invent an appropriate large-scale plot on their
own. Traditional if alien patterns were of course available. The
tried plots of Victorian fiction tempted many a local colourist, but
they shifted rather than solved the problem of unity. They belonged
to conventions which were at odds with local colour, since they
stressed the representative rather than the eccentric in human behaviour. Nor were their typically melodramatic conflicts a suitable

mode for the complacent local colourists. Duncan Campbell Scott spoiled much of the unity of *In the Village of Viger* by concocting plots about madmen and murderers which clashed incongruously with the charm of his atmosphere and his French- Canadian characters.

The local colourists wanted to record a society in which neither disaster nor evil occurred. Tragic patterns were unthinkable, and so too was robust satire: there were no evils, it seemed, to attack. For, luxuriating in the best of all comfortable worlds, genial humour naturally became the staple mode. Again the local colourists were tempted into a difficult artistic form. Genial humour is fairly rare in literature; it is much more elusive than satiric wit. Several local colourists, like L.M. Montgomery, managed plot and humour nicely at the level of children's stories, particularly when growing up was the unifying device. But most, including L.M. Montgomery, were childish when they turned to adult life. It took a great genial humorist to meet the varied challenges—a Mark Twain or a Stephen Leacock.

Sunshine Sketches of a Little Town contains all the familiar ingredients of typical local colour, although in this version they look a little strange because the most memorable characters are more elaborated and more integrated into a larger purpose than usual. Yet in the background there are several quaint characters who have not been developed. The village drunk—here schoolteacher Diston who never gets a raise—is a staple of local colour fiction; and the undertaker Golgotha Gingham is similarly extraneous to plot and theme. More developed but still peripheral vignettes include Yodel the auctioneer, Mullins the banker, and fiery Judge Pepperleigh. A local custom which comes right out of the tradition appears in the opening chapter, when the steam merry-go-round comes to Mariposa town and the calculating innkeeper Josh Smith treats all the children. Such characters and incidents justify the claim of the opening sentence that there are "a dozen towns just like it," but they also recall Canadian literature as much as Canadian life. They help to evoke the familiar golden atmosphere of "a land of hope and sunshine," as Leacock put it in his preface. But the atmosphere gains much more strength from the more developed incidents, which are all Leacock's own.

From the first Leacock presents Mariposa not so much in the

usual formless collection of odd characters and bizarre incidents as through a pervading sense of a whole life. With a typical sense of being at the centre of the universe, the townsfolk talk of "main street" and the "lake" from the first page on, ignoring the proper Indian names. They display their self-centred pride even more actively by comparing the width of Main Street favourably with that of Wall Street. These mannerisms are merely amusing, but Leacock uses other special customs and features of the environment to help define the four seasons of the year in Mariposa. By winter the electric light is as strong as coal oil lamps, by spring the farmers from Missinaba County stroll through Mariposa like dangerous lumbermen, by summer the seven cottages on the lake are rented, and by autumn the Salvation Army sings on street corners under naphtha lamps. In such a description Leacock goes beyond typical local colour, and beyond his typical humour too, using both as a means of comprehending a whole society.

In terms of characterization, the simply quaint figures like Diston the drunk schoolteacher merely lurk in the background of the stories. For the two bank clerks, in contrast, Leacock uses a sort of inverted quaintness by stressing their city-like similarity (the one with the cameo pin and the face of a horse, and the other one with the other cameo pin and the face of another horse). A central figure like Josh Smith may look at first like "a character" (and "an over-dressed pirate"), but he quickly becomes a rounded, vigorous and amiable representative of the small town at its best. Most unexpected of all, the town barber Jefferson Thorpe plunges right through the layers of quaintness and reveals a pathetic man of high principles who automatically assumes the money losses of townsfolk who have speculated foolishly on his advice.

This example of exceptional integrity indicates both a final trait which Leacock shares with the lesser local colourists and at the same time the insight which makes his version great. Like them he assumes that no evil or tragedy worthy of the label is possible in the small town of the story. Leacock can be funny on this topic too, putting the perspective of humour between himself and the small town. When the *Mariposa Belle* sinks in six feet of mud in the "lake," he tells us that disasters such as mass drownings never occur in Mariposa. The quip sounds satiric, but in effect it is whimsical. Leacock clung to his love of the small towns for a lifetime just because dreadful things really did not happen in the "land of hope and sunshine." Yet he had the insight to recognize that men can be double-faced in Mariposa just as they can be anywhere. The most successful citizens are in fact hypocrites: Judge Pepperleigh orders the tavern shut down because he was kept out after hours, and Josh Smith ensures that it keeps operating by banqueting the leading citizens daily in his restaurant until his liquor license is renewed. Leacock laughs at both men, but he laughs with kindness. He recognizes human traits which almost every local colourist pretended did not exist in his town, yet they do not infuriate him as they do most humourists, who unlike him are satirists. To him they do not, cannot, constitute evil.

There is in fact a rare perception in *Sunshine Sketches* that has fundamentally nothing to do with humour, which is only the means of expressing it. In contrast to the typical thin glimpses of small town life, Leacock's view comprehends all of small town life, giving us for example a sense of the whole town, rather than just a family at play, on the occasion of the annual picnic of the Knights of Pythias. At a more serious level, nothing fires interest in a real small town more than an election, but very few story-tellers besides Leacock have told about one. Josh Smith wins the riding of Mariposa with a typical double-dealing trick, but deservedly, for he is also the ablest candidate. Smith is in fact a hypocrite using his talents to serve the best interests of Mariposa, as when he solves the crisis of the church building fund by setting fire to the old building for the insurance money. In drawing him Leacock has indeed made hypocrisy a neutral quality, which can even end in benevolence, as when Smith keeps the lavish restaurant open after his liquor license has been renewed.

This local colour is in fact both positive and mature. For Leacock the small town offered the best of all practical worlds. The sad, ruined Jeff Thorpe is really fortunate not to have gained the means to leave Mariposa:

> It seemed to spoil one's idea of Jeff that copper and asbestos
> and banana lands should form the goal of his thought when,
> if he knew it, the little shop and the sunlight of Mariposa was
> so much better.

The real tragedy is that of the old boys who have left and, in their prosperous old age in the city, long for small town life. *Sunshine*

Sketches in fact ends on this unhappy scene, with their dissatisfied dreams of a better way of life back in Mariposa, and of
the trainmen calling out the station:

> And, as we listen, the cry grows fainter and fainter in our
> ears and we are sitting here again in the leather chairs of the
> Mausoleum Club, talking of the little Town in the Sunshine
> that once we knew.

Independence and Leisure were the keystones of Leacock's
philosophy of life, and he tells us in his "Preface" that he enjoys
"more in the four corners of a single year than a business man
knows in his whole life." That is why he escaped as often as he
could from Montreal to his country home near Orillia.

When applied to such a heart-felt purpose, the nonsense
humour is also unusually positive and mature. Although a few of
the quips and brief character sketches in *Sunshine Sketches* are as
gratuitous as some of the background local colour, most of them
serve the larger purpose. The humour itself can penetrate the
degrees of pettiness in the citizens, but its genial tone provides
for an acceptance of them all. Thus the sinking of the *Mariposa
Belle* reveals the shallow faith of the lesser citizens, as when the
student minister in the lifeboat assures the passengers that they
are "in the hands of Providence," but "he was crouched and
ready to spring out of them at the first moment." Meanwhile Josh
Smith with his more practical faith corks the hull, lets the ship
float, and sails it home before the lifeboat passengers can walk
back. In the same incident, Leacock with his nonsense combi-
nations extends his perspective momentarily to make fun of the
national image: the boat began to sink just as everyone was singing "*O—Cana-da*"; but those who stay with the ship are still
singing it when Smith steers the refloated *Mariposa Belle* into
harbour. Here a rare symbolism adds to the maturity of the
humour. At the same time the sense of latent determination here
and in almost every sketch, however oddly implied, builds up the
mood of stability necessary for a positive presentation of the
small-town way of life, and gives an exception to Carl Van
Doren's sound criticism:

> The local colourists were not very realistic observers. Ordi-

narily provincial, but without the rude durability or homely truthfulness of provincialism at its best, they studied their world with benevolence rather than with passion. Nor were they much differentiated among themselves by highly individual ideas or methods.

And yet at the same time technically Leacock's humour is still the same combination of incongruous extremes as in his score of other books. Anthologists can select individual sketches from *Sunshine Sketches* and print them side by side with ones from all the other books without jarring a single tone of humour. Nevertheless the anthologists do injustice to *Sunshine Sketches*. It does develop an over-all unity which goes far beyond the unity of tone in *Nonsense Novels*. Leacock's philosophy of the happiest way of life makes the chief contribution to this larger unity. Yet although the special Leacock humour produces a unified tone, and the sense of wholeness in the local colour scene a unified atmosphere, both are essentially static, and although a single set of characters and incidents may unify as many as three sketches for a change, and Josh Smith and others recur in several different stories, *Sunshine Sketches* is still episodic. Nor does Leacock show any inclination to develop original plots in the individual stories. Chiefly he borrows conventional patterns like those he had parodied in *Nonsense Novels*, still inverting them amusingly. Not only does the sinking ship fail to sink, but the bank robbery is after all not a robbery, and the hopeless romance of young lovers turns out to have been prearranged by the parents. The effect just suits *Sunshine Sketches* with its happy balance of many interests, but it promises little help for future books. Leacock created a great book because his concern for his topic absorbed his regular talents and gave them direction. He did not hit on a plot pattern or a philosophy which offered a means to overcome his continuing problem of disunity and shallowness.

Gerald Lynch
The Train to Mariposa[33]

... "L'Envoi. The Train to Mariposa" takes the completed picture of Mariposa and throws a new light on *Sunshine Sketches* by applying its perceptions of the little town to life in the city. In a manner that parallels the movements between reality and illusion within each previous sketch, there is in "L'Envoi" a quite literal traffic between reality and illusion—"the train to Mariposa."

As this train crosses the bridge over the Ossawippi and moves ever closer to Mariposa, the narrator exclaims, "we must be close now!" In a manner that resembles a technique of the dramatic monologue, the auditor interrupts the narrator's anticipation with an unrecorded, though apparently apprehensive, remark. The narrator considers the cause of his companion's anxiety: "What? It feels nervous and strange to be coming here again after all these years? It must indeed. No, don't bother to look at the reflection of your face in the window-pane shadowed by the night outside. Nobody could tell you now after all these years. Your face has changed in these long years of money-getting in the city. Perhaps if you had come back now and again, just at odd times, it wouldn't have been so." The mirror image here focuses the concerns of "L'Envoi": self-identity in relation to Mariposa. The narrator admonishes his auditor for the relentlessness of his "money-getting in the city," a relentlessness that has told on his features, making him unrecognizable to those who have remained in touch with their Mariposan roots. However, the narrator is not suggesting that his auditor go home again, only that he should "perhaps" have "come back now and again, just at odd times." Note, also, that the nostalgically maudlin and simplistic perception of Mariposa as "home" is not the narrator's; it is, rather, the homesick auditor's.

The reader of the *Sketches* may experience at "L'Envoi" a sense of dislocation similar to its auditor's sense of displacement.

---

[33] From *Stephen Leacock: Humour and Humanity* (Montreal: McGill-Queen's University Press, 1988), pp. 111-20. Used by permission.

Here, for the first time since the preface, the reader is outside of Mariposa. He is situated now in the "dull" Mausoleum Club, and like the auditor, he may yearn to return to colourful Mariposa. But before such an imaginative return can be attempted, the narrator must first correct his auditor's misperceptions.

The narrator initially suggests his auditor's displacement and ignorance of Mariposa by remarking continually on what he "knows" and does not "know." The auditor does not know—or remember—that there is a train to Mariposa, though he came "from the little town" and once spent many an evening yearning after the returning train. The auditor does not have a definite reference for the repeatedly emphasized word, "home." Home once referred to Mariposa, but now home "means that big red sandstone house ... in the costlier part of the city," or "'Home' means, in a way, this Mausoleum Club." And, finally, home can once again mean Mariposa when the auditor sits "reading in a quiet corner somewhere such a book as the present one." Essentially, *Sunshine Sketches* is a reminder of what "home" is, and "L'Envoi" is a concluding lesson in how memories of Mariposa should be employed. But the reader would be as ignorant as the auditor to presume that Mariposa-as-home is an ideal to be set apart in some nostalgic, musty and maudlin corner of a Mausoleum Club—an ideal concept that is occasionally dusted off and shined up. The reader, who is familiar with Mr Smith and with Drone's "beacon," should know better. The narrator is determined to correct just such a misperception of Mariposa. He does not want his auditor to misread *Sunshine Sketches* and misapply the lessons that it contains.

The narrator proceeds to recount his auditor's career. Upon first arriving in the city, the auditor, a homesick boy, had planned to "make money," to become "really rich," and then to return to Mariposa and build an ostentatious house—the best that money could buy." The narrator remarks that such a house would be "much finer in true reality, than the vast palace of sandstone with the porte-cochère and the sweeping conservatories that you afterwards built in the costlier part of the city." No doubt the narrator's perception is to some extent "true reality": such a house in Mariposa would be "much finer" than a "palace of sandstone" in the city. The ostentatious house that the auditor had dreamed of building in Mariposa dwindles, however, in compari-

son with the enchanted home of Peter and Zena Pupkin, which
home is located in the "newer part of town." Cost has little to do
with the relative enchantments of a Mariposan home; in fact, it
can effect enchantment inversely, for, as the reader knows,
"some of the most completely enchanted [homes of Mariposa] are
the cheapest." The auditor's early ambition betrays his dream as
the gaudy dream of the *nouveau riche*: the small-town boy makes
a pile and returns to impress the locals.

The salient characteristics of the auditor are his desire for
wealth and his mistaken, nostalgic perception of Mariposa as
"home." When he left Mariposa, the auditor changed and lost a
part of himself. A large part of the cause for his change and loss
is that to which the narrator later refers in the central passage on
self-identity—"these long years of money-getting in the city."
The auditor's obsessive desire for material riches suggests further
that he possesses something of a Smithian bent. His ambition also
recalls Jeff Thorpe's mistaken desire for impressive wealth and
Dean Drone's mistaken faith in his ostentatious church. And yet,
though the auditor is uninformed in his nostalgic perception of
Mariposa and mistaken in his desire for riches with which to
build an impressive home in Mariposa, he is nonetheless still
thinking of Mariposa. Mariposa remains his reference point. The
more threatening trouble arises when he begins to forget Mariposa.

The narrator regrets that his auditor has "half forgotten Mariposa, and long since lost the way to it." He notes that his auditor
is in this respect "only like the greater part of the men in this
Mausoleum Club in the city." And it is here that "Mariposa"
begins to acquire a degree of abstraction, for it is difficult to conceive that "practically every one of the [the Mausoleum Club
members] came from Mariposa once upon a time." Rather,
"Mariposa" is intended to suggest collective origins and the past,
an interpretation supported by the fairy-tale "once upon a time"
which assists temporal suspension. (Recall that Leacock con-
cludes his author's preface, "the inspiration of the book ... is
large enough.") Like the auditor who "half forgets" his origins,
the members of the Mausoleum Club are "half ashamed to own"
their beginnings in "Mariposa." Just as the earlier comparison of
houses recalled the enchanted houses of the three-sketch love
interest, the most favourable treatment of Mariposa, so here the

restrained criticism of forgetting and disowning remembers the three sketches on Mariposan religion, the most unfavourable treatment of Mariposa. The auditor and his fellow clubbers are forgetting "Mariposa" in a manner that parallels the way Mariposa discarded the quaint old church which, "like so much else in life, was forgotten." In an attempt to induce his auditor to remember correctly his origins and the value of Mariposa, the narrator begins to recall for him some of Mariposa's allurements and to lead him to board, in his imagination, the train to Mariposa. Only such an imaginative re-affiliation with his origins can offset "the long dull evening" of the Mausoleum Club—a place which, judging from the auditor's anxious reaction to his reflection in the window of the train to Mariposa, effectively buries the hope of his achieving an integrated personality.

The narrator first entices his auditor with a sensuous appeal. The auditor is asked if his club meals can compare to the fish and fowl that he once caught near Mariposa. (Perhaps memory must begin so, with the body, in order to counter the maudlin musings of the mistaken mind. Certainly Proust thought so.) By a sudden leap of imagination, the narrator and his auditor are suddenly aboard the train to Mariposa. "The joke is" that the city dwellers do not realize that the suburban train transforms into the Mariposa train. This may well be "the joke"—the humorous purpose —of *Sunshine Sketches*, for, like the train, the book itself provides access to Mariposa. That is, *Sunshine Sketches* provides the only opportunity for an imaginative return to "Mariposa"—to the past, to home, to origins. The community is transformed in Leacock's humorous vision so that it is perceived simultaneously as more real and more illusory, as ironically revealed and colorfully heightened. It may be, moreover, that the shift to the train is not so sudden a leap of imagination. The narrator began by recalling Mariposa and then unapologetically required his auditor (and the reader) to board the train, suggesting that *informed* memories of Mariposa make possible the beginning of an imaginative return.

By feigning ignorance of the appropriate, fashionable terminology, the narrator not only insinuates an opposition between himself and his travelling companion but also identifies himself with the temporarily displaced Mariposans aboard he train: "Those people with the clothes that are perfectly all right and yet look odd in some way, the women with the peculiar hats and the—what do you say?—last year's fashions? Ah yes, of course, that must be it." While in the city, the Mariposans are not individualized. When the narrator points out "one of the greatest judges that ever adorned the bench of Missinaba County" and "that clerical gentleman ... who is explaining to the man with him the marvellous mechanism of the new air brake (one of the most conspicuous illustrations of the divine structure of the physical universe)," the references are, of course, to Judge Pepperleigh and Dean Drone, although neither is named. In a sense, Pepperleigh and Drone are here accorded a degree of abstraction similar to "Mariposa," in accordance perhaps with Leacock's claim in the preface that his characters are types. More important, the references to Pepperleigh and Drone pointedly recall the most favourable treatment of Mariposan life (the romance) and the most disillusioning aspect of life in the little town (the new church). Only as a result of temporal and spatial distance—such as the auditor has interposed—is Mariposa remembered incorrectly as the ideal "home" or as an untroubled idyllic community. As the train moves towards Mariposa, the two characters of Pepperleigh and Drone emerge hazily to suggest the good and the bad of Mariposan life. "But of course you hardly recognize them while the train is passing through the suburbs and the golf district and the outlying parts of the city area."

As the train departs from city environs, it undergoes a transformation reminiscent of the electricity which "turned into coal oil again" by the time it entered Mariposa. The electric locomotive "changes its character" and turns into an "old wood engine ... with sparks enough to light up a suit for damages once in every mile." Metaphorically, the city and the present are set afire by the retreating train and left in the distance as the train to Mariposa enters the country and the past and continues "thundering and pounding towards the north ... up to the higher ground of the country of the pines and the lakes." It is at this juncture that the narrator instructs his auditor to "look from the window as you go." And there are strong hints here that the auditor's fleeting journey towards Mariposa/home reflects his country's, Canada's, ongoing struggle for the preservation of a distinctive identity vis-à-vis the United States of America.

In a passage that anticipates the ultimate indictment of the auditor for having half-forgotten Mariposa, the narrator regrets that it is not a lack of opportunity that has kept the auditor away from Mariposa:

> As you sit back half dreaming in the car, you keep wondering why it is that you never came up before in all these years. Ever so many times you planned that just as soon as the rush and strain of business eased up a little, you would take the train and go back to the little town to see what it was like now, and if things had changed much since your day. But each time when your holidays came, somehow you changed your mind and went down to Naragansett or Nagahuckett or Nagasomething, and left over the visit to Mariposa for another time.

Rather than coming up to the country of his origins and affirming his bond with its changing reality, the materialistic auditor has spent what free time he could steal gong down to vacation in the United States. (Narragansett is a resort town and its adjoining bay in Rhode Island; Nagahuckett appears to be a conflation of the names of two other US resort areas, Naugatuck in Connecticut and Nantucket Island off Massachusetts.) Compared to the mellifluous Mariposa—the Spanish word for butterfly—the US names suggest the grinding gears of a machine. These areas are the vacation spots that the auditor has chosen—"you changed your mind and went down."

The narrator then contrasts this Nagasomething to the Mariposan countryside which the auditor has been avoiding: "At every crossway we can hear the long muffled roar of the whistle, dying to a melancholy wail that echoes into the woods; the woods, I say, for the farms are thinning out and the track plunges here and there into great stretches of bush,—tall tamarack and red scrub willow and with a tangled undergrowth of brush that has defied for two generations all attempts to clear it into the form of fields." This is suggestively a view of (to borrow from the title of an Al Purdy poem) the country north of Toronto. This view is offered in opposition to "the city," but it is contrasted also to those vacation spots in the US that were referred to in the immediately preceding paragraph. A recalcitrant land that defies "all attempts to clear it into the form of fields" is a strikingly poetic image that echoes forward to several later Canadian works. Here is an approach to the Canadian landscapes of Lawren Harris, F.R. Scott, and A.J.M. Smith, and Leacock has captured the spirit of the land in one seemingly endless sentence. (Of course, the implications arising from the image of a land resistant to "the form of fields" are ones to which later modernists such as Purdy and Margaret Atwood have devoted much literary exploration.) For Leacock the Canadian hinterland—"the higher ground of the country of pines and the lakes"—is the place "where the town of Mariposa has lain waiting for you ... for thirty years." Mariposa has lain waiting to reaffirm the auditor's sense of self and identity. Mariposa waits as the place to which city dwellers (Mausoleum Clubbers) may yet return, and should return, to revitalize their lives—both individual and collective. But the auditor has "half forgotten" Mariposa, having dismissed the train to Mariposa to ride instead the "Empire State Express" and the aptly named "New Limited." The auditor is aboard the train to Mariposa only because the narrator has brought him there. By extension, the representative auditor is aboard only because "such a book" as *Sunshine Sketches* has provided memories and induced imaginings of Mariposa. Still, Leacock does not portray the auditor as a hopeless case. The auditor is on the train in a "half dreaming" state, which suggests an equal mixture of romance and reality and, consequently, the possibility of insight into his condition. Furthermore, the positive side to "half forgotten" is that the auditor has "half remembered" Mariposa and so has read such a book as *Sunshine Sketches*.

Significantly, when nearing Mariposa the narrator feels none of his auditor's anxiety. Having alternated his narrative mode from "you," to "they," to "you," the narrator finally clarifies his own position in a passage that employs the first person, thereby reaffirming his identification with the Mariposans as the train approaches its destination. He refers to some other of the world's fast trains and proceeds in what might be termed a Maripocentric manner:

> But what are they to this, this mad career, this breakneck speed, this thundering roar of the Mariposa local driving hard to its home! don't tell me that the speed is only twenty-five miles an hour. I don't care what it is. I tell you, and you can prove it for yourself if you will, that that train of mingled flat

cars and coaches that goes tearing into the night, its engine
whistle shrieking out its warning into the silent woods and
echoing over the dull still lake, is the fastest train in the
whole world.

Yes, and the best too,—the most comfortable, the most
reliable, the most luxurious and the speediest train that ever
turned a wheel.

In a sense the wheel is coming full circle. The narrator's childish
petulance and pride in *his* "Mariposa local" as the best, most
comfortable and speediest "train in the whole world" is of course
quintessentially Mariposan. Most important, he desires to be
wholly Mariposan because the Mariposans aboard the train are
"the most genial, the most social" of people; having shed "that
dull reserve" of the city, they call to one another by name "as if
they were all one family." Many times throughout the *Sketches*
the virtues of just such a communal familiarity—in contrast to the
individualistic machinations of Mr Smith and the image of "the
city"—prove overwhelmingly attractive to the narrator.

In the passage that describes the auditor's anxiety over his
reflection in the window, the narrator at once sympathizes with
his apprehensiveness and forthrightly reveals its causes. The
indictment is twofold: the auditor is guilty of an over-emphasis
on "money-getting" and of going down to the US instead of occasionally returning to the typically Canadian and somewhat northern town of Mariposa. The two offences—materialism and a US
bias—are suggestively related. Leacock may well be implying
that the obsessive desire for material gain nurtures an affinity for
the "home" of liberal individualism. Such a relationship is suggested in "L'Envoi," though it would be mistaken to over-empha-
size its implications: the auditor lives, after all, in a Canadian
city. Rather, *Sunshine Sketches* disparages unrestrained individualism and crass materialism in favour of the humane virtues of
the Mariposan community. And yet, individualism and materialism are gaining ground in Mariposa; these are two of the changes
the auditor would have noticed had he "come back now and
again, just at odd times." Had he met the *arriviste* Smith or
attended services in Drone's (or Mr Uttermost's) new church, the
auditor would have seen that "things had changed." Perhaps the
incongruity between his mistaken nostalgic memories of "home"

and the reality of change for the worse would have prompted him to perceive and arrest such developments within himself.

In fulfilment of his credo that humour be "kindly," Leacock portrays the narrator's final position as one of sympathetic identification with his auditor's plight. "L'Envoi" could have ended with the train's arrival in Mariposa, with "the cry of the brakemen and the porters:

"MARIPOSA! MARIPOSA!"

The cry recalls the conclusion to "The Marine Excursion," that other, most Canadian of the sketches: "O-CAN-A-DA!" The cry "Mariposa" would seem similarly to offer a fitting conclusion to *Sunshine Sketches*, but only if the reader is unrealistically predisposed to the idyllic, mostly escapist fiction of small town life that enjoyed such popularity at the turn of the century. A physical and permanent return to Mariposa was never the narrator's intention, either for himself or for his auditor. The auditor should have returned "now and again." For the book to have terminated with the train *in* Mariposa would have been to leave the reader with a falsely comfortable impression, an impression that satisfies an emotional indulgence similar to the auditor's mistaken nostalgia. And, of course, a successful return to and entry into Mariposa would have devalued the criticism of materialism and uninformed memories that the narrator levels at his auditor.

The final paragraph (the postscript, as it were) of "L'Envoi" serves two critical purposes: first, it shows that the narrator sympathizes with the plight of his auditor. The narrator adopts the narrative mode "we," thus effectively unifying himself and his auditor back in the Mausoleum Club at precisely the point where an escape into an idealized "Mariposa" appeared imminently realizable: "And as we listen, the cry grows fainter and fainter in our ears and we are sitting here again in the leather chairs of the Mausoleum Club, talking of the little Town in the Sunshine that once we knew." With Maripocentrism as its communally binding force, the little Town in the Sunshine gathers to its enchanted heart those residents who have visited the city. Leacock closes his circle of affection, but he sympathetically leaves his philosopher-guide, the narrator, with the auditor. The pair, now a community of two within the world of the Mausoleum Club, are returned to the real world. The conclusion of "L'Envoi" displays Leacock's humanism: an imaginative and visionary journey out of the self and the present to a somewhat northern, ideal community is followed precipitously by a return southwards to the world of men. A conclusion that left the narrator and his auditor in "Mariposa" would have suggested a *contemptus mundi* that was foreign to Leacock's humanistic vision.

The second purpose of the "postscript" is to emphasize what has become increasingly clear throughout "L'Envoi": there is no literal "train to Mariposa." In the context of "L'Envoi," there is in fact no real Mariposa. Mariposa is geographically real to the narrator of the sketches, but it is not so to the slightly different narrator of "L'Envoi." For the Envoi narrator, "Mariposa" is an abstraction, that extrapolation finally from "seventy or eighty" Canadian towns that Leacock insisted upon in his preface. "We are sitting here in the leather chairs of the Mausoleum Club," which, of course, "we" never left physically. The real and only "train to Mariposa" is *Sunshine Sketches*. Imaginative literature— "such a book as the present one"—provides access to a correct perception of the past, of origins both individual and collective; and such fiction helps make available in the present the informed memories from which imagination can fashion a vision of the future.

The narrator stresses the importance of periodic, imaginative "returns" to Mariposa and demonstrates that, in imagination, by means of realistically and romantically informed memories, he is quite capable of reaffirming his bond to Mariposa. If Mariposa remains only "the little Town in the Sunshine that once we knew," if "we" forget and deny our origins, then "we" are condemned to remain entombed in a Mausoleum Club, waxing nostalgically and with mistaken eloquence on misconceptions of Mariposa as "home." It is just such an ignorance of Mariposa that allows the auditor to fancy that he possesses the proper feelings, thereby freeing himself to pursue competitively his materialistic, individualistic ends. However, the threatened fracturing of the representative auditor's identity, which he experiences when his face is reflected on the window of the imaginative train, is but one of the consequences of forgetting Mariposa. Without realistically informed memories of Mariposa, the auditor also lacks the material of imagination from which to fashion a future based on a correct understanding of the worthwhile from his and his country's past. The narrator of "L'Envoi" shows him, as *Sunshine Sketches* shows us, how such an imaginative recreation operates.

Bibliography

Anderson, Allan. *Remembering Leacock: An Oral History*. Ottawa: Deneau, 1983.

Berger, Carl. "Other Mr. Leacock." *Canadian Literature*, 55 (Winter 1973), 23-40.

----------. *The Sense of Power: Studies in the Ideas of Canadian Imperialism, 1867-1914*. Toronto: University of Toronto Press, 1970.

Birbalsingh, Frank. "Stephen Leacock and the Canadian Literary Sensibility." *The Canadian Literary Review*, 1 (Fall/Winter 1982), 73-83.

Bissel, C.T. "Haliburton, Leacock and the American Humorous Tradition," *Canadian Literature*, 39 (Winter 1969), 5-19.

Bowker, Alan. Introd. *The Social Criticism of Stephen Leacock*. The Social History of Canada. Toronto: University of Toronto Press, 1973.

Bush, Douglas. "Stephen Leacock." In *The Canadian Imagination: Dimensions of a Literary Culture*. Ed. David Staines. Cambridge: Harvard University Press, 1977. Pp. 123-51.

Cameron, Donald. *Faces of Leacock*. Toronto: Ryerson, 1967.

Clever, Glenn. "Leacock's Dunciad." *Studies in Canadian Literature*, 1 (Summer 1976), 238-41.

Cook, J.R. (Ramsay). "Stephen Leacock and the Age of Plutocracy." In *Character and Circumstance*. Ed. J.S. Moir. Toronto: Macmillan, 1970. Pp. 163-81.

Curry, Ralph. *Stephen Leacock: Humorist and Humanist*. Garden City, N.Y.: Doubleday, 1959.

Davies, Robertson. *Stephen Leacock*. Canadian Writers, no. 7. Toronto: McClelland and Stewart, 1970.

Doyle, James. *Stephen Leacock: The Sage of Orillia*. Toronto: ECW, 1992.

Edgar, Pelham. "Stephen Leacock." *Queen's Quarterly*, 53:2 (1946), 173-84.

Ferris, Ina. "The Face in the Window: *Sunshine Sketches* Reconsidered." *Studies in Canadian Literature*, 3 (Summer 1978), 178-85.

Innis, Harold. "Obituary: Stephen Butler Leacock (1869-1944)." *Canadian Journal of Economics and Political Sciences*, 10 (May 1944), 216-26.

Kimball, Elizabeth. *The Man in the Panama Hat: Reminiscences of My Uncle, Stephen Leacock*. Toronto: McClelland and Stewart, 1970.

Kushner, J. and R.D. MacDonald. "Leacock: Economist/Satirist in *Arcadian Adventures* and *Sunshine Sketches*." *Dalhousie Review*, 56 (Autumn 1976), 493-509.

Legate, David. *Stephen Leacock: A Biography*. Toronto: Doubleday, 1970.

Lomer, Gerhard Richard. *Stephen Leacock: A Check-List and Index of his Writings*. Ottawa: National Library of Canada, 1954.

Lower, A.R.M. "Mariposa Belle." *Queen's Quarterly*, 58 (Summer 1951), 220-26.

Lucas, Alec. "Leacock Writes for Truth." *Studies in Canadian Literature*, 1 (Summer 1976), 254-58.

Lynch, Gerald. *Stephen Leacock: Humour and Humanity*. Montreal-Kingston: McGill-Queen's University Press, 1988.

----------. "Leacock's Debt to Daudet." *Canadian Literature*, 107 (Winter 1985), 186-89.

MacDonald, R.D. "Measuring Leacock's Mariposa Against Lewis's Gopher Prairie: A Question of Monuments." *Dalhousie Review*, 71 (Spring 1991), 84-103.

MacLulich, T.D. "Mariposa Revisited." *Studies in Canadian Literature*, 4 (Winter 1979), 167-76.

Magee, William H. "Genial Humour in Stephen Leacock. *Dalhousie Review*, 56 (Summer 1976), 268-82.

----------. "Parody and Perspective: Form in Leacock's Sketches." *Thalia*, 3 (Fall/Winter 1980-81), 31-37.

----------. "Stephen Leacock, Local Colourist." *Canadian Literature*, 39 (Winter 1969), 34-42.

Mantz, Douglas. "The Preposterous and the Profound: A New Look at the Envoi of Sunshine Sketches." *Journal of Canadian Fiction*, no. 19 (1977), 95-105.

Marshall, Tom. "False Pastoral: Stephen Leacock's Conflicting Worlds." *Journal of Canadian Fiction*, no. 19 (1977), 86-94.

McArthur, Peter. *Stephen Leacock*. Toronto: Ryerson, 1923.

Moritz, Albert and Theresa Moritz. *Leacock: A Biography*. Toronto: Stoddart, 1985.

Norris, Darrel A. "Preserving Main Street: Some Lessons of Leacock's Mariposa." *Journal of Canadian Studies*, 17 (Summer 1982), 128-35.

Pacey, Desmond. "Leacock as a Satirist." *Queen's Quarterly*, 58 (Summer 1951), 208-19.

Priestly, J.B. Introd. *The Bodley Head Leacock*. 1957; rpt. Toronto: McClelland and Stewart, 1969.

Rasporich, B.J. "Charles Dickens and Stephen Leacock: A Legacy of Sentimental Humour." *Thalia*, 3 (Fall/Winter 1980-81), 17-24.

----------. "Leacock Persona and the Canadian Character." *Mosaic*, 14 (Spring 1981), 76-92.

----------. "The New Eden: The Source of Canadian Humour: Mc-Culloch, Haliburton, and Leacock." *Studies in Canadian Literature*, 7:2 (1982), 227-40.

Sandwell, B.K. Leacock Recalled: How the 'Sketches' Started." *Saturday Night*. Oct. 1942, p. 4.